THE ONE-EYED JUDGE

THE ONE-EYED JUDGE

A Novel

MICHAEL PONSOR

INTEGRATED MEDIA
NEW YORK

Cover design by Mauricio Díaz

978-1-5040-3525-5

Published in 2017 by Open Road Integrated Media, Inc.
180 Maiden Lane
New York, NY 10038
www.openroadmedia.com

To Christian, Anne, and Joseph, and to all children.
And to Nancy, another love song.

THE ONE-EYED JUDGE

Alice Liddell, age 6, the inspiration for the central character in *Alice's Adventures in Wonderland,* costumed, posed, and photographed by the author, Charles Dodgson, aka Lewis Carroll

PART ONE

INITIAL APPEARANCE

1

Elizabeth Spencer was halfway through her report when someone knocked sharply on the front door. Professor Cranmer jumped up from his chair by the coffee table, where Elizabeth had spread out her file. He shuffled across the room to see who the intruder was, muttering under his breath.

At least he's not still in his pajamas this time, Elizabeth thought. She would later testify about how hot it was that May afternoon—so warm that, with the blinds drawn and the AC turned up, they could hear almost nothing from the outside.

Elizabeth had been Cranmer's intern since the start of the semester in January, and for the first couple months, things had gone more or less fine. She'd begun to like him, sort of, and had even gotten interested in the research he had her doing. He'd hinted that he was concocting the work-study project to help her out, and she appreciated the supplement to her grant. In addition to doing a good job, her payback to the professor, she knew, was to make sure she looked good when they got together. She could tell he liked her smart and pretty.

Professor Cranmer was an odd, mousy man, shorter than Elizabeth, sometimes bad tempered, but very smart, and in their first weeks, often very funny. He was in his late sixties, and he'd been at Amherst College forever, teaching nineteenth-century English literature and the modern novel. He had two cats, Mick and Keith, but no wife, and he was a hard grader. Elizabeth's boyfriend, Ryan, thought Cranmer was a pretentious old fossil, but if you got an *A* from him, which Elizabeth had, it meant something.

In the beginning, she usually met Professor Cranmer at his office on campus, though occasionally he'd had her drop by his small Cape-style house on a side street off the quad, where he lived with his mother, Doreen. Elizabeth only saw Doreen once. On her first visit to the house, Professor Cranmer had taken Elizabeth to the doorway of the TV room for introductions. She had a glimpse of a very old, very fat woman sprawled in a recliner, with an ashtray and an iced drink on the table next to her. A soap opera was on. When Professor Cranmer called out, Doreen shoved herself up and twisted around to have a look back.

"Well, hello there." Doreen's voice was scratchy. "Aren't you a cutie though."

Those were the only words Elizabeth ever heard from Doreen. She died two weeks later, quite suddenly, which was when Professor Cranmer had his meltdown, and Elizabeth's internship took its weird turn.

The loud rap on the door that afternoon turned out to be another delivery. For weeks since his mother's death, the professor had been ordering all sorts of miscellaneous junk off the Internet. Stacks of cardboard boxes crowded the corners of his living room. The exchange Elizabeth overheard between Professor Cranmer and the UPS guy did not seem unusual at the time.

"You Professor Sidney Cranmer?"

"Uh-huh."

"Expecting a package?"

"Wouldn't surprise me."

Then the UPS guy said, "Sign here." Professor Cranmer signed and took the package, and that was how it went down.

The item this time was a square DVD mailer. Professor Cranmer held it up to his nose, sniffed, and looked at it, either pleased or puzzled. He made some kind of noise, like *Hmmp*, walked over to his rolltop desk, and picked up a pair of scissors.

"Just a sec."

He was wearing wrinkled khaki shorts, a purple Amherst College T-shirt, and flip-flops. The sight of his hairless, old-man's legs was always gross, and Elizabeth looked away. Still, he was a lot better than he had been. His hands had stopped shaking, he shaved most days, and he wasn't wearing his disgusting brown bathrobe all the time. In the weeks following Doreen's funeral, Elizabeth sometimes came to his house an hour early on class days to make his coffee, bug him to get dressed, and check to be sure he'd zipped his fly, brushed his teeth, and used deodorant to cover up the smell of the booze. Most mornings, he'd have been up all night watching old movies or surfing the Internet. The house, except for the day after the cleaner came, was always a disaster.

Besides herself and the cleaner, the only other visitor Elizabeth noticed over the months was a tattooed handyman, who was gutting Doreen's old bedroom, replacing the windows and installing custom bookcases. The lingering smell of his mother was too much, Professor Cranmer said, and the aroma of sawdust and wood glue helped.

Despite the professor's personal problems, Elizabeth was enjoying the research project, which focused on the writer who'd made Sidney Cranmer famous. Early in his career, he had written an authoritative biography of Charles L. Dodgson, the Oxford mathematics professor who had published *Alice's Adventures in Wonderland* under the nom de plume Lewis Carroll in 1865. Apart from mathematics and writing, Dodgson's passion had been photography, something new at that time. What made his hobby controversial was that many of Dodgson's photographs were of very young girls in seductive poses, partially dressed or entirely naked.

Speculation persisted that Dodgson was a pedophile. A British journalist had uncovered Dodgson's bank records, which showed regular, substantial withdrawals that could not be accounted for. These mysterious transfers, the journalist hinted, might signify payments to a blackmailer. Professor Cranmer thought this was preposterous. He assigned Elizabeth to go through the thousands of pages of old bank documents, track down every expenditure she could, and prepare summaries for the professor to use in the article he was working on.

As Professor Cranmer was standing by his desk, clipping the end off the cardboard mailer, a tremendous thumping and shouting burst out at the front door, so raucous and abrupt that it startled Elizabeth badly. Professor Cranmer quickly stuffed the mailer into a drawer and trotted back across the room, calling out, "I'm coming. I'm *coming*."

When he opened the door, things suddenly got very frightening. Several large people, including at least one woman, pushed right past him and fanned out into the house, moving fast. A black man in a sports jacket stepped inside and put his hand in the middle of Professor Cranmer's chest, pushing him backward—not rough but very firm. Elizabeth was so shocked, she leaped up, wondering if she ought to run.

The black guy, who was holding out some kind of metal badge, spoke aggressively. "FBI. We have a warrant for your residence." He lifted his head and shouted, "Clear the second floor." Then he looked down at Professor Cranmer. "Are you Professor Sidney Cranmer?"

"Yes, of course I'm . . ."

"Sit down, Professor. I need to talk to you." He kept nudging Professor Cranmer farther into the living room. Elizabeth noticed that the agent seemed to have a limp.

"Take a seat on the sofa, please." When Professor Cranmer didn't immediately move, the man nodded into the room and said more distinctly, pointing, "Professor? I need you to have a seat on that sofa. Please." Then, softening his tone a little: "Just while we check out a couple things. Help me out here, okay?"

More people were entering now. Elizabeth lost count of exactly how many in the burst of voices and the thumping of feet. When one of the men lifted his hand to point upstairs, she saw a gun bulging out from under his shirttail.

At this point, the black FBI agent noticed Elizabeth and nodded at her. "Who's that?"

"That's my intern." Professor Cranmer dropped onto the sofa. "What the hell is going on here?"

The FBI agent looked like Colin Powell. He had a touch of silver on his temples, and he wore rectangular black glasses.

"Hang on." He limped over to the bottom of the stairs and called up. "Ginnie! Would you come here for a minute, please?" He turned to Elizabeth and gestured toward the far end of the living room, where the professor had his dining table and sideboard. "Have a seat over there, would you please, miss? At that table?"

Elizabeth walked three or four steps to the dining table and sat. The FBI agent lowered himself into the wingback chair facing the sofa and began talking to Professor Cranmer, still louder than necessary.

"Couple quickies first. Anyone else on the premises? Any weapons, firearms of any sort?"

Professor Cranmer looked over his shoulder as more people entered the house. "No one here but me and Ms. Spencer. And, yes, an automatic in the nightstand, a .45. What the Christ is going on?" He sounded nervous, but also irritated.

"Loaded?"

"Of course. What's the point otherwise?"

"Got a permit?"

"Oh, for heaven's sake." The edge in the professor's voice got sharper. "It's right in the drawer. Is that what this is about?"

A woman in khaki chinos and a forest-green polo came down to the foot of the stairs. Her auburn hair was in a ponytail. The black FBI agent pointed at Elizabeth.

"Take care of the young lady, would you please, Ginnie?" Then he yelled up the stairwell again. "Loaded .45 in the nightstand." A man's voice called back, "Got it. Clip's out. It's secure."

The female agent walked over and stood in front of Elizabeth, smiling. "Hi, I'm Ginnie O'Brien. I work for the postal inspector. Who are you?"

From her seat at the dining table, Elizabeth could see the black agent placing a sheaf of papers on the coffee table. She heard him talking.

"My name is Mike Patterson," he was saying. "I'm a special agent with the FBI." He poked his chin toward the second floor. "The folks with me are federal law enforcement agents, okay? Working with the postal inspector." He shoved the papers closer to Professor Cranmer. "This is a search warrant for your house issued yesterday by the federal court in Springfield."

Agent O'Brien poked Elizabeth lightly in the arm to get her attention. "Hello?" She was still smiling, but she was looking at Elizabeth carefully. "I'm Ginnie O'Brien," she said again. "Who are you?"

"Sorry. I'm Elizabeth Spencer."

"Spencer with an *S* or with a *C*, Elizabeth?"

"It's a *C*."

"What are you doing here, Elizabeth Spencer?" O'Brien smiled again.

A stocky white man in a purple-and-gold rugby shirt came through the kitchen and stood in the entry to the living room. He pulled a handkerchief from his back pocket and wiped his face.

"Basement and upstairs are clear."

"I'm Professor Cranmer's student intern. We were going over some work I'm doing for him."

"Uh-huh. That's nice," O'Brien said.

"Good," Agent Patterson said. "Tell Jack to bring the video cam. Subject says there's no one else here—and no other weapons." He nodded down at Professor Cranmer. "Correct?"

"Yes, yes. I told you."

Agent O'Brien stepped a little closer. "Would you do me a favor, Elizabeth? Would you stand up and hold your arms straight out like this?" She stuck her arms out. "I just need to give you a quick pat-down." She shrugged apologetically. "Standard procedure."

Elizabeth stood and held her arms out.

Agent O'Brien continued talking while she was patting her down. "You're at Amherst College here?"

"Yes."

"Live on campus?" She was feeling around Elizabeth's waist.

"During the year. I have a sublet for the summer."

"Great. What are you studying?"

Patterson spoke to the agent in the rugby shirt. He pointed at the desk. "Start with that. I saw him through the window standing over there." Then he leaned back in the chair and looked at Professor Cranmer with a sour expression, as though he were disgusted with him for some reason. The agent in the rugby shirt walked over to the desk and began rummaging through the drawers.

"What are you studying?" O'Brien asked again. "Thanks. You can sit down."

"I'm a bio major." Elizabeth took a seat.

"Med school someday?"

"Hope so."

"Good for you. How long have you been working for Professor Cranmer?"

"Just about five months."

"Uh-huh. Since the start of the year?"

"Yes."

"I see. Nice."

Elizabeth's eyes kept drifting back to the coffee table and Professor Cranmer. He was twitching around, and she was worried he might blow his stack. Despite her confusion, she registered that the FBI agent, Patterson, was better dressed than the others, in buff pants, a yellow shirt, and a tan tweed jacket. Polished shoes instead of the high-tops and khakis or jeans the other agents had on.

She heard Professor Cranmer ask Patterson, "You were limping. Did you . . . ?"

"Never mind that."

O'Brien leaned toward Elizabeth. "Would you do me another favor, Elizabeth, and stay right here for a minute?"

"Okay."

"I'll be right back."

Another man appeared halfway down on the stair landing, leaned over the railing, and spoke out to Patterson. "Save a lot of time if your pal would give us the computer passwords."

"Just a sec, Jimmie." Patterson took a wallet from his inside jacket pocket and pulled out a card.

"Bingo!" the agent by the desk called out. "Little prick had it open already." He was holding the cardboard DVD box with a small pair of pliers. "Hey, Professor, does this belong to you?"

Professor Cranmer waved at it without looking. "Of course. It just arrived."

Patterson spoke. "Professor Cranmer? You have certain rights, and I want to be sure you understand them." He began reading from the card. "You have the right to remain silent." He glanced up. "Do you understand?"

Professor Cranmer didn't say anything. He was looking at the front door, where two more people were entering as if they owned the place. Something fell over upstairs with a thud that made the chandelier over the dining table jingle. Mick and Keith would be cowering under Doreen's old bed.

"Anything you say may be used against you in a court of law. You have a right to an attorney. If you cannot afford an attorney, one will be appointed to represent you. If you begin to make a statement, you have a right to stop at any time. Do you understand these rights as I have read them to you?"

"Yes. I suppose." From the side, Elizabeth saw Professor Cranmer give his nervous little smile. "Sounds like TV, so it must be true."

"Having understood these rights, do you wish to speak to me at this time?"

"Mr. Patterson, I really . . . What in the hell is all this? Can you . . ."

"Jesus!" The man over by the rolltop desk was drawing the DVD out of the mailer. "Oh, Christ!"

Patterson repeated, "Having understood your rights, do you wish to speak to me at this time?"

The man walked over and held the DVD out. His mouth was pinched down. "This yours?"

"Give us a minute here," Patterson said.

Professor Cranmer, dangerously annoyed again, measured out his words. "Yes. As I told you a minute ago, it just arrived, okay?"

"Having understood your rights, Professor," Patterson repeated again. "Do you now wish to speak to me?"

"What am I supposed to say?"

The heavy man in the rugby shirt broke in. "How about starting with this?"

Using the pliers, he placed the DVD on the coffee table. Professor Cranmer glanced down at it and quickly turned his face away. "Oh my God!"

O'Brien leaned over Patterson's shoulder and said something that Elizabeth couldn't hear. Patterson nodded.

O'Brien waved from across the room. "You're all set, Elizabeth. You can take off now."

Elizabeth got up and walked across the room past the coffee table, heading toward the front door. Patterson had folded his arms and was staring at Professor Cranmer, frowning. Professor Cranmer was turned to the side, looking down at the rug and away from the DVD.

She couldn't see the professor's face, but as she went past, Elizabeth got a good look at the color photo on the front of the plastic DVD sleeve. It showed a small blond girl, about four years old, naked, tied to a table with her legs spread apart. Above her, the lower half of a man in an open lab coat was visible, both hands grasping his erect penis. The girl's eyes were wide with terror, and her mouth was open. It looked as though she was screaming.

2

At the urging of two department colleagues who were dying of curiosity, Professor Claire Lindemann decided that it was time to bring her semifamous boyfriend into the center of her world. She asked David to come to President Cabot's annual Amherst College Garden Party.

The Honorable David S. Norcross had been in the spotlight a year before, when he had presided over a rare death-penalty case, *United States v. Hudson*. He was known these days by some members of the local bar as the "one-eyed judge," but the sobriquet was something of an exaggeration.

Judge Norcross had both his eyes. He just couldn't see very well out of his left one, a result of an injury toward the end of *Hudson*, when a loopy *pro se* litigant had discharged a pistol in his face. In the months while the eye had been healing, he'd sported a leather patch on the bench, but now all that remained of the episode, physically, was a fine web of scarring, a slightly drooping left eyelid, and limited depth perception at night.

The area around the eye sometimes tingled or itched, and Claire noticed that David had fallen into the habit of rubbing at it, especially when he was tired or worried. Combined with his tendency to pull on his nose and sniff, and to scratch his ear, her boyfriend's performance under stress sometimes reminded Claire, who was an avid baseball fan, of a third-base coach orchestrating a suicide squeeze.

Her friend's offhand response to the garden party suggestion—"Sure, sounds like fun"—struck Claire as one more expression of David's obliging cluelessness.

"I don't know how much fun it will be," Claire replied. "It's mostly a lot of faculty standing around drinking lukewarm chardonnay while the president praises our hard work and gushes at the donors who've shown up. A few of my friends are eager to meet you, though." She paused, watching David closely. "So I thought we might go."

"I don't have to go without a tie, do I?"

David stayed over at Claire's house the evening before the party, something he and his dog, Marlene, did two or three times a week now. He seemed preoccupied during dinner, which worried Claire. Then, he was uncharacteristically distant after they went to bed—usually, they tucked themselves together like two puzzle pieces—and his restless tossing kept them from getting much sleep. Claire was concerned that David's touch-me-not mood reflected his discomfort at the prospect of standing around with a lot of prying academics. Around two a.m., when she was sure he was awake, she rolled toward him and touched his arm.

"David?" she whispered.

"Hmmm?" He turned toward her in a puff of warmth, faintly scented with Old Spice.

"We can skip the garden party if you want. It's not that big a deal."

"Oh, gosh, no." David lifted his head off the pillow. "It's not the party." He twisted around and, with some bouncing, managed to push himself up against the wall. "I'm kind of a public guy, you know. I don't spook that easily. What . . ." He paused and wiped his hands over his face. "What I can't seem to rinse out of my mind . . . Oh crud, hold on. Let me get the light."

He reached over and switched on the reading lamp next to the bed, shoved the pillows up behind him, leaned back, and let out a sigh. "The postal inspectors . . ." He glanced down at her. "It's so ugly I hate even mentioning it. The postal inspectors brought me another warrant application for child pornography yesterday. I had to review the material to be sure there was probable cause to authorize the seizure."

Claire propped herself on an elbow, looking up at David. His weary, tousled expression was somehow very endearing.

"The pictures of those poor, skinny little kids . . ." He pressed his hands against his temples and squeezed his eyes shut. "They're so . . ." He dropped his hands and searched for words. "So far beyond anything merely disgusting—doing those things to a helpless child, and making a video of it. It . . ." He shook his head. "It makes me ashamed to be human."

"God, I'm sorry, David. Assholes." A silence drew out. Finally, Claire said, "I'm trying, but I honestly can't come up with a single consoling thing to say. It's too sickening."

"There's nothing to say. People do terrible, vicious things, that's all."

"Would a back rub help?" Claire asked.

He looked at her and gave a relieved smile. "That would be fantastic."

David swung his legs onto the floor, and Claire got behind him and began kneading the base of his neck and shoulders.

"The scenes hit your brain like boiling acid," David said. "Wow. That helps." He inhaled deeply. "Just looking leaves a scar. I keep seeing this one little girl. I can still hear her . . ." He trailed off.

"I can't imagine." Claire pressed her thumbs into his shoulder blades. "I don't want to imagine."

After another long silence, David's shoulders began to relax. He turned and kissed Claire. "Thanks. You're a true sweetheart. That's a lot better."

He switched off the light, and in a few minutes, he began breathing regularly. Claire, however, lay awake for a long time. David's distress was painful to see, but it was also a troubling sign for their relationship. A few weeks before, they'd enjoyed a romantic, champagne-drenched evening at the Blue Heron, a swanky local restaurant in nearby Sunderland. Over dessert, David had slid a black felt box containing a beautiful diamond-and-sapphire ring across the table and asked Claire to marry him. It was so sweet—she'd actually blinked back tears, which was unusual for her—but she hadn't given him her answer yet.

The problem was, she wanted children, and she wanted them soon. David did not seem to want children, certainly not soon and maybe not ever. His wife, Faye, had died pregnant, and his life in court made him doubt that the world was a fit place for anyone, let alone a helpless toddler. Claire could see no point in a wedding if kids were off the table. On the other hand, she had to smile at herself: She might not like the idea of marriage without children, but she certainly liked that ring.

This child porn sewage definitely would not help things. Claire sometimes wondered fleetingly whether she should be with David at all. Maybe she should be trying for someone else who was ready for a family. Other men, including one in particular, a highly available colleague whom she'd had a couple lunches with, were making friendly noises.

But these thoughts never stayed long. David, in his earnest, semi-dorky way, was unbearably lovable. Things had reached the point where the notion of being without him literally made her sick. The kid issue was painful, she told herself, but it was one of those tough things a couple had to work through.

The darkness was thinning and the first birds were beginning to call before she finally dropped off.

The afternoon of the party turned out to be hot for May. As Claire pulled into the parking area near the Amherst College quad—she usually did the driving now—bubbles of tar popped under her tires. When they got parked, she looked over at David and saw him checking her out, his eyes going shiny with affection.

"Okay, showtime!" He punched her lightly on the shoulder. "Let's go party."

David's act was so typical it brought a smile to Claire's face. She knew that she was no longer in her twenties, or even early thirties, and she knew that her behind was slightly larger, and her upper arms slightly puffier, than was strictly ideal. Yet every time she got into a nice outfit for events like this and put on a little makeup, she'd catch him, no matter how wiped out or distracted he might be, giving her this look, as though today was his birthday and she was the ice-cream cake.

As they exited the car and began walking toward the crowd gathered on the lawn, Claire worked extra hard to maintain her poise. Was it her imagination, or were heads already turning toward them? She'd been at the college twelve years, and nearly everyone knew about her painful divorce. A lot of people would be pulling for her now, but it was not clear that their wagging and sniffing would make the next hour and a half any easier. The situation was made even more fraught by the fact that, according to rumor, Claire was in the running for the much coveted Senior Class Faculty Award, which would be announced at the party.

She hadn't told David about this in case she didn't get it, but she wanted him to be on hand if she won. Silly, she had to admit, but still.

As they passed through the sweltering parking lot, something caught David's attention that pushed him close to profanity.

"Oh, boy!" Then louder, "Oh, darn it all!"

He was leaning over, squinting into the rear driver's-side window of a large black BMW parked in the blazing sunlight.

"What's the matter?"

He was cupping his hand against the glass. "Some . . . Some . . ." he sputtered. He stood and pointed. "Some jerk's left his dog in there." He shook the door handle; the car was locked. "Man!"

Claire peered inside and saw a golden retriever on the backseat, panting and shifting position to find some shade.

"They can't have been gone long," she said. "They'll probably be right back."

"I guess." As they moved on, David kept glancing back over his shoulder. "Dogs trust us. I hate it when . . ." He shook his head, trailing off, his face dark.

A few minutes later, Claire was swept up in the flurry of introducing David to her intrigued friends, most of whom knew him through newspaper stories about his capital trial or from one of his other high-profile cases. A few people asked questions about his work, and Claire noticed how adroitly David steered around them, making jokes—usually about himself—and changing the subject.

Claire realized that she was unfamiliar with this public side of him, a persona both amiable and inaccessible.

During one unfortunate interval, for the better part of five minutes, they found themselves glued to Dixwell Pratt, an old high-school classmate of David's from Madison, Wisconsin, now an associate dean at the college, who introduced David as the Lord High Executioner many, many times, laughing in exactly the same way with each rendition, like an audio loop. They were rescued by Claire's gorgeous, dark-haired friend Celine, from the French Department, who dragged David off to introduce him to a professor in legal studies while Claire escaped to refresh her wine.

As she was waiting to be served, a department colleague, Darren Mattoon, approached her, smiling. "Have mine," he said, holding out his glass. "Our sophomore-slump bartender is taking forever."

When Claire looked dubious, Darren's grin broadened. "Don't worry. It's like me: fresh. I haven't taken even a sip. See?" He held his glass up, full to the brim.

Darren Mattoon had been on the faculty for four years and was coming up for tenure. Claire's letter setting out the department's assessment of him would be a key factor in the ultimate decision. Since he was unabashedly ambitious, Claire knew that Darren's courtesy was, at least in part, an attempt to grease her. On the other hand, to complicate matters, he was also handsome, smart, and single. Tall and broad shouldered, he had thick blond hair and an aquiline profile accented by trendy black, round-frame glasses—a surfer dude with a brain.

During two very amusing lunches, without being pushy or indelicate, he had been transmitting unmistakable sunbeams. He'd worked for several years selling real estate in Southern California—and, according to the gossip, making a pile of money—before going for his PhD. He was younger than David, roughly Claire's age.

"You know," Claire said, receiving his glass. "I think I'll take you up on that."

"Better move fast." Darren raised his eyebrows and, still smiling, nodded across the crowd in David's direction. Celine was lingering next to him, laughing.

"She's a friend." Claire sipped her wine. "I'm not too worried."

"Friends are good." Darren looked to the side, poked his glasses up his nose, and turned back to Claire. "Speaking of which, have you heard the news? The National Endowment has a traveling exhibition of one of Shakespeare's First Folios—the real deal, published in 1623—and it's coming to the college art museum next month. I know the lady who's chaperoning it. Care to join me on a private viewing?"

"Wow, sign me up," Claire said distractedly. Celine had put her hand on David's shoulder, as if to steady herself. "I better mingle."

"Good idea. We'll talk later."

When Claire approached, Celine moved off with the legal studies professor. As she passed, she elbowed Claire in the side and whispered, "I hate you!" She was, Claire knew, on the hunt for a husband and a baby, not necessarily in that order.

Eventually, Claire and David found some shade and stood together watching President Cabot as she offered her occasionally funny remarks. From time to time, they let their hands touch discreetly. To Claire's irritation, she felt her tension over the imminent award announcement rising.

"I almost forgot!"—Cabot was smiling—"Now, it's time to announce the winner of this year's Senior Class Faculty Award. This recognition, which has been bestowed annually for nearly fifty years, goes to the college faculty member who is most respected by the graduating class as a teacher, mentor, and academician."

Someone handed Cabot a small plaque along with an envelope, which she fiddled with, apparently having trouble getting it open. She let her hands drop and continued. "By tradition, the election is solely by vote of the seniors, and the seniors alone." She rolled her eyes in mock frustration. "Even I don't know who it is!" When she wrestled the envelope open and read the slip of paper, a smile lit up her face. "And this year it goes, most deservedly . . ."—she paused to let the anticipation swell—"to our dear colleague and friend, Professor Claire Lindemann!"

An enthusiastic burst of applause followed, punctuated by one or two whoops, and Claire was delighted to look up into David's amazed, beaming face. His arm snaked around her, and he hugged her to his side, kissing her on top of the head.

By the time they'd finished fielding the stream of well-wishers—including, of course, Darren Mattoon, who was effusive—and drifted back to the parking lot, many of the cars had left, and Claire was ready, first, for a bathroom and then for a quiet hour to sit and read.

The ordeal seemed to have energized David. "That was fabulous!" he said, smiling at her. "I had no idea you were such a star! Fabulous! What in the world are you doing with a clod hopper like me?"

"I crave your bod, that's all."

"Who was that lantern-jawed Mattoon fellow?"

"Junior faculty. Nobody."

"Let's hurry home."

They were approaching Claire's car when David noticed the black BMW, still parked in the same place. He veered off in his gangling stride, head bobbing, like a giraffe on a mission.

"David?"

"Just checking," he said over his shoulder. Then, as he bent down to the window, he added angrily, "Oh man!" He stood and glared at the car. "This is my fault. I should have done something before."

What Claire saw when she joined David was not good. After ninety minutes in the broiling car, the dog's eyes were closed, and its rapid, shuddering breaths made its ribs stand out. The poor animal's rear haunches were on the floor, and its upper body and head were on the leather seat in a small triangle of shade. Its gray tongue lolled out.

"Shit!" Claire leaned down. "His heart is beating like crazy. You can see it under his leg."

"It's a she, not a he." David looked grim, almost dangerous. "Like Marlene. Stay here, okay?"

Claire stood by the car while David marched quickly back up the hill, searching, she assumed, for whomever the Beemer belonged to. She had a passing concern that he might get angry or rude, but dismissed it. David could be direct, but he did not make scenes.

As she waited, Claire continued to peer anxiously into the car. The dog looked as though she might expire before David returned. The poor animal's desperation, and Claire's growing concern, contrasted with the peaceful scene around her. The air was still very warm, but the sun had dropped lower, and the diagonal light was going peach. Bordering the parking lot were swishing sugar maples, already deep green, and well-manicured paths containing an occasional jogger or strolling couple.

Gazing around, Claire's eyes focused on her friend Sid Cranmer's tidy white house, a block down a side street. A bunch of cars were clustered around it. One, a black monster SUV, was even squatting on his lawn, partly crushing his hydrangea. Sid had turned down President Cabot's invitation to the party, and Claire's phone call the night before to prod him to change his mind had only reached his answering machine. He'd been through a rough patch since his mother died, and even his recorded message sounded reedy.

Much as she liked Sid, Claire had found his absence from departmental meetings a relief. As chair, she had the task of presiding at these powwows, and Sid, when he went off on one of his toots, could be a massive pill.

The question was: What was he doing with all the visitors?

David's appearance in the distance interrupted her speculation. He was coming down the incline, staggering a little and carrying something against his stomach. As he drew near, Claire could see that he had a big, cut-glass bowl, half full of melting ice and water. Some had slopped onto his pants, spilling a dark stain from his crotch to his knee.

"She's worse, I think," Claire said as he approached. "Where'd you get the . . ."

"Pinched it off a table." David bent down and set the bowl next to the rear door of the BMW. "Stand there and screen me, okay?"

"She's really . . . Whoa!" Claire exclaimed as David pulled a misshapen half brick out of his pocket. She swept her eyes over the parking lot, checking for witnesses.

"Just stand like this?" He took her shoulders to position her. "Right like that. Act nonchalant." David hefted the brick, which was partly covered with mortar, and swung it a couple times experimentally. "Heck of time finding this," he muttered.

"Da-vid?" Claire's voice went up, drawing out the two syllables. "Is this legal?"

"Possibly." He eyed the window. "Some precept I dimly remember about committing a small crime to forestall a larger one. Not sure if it applies." He braced himself, leaning one hand on the door frame. "Anyway, here goes nothing."

Claire, looking up at the sky in a ludicrous pose of casualness, heard a grunt from David and a sharp whack as he swung the brick into the BMW's rear driver's-side window.

"Jeessuss!" she hissed. From the sound of the impact, not much had happened. A peek over her shoulder revealed only a modest spiderweb of cracks.

David kept at it, his words punctuated now by the sound of blows. "It doesn't happen very often"—*whack!*—"but sometimes"—*whack!*—"what you need to do"—*whack!*—"is pretty obvious." Pieces of mortar or window bounced off the side of Claire's leg.

At that moment, casting her eyes toward the grassy incline at the end of the parking lot, Claire noticed something that hoiked up her stomach and dropped it heavily. From the crest of the hill, coming out of the trees, a patrician-looking couple was ambling its way in their direction. The two were arm in arm, and the male was pointing up at one of the dormitory buildings.

"Step back a little," David said.

He finished the job with a couple fierce, roundhouse strokes and tossed the brick on the ground.

"David, I'm pretty sure somebody's coming."

"It's okay. I can reach in and . . ."

When the two aristocrats stepped out of the shade of the trees, Claire could see the man's silver hair and tanned, beefy face. She recognized him as the head of a foundation that had made several stupendous donations to Amherst College. The woman, much younger, was wearing one of those skimpy summer dresses that run up into four figures.

David was muttering to himself. "Staying calm, staying calm." There was the sound of the door opening, and a gust of hot air boiled out of the interior. A soft thump told Claire that the dog, wheezing hard, had slipped entirely off the seat onto the carpeting.

"Here you go, girl." David reached in and gently pulled the animal out, wrapping his arms around her rib cage and setting her on the pavement in front of the bowl.

The man and woman had crossed the boundary of the parking area but were still lost in their own conversation. They swiveled and looked admiringly back up the hill. Claire heard the sounds of slurping, dribbling, and heavy panting. Now the couple turned to resume their walk into the parking lot, on a beeline toward them.

"David," Claire said. "Time to be running along."

"You're okay, girl." David's voice was tender, reassuring, and apparently oblivious to danger. To Claire's horror, he bent down and began stroking the dog's head.

"Come on!" She yanked him up by his armpit and began dragging him toward her car.

David followed reluctantly, looking over at the dog until Claire shoved him into the passenger seat and danced around to the driver's side.

"God, David!" she said as she slammed her door. "I adore you." She flipped her plaque onto the backseat and patted his cheek. "But for a quiet type, you can be fucking crazy."

"We could stay and explain . . ." David began.

"I think not," Claire said, pressing down on the accelerator and negotiating a brisk U-turn.

As they cleared the parking lot, the couple reached the BMW, and the silver-haired man leaned over the dog with his hands on his thighs. Claire's last glimpse was of the girlfriend looking around indignantly, but fortunately, not in their direction.

"Serves them right," David said, beginning to smile. He and Claire looked at each other, burst out laughing, and performed a clumsy high five.

David leaned back, pulled on the end of his nose, and sniffed. "I had no idea that a simple, well-executed criminal act could be so exhilarating."

"My favorite part was the hair-raising, last-minute escape."

How can someone who would do that for a dog, Claire thought, *keep fending off the chance to be a dad?* She looked over at David and smiled.

"What?" He smiled back.

"Nothing."

A little later, Claire got a closer look at her friend Sid Cranmer's house. "Wonder what's up at Sid's. Look at all those cars!"

"Name again?"

"Sidney Cranmer, a buddy of mine in the English Department. Great Victorian scholar. Famous for his F-bombs at faculty meetings." She craned her neck. "He may not actually be bipolar, but he's certainly bipolar-ish. Jeez, they're carrying things out of his house. I hope he's all right. Let's just stop for a minute." She began to slow down. "He's been a total mess since his mom died."

"Cranmer." David's face had fallen. "Uh-huh."

Claire eased around the double-parked cars, twisting her head to stare, speaking quickly. "Sid's a complicated guy, but sweet once you get to know him. Turned out he got some big medal in Vietnam. Nobody knew. He rescued me once from a really nasty situation." As they crept along, she caught sight of her friend being walked out of the house toward the black SUV, with his hands behind his back. "What the hell!"

David's face was looking very tired again. He rubbed under his eye and blinked. "I think we'd better just get on home."

3

He liked to call his little girls "Happy Meals."

It was 11:30 p.m., the perfect time to troll. Homework was done—if the naughty darlings did any homework—the TV was off, and Mom and Dad had gone to bed.

He'd moved north years ago, finally giving up on college, and now he lived alone, deep in the woods, which was how he liked it. A barred owl lived in the hemlock grove behind his house and kept pushing its question into the silence: "Who cooks for you? Who cooks for you?" Nice.

He preferred to cook for himself and to do his fishing alone. In the glow of the computer, he paddled from one site to another, tending his many lines. This evening, one minnow was making his bobber dance. Li'l Sis. It was their third chat. Don't rush it, he told himself.

LS: u wouldnt want to go out w/me.
2Kool: yea i would why would u say i wouldnt want to go out w/u.
LS: cuz im not cute :(

He typed: "aw your cute i bet your really beautiful." He looked at the screen thoughtfully, sipped his coffee, struck the line out, and after a few seconds, replaced it.

2Kool: i bet your cute anyway its not whats outside its whats inside that matters and you are pretty inside and outside 2 that's what i like anyway maybe im weird

The response was a quick tug.

LS: omg no way no guy is like that here they just want a hot girl and a bj
2Kool: maybe im weird im not like other guys
LS: yur not weird yur sweet :)
2Kool: hey im looking at your yrbk pic, and i think u are hot i would love to have u as a gf if u want me as a bf
LS: *blushes* i dont really look 2 much like that pic irl i mean sorta but not 2 much
2Kool: spell right i cant read it
LS: sowwy what cant u read? :(
2Kool: whats irl?
LS: u dont know irl??
2Kool: no i dont do this that much so u need to help me sowwy :(

He knew "irl."

LS: irl means in real life u r so funny u probably don't even know what LMAO means
2Kool: haha i know that one how about sweet<3? thats what i want u 2 be
LS: *giggles* how about dwpkotl
2Kool: ????
LS: deep wet passionate kiss on the lips!!! :) ;)
2Kool: !!!!! u make me so hot
LS: i better slow down then **//

He smiled, slipped his hand up under his T-shirt, and scratched his stomach. "**//" meant "wink, wink, nudge, nudge." This was the second time Li'l Sis had used it. He gave her some line.

2Kool: slow is ok we don't have to hurry this is so 1daful and u are so kool u make me smile :) maybe u can send me a better pic that looks more like u and i can be your bf
LS: *blushes* but what about age? where i am high school guys don't even look at middle school kids
2Kool: 4 yrs is not 2 much besides 2 me how old u are is just a # but if u don't want to be my gf its ok but i will be sad :(
LS: wow i think the same thing about #s my mom says im 2 young for a bf but i think i would go out with u and be your gf if u wanted, but i don't think u wld want to if u saw me irl u make me smile and keep smiling :) :) :)
2Kool: u can send me pics I bet u r beautiful
LS: p911 gotta go luv u talk 2moro

The p911 code meant one of Li'l Sis's parents was around, and she was hiding their chat, which was excellent. The lazy stirring in his crotch intensified. Soon.

The owl's questioning had stopped. It must have snagged some vole or chipmunk and flown deeper into the woods to enjoy its meal. He let his right hand drift down. Bedtime. 2moro was another day.

4

All rise!" The voice of Judge Norcross's deputy, Ruby Johnson, filled the courtroom with its formal, honeyed Jamaican accent. The case of the "porno professor" had gotten a boatload of media play, and the usually empty gallery was filled with reporters and curious onlookers who had come to see the defendant's initial appearance in court. Ruby's no-nonsense summons had the throng jumping to its feet. Somebody dropped something with a clatter and the murmuring died.

The judge moved quickly from the doorway up the three stairs to the bench. Chitra and Erik, his two law clerks, followed him and peeled off to their table at the side of the courtroom.

"All persons having anything to do before the Honorable David S. Norcross, judge of the United States District Court for the District of Massachusetts, Western Division, may draw near, give their attention, and they shall be heard. God save the United States of America and this honorable court. The court is now in session. You may be seated."

Judge Norcross slipped into his high leather chair, arranged his robe over his knees, and deliberately nodded, as he always did, once to the assistant United States attorney and once to defense counsel. This habit allowed him to make eye contact and to check the lawyers' facial expressions for clues. Initial appearances were usually routine matters; the trial, assuming the defendant didn't plead out, was still many months away. But today's proceeding might be different. What was he in for this morning?

Ruby continued: "Now before the court is the case of *United States of America versus Sidney C. Cranmer*, CR16-30106-DSN."

The AUSA, Paul Campanella, had joined the Springfield U.S. attorney's office a few months back, and the judge was only gradually getting to know him. Slightly plump, Campanella was in his late twenties and either prematurely bald or shaving his head. He stroked his goatee and bobbed lightly on his toes, getting ready to launch into his pitch. In two or three previous appearances on minor motions, the judge had been impressed by Campanella's eager, happy-warrior energy. As far as Norcross knew, this was the man's first time representing the government on his own in a major felony case.

Defense counsel, Linda Ames, was an old hand who had appeared before Norcross many times. She was a square, sturdy woman with short brown hair, and she knew her stuff. The judge respected and liked her, in spite of the fact that her bulldog efforts on behalf of her clients tended to make extra work for him.

"Please be seated." Norcross cleared his throat.

Campanella kept standing. "Your Honor . . ."

"Have a seat for a minute, Mr. Campanella, would you please? I want to put something on the record."

"I just . . ." Campanella began. Then, catching the judge's look, he said, "Sure, of course," and sat down.

"I want to make counsel aware of some minimal out-of-court contact I've had with this case. Not enough to create concerns in my own mind, but, if it comes out, I don't want anyone wondering why it wasn't disclosed."

The atmosphere in the courtroom tautened slightly, like a sail struck by a puff of breeze, as it always did when something broke the routine. Campanella went motionless, his hand frozen on his chin. Next to him, an African American man with black-framed glasses, probably the case agent, was scrutinizing the judge with an intensely focused but unreadable expression. To the judge's left, defense counsel and Cranmer formed a tableau, with Ames shifted to one side in the direction of her client, within whispering range, and the defendant's head tilted toward her, ready to listen.

As Norcross inhaled to speak, Cranmer turned his face up to the bench, and the judge got a look into the man's eyes. They exuded such a shocking degree of despair that Norcross was stopped in midthought.

A high level of misery was not unusual for defendants, especially white-collar defendants, at their initial appearances in court. They'd been arrested, often for the first time, booked and fingerprinted, jailed for up to forty-eight hours, and publicly mauled by news reports. On the shame and humiliation scale, defendants charged with child pornography offenses, like this creature, had it the worst, which was probably what they deserved.

The misery made sense. Cranmer's legal position was about as bad as it could get. Receipt of child pornography was a violation of both state and federal law—the crime could be prosecuted in either jurisdiction—but the penalties under federal law were much tougher than under state law. This case was surely before Norcross because the authorities wanted to crucify a high-profile defendant. The minimum sentence was five years, and this guy was probably looking at much more.

Welcome to hell, Professor Cranmer.

The judge pushed on. "Yesterday, I was attending a function at Amherst College with a close friend who happens to know the defendant." He nodded down at Cranmer. "As we were leaving the event, we passed the defendant's residence. We saw Mr. Cranmer, Professor Cranmer here, being escorted out. My friend mentioned that she liked and respected the defendant . . ."

Cranmer's face twisted, and he dropped his head.

". . . and wondered what might be happening. Professor Cranmer, my friend said, was a colleague at Amherst College. She disclosed to me that he was a well-reputed scholar and that he'd served in Vietnam and received some kind of decoration. She told me his mother had recently died, which had been a painful loss for him. That was basically it. Obviously, there will be no further out-of-court discussions about this case on my part—with anyone. Counsel now know everything I know."

This summary was the truth and nothing but the truth, but not quite the whole truth. Judge Norcross was certainly not going to mention the quagmire he and Claire had spiraled down into after he had confessed to her that he'd approved the warrant authorizing Professor Cranmer's arrest and the search of his house. The affidavit supporting the application had revealed that the target was an Amherst College professor, and as Norcoss was reviewing it, he vaguely recalled that Claire had mentioned Cranmer's name once or twice in the past year. He, of course, hadn't been able to let Claire know about the search ahead of time. The papers didn't reveal Cranmer's department, and Norcross had told himself that, even if she knew him, the target was unlikely to be someone very close to Claire.

Claire's questions about what would be happening to her friend had gotten increasingly pointed as the evening wore on, but because the case was still under seal, he couldn't say much. Claire understood this—she knew and mostly respected the constraints he worked under—but her concern for Cranmer clearly put her in a painful position. Over dinner, the clicks of her knife and fork were sharper than usual, and Norcross could see she was struggling to resist coming back to the topic. When she'd told him that Sid's mother had recently passed away and that her death had hit him hard, he'd had to ask her again to please drop the subject. Everything she said to him, everything that went into his head about Cranmer, would have to be shared with the lawyers. He couldn't have private information.

After this, their conversation lapsed into longer and longer silences. There was an elephant in the room, and if they couldn't talk about that, it was hard to talk about anything. Even Norcross's attempt to reprise their happy adventure with the dog in the parking lot fizzled.

From his perch on the bench, Norcross moved his gaze from Campanella to Ames and continued. "Based on the scenario I just described, where I've had no direct personal contact with this defendant, I've concluded it would not be proper for me to recuse myself on my own initiative, *sua sponte*." He nodded at the attorneys. "But I'm happy to hear counsel if you have concerns." He saw Ames lean back, whisper something to her client, and shake her head. She had no problem. AUSA Campanella, however, might feel differently.

Now that he'd put his position on the record and could not go back, it struck Norcross even more painfully that he didn't know how he was going to untangle things with Claire. The defendant was, it turned out, someone she knew pretty well and apparently liked, and it might take him months to dispose of the man's case via a guilty plea or trial. If he imposed a long prison sentence on Cranmer, which he almost certainly would, Claire might never forgive him.

She had asked him—later in their conversation, as things were getting badly out of hand—why he couldn't just pass the case off to some other judge, recuse himself, now that he knew Sid was her colleague and friend. All the judges had hundreds of cases; one more couldn't be that big a deal. He'd responded, reasonably, that it would be an imposition on the judge who would inherit the file, that everyone disliked these child pornography cases, and that the applicable authorities simply didn't support recusal in these circumstances—all of which was true and okay. But then, when she kept pressing him, he'd gone on to say that a judge couldn't toss a case every time someone he was dating happened to know a defendant, which he could now see was a horrendous flub on his part. Claire had responded, "Oh, is that what we're doing? Dating?" Which was when she had gone upstairs, closed her door with a medium bang, and he and Marlene had departed.

Norcross's guilty knowledge that he had not been entirely honest with Claire about his reasons for declining to recuse himself compounded things. The whole truth was that, only a month before, he'd passed off a jumbo securities case involving Massachusetts Mutual, a local employer that he held stock in. The case had bounced over to a dear friend in Boston, Judge Bertha Weinstein, who was struggling through chemotherapy and needed a twenty-defendant securities class action like a hole in the head. He just couldn't bring himself, so soon after that, to duck yet another messy trial and have it redrawn to a new judge. He probably should have told Claire all this, except he couldn't see how it would help.

AUSA Campanella had been leaning toward the case agent, conferring in low tones. He now stood. Attorney Ames turned away from her client and gazed over at Campanella with a look of amused expectation. Campanella might be uncomfortable with where this was going, but there was little he could do about it. Absent facts much more compelling than this, the recusal decision was within Norcross's discretion.

Campanella started on easy terrain. "Your Honor, let me begin by introducing Special Agent Mike Patterson of the FBI. He's up here from Washington, and he will be the government's case agent."

The judge nodded. "Welcome."

Patterson nodded back with one-tenth of a smile, and Campanella went on.

"With regard to your friend's acquaintance with the defendant, might I inquire?"

"Of course."

"I think you said she was a close friend of yours?"

"Right."

Campanella shifted his weight over to his right foot and scratched the back of his head. How much, Norcross wondered, did the AUSA know about his relationship with Claire? In the greater Springfield legal community, everybody basically knew everything about everybody, but Campanella was new in town, still green, and Patterson was just joining the local FBI office. Did the prosecutors pass around gossip they'd heard about a judge's private life? He'd certainly done that, back when he was trying cases. Every little bit helped.

"Would Your Honor be comfortable, um, revealing the name of your friend? I could approach side bar if you'd prefer."

"Professor Claire Lindemann."

The second the words were out of his mouth, Norcross regretted uttering them. The very competent *Springfield Republican* reporter was in her usual corner of the gallery, jotting away. On the one hand, the judge reminded himself, he didn't want to come across as though he had something to hide. On the other hand, it would probably irritate Claire if her name got into the papers, and that would make it even harder to iron things out between them. He should have provided the name off the record or found some way to avoid mentioning it at all. In fact, he realized, he probably should have passed the case back to the clerk to be redrawn to another judge, no matter how guilty it made him feel. But it was too late to jump now. It would look as though he'd chucked the case because he'd been scared off by Campanella's question.

Norcross didn't want to appear flummoxed, so he fell back on a technique he regularly used when he couldn't trust his face. He popped a Kleenex out of the box he kept under the bench and began cleaning his glasses. If he got really ruffled, he'd bend over and retie his shoes.

Campanella examined the surface of the counsel table and rotated his mouth in a circle several times. Linda Ames folded her arms and cocked her head to one side, just short of chuckling.

"Well, obviously," Campanella said finally, "if Your Honor is not concerned, the government has no objection."

Judge Norcross turned to Attorney Ames and raised his eyebrows inquiringly. Out of the corner of his eye, he noticed Agent Patterson writing something down. Would they be doing a background check on Claire now? Terrific.

Ames bobbed to her feet. "Defense has no objection, Judge."

"Okay, then, we'll get started." He turned to the defendant. "Mr. Cranmer, I have some information for you, and some warnings I need to pass on to you. Can you hear me all right from there?"

Cranmer nodded, and after a nudge from his attorney, sat up straighter and said, "Yes, very well. Thank you."

Judge Norcross fell into the stock series of questions he employed at all arraignments, beginning with: "For the record, do you have any difficulty with the English language?"

In response, Cranmer sagged and grimaced, bringing home to Norcross the irony of posing this question to an Amherst College English professor. The judge was tempted to observe that he routinely asked this question, that it was merely a formality—maybe even find a way to lighten things up with some humor—but decided against it. Excessive explanation or waggish remarks, he'd learned, tended to complicate things. Stick to the script.

A rustle from the back of the gallery brought the judge's attention again to the *Republican* reporter, who was scribbling fast and muttering something to the man next to her. The exchange about whether Cranmer had problems with English might make a nice lead to her story. The case was certainly going to sell newspapers.

"No, Your Honor," Cranmer said. He smiled wanly. "Not so far."

The reporter's smile widened; she drew an underline and looked up happily.

The next portion of the process followed a well-trodden trail: making sure the defendant had received a copy of the indictment, reviewing the charges, reminding the defendant again of his rights pursuant to *Miranda*, confirming that he was retaining his own lawyer and did not need one appointed, and entering his pleas of not guilty to the various counts. The trick was to cover all this very standard stuff in a way that was sufficiently fresh and pointed to penetrate the defendant's reeling brain.

Professor Cranmer seemed to get the gist. At least, he nodded at the right moments. Then came the hard part. Norcross turned to the AUSA.

"Mr. Campanella, I understand from your written motion that the government is moving for pretrial detention. Is that correct?" The muted phone on Ruby Johnson's desk below him emitted a soft buzz, and he noticed Ruby picking up and whispering.

Campanella quickly stood, squaring himself like a man preparing for hand-to-hand combat. His posture instantly told the judge that he was not entirely confident of his arguments, or at least had doubts about their reception by the court.

"Yes, Your Honor. It is the government's position that the defendant, if released prior to trial, would present both a danger to the community and a risk of flight."

Ruby, who had been scribbling on a sheet of paper, now turned in her chair and handed up a folded note to the judge. When he opened it, it read: "Your brother's office is on the phone. Important. Holding for you in chambers."

Judge Norcross considered these words, half weary and half wary. His brother, Ray Norcross, the former governor of Wisconsin, was now the country's secretary of commerce. His influence had been key in getting David Norcross his job on the federal bench. From childhood, Ray had always viewed minor inconveniences to himself as extreme emergencies justifying any and all demands upon others, especially upon his younger brother. Still, it might be something about their mom, who had late-stage Alzheimer's. Norcross had no choice.

Campanella was rattling forward, carried on by his own momentum and ignoring the fact that the judge was distracted by the note. "There are three compelling reasons, any one of which . . ." he was saying. A more experienced lawyer would have waited with an expression of sympathy until he had the judge's full attention.

"Very sorry to have to do this," Norcross interrupted. "Something has come up I have to deal with, and I'm going to need to take a recess." He looked over at the deputy marshals. "You can take the defendant down to the lockup. He may need to, you know . . ." He tipped his head toward Cranmer, and the deputies nodded back, understanding. The poor guy might need to pee, or throw up. "Fifteen minutes. Possibly a little more. Ms. Johnson will call you when we're ready to resume."

5

The defense attorney, Linda Ames, had three passions: her son, Ethan; Weight Watchers; and defending criminals.

Ethan, nine, was the product of a three-beer fling with a roofing contractor who'd dropped by one winter evening to discuss her leaky porch. Ames had considered terminating the pregnancy, but she figured (a) at age forty-one, it was probably her last chance at motherhood and (b) Charlie Buchannon was a healthy, easygoing man who looked like he had decent genes. Charlie soon drifted to the margin of her life, never more than sorta-kinda acknowledging that Ethan was his, which was fine with Ames. The baby, however, plopped right down in the center of her world: the absolute coolest person Linda Ames had ever known.

Ames's romantic life over the years had been a patchwork of both men and women. She never understood why a person had to choose. It was like Chinese versus Italian food. Depending on the quality of the ingredients and the skill in preparation, they could both be delicious. For a while now, things in that department had been in suspension anyway. The fires had died down, and she was too busy with her fabulous boy and her creepy clients to worry much about Valentine's Day.

A second time-sucker was Ames's obsession with Weight Watchers, which had her counting points and filling a small wire-rimmed notebook with scribbles in her endless campaign to drop ten pounds. On the morning of Sid Cranmer's arraignment, Ames was on a roll—low-fat yogurt with berries, two tablespoons of sliced almonds, and black coffee for breakfast, leaving her twenty-one of her twenty-six points available for the rest of the day. With salmon and peach salad and a Diet Coke for lunch, she'd have space for a five-ounce glass of Australian red (four points) with her bunless veggie burger at dinner.

Unfortunately, her meager breakfast had provoked in Ames a yearning for sugar so intense it was reaching what saints must feel for God. Sitting in court, she reflected that she would have given anything for a sticky bun, even if it meant she'd be on celery and herbal tea until a week from Wednesday.

Ames acquired her third passion, criminal law, while watching *Perry Mason* reruns as a grade-schooler. She was a patient person who moved slowly but thought fast, and she had the rare ability to ask blunt questions without being offensive—all of which made her very good in the courtroom. In law school, she took every criminal law course available, and she summered at the public defender's office. After graduation, she worked for two years for Bill Redpath, a very skillful Boston defense lawyer, before moving to the greener pastures, and the smaller pond, of Amherst. The one drawback in her professional life was that in twenty-five years defending criminals, she'd had to adjust to the fact that, unlike her hero Perry, she nearly always represented guilty people.

Innocent clients, in her practice at least, came along about as often as buffalo nickels, and Professor Sidney Cranmer did not look like one of them. The big tip-off was that he was obviously holding out on her. Ames's rare innocent clients were usually so outraged and hysterical she couldn't shut them up. Guilty clients tended to be vague and cagey, surrendering the truth in teaspoonfuls, which was what Sid Cranmer seemed to be doing. On the other hand, she only liked about a quarter of her creeps, and she was getting concerned that poor Sid might end up being one of these. Hard to say why. The charge against him was certainly putrid, and she assumed he was guilty. Maybe it was just that he had half a brain, which most of her clients did not, or that he was so totally screwed. It was always painful when one of her guys, even someone disgusting, fell into the yawning black mouth of the Bureau of Prisons, and for Sid it was going to be a very long drop.

The Amherst College Dean's Office had put Professor Cranmer in touch with Ames after his arrest, based on her recent victories with two college faculty members facing DUI charges. This was rash, since DUIs were Pop-Tarts compared to federal child porn trials, but they'd been lucky to stumble onto her. She actually had handled porn cases, one in federal court in Worcester, one in state court up in Greenfield, both guilty pleas with decent outcomes (prison terms, but survivable), and she had plenty of experience before Norcross doing drug and gun cases. He wasn't going to give her any special breaks—he didn't give anyone special breaks—but she could tell he respected her, and the feeling was mutual.

The U.S. Marshal's area on the first floor of the courthouse contained a row of cubicles and an array of surveillance monitors and electronic equipment along one wall. Making her way past the desks, Ames nodded to the deputies, all of whom knew her. As she turned down the windowless corridor leading to the attorney-client conference rooms, she breathed in the aroma of hot coffee. It made her think of pecan rolls.

Sid was waiting in the room set aside for them, slumping to one side as though someone had tapped all the blood out of him. The area, roughly eight by six feet, was arranged so that the detainee came in through one door and the attorney entered through another on the opposite side. The air was stuffy and smelled of Lysol. Sid was seated on a round metal stool that was bolted to the floor to keep it from being used as a weapon. Ames eased herself into one of the two chairs on the attorney's side. A scratched steel counter and a heavy mesh screen separated them.

If the screen hadn't been there, Ames might have been tempted to pat Sid on the shiny crown of his head, which was tipped toward her dolefully. His meager hair hung in gray commas over his collar. Some helpful deputy must have shown him that morning's *Republican* story, detailing the child porn charges and the news that Amherst College had suspended him.

"How you doing?" Ames asked.

"I'm alive." He looked up at her. "That's about it." He squirmed on the metal stool, and the humming fluorescent light reflected off his glasses. "One night in the slammer, and I'm already picking up some new vocabulary. My fellow inmates refer to me as a 'diddler,' which seems to be their word for a pedophile."

"Are they getting on you? I can talk to the sheriff . . ."

Criminals, Linda knew, had a harsh code of morality, and the drug dealers and gang members bunking with Sid could be very tough on sex offenders, especially child abusers.

"So far, so good." Sid pushed his glasses up his nose and blinked. "What are my chances of getting out of here, Linda? Tell the truth, it's a fucking nightmare. I already miss . . ." The face he tipped up to her was painful to see. He looked like a man struggling to bend his mind around a terminal cancer diagnosis. "There isn't a single thing I don't miss." He breathed in shakily. "The bed is killing my back, the cell smells like puke, and most of the other men I've seen scare me to death, even the guards."

"I can't promise anything." Ames shook her head. "Campanella's a world-class drip. He can't seriously think you're going to flee or endanger anybody. My guess is, one, he's showing off for his FBI agent up from Washington, who's trying to frighten me with his big, intimidating game face. And, two, he wants you detained to soften you up so you'll plead. Problem is, Norcross might just buy what he's selling. I can't . . ." Ames paused to emphasize the bad news. "I can't honestly predict what he'll do, Sid."

Her client's detention would make trial preparation much harder. Worse, after seven or eight months moldering inside a cell, the professor, even if somehow he were innocent, would look exactly like the pasty-faced pervert the government wanted the jury to think he was.

"It's just . . ." Sid dropped his eyes and shook his head again. "I know it sounds silly, but the cats will be freaking out. My intern is feeding them. The poor girl was there when they showed up. The problem is, she can only come by every other day or so, and the cats are Siamese. They hate being alone." He broke off, staring straight ahead but obviously seeing nothing. "I still can't believe what's happening. It's a cliché, I know, but I keep hoping it's just some bad dream, and I'll wake up."

"It's horrible. It always is." Ames leaned forward, placing her hands on the cool metal counter. "We don't have much time here, though. I need your help on a couple things if we're going to have a chance at getting you out." Ames watched Sid as he looked back at her warily. This was only their second meeting. She was still trying to figure him out, and he was still deciding whether he could trust her. How hard should she push?

"Tell me some more about this DVD."

"Like I told you, I do remember getting a flyer about it with an order form."

"And you didn't just toss it?"

"I couldn't figure out where it came from. It weirded me out."

"The postal inspectors must have gotten wind somehow that you were interested in this sort of stuff. Maybe from a chat room they were monitoring?"

Sid groaned. "Chat rooms." He put his hands over his face and talked through his fingers. "I spent a lot of time in them after my mother died. Late at night." He dropped his hands. "I can't even remember half the places I went, or the stuff I said. A lot of idiotic things, I know that."

"Campanella showed me a couple juicy passages they recovered. Not good. They must have seen what you were saying and decided to mail you the brochure, toss you some bait as part of their sting operation. Its code name is 'Window Pane.' It's all over the country."

"Can they do that? Isn't that, like, entrapment or something?"

"Not if they just give you the opportunity to commit the crime and you bite. It's only entrapment if they keep pushing you to do something you don't really want to do." This was a quick and dirty explanation of the law; Ames was more interested in other things. "I'm just trying to figure out what I can say when Campanella tells the judge you deliberately ordered that DVD."

"I can't believe I ordered it." He shook his head.

"Really."

Sid's answer had two possible meanings: (1) He didn't think he ordered the DVD, or (2) he knew he ordered it, but he couldn't believe how stupid he was for having done it. This sort of roundabout bibble-babble was typical of Linda's white-collar clients. Whether it was a Ponzi scheme, embezzlement, or child porn, it took these clients forever to cough up what they'd done. She'd have to give it time.

"I don't know." Sid looked at her. "Like I told you, I've been pretty . . . I haven't been myself for a while. I could have done a lot of things, I guess, but I honestly can't believe I ordered that DVD."

"Okay." Ames let Sid see she was examining him carefully. His nonexplanation was not going to do him any good with Norcross, let alone with a jury. "Campanella told me before court that you admitted to the raid team that you were expecting the DVD, that it was yours."

Sid looked shocked. "That's bullshit! I never admitted anything of the sort. I couldn't have." He looked into the distance again, trying to absorb this new blow. After a few seconds, he turned to her, glaring. "Can they just lie like that?"

"Campanella says his agent will testify that you said you weren't surprised when it arrived, or something like that." Ames paused, continuing to keep her eyes on Sid, who had collapsed back into his six-weeks-to-live stare. "Could be Campanella's pretending he's got more than he has." She pushed on. "But they've got the form, Sid, filled in with your credit card number and security code, your address, et cetera. Any memory of that?"

"Zip. I don't see how . . ." He started to say something, then stopped and shook his head. "I just don't see how I could have done that. I'm not into that stuff."

This all sounded pretty soupy. If she were forced to bet, Ames would put her money on Sid's having ordered the DVD deliberately. In the one-in-a-hundred chance that he really was innocent, or the one-in-ten chance he couldn't stand up and admit he was guilty, which would knock out any possible plea deal, this case was going to be a back—and heart—breaker.

Ames decided to move on to a more pressing issue and leaned forward, dropping her voice.

"You don't have any other material like this sitting around anywhere they didn't think to look, do you? Any stuff they missed?" The Marshals' attorney-client conference room was supposed to be private, no cameras and no microphones, but Ames never entirely trusted that.

Sid's face twitched up to her. "No, for heaven's sake, I don't think I ever had *any*. . . ."

"Campanella tells me they dug out a fair amount of porn on your home computer, including some underage material. How about a work computer or an iPad? Hard copies stuffed in a folder somewhere?"

Sid jumped at the sound of a sharp clang in the distance followed by a male voice shouting.

Ames recognized the groan of the big steel door that opened on the courthouse's sally port. The Marshals must be bringing in more prisoners.

"They'll find some fairly . . ." He hesitated. "Some fairly ugly pictures and video clips, okay? I'm not even sure what." Sid looked anxiously in the direction of the noise, which now had a sinister, metallic tone, as though it were a huge, dying robot.

"It's okay," Ames said. "Just the sally port with some more customers."

"But nothing like the DVD, okay? I'm not into that."

She pressed a little harder. "Nothing you've ordered on its way to you in the mail?"

"No fucking way." He hesitated, flushing. "They'll probably, like I say, find . . ." He paused again, struggling. "Some, probably some pictures, probably some videos, on my computer. I can remember sites, I think, like 'Barely Legal' and 'Horny Teens.' That kind of crap." He looked up at her with a pained expression. "But doesn't everyone look at that stuff once in a while? In the army, porn was like comic books at summer camp. Nobody thought twice about it."

"Adult porn's not a problem, Sid. Even I've checked it out once or twice." Ames sniffed. "Heck, I bet even our buddy Campanella has, if he's human. I'm talking about little kids."

"No. There was some of that in Saigon, underage Asian prostitutes and that sort of thing. It didn't shock me—people needed money—but it never did anything for me. I . . ."

"Sex with a minor in a foreign country gets you fifteen years nowadays, mandatory minimum."

"Well, that's one thing we don't have to worry about." He

hesitated and swallowed. "I paid for sex a couple times over there—everyone did—but never with a child. Jesus!"

"I hear you, but I also need you to understand. Patterson and his team will be on the lookout, and if they find more pictures or videos like this DVD, you will be, pardon my French, shit on a stick."

There was a long silence. Finally, Sid just said, "They'll find evidence on my hard drive that I've visited porn sites, okay? Adult porn sites. It's embarrassing enough to have to admit that." He paused and a look of disgust came over his face. "I flat out lied to my intern when I finally got her on the phone about the cats. Told her I wasn't into porn at all. But I honestly can't believe I ordered that video."

"Okay, fine. We'll leave it at that." Ames nodded. "New topic: Have you got a mortgage on your . . ."

A deputy marshal, a Hispanic woman with dark, curly hair, poked her head through the door behind Sid. She'd obviously been monitoring the room, just out of earshot. She tossed Sid a sandwich in a plastic baggie.

"I'd eat up," she said. "Judge sends you back to Ludlow, and this will be your last bite until dinner. You're going to miss lunch."

Sid stared down at the sandwich as if it had just landed from outer space.

Ames broke in. "Give us a minute, okay, Carmen?" The deputy disappeared, and Ames turned back to Sid. "Have you got a mortgage on your house?"

Sid looked surprised. "No, I . . . I paid it off with mother's insurance."

"Any problem giving the government a deed to secure your appearance and good behavior if we have to?"

"I don't understand."

Ames spoke quickly. "You sign a deed transferring your house to the government. They don't record the deed, just keep it in their files. But if you skip out, or get into any monkey business, they trot down to the Registry, record the deed, and they own your house. Simple as that. It's a form of bail. If there are no problems, they tear the deed up once the case is over. You willing to do that?"

"The house is about all I have, Linda, but I'll do anything to get out of here."

"Even if Norcross goes for it, you won't get out today. We'll need time to get the paperwork done and a good real-estate lawyer, my friend Bruce Brown." Ames's retainer was $50,000, and with extra expenses, it would evaporate quickly even at her below-market rate of $350 an hour. If the case went to trial, Sid would probably end up paying her at least $300,000, probably more, and even then Ames could end up taking a bath on the case.

"How do you feel about home confinement?" she continued.

"It would be a big improvement." Sid shrugged. "Except for classes, I haven't been getting out much lately anyway."

6

The FBI had no assigned space in the Springfield courthouse, so Mike Patterson was camping out in the U.S. Marshal's area, using a spare office with a dented metal desk half buried under file cartons. Assistant U.S. Attorney Campanella pursued Patterson downstairs during the recess, obviously looking for feedback about how his pitch to Norcross was going. Patterson tried to walk quickly to let Campanella know he had something else he needed to get to, but his bum ankle slowed him down.

He hated that his injury from Afghanistan was acting up again. If the ankle didn't improve soon, he'd be looking at a disability retirement, a depressing prospect. At fifty-one, he had twenty-two years with the Bureau, continuous except for his reserve deployments. He loved the work, and he took pride in being a role model for the younger black agents.

"Why do you think he took the recess?" Campanella asked as they stepped into the cramped office.

Patterson spoke over his shoulder. "Probably needed to take a shit."

He draped his navy suit jacket over the back of the chair, lowered himself into the seat, and began pulling out drawers to find something to write on. Some ideas were floating around in his head about another, much more serious, case he was working on, and he wanted to jot them down before the recess was over.

"I doubt he needs a note from his deputy for that." Campanella was standing in the doorway. "So what's your take on how things are going? I don't like this wild-card stuff about Norcross's lady friend knowing the defendant."

"We'll check her out." He found a yellow pad and began writing.

"Cranmer doesn't belong on the street, that's for sure," Campanella was saying. "Do you think I should have pushed for recusal?"

"Never piss a judge off unless absolutely necessary." Patterson finished his note and tossed his pen down. He leaned back in his chair and pointed at Campanella. "I'd like this guy locked up, too, but it's not going to be easy to sell that to Norcross."

Campanella started. "Really? The guy could run, and he's a child molester. I mean . . ."

"Norcross is going to wonder where Professor Dumbledore might run to. Hogwarts? My son was a big Harry Potter fan. You have kids?"

"Just one, a boy. But he's only two. Not reading yet." A happy look came over Campanella's face. "He's such a great little guy."

Patterson touched his heart. "Girl and a boy: sixteen and fourteen. Best things that ever happened to me." He leaned over the desk and steepled his hands. "Cranmer's not going to take off, Paul. He's nearly seventy, for God's sake. A bigger risk is that he'll escape riding downstream on a bottle of Seconal—everyone's favorite ticket to the next world. I've had that happen." Patterson reached around, took a bag out of his jacket pocket, and held it out. "Want a pistachio?"

Campanella shook his head. "He could hurt some child or . . ."

"I'm on your side, Paul, but I really doubt it." Patterson poured a small pile onto the desktop and began prying the shells open. Courtrooms, for some reason, always made him hungry.

Campanella scratched the back of his neck. "So what's the . . ."

"My take is Cranmer's a looker, not a toucher. Typical of the type. Middle-aged adult male. Lives alone or with a parent. Sits in front of his computer with his Kleenex box late at night, brings up his favorite kiddie porn, watches for a while, and jerks off. Then he wipes up and goes to bed. That's his love life. It's pathetic, but very few of these guys actually hurt anybody, at least not directly." He paused to finish chewing, swallowed, and resumed. "Judges, at least where I come from, tend to release these guys to await trial, even if they know they'll clobber them after they're convicted. So, take your best shot, but my advice? Don't expect much help from the court, not at this stage. Save your ammo for the sentencing hearing."

"Love life," Campanella muttered, shaking his head. "I'm sorry, Mike, I probably shouldn't say this, but I hate these guys. Even if they only look, they make me sick. Some of these kids are as young as my son."

"Ugly, and the more you see of it, the uglier it gets." Patterson swept the small pile of shells into his hand and dumped them into the wastebasket. He pointed at Campanella and then at himself. "On the other hand, there's many a lonely college boy who's done something like the same thing, right? They're just not into five-year-olds, that's all."

Sirens started up in the distance. A fire station occupied a corner a few blocks from the courthouse, and emergencies constantly called the trucks out. Campanella, still frowning, glanced up in the direction of the increasing racket.

"That's a big difference, Mike. Going to the *Penthouse* website is not the same."

"True, but I doubt we'd have bothered with this runt if he weren't a hotshot professor. We get headlines, and that means a big bang of deterrence for a popgun prosecution. His tough luck."

"Popgun? Come on."

"Sorry. Let's just call it a fish-in-a-barrel child-porn consumer case. Here's how it will go. Our professor will whine about how unfair it all is. His lawyer—watch out for her, by the way, she's a weasel—will beat him over the head with a polo mallet until he pleads guilty. After he squirms for a while, he'll take the mandatory five years, because if he doesn't, the jury will convict him, and he'll end up with eight or nine years, or even more if Norcross gets really steamed at him. The five years will put a big crimp in his life. He'll lose his job and have to register as a sex offender and so forth. Two years, or even a year, would probably be plenty for a sad sack like him. But you know what?" Patterson took off his glasses and tossed them on the desk. "To coin a phrase: Frankly, I don't give a damn. The kids in those videos have their lives messed up a whole lot more than his ever will be. And why? Because respectable types like him look at this garbage, buy it, and swap it over the Internet." Patterson sat up, wincing, and scrubbed his hands around his eyes. "He deserves what he gets. Did you see the report about what happened to the girl in his DVD?"

"Yeah. It will be part of my pitch to Norcross."

The sirens were fading, heading west toward the interstate. One of the marshals down the hall must have been monitoring the fire department frequency. He called out: "Eighteen-wheeler on its side on I-91."

"Well, good luck. I'm all for locking the guy up right now, instead of waiting for him to plead guilty. He won't have an easy time in detention, that's for sure."

Campanella turned to leave. "Well, thanks. I can see you've got stuff to do." He hesitated. "I've second-chaired a lot of trials, but this is my first one solo. I appreciate the help."

Patterson's experience made him sensitive to the odd situation he and Campanella occupied. As the responsible AUSA, Campanella was technically in charge; he was Patterson's superior, subordinate only to the U.S. attorney in Boston, Buddy Hogan. But Patterson was vastly more experienced with these prosecutions. The setup reminded Patterson of the army, where a hairy-knuckled master sergeant with twenty years of active duty might find himself taking orders from a second lieutenant fresh out of some college ROTC program. The trick was to manage the new man tactfully—try to keep him from screwing up and getting them both killed.

"You'll do fine, Paul. This one's not going to be hard." As Campanella started to leave, Patterson glanced at his watch. "This recess is going longer than I thought. Have a seat for a second." He pointed. "Shove that box over there."

Campanella hefted a carton off the chair facing the desk onto an adjoining stack and sat down. The box had a notation, "U.S. v. Hudson," on its side in black Magic Marker.

"Let me tell you the real reason I'm here, and what's put me in such a ratty mood," Patterson said. "This case of yours just happened to come along. I'm here on a temporary transfer, one year max, to help out with the A.G.'s 'Project Safe Childhood' initiative targeting the big-time touchers, the worst of the worst. Don't want to hurt your feelings, but I wouldn't be up from DC for a penny-ante case like Cranmer's." He took the bag of pistachios out of his pocket again and poured another small pile on the desk. "My wife and the kids will move up at the end of the summer, once Fran has our place rented." He paused and shook his head. "Right now, I'm supposed to be coaching my girl's summer-league softball team. They got toasted in their last two games." He was looking down, busily prying open shells and frowning. "Margaret, my sixteen-year-old, is a slugger, but I can't get her to pick her pitches. She keeps popping up."

"Sounds frustrating." Campanella spoke automatically, being polite but looking unhappy. The "penny-ante" reference had clearly stung.

"Here's why I'm here," Patterson said. "Like I said, we have the lookers and touchers. The lookers are the sad guys; the touchers are the bad guys. The lookers are mostly so depressing, they make you want to migrate to another planet. The touchers make you want to commit murder."

"I haven't drawn one of those yet."

"Some of these guys—they're always males, and, by the way"—he gave Campanella a steely look—"they're nearly always white. Child porn is mostly not a black sport. If it were, the penalty would probably be mandatory life, not just five years." He shifted in his chair, and an angry expression washed over his face. "Anyway, some of these guys have a real scary grasp of adolescent psychology. They circle over certain Internet chat rooms like buzzards, pretending to be teenagers, and they are very, very skillful at grooming vulnerable underage girls they connect with."

"Right. We had a seminar in Atlanta about this."

"So you know. Pretty soon, it's him and the girl, Romeo and Juliet, against the cold, hard world. He'll talk her into sending him pictures. Then he'll get her to send live images of herself that are more and more explicit. Masturbation. Bananas. Beer bottles. That sort of thing. He'll store the videos in his collection of stroke shows to swap with his buddies."

"We should just execute these guys, Mike. I'm serious. I know I'm not supposed to say that, but really . . ."

"Yeah, but the worst comes if he can sweet-talk the girl into meeting him somewhere. Once she's in the car or the motel room, it's game over. Sometimes they just disappear."

"Just take a chain saw and . . ."

"We think you've got one of the worst in your neighborhood." Patterson held up three fingers. "Three girls, two thirteen-year-olds and a fourteen-year-old, have gone missing in the last year after Internet chats with what sounds like the same guy. In each case, he convinced the girls to meet him. We think the groomer might have a partner who helps with the grab. Anyway, the girls have vanished. The families are out of their minds."

"I didn't know anything about this, Mike."

"Yeah, and you still don't. If we track him down and get an indictment, they'll probably bring in someone from Boston or DC to handle the case. No offense."

Campanella's face got hard. "They may be underestimating me." He reached toward Patterson's pile and took a handful of pistachios. "How do you know this guy is around here?"

"First, the IT people tell me that unless Henry has a very high-tech computer, he must be somewhere in western or southern New England."

"Who's Henry?"

"I always call these guys Henry. I don't know why." He shrugged. "It's easy to read the incoming messages off the girls' computers, but hard to trace the sender. Anyone with any smarts can use programs that bounce encrypted transmissions through different servers. The most they can tell me is that Henry is probably within driving distance, three or four hours of where we're sitting now."

"Okay."

"Second, the missing girls all come from this area: one from down in Enfield, Connecticut; one from South Hadley, just up the road; and one from over in the Albany area. It seems likely that Henry is not too far away if he's driving to meet them. Finally, I have my own theory, which is probably why I got sent up here."

"No good deed goes unpunished."

"Right. Henry used the same phrase to groom all three of the victims: 'Refuse to Lose.' He tells them that they should be tough, be themselves, and refuse to lose. That ring a bell?"

"Not really."

"You're not a basketball fan?"

"Once in a while, I catch a Celtics game. That's it."

"'Refuse to Lose' was the motto of the 1996 University of Massachusetts basketball team, the last UMass team to make the Final Four. I'm betting this guy has, or had, some connection to the University of Massachusetts up in Amherst." Patterson swept his pile of nutshells into the metal wastebasket. They made a faint clatter. "That's why I'm here. I'm going to find Henry. And when I do, I'm going to tear his balls off."

"Save one for me." Campanella stood up. "I better go. I need to check on a couple things before we head back in."

"Good luck. Let's see if you can convince Norcross to stick Professor Snape in Azkaban."

7

You don't have children, Chitra. Just wait."

"Erik, I'm a raging feminist. If it were up to me, I'd ban adult pornography and child pornography both. It's all disgusting. But you can't dictate what some loser pulls up onto his computer. It's like trying to ban what a person can read."

Chitralehka Vaidyanathan's mom and dad came from Chennai, India, but she was born in Palo Alto where her father taught at Stanford. She was leaning in through the doorway to Erik's small office. Her dark hair was, as usual, piled high on her head in an effort to compensate for her small stature. A yellow pencil stuck out of the side of her coiffure. She'd been Judge Norcross's law clerk, her dream job, for the better part of a year.

Her co-clerk, Erik Blanchard, was sitting at his desk, his chair tilted back against the wall as though pinned there by Chitra's vehemence. His family came from Provo, Utah, where Erik had been an All-American rugby player. His hands were the size of snow shovels, and everywhere was too small for him. Even his desk looked undersize. He'd married right after college and now had three kids, with a fourth on the way. In contrast to Chitra, who liked to gab, he hardly ever talked, unless provoked.

Erik liked Chitra very much—he secretly hoped that he'd overhear some guy, preferably some large guy, being rude to her so he could flatten him—but it was fair to say that Chitra did provoke him, sometimes almost to loquacity. The two clerks were very smart, and they disagreed strongly about child pornography.

During the court recess, Judge Norcross had disappeared into his private office at his end of the chambers and closed his door to take the phone call. The two clerks had been battling ever since, with Chitra pursuing Erik like a fox terrier nipping at the tail of a rhinoceros.

"Chitra," Erik began, but his co-clerk broke in.

"It's just as futile as banning adult pornography was back in the sixties." She waved her fingers behind her. "Except worse, because now we have the Internet."

"It's not the same. This is . . ." Erik flushed and tapped his desk with the point of his pencil. He'd been underlining passages in Cranmer's pretrial services report, reviewing the pros and cons of detaining the professor in case Norcross wanted to confer.

Chitra pressed over him. "Until the early 1970s, if I remember, a person could go to prison for possessing any material, including sexually explicit adult material—let's see if I can do this—'whose dominant theme . . .'"

"'Taken as a whole . . .'" Erik inserted.

"'Appealed to prurient'—boy, that's an odd word, hard to pronounce too—'prurient interest in the mind of the average person . . .'"

"'Applying contemporary community standards.'" Erik completed the formulation.

"And this test allowed the police to arrest Lenny Bruce for using the word *cunnilingus* during a comedy routine."

"Right." Erik's face squirmed with distaste. "But the Supreme Court put an end to that in *Stanley v. Georgia*." He tried to return to underlining the pretrial services report but instantly broke the point of his pencil. "Dammit."

"They had to. The justices had been stuck applying the wacky *Roth* test, film by film, magazine by magazine. Justice Stewart's version of the standard—that he couldn't define pornography, but he knew it when he saw it—meant that they were forever watching dirty movies. You remember poor Justice Harlan?"

"It's an old story, but child porn is totally different. The Supreme Court said so in *Osbourne*."

"The poor man was losing his eyesight, and he had to have a law clerk sit next to him and describe who was inserting what into where so he could decide if it was prurient. Here, take this one." She pulled the pencil out of her hair and handed it to him. "Nowadays, they keep porn in doctors' offices to hand out to sperm donors. It's in the best hotels. It's on HBO, more or less. Fifth-graders look at it when their parents aren't around."

"Are you saying it should be the same with videos of five-year-olds, Chitra? Raping a toddler as a form of entertainment? Give me a break."

"It's revolting, I agree. But the Internet is like the river Ganges, divine and swollen with garbage." She nodded at Erik's computer. "Four or five clicks on that, and you can watch some poor journalist having his head removed. You can watch suicides and murders in real time. You can watch the dead bodies of American soldiers being mutilated and dragged through the street. And, yes, you can watch little children being raped. The people who do it, the people who film it, and the people who distribute it as a business should be chucked into a giant food processor. I have no problem with that. But some curious teenager? Some depressive with Asperger's or whatever who just looks at this muck? Five years in prison for looking? We punish people for what they do, Erik, not what they look at."

Erik shook his head. "It's the only way to suppress the industry. And some of these guys are not just losers. They sit at their computers . . ."

"Okay, sleazebags."

"Lots of them aren't just that."

"Dirtballs."

"Whatever. Lots of them sit at their computers, like I'm trying to say, Chitra, and they crow about their collections, trolling for swaps, buying it, and trading information on the best sites. These creeps keep the whole horror show going. Children are tortured, and these pictures get made, because guys like Cranmer enjoy looking at them." Erik dropped his head, exhausted by all the talking, and muttered, "Some things just have to be off-limits." He nodded up at Chitra. "Like I said, wait until you . . ."

"Excuse me. Could I break in?"

Both of them jumped. Judge Norcross rarely came down to their end of chambers, and the carpeting had muffled his approach.

When Chitra turned to face him, she knew immediately that something awful had happened. Judge Norcross was looking down, with his mouth open as though he were still trying to catch his breath.

"I've just had a pretty rough phone call."

Erik untangled himself from his desk chair and stood up. "Who was it?" He broke off, perhaps realizing he was too pushy. "I'm sorry, I mean if . . ."

"My brother Ray's chief of staff." Norcross inhaled, steadying himself. "It will be in the newspapers tomorrow." He paused. "Probably online this afternoon. There's . . ." He cleared his throat. "There's been a plane crash."

"Oh no." Chitra's eyes instantly welled up. She started to touch the judge's arm and pulled her hand back.

"Ray was on a fact-finding mission to Croatia, and they were approaching, uh, the Dubrovnik airport in fog. Two hours ago. About forty people on the plane." Norcross looked to the side and swallowed. "They overshot the runway, and the plane . . ." He paused to swallow a second time and clear his throat. "Sorry. The plane went into a stand of trees and caught fire. Half the passengers were killed immediately, including Ray's wife, Sheila." He reached around to the back of his neck and rubbed hard. "She was traveling with him, I guess."

The judge's secretary, Lucille, came up and joined the group, her face grave. Back at her desk, the phone began ringing. When Chitra said, "Let me get it," and turned to go take a message, Lucille put a hand on her shoulder and said, "Let the machine do it."

The judge leaned back against the wall and folded his arms. He looked devastated. Chitra wondered how she would handle news like this if it were one of her brothers. The Vaidyanathan family was very close.

"Ray was alive when they pulled him out, but in bad shape." Judge Norcross closed his eyes, waited a few seconds, and opened them again. "Unconscious. They're trying to get him on a plane to Germany." He looked at Lucille, then Erik, and then Chitra. "Ray's my only brother." He wiped his hands over his face. "I just called my dad. He's pretty cut up."

"Did they have—" Erik began and broke off, shaking his head. "I'm sorry. Never mind, I . . ."

"It's okay. What is it?"

"Did they have any kids?"

"Two. Two girls. A teenager and a . . . a . . ." The judge lowered his hand, palm down, to indicate kindergarten height. "A littler one. Jordan. Right after we finish up in court here, I'm headed to Bradley. The Secret Service has a plane waiting. Ray's staff asked me to come and break the news to the girls. Just to . . ." He hesitated. "They're not sure what to do with them."

"Judge, we can postpone this hearing." Erik twisted his large hands into a tangle at his waist, pulling on his thumb. "Really."

Chitra said. "Or you can send it to Boston to the emergency judge. We can draft the order. It wouldn't take—"

"No, I'm . . ." The judge pulled on his nose and sniffed. "I just have to flip the 'off' toggle here. Just for an hour. We'll do this, and then I'll have it done. Tell the truth, it might help." He looked at Lucille. "Call Ruby, please. Ask her to round up counsel. We're going back in."

8

He didn't think much of people, but he loved birds. The field down below his house was full of song sparrows and at least two eastern meadowlark pairs. In the evenings, he'd sit on his porch just riding the music, listening to the males marking their territory. His favorite was the hermit thrush. You could never find him, but his call was sad and sweet, like a voice from a better world. A couple nights back, he thought he heard a bobolink.

He'd been out that morning running errands, picking up bags of seed from the Garden Center for the chickadees, nuthatches, and finches that mobbed his feeders. As he drove, he kept turning over in his mind ways to move things along with Li'l Sis. He hadn't pushed to get her address—he'd once frightened off a perfect sweetheart who might have been his best catch ever by yanking too hard. One minute, you had them eating out of your hand, ready to do anything, and the next minute, they'd slip off the hook and disappear, and you'd never know why.

But with some patient play on the line, he'd learned that Li'l Sis was in the eighth grade and lived somewhere in Massachusetts. When the name of her horribly unfair, stupid social studies teacher slipped out—McCauley—it took him less than an hour on the Internet to discover that Li'l Sis had to be living somewhere in the Amherst-Pelham school district.

It was only three hours' drive down there, and he had a nephew in the area, Buddy, who enjoyed Playtime and would be happy to help out.

He bounced his Jeep up into the garage, pulled the brake, and popped the hatch. After the car died, there was only the sound of the birds and the wind in the trees, which was how he liked it. To the west, a grassy field, spotted with wildflowers, sloped down toward a pine copse. Two ruts ran through it, leading to a narrow dirt road through the trees and eventually to a small pier he kept on the water with a motorboat tied up. The Lake Champlain frontage had been his grandfather's, and he'd inherited it years ago along with a little bit of money. That was when he decided that six semesters chasing a UMass degree was enough. He had everything he needed anyway. The place was completely private. No neighbors for a quarter mile on either side and so shut in by trees it was practically invisible both from the road and the water.

Apart from the money and the land, he'd inherited a love of Lake Champlain itself. The lake was vast enough that it even had its own monster, now nicknamed Champy, with legends trailing back to before the time of the white man. He'd never seen Champy, but he could feel her down there in the dark water. The middle of the lake was very deep. When something went into it, properly weighted, Champy never gave it back.

A squad of blue jays in the sugar maple alongside the garage was bombarding him with indignant squawks. Their insults made him smile. At the back of the car, he began pulling out bags of sunflower seed, cracked corn, and suet blocks. Over to the side, next to the jack, he kept his traveling kit: a small green duffel with a teddy bear sporting an I LOVE YOU! *T-shirt with a large red heart, some petite-size gauzy pajamas, a blindfold, a gag, two tubes of lubricant, and duct tape.*

9

As he scrutinized the defendant, Judge Norcross found himself beginning to worry.

"The government, Mr. Cranmer . . . Professor Cranmer, are you with us?"

Cranmer was slumped, motionless, staring blankly into his lap like a crash-test dummy after the collision. Norcross tilted his head to one side to try for a better look at the guy. Defendants in child pornography cases were a high risk for suicide. Should he order a psychiatric evaluation? The defense wasn't seeking one. He'd have Erik swat up a memo on the circumstances that would justify having someone like Cranmer examined on the court's own initiative. Two of his defendants had died while charges were pending against them, one of AIDS and one in a carjacking. He didn't want another fatality, certainly not one where the defendant took his own life.

Death, indeed, seemed to be everywhere. He hadn't known Ray's wife, Sheila, very well. She and Ray had met in Madison after he'd left the Midwest for his Peace Corps stint in Kenya and then law school. Little bits of things about her stuck in his mind. She was a late only child whose parents had passed away years ago.

She liked flowers in the house. She and Norcross's wife, Faye, had never clicked. Sheila had a routine, each time he met her, of putting a hand on his shoulder and kissing him quickly on the cheek, then backing up, looking him in the eye, and smiling. The gesture felt practiced, the act of a politician's wife, but it might have just meant she was shy. He and Sheila had been related by marriage for almost twenty years, but he couldn't recall even one phrase of any conversation they'd shared. What on earth was he going to say to her children?

These thoughts flickered through Norcross's mind in less than a second while Cranmer finally woke up to the fact that the judge had spoken to him. The professor twitched and cranked himself upright. "Yes, Your Honor. I'm with you. Sorry."

"Good. The government takes the position that you should be detained pending your trial, which may be some months from now. Ms. Ames, have you gone over this with your client?"

"Yes, Judge." She stood and shook her head wearily. "And it's cuckoo. My client's, you know, an English teacher. He's lived in western Massachusetts for more than thirty years. He's no threat to anyone, and he's not going anywhere. We're happy to post his house, which has no liens, if you feel it's necessary. Brother counsel over there has lost his marbles."

But Campanella was already on the move, shifting from counsel table to the podium in the well of the court, buttoning his suit jacket and quickly adjusting his tie. He didn't twitch at the "marbles" dig or even deign to glance at Attorney Ames.

"Your Honor, if I might be heard?"

"Proceed. Ms. Ames, have a seat, please. My time is limited this morning, Mr. Campanella. I can give this matter about twenty minutes."

Campanella positioned his yellow pad in front him. The top of his bald head caught the ceiling lights. "Okay. First, let's look at the weight of the evidence, okay? It's overwhelming. The case is not triable, and sister counsel knows it. Getting a conviction in this case will be child's play. The defendant has been participating for at least the past month, probably longer, in a disgusting . . ."

Judge Norcross interrupted. "You're talking about child's play?

In a pornography case?" Campanella stopped abruptly. His car was already in the ditch. He glanced back at Patterson.

The top of his head turned pink. "I'm sorry, Your Honor. That was unintentional."

"It happens. Proceed."

Campanella consulted his notes, backed onto the highway, and pressed down on the gas. "The defendant has been participating for several weeks, probably longer, in a notorious chat room, the so-called Candyman E-Group, used by pedophiles to discuss fantasies about child sex abuse and exchange pornography." Campanella flipped a page and looked up at the bench, dropping his voice. The change in tone conveyed the feel of an ad-lib, but it obviously wasn't. Norcross could picture Campanella practicing it in his office.

"Actually, I shouldn't say fantasies, because based on some of that man's"—Campanella pivoted in the same transparently rehearsed way and pointed at the defendant—"comments, he may have actually abused children." Then Campanella returned his gaze to the judge. "We know from his own words that he'd very much like to. Your Honor has the transcripts of some of his conversations attached to the government's sealed motion. Defendant appears under his chat-room code name 'Luv2look.' At one point, he brags about molesting his niece. I quote, 'I love to rip her little diaper off, and stick my—'"

"I've seen the transcripts, Mr. Campanella. You don't have to quote them."

This was going to be Page One already. Too much lurid pre-trial publicity, and he'd never be able to piece together a neutral jury. Besides, it was piling on, which reminded him of Ray.

Judge Norcross felt a plunge in his stomach at the possibility that his brother's aggressive, buccaneer spirit might pass from the world entirely. The man was not easy, but he was rooted in Norcross's heart. What would happen to the girls? And how would his father, already weighed down with his mother's illness, ever survive this new blow?

Campanella had paused and was looking up at the judge, stroking his goatee.

"Okay," he said uncertainly. He'd clearly been relishing the prospect of two or three nauseating quotes. He flipped two pages of his yellow pad and soldiered on. "Very good." He took a deep breath and exhaled. "Okay. Then there's the DVD itself. Which he personally ordered in response to a flyer sent out by the FBI as part of its 'Window Pane' sting. The title of the video, which includes the phrase 'Playing Doctor,' is too disgusting to repeat in full. I assume Your Honor has seen it? The video was purchased with the defendant's MasterCard, including both the number, expiration date, and the security code." Campanella glanced back at Patterson to confirm this. The agent, without expression, nodded. "Okay." Campanella paused and looked down at his notes. "When the agents arrived to execute the search warrant? The defendant gave a voluntary statement essentially confessing to the crime, admitting that he ordered the video, and confirming that it was his." Campanella gave the judge a full blast of eye contact. "I assume Your Honor has viewed the video in its entirety?"

Norcross was not going to be pushed. He leaned forward and returned Campanella's stare. "I have reviewed all the material the government has submitted."

"Respectfully, has Your Honor viewed the last four minutes, where—"

"Mr. Campanella," Judge Norcross interrupted, tapping the bench with the butt of his pen. "I just told you I have reviewed all the material."

This was mostly true. The court of appeals had made it clear that a judge was required, before issuing a search or arrest warrant in these cases, to actually look at the targeted pornography. Norcross, however, did not interpret this precedent as binding him to sit and watch the entire ghastly DVD—only enough to get the gist. If Campanella was concerned that Norcross had not had his stomach turned or his heart wrenched, he didn't need to worry.

"Let's move on. What can you tell me about the potential penalty the defendant is facing?"

"Fine." Campanella looked down and flapped another page. "It's, Your Honor, it's enormous—basically life, given the defendant's age. Calculation of the sentencing guidelines will include enhancements for use of a computer, number of images, depictions of sadomasochistic conduct, and images of prepubescent children. We estimate that with these adjustments, the applicable guideline range will be two hundred and ten to two hundred and seventy-six months, roughly eighteen to twenty-three years, with a minimum mandatory sentence of at least five years, lifetime supervised release, and a requirement that he maintain registration as a child sex offender for life."

At the periphery of his vision, Norcross could see that Campanella's words were landing on Cranmer like repeated blows over the head. The defendant seemed to be slipping lower in his chair each time Campanella flicked a hand at him. It was hard to imagine that a person would respond this way if he were innocent. The guidelines range was obviously too high, but the sentence would almost certainly come in well above the minimum five years. *Hasta la vista*, Professor Cranmer.

The defendant would likely die before he finished his sentence. A colleague in Boston had once sentenced an aged mobster who protested that he would be in his grave before he could serve out his lengthy prison term. "Just do the best you can," the colleague had replied. "Just do the best you can." Even if Claire eventually accepted the truth that her friend was guilty, which she might not, the severity of his sentence would break her heart.

The thought of Claire's distress made Norcross think once more of how much he needed to speak to her, to get her help about what he should say to his nieces. Would they cry? Of course, they would cry. Would he? Claire was the only person on earth he could talk to about this.

He knew Lindsay, the older girl, a little. They'd had some contact when she'd briefly attended nearby Deerfield Academy, but she'd been a poor fit for boarding school and had returned to Washington after a semester. An essay she'd written condemning the death penalty had gotten into the newspapers during his capital trial. Her few months in western Massachusetts hadn't brought them close. Jordan, whom he'd only seen at occasional family holidays, had so far been too young for much conversation. Some years back, one Thanksgiving at Ray's when Jordan had been a toddler, she'd hopped up into his lap to watch a football game. He'd enjoyed feeling her curled warmly against his chest, but she'd gotten bored and hopped down after a few minutes. How would he manage to make a home for these girls, even temporarily, if they needed a place to stay while Ray recovered? And what if Ray didn't recover? Norcross didn't even know what they ate for breakfast.

Campanella kept rattling along. His argument regarding the defendant's supposed dangerousness was feeble. The pretrial services report informed the judge that Cranmer was sixty-eight years old, with no prior criminal record of any kind, and had been living with his mother. In Norcross's experience, all child abusers looked at child pornography, but relatively few people who looked at child pornography ever laid their hands on actual children. Like this soggy morsel, they mostly just "loved to look." Beyond the pornography itself, which was bad enough, the record so far offered no evidence that the professor would do anything to hurt anyone, or cause any sort of problem, if he were released pending trial.

The risk-of-flight argument was stronger. If the defendant stuck around to be convicted, his life would basically be over, except in the very unlikely event that he was found not guilty, and defendants rarely beat child pornography charges. Under the circumstances, who wouldn't think about heading for the hills? He certainly would, especially if he knew that certain European countries would not extradite for this class of offense.

Linda Ames, however, seemed unfazed by Campanella's rhetoric, looking at him with a half smile that suggested she was about to burst into laughter, totally unimpressed. She was good, but what would she come up with?

"Thank you, Mr. Campanella." The tone of Judge Norcross's voice should have made it clear that it was time for Campanella to sit down. He'd scored all the points he was going to score, and he was in fairly good shape. Unfortunately, he lacked the experience to know when to stop.

"If I might have just thirty seconds?" Campanella held up a finger. "For a word with Agent Patterson?"

After receiving Norcross's nod, Campanella stepped around to the back of counsel table and lowered his head to confer with the case agent. The purpose of this, the judge knew, was to confirm that Campanella had not left anything important out. Usually, the agent's response was a shrug or a quick nod, but in this case Patterson had something to say that took up most of Campanella's half minute. As they finished up, Norcross noticed that Patterson briefly patted

Campanella's arm, like a lineman encouraging a running back as they broke the huddle.

The emotion that this gesture provoked in the judge took him by surprise. He felt something surge into his throat, and he quickly bent over and began retying his shoe. In two or three hours, he would be talking to his nieces. Very likely, by the time he got there, his only sibling, like his wife, Faye, would be dead. Darkness was waiting for everyone.

As Campanella returned to the podium, Patterson's eyes followed him.

"Okay," Campanella said. "One final point, if I might, for just one more minute?"

"I'm watching the clock."

"I want to emphasize that the existence of a market for this material, with customers like that man"—he pointed once more at Cranmer—"ensures that this sort of incredibly cruel, heartless abuse keeps happening."

Norcross broke in, with an edge to his voice. "I'm very aware of that, Mr. Campanella."

"I know, but in this case, Agent Patterson informs me that they have uncovered the actual names of some of the victims in the videos and still pictures the defendant has been sharing around. These are real, identified children, Judge, with real, terribly damaged lives." Campanella pushed forward, finally ignoring his yellow pad, speaking extempore and more confidently, with increasingly intense eye contact to keep the judge with him. "The little blond girl you saw in the DVD? She now lives in eastern Oregon. She's fifteen, Judge. She's in foster care. She participates in twice-a-week psychotherapy to deal with her anorexia. She already has a serious drug problem."

Campanella looked to the side and took a deep breath, gathering himself and trying to get his fury under control. He'd been speaking fast. Now he turned to the bench and continued, more slowly.

"Fifteen, Your Honor. We have a statement from the victim's aunt about what this abuse, which went on for years, did to her. She also tells us what the ongoing distribution of this video, which will go on forever—for as long as people like this defendant continue to order or download it—still does to her to this day. The charge here may be just receipt, but it is not a victimless crime, Judge. It is *not* a victimless crime. Thank you."

This worked. No one in the crowded courtroom made a sound as Campanella returned to his seat. No one even moved, except Linda Ames, who was shaking her head slowly. Patterson turned and gave Campanella a brief approving look.

Norcross looked down at defense counsel. "Ms. Ames? What do you say?" Linda Ames rose.

"What I say is that no one has argued to you, or is going to argue to you, that this is a victimless crime. That's a straw horse. What I also say, respectfully, is that the nature of this crime is irrelevant at this point. That's what we have trials for." She placed her hand on her client's shoulder. "And finally what I say is that Sid Cranmer is presumed innocent unless and until he is proved guilty beyond a reasonable doubt, which is something that I suggest brother counsel over there conveniently forgot."

She dropped her hand and moved to the podium. She took no yellow pad.

"Pretrial detention—as you know, Judge—is not intended to be punishment. It is only justified in two narrow circumstances. First, when the government can prove by a preponderance of the evidence that a defendant is likely to flee. Or, second, where the government can carry the even heavier burden of proving by clear and convincing evidence that a defendant will present a danger to a specific person or to the community generally."

She paused and pointed at Campanella. "For the past ten minutes, my brother has put on a performance for you designed solely to sell you the sizzle instead of the steak." She held out her hands palms up and lifted her shoulders. "Pardon me, but where was the evidence relevant to either of the issues you're actually supposed to be deciding? All sizzle, no steak."

"I get the barbecue metaphor."

"We all love children, Judge. I have a son. If anybody tried doing that stuff to him, I'd kill them." Ames glared over at Campanella, as though Sid were her child and the AUSA was abusing him. "I really would. It's not that tough to go ballistic about how abusing little kids is bad. It's bad. It's horrible. But the first question, the first relevant question, today is: Will Sid run if you release him? And the answer is: Of course he's not going to run. He'd be nuts to try running with the conditions you can set for his release. He's almost seventy years old, for heaven's sake. If he tried to run, he'd just get caught, and he'd be a dead duck. If you have any worries, you can have Sid post his house, you can put him on a curfew or on home confinement, you can have a probation officer monitor him with an ankle bracelet."

As Ames's argument gathered momentum, Judge Norcross felt his mind being drawn away from his brother and his nieces and into difficult but blessedly familiar terrain. In about five minutes, he was going to have to decide where Professor Cranmer would be sleeping for the next six or eight months. Norcross had been leaning toward detention, but it was central to the discipline of judging that, while he could prepare ahead of time, he could not, without cheating, decide ahead of time. He had to listen.

Each time, as he approached the moment when he would need to make a hard call, he felt like a man being carried slowly to the top of an old-fashioned roller coaster, click by click to the summit. When he reached the peak, he'd have heard all he was going to hear, he'd open his mouth, and words would plummet out, formed into sentences—conveying to counsel, to the courtroom, to the transcript, to the court of appeals, and to all of posterity exactly what his decision was and why. As Ames shifted to the next segment of her argument, Norcross had only a shadowy idea of what his decision would be. All the glow lights of his brain were lit up with the effort of taking her argument in and weighing his decision. He was getting to the top, and, thank heaven, the steady rise to the precipice was, for the moment, blotting everything else out.

"Now let's talk about the crime," Ames was saying. "Used to be, you had to go to the grimiest part of town and knock on some back door to get this garbage. You'd have to be desperate, maybe dangerous, to even get your hands on it. Now it's available at any time to anyone in the world, anyone in this courtroom, including, respectfully, Your Honor, with a few clicks of a mouse in the privacy of your home or anywhere. There's an ocean of this manure floating around out there. Anyone can dive into it, anywhere, any time. It's practically a new form of spam. And"—she held up a finger—"if you intentionally pull it up on your screen, even if you are just curious, you've committed a felony, and the government can stick you in prison to serve a five-year mandatory sentence just for looking at it. That's where we are. That's where technology has taken us."

Ames shifted around and nodded at her client. "Sid Cranmer poses no threat to any child and never has. As Mr. Campanella knows very well, my client has no brothers or sisters. He's never married. He has no niece, and no nephew either for that matter. I'm not going to defend what was said by Luv2look in that chat room. It makes me want to throw up. But I have to point out that speaking those words, awful as they were, was not a crime. More than that, if the government wants to put those words into evidence, they're going to have to convince you that they're somehow relevant, and that they actually came from Sid Cranmer. Neither of these things will be easy."

As Ames's argument moved toward its climax, Norcross found himself grappling with the most difficult dilemma these bail hearings posed: the problem of the visible mistake versus the invisible mistake. If he released Cranmer and the man absconded or hurt a child, Norcross would have made a very serious, very visible mistake. Everyone, including him, would know it, and there would be painful blowback on many levels. People would hate him. He might even hate himself; he'd certainly hate his mistake. On the other hand, if he detained Cranmer when it was not necessary—when Cranmer would never have fled or hurt anyone—the defendant's loss of liberty would be an invisible mistake. Nobody would ever know it, not even him. It was always tempting to avoid visible mistakes simply by making sure only to commit invisible ones. Bad judges did that.

Ames turned from her client to face the bench. "Let me tell you what's really going on here, Judge. The government wants to punish my client, an Amherst College professor with no criminal record and a multidecade history in the community, and make headlines without ever having to prove he's committed the crime he is charged with—or any crime. That's not right. Sid Cranmer's no danger to anyone, and he's not going anywhere. He's entitled to be released on his own recognizance or with a minimal unsecured personal bond."

Ames turned and sat; she knew when to quit.

Campanella immediately rose, "May I be heard, Your Honor?"

"There's no need."

"Just one point I overlooked, if the court please."

Norcross nodded, not happy. "All right, but be quick." Ninety percent of the mess occurred in these proceedings after ninety-nine percent of the useful argument was at its end. Things could unravel over nothing. "I have a lot on my plate today."

Campanella spoke from behind counsel table, avoiding the podium as a way of indicating he would not be long. "It is significant that Professor Cranmer's academic specialty is the writer Lewis Carroll, a well-known pedophile."

At this point, as Norcross had feared, things began to go frizzy. The defendant lifted his head, looking angry, and began whispering furiously to his attorney.

"Oh, come on, Mr. Campanella." Norcross was genuinely irritated. This was a waste of his time. "The author of *Alice in Wonderland*? Please."

"Infamous." Campanella pressed on. "And Carroll is also known to have distributed child pornography, photographs of children he took himself, that would have earned him a heavy prison sentence if he'd done it today. This is the man we—"

"What does this have to do with anything?" It was time to cut this off. Norcross felt his scalp begin to prickle, a sign of gathering anger he'd have to control.

The defendant was leaning forward, his hands pressed down on the surface of counsel table, with a furious, determined expression. Was he going to get on his feet? The wisps of hair on top of his head were practically standing on end. He was speaking to Ames in tones just beyond the judge's hearing.

But not, apparently, beyond Campanella's. His head darted to one side in surprise, and he looked up at the court indignantly. "And do you know what I just heard this defendant say to his attorney in response to my comments? He said—"

At this, Ames stood up, smacked her right hand hard on counsel table, and said, very loud, "Objection!"

"What he said was—"

Ames repeated, even louder, "Your Honor, I object. I object! That was a comment made to counsel."

Campanella responded, equally loud, pointing over at Ames, "The attorney-client privilege does not protect remarks made within the hearing of third parties."

"Okay." Judge Norcross tapped the butt of his pen on his microphone. "Everybody just settle down."

Ames grabbed the floor. She dropped her voice but spoke with focused intensity.

"The only point my client wished to make, wishes to make, is that there is no evidence, no credible evidence, suggesting that"—she nodded down at the defendant who was still muttering to her heatedly—"Charles Dodgson, an Oxford professor who wrote *Alice's Adventures in Wonderland*"—Ames looked down at Cranmer again and nodded impatiently as he continued to bug her with whispered muttering—"and *Through the Looking-Glass* under the pen name Lewis Carroll, was a pedophile. It's okay, Sid." Ames nodded at Cranmer, who was still trying to get her attention, then looked up at the bench with an expression of exasperation, to make sure Norcross knew that the controversy over Lewis Carroll was news to her.

"As Your Honor can see, my client seems to feel strongly about this academic dispute. Personally, I don't give a hoot about Lewis Carroll or Charles Dodgson or whatever he called himself. The guy died, like, a hundred fifty years ago. I'm more interested in what happens to Sid Cranmer in this courtroom in the next five minutes." She looked pointedly down at her client to make sure he got the message.

Campanella, still standing, broke in, once more gesturing at Ames and Cranmer. "That's all very well, but the defendant also just said something very significant that perhaps Your Honor didn't hear. He said that just because a person takes photos of naked children doesn't mean he's a—"

Ames smacked her hand on counsel table again, not quite so hard this time. "I object! I already said I object twice, and I still object. I object strenuously. This is unfair."

"I don't care what the defendant said," Norcross interrupted. "Everybody sit. I've heard enough. Here's what I'm going to do."

10

In her book-lined office at Amherst College, Professor Claire Lindemann sat and stewed. She was positive her friend Sid was not into child porn. How could he be? He had to be innocent, and she was going to stand by him, end of story. She couldn't imagine what she would think if he turned out to be guilty. It was too upsetting to contemplate.

Claire couldn't say that she "loved" Sid Cranmer, even in a sisterly way—sometimes she didn't even like him—but she was fond of him, respected him as a colleague, and, knowing his frailties, felt protective of him. What was happening was a travesty, and it was making her angry at David, which was even more distressing. David apparently felt more allegiance to the overrefined niceties of his judgy world than he did to her. She knew she was being unfair, maybe, but she didn't care.

Her loyalty to Sid stemmed, in part, from a particular, perfectly awful, incident. One afternoon, years ago, when she'd been new at Amherst, she had been hurrying across campus when her former husband, Ken, had stepped out from behind a tree into her path, drunk and demanding to talk. Claire didn't frighten easily, but her ex's out-of-the-blue appearance rattled her so badly, she just froze. Sid Cranmer happened to see the two of them from a distance and, somehow, picked up on what was going on. Though he barely knew Claire, he hurried over and actually pushed himself in between Ken and her. Claire couldn't recall exactly what Sid said, but he got right up in Ken's face, almost butting chests with him and making it clear that, while he might be a small dog, he could bite hard if things got nasty. Before long, Ken staggered away, flinging curses. It was the beginning of Claire and Sid's friendship.

One peephole into Sid's situation might be Elizabeth Spencer, Sid's erstwhile research assistant and the belle of Amherst College. As chair of the English Department, Claire was going to have to dig up someone to take over Elizabeth's summer supervision now that Sid was suspended, and this would give her a chance to have a chat with the girl. Sid had mentioned that Elizabeth was doing some research for him on his specialty, Charles Dodgson. Claire was generally familiar with the controversy over Dodgson's photographs of very young girls. The potential relevance of this academic brouhaha to Sid's criminal charges was obvious and worrying, but she pushed the feeling aside. She simply refused to believe Sid was a pedophile.

After pondering the matter, Claire decided she would take over supervising Elizabeth herself. Elizabeth was practically the only person who'd seen Sid outside class for weeks, possibly months, since his mother died. She might know something.

Claire texted Elizabeth asking her to drop by her office when she had a minute to discuss her research stipend in light of the change in Professor Cranmer's situation. A return text arrived from Elizabeth almost immediately, thanking her and saying that she could come by right now if that was okay.

Fortunately, Claire knew Elizabeth Spencer fairly well. It was hard to miss her. She possessed all the qualities that in Claire's experience provoked poetry in men: soft, deferential brown eyes, creamy skin, a slim waist, larger than average breasts, the voice of an earnest child, and a way of wearing her clothes that tended, with reasonably good taste, to get the goods in the window.

She had also taken Claire's Renaissance drama course and received a well-deserved *A*. She might be cute, but she was no airhead. Her insights into the plays of Shakespeare, Marlowe, Ben Jonson, and John Webster had been impressive, particularly considering she was a biology major. Elizabeth had folded her future professional interests into a final paper entitled "Renaissance Corpses," in which she examined, from a medical and thematic viewpoint, the interesting methods employed by sixteenth- and seventeenth-century playwrights to kill off various characters. The cardinal's murder of his mistress, Julia, in Webster's *The Duchess of Malfi*—using a poisoned bible—struck Elizabeth as especially ingenious.

Claire kept an eye out the window and soon saw Elizabeth strolling across the quad with her boyfriend, Ryan Jaworski. Ryan had taken the course with Elizabeth, though he'd been content with a gentleman's *B+*. Certain stylistic similarities between Ryan's final paper and Elizabeth's made Claire wonder whether Elizabeth might have been his ghostwriter.

Claire's suspicions were compounded when she learned that Ryan had taken Sid Cranmer's seminar on George Eliot, without Elizabeth's company—an act of ridiculously lousy judgment—and pulled a disastrous *C–*. His appeal of the grade, supported by a fire-breathing letter from his father, a Chicago attorney, went all the way up to the dean before expiring without success. Scandals over grade inflation had finally given the administration a little backbone.

The two paused before the entrance to Claire's building, just below her window, and Claire watched as Ryan, laughing, put his hands around Elizabeth's throat and shook her head back and forth as though she were a doll. Presumably, Ryan found this to be good fun, but as he walked away, Claire noticed Elizabeth rubbing the back of her neck and frowning after him.

A minute later, as she took a seat opposite Claire, Elizabeth apologized for her outfit, white running shorts and a lavender racerback top that went well with her light brown hair.

"Ryan and I were about to go for a run, but I wanted to come right over. I hope it's okay."

"Don't worry about it," Claire said with a wave of her hand, and they dived into the new arrangements for Elizabeth's summer research. They quickly agreed that Elizabeth would continue plugging away on the Dodgson material. This was not Claire's area, but she knew enough to keep Elizabeth on track.

"I'm going to be away for a good bit of the summer, so we'll have to stay in touch by email or Skype. Are you all right with that?"

"Oh, that's not a problem. Thank you so much, Professor Lindemann," Elizabeth said. "My parents will be relieved. Me, too." The Spencer family was not well off. Elizabeth was on scholarship and must have been counting on the summer stipend.

"Glad to do it," Claire said. She shifted to sit sideways behind her desk, propping her feet on her computer table. Without making eye contact, she asked briskly, "So how have you liked working for Professor Cranmer?"

"He was really sweet at first." Elizabeth smiled. "I'd bring him cookies. He'd make muffins. Sometimes we had almost, like, baking contests. Once, we let the cleaning guy, Jonathan, act as judge." She chuckled and shook her head. "Poor Jonathan. He's so quiet. He hated having to choose.

"Anyway, after Professor Cranmer's mom died, all that stopped. Sometimes, he wouldn't even come out of his bedroom. He showed me where he kept his key outside, so I could just ring the bell and let myself in if I had something to drop off. When he was really bad, I helped him get ready for class a few times."

Claire kept her face neutral. "We're all shocked about this stuff in the news."

Elizabeth shook her head. "It was really awful, Professor Lindemann. I know he didn't do it. He couldn't. If he did, I'd . . ."

"Please call me Claire."

"I was there when, you know, the cops showed up. It was just like, *wham*, they came through the door like the Gestapo or something."

"God, Elizabeth. I didn't know that."

"People mostly call me Libby. Anyway, we were going over the research when it happened. The first couple minutes, I was, like, totally freaked. I didn't even know who these guys were. Later, he called from the, you know, from the jail, and asked me to go in and feed his cats and stuff."

"They took things from his house?"

"From everywhere. There were at least a dozen of them, running all over the place. The worst was the DVD. I got a look at the front of it. It was really . . . I don't even like to think about it. It was really bad."

"Damn. It was . . ." Claire hesitated. "A child?"

"A girl, younger than my little sister. It was horrible."

"Shit."

"I don't know what happened. He said he never ordered it." She bit her lip and shook her head. "Ryan says the college is bound to get him off."

"I doubt there's much they can do."

"Well, I don't know. Ryan is sure they'll do something." She looked to the side with a worried expression before turning back to Claire.

"It's kind of strange," she said, her voice changing. "Lewis Carroll liked—Dodgson liked—to take photographs of naked children, especially little girls."

"Right." Claire tipped toward her lecture mode. "The Victorians saw no problem with that. The girls' parents were often present, and he stayed friends with some of his models even into adulthood. The pictures were considered esthetic, just pretty little flowers."

"Spiritual almost, I know," Elizabeth said. "It wasn't porn exactly, but some of the poses . . ."

"Yeah, they were . . ."

"*My* mom and dad sure wouldn't have let anyone take pictures of me like that. A few of them are really borderline. Even some of the ones in the published biographies." Elizabeth leaned forward, and Claire was impressed at the competence and animation that came into her voice. "The 1995 Cohen biography includes some photographs, especially the ones of Beatrice and Evelyn Hatch, taken in the mid-1860s, that would definitely be a problem if someone took them today. Especially if he sent them around to his friends, the way Dodgson did to his Oxford buddies." Elizabeth stopped, as though she was considering whether to say more.

Claire waited. Silence often got a fuller response from students than questions. Unfortunately, her cell phone wrecked the moment by breaking in with its maddening hum. She quickly looked at the screen: David.

"I'll deal with this later." She turned off the ringer and popped the phone into a drawer. "You were saying?"

"Sid—Professor Cranmer—has a separate accordion folder with a bunch of Dodgson's published and unpublished photographs. There's an original print of the famous one of Alice Liddell—the real-life Alice—six years old and dressed up like a prostitute, in torn clothes with her chest exposed." She looked at Claire, embarrassed. "Some of the unpublished ones are even worse. I only saw a couple before he put them away, but they were . . ." She hesitated and grimaced. "Gross is the only word I can think of. It was a pretty fat file."

"Oh, dear." Claire shook her head. "That's not going to help, that's for sure."

"The file's still there in a sort of hiding place. The cops didn't find it."

"Aha. Hmm."

"Should I . . ." Elizabeth hesitated and scratched the top of her knee. Her fingernails were perfect. "Should I take it away and put it somewhere? I'm going to be at Sid's house, using the bank records he scanned from Christ Church College. Sid told me to come by as often as I can." She smiled. "He says I can even sleep over if I want to. The cats like it."

"You don't want to get any more involved than you are, Libby. If I were you, I might just forget I ever saw that file."

A silence followed, with both of them drifting off. Outside, the buzz of a lawn mower approached and retreated, then the purr of a plane passing overhead. Some students walked under the window three floors down, chatting and laughing. The breeze through the window carried the aroma of the cut grass.

On an impulse, Claire gestured at her laptop, which was sitting open. "Have you ever used Professor Cranmer's computer?"

Elizabeth nodded. "Oh yes, all the time when I'm at his house. I pull up the records on his desktop computer and draft the summaries on my laptop." She sighed and looked down at her knees. "It was bad after his mother died, but he was finally getting better. He was playing his harpsichord again."

"Was there a password for the computer?"

"If there was, I didn't need it. The computer was just always switched on when I got there. He was using it a lot, I guess." She ran a finger under the upper hem of her top and scratched thoughtfully, then seemed to realize what she was doing and pulled her hand away. "He had a yellow sticky on the side of the screen with some numbers on it. I don't think . . ." She shook her head. "Sid—Professor Cranmer—is not very security minded."

Looking out the window, Claire saw Ryan Jaworski trotting slowly across the quad in his running shorts and T-shirt. He was looking up at the building with a blank expression.

"I see Ryan's here," Claire said. "I'd better let you go. But let's keep in touch about the research and anything else you need to discuss. I'll want to be in touch with you at least once a week, either in person or, if I'm away, by email, okay?"

"Fine. This is so great," Elizabeth said, standing up. "Thank you so much, Professor Lindemann. Claire. I appreciate it. I really do."

Claire swung her legs off the computer table and leaned toward Elizabeth. "Can I give you some advice, Libby?"

"Sure." Her voice was tentative. "Of course."

"When I was about your age, I went crazy for this one guy I'd met. I sort of let him take charge of me. It didn't work out." Claire nodded down in the direction of Ryan Jaworski. "In fact, it got to be quite bad, which was mostly my fault." She looked at Elizabeth. "You have a good brain, Libby, and a great future. My advice is: Beware of being too sweet. Sometimes you can end up attracting flies."

Elizabeth, relieved, broke into a tinkling laugh. Her white teeth were perfect.

"Oh, Ryan—I know what you mean!" Elizabeth shook her head, still smiling, and scratched her top again, obviously thinking of something that amused her. "He's better than he looks, better than he acts sometimes. I can deal with him." She stood up. "Thanks for the advice, though." She tapped her temple. "I'll store it away."

The conversation with Elizabeth left Claire late for her usual lunch time, and afterward, she hurried across campus to the faculty dining room, starving. Just as she was taking her seat, her cell phone started vibrating with another call from David. The interruption created at least two species of headache. First, while talking on a cell phone was not explicitly forbidden in the dining room, it was definitely frowned upon by everyone, including her. Second, given the Sid mess, she wasn't sure she was ready to talk to David just yet. To complicate matters further, her colleague Darren Mattoon was bearing down from across the room, clearly intent on joining her and ruining the quiet half hour she needed to process her chat with Elizabeth.

She let the phone take another message. David wouldn't be surprised not to reach her.

They never talked at this time of day.

As expected, Darren's shadow was soon hovering over her table.

"Mind if I join you?"

"Not at all."

He slipped into the seat opposite and began unloading his tray. When he looked up and took in her face, his expression melted.

"Whoops," he said. "Do you really want company, Claire?"

"No, it's . . ."

"I can see you've got things on your mind." He put his hands on the table, preparing to stand. "I always enjoy seeing you, but we can do this some other time. Really."

His face was empty of pretense, and it seemed so clear that he truly did sympathize that Claire was tempted to take him up on his offer. But there were other faculty in the room, and it would look strange if he reseated himself at another table. Besides, he was being nice, and she was touched.

"No, no, I mean it. It's okay."

If Darren was flirting, Claire was pretty sure he was wasting his time. Even forgetting David, it had taken her only five minutes after meeting Darren to go from *Hmmm?* to *I don't think so.* He'd taken a while getting his PhD, so he was the right age, but there was something slick about him that bothered her, maybe something that lingered from his years selling condos in San Diego. It also didn't help that he had a bitchy relationship with Sid, hinting to everyone that he considered Professor Cranmer's deconstructionist theories over the hill. Sid had caught wind of this and responded, during a faculty meeting, by publicly describing Darren's scholarship as "California Dreamin'." The air in the meeting had crackled.

Despite all this, she had to admit it wouldn't be the end of the world if she and Assistant Professor Mattoon happened to find themselves stranded on a desert island for a few hot nights. He certainly was easy on the eyes, and his second book, which had come out that spring, was a good read—just the right blend of cultural analysis and new historical research, with a soupçon of wry, superior humor. The lavish *New York Times* review had marked its status as far above the typical, going-nowhere tenure tome. Whatever Sid thought, Darren looked like a dead cert for tenure.

Claire glanced up as Darren took a bite of his grilled chicken salad. Another point in his favor was that, unlike many of the older males on the faculty, he did not talk with his mouth full or dribble things down the front of his shirt.

"You're worried about Sid, I bet." He dabbed the corner of his mouth with a napkin.

"Is it so obvious?" Claire was surprised.

"Everybody's worried about Sid." He sipped his coffee and swallowed. "People can't talk about anything else." He peered around the room and began nodding at adjoining tables. "I bet they're talking about Sid, and I bet *they're* talking about Sid . . ." He raised his thick blond eyebrows and smiled. "Everyone's talking about Sid. 'The sword of Damocles,' as one of my students said, 'is hanging over Pandora's box.'"

Claire shared a laugh with Darren over the idiotic quote.

Darren quickly followed up. "But I hope you know I'm taking no pleasure in this latest catastrophe, Claire."

"Well, in a way, I wouldn't be surprised, I guess. You two are kind of . . ."

"It's true, I didn't appreciate his public dig, and he knows that I think his 1970s-style, 'sense of nonsense,' postmodernist analysis of *Alice's Adventures in Wonderland* is paradoxical poppycock." He paused, set down his fork, and leaned toward Claire. "But this latest thing is appalling and, I truly hope, totally undeserved."

"Of course it's undeserved. It's awful." She looked around the murmuring room. "And, you're right, the gossip must be brutal."

"Besides that, you, um, you know his judge." He smiled primly. "That's another topic on everyone's lips."

"Well, people saw us at the garden party. . . ."

"Garden party, nothing. You were mentioned in court this morning. Someone at the college picked it up off a Twitter feed, and the news has been tearing around campus ever since." Claire could see her startled reaction reflected in Darren's face. "Didn't you know? It's already in the online edition of the *Republican*." Darren spread out his hands to frame the headline. "'Judge Discloses Amherst College Connection.' He told the attorneys you were a close friend." Darren speared a piece of chicken and peered at Claire over the top of his glasses. "You're a celebrity."

"Shit." Claire put down her fork. "I can't believe this."

"I guess a lot of people didn't know that the two of you were . . ." He paused for a beat and cleared his throat significantly. "Close friends."

Claire took a deep breath. She hated the idea of being talked about.

Again, she noticed Darren was watching her closely. Claire was beginning to be bothered by her own transparency.

"Sorry," Darren said. "I'm overdoing this. We can talk about something else."

He busied himself buttering a roll, giving Claire time to initiate some other topic. She didn't say anything, simply chewed without tasting. To her left, the magnificent view from the dining room's south-facing windows fanned out into the distance. The vista over the green hills and church steeples of South Amherst and off into the Holyoke Range was one of the cherished perks of the college faculty. The outline of the range's promontories in the distance was like the profile of a giant sleeping under a nubbly green blanket. She and David would get through this, of course, but it was going to take some work.

After a few minutes, she realized the silence was getting awkward. "Sid is an old friend and a dear man."

"*Old* may be the operative word. Really. Putting this latest horror aside, don't you think he's kind of edging up on his sell-by date?"

"You're the new kid on the block, Darren. You frighten Sid, so he acts like an asshole. Cut the poor guy some slack, for heaven's sake."

"Ignore me," Darren said. "Professor Cranmer's a fine teacher, and I'm sounding like a jerk, doing the classic young buck–old bull thing. Predictable but dreary. I'm sorry."

A large silver-haired man at an adjoining table pricked up his ears at the sound of Sid's name. It was Harlan Graves. Like Sid, Graves was an English Department dinosaur. The two old professors had been at swords' points for decades. Graves leaned toward them with a merry smile.

"Poor Professor Cranmer! Who would have thought it!" He rubbed his hands together and his eyes lit up. "Did you hear the limerick that's going around? One of my students shared it with me after class this morning. Let's see if I can remember it." Professor Graves turned to the view, making a show of reaching into his memory. It did not seem to Claire that he needed very long to bring back the words.

"Something like this." He lifted his hand and beat out the measure, like an orchestra conductor. "A worn-out professor named Sid. Had a hobby he had to keep hid. While his lectures weren't prime. He had a great time. Having sex with a nine-year-old kid."

Darren frowned at Graves. "That's a cheap shot."

"My God," Claire said quietly. "Have things already gone this far?"

"It may have been 'five-year-old kid,'" Harlan Graves said, knitting his brows. "I can't quite recall."

11

Elizabeth Spencer was the best thing that was ever going to happen to Ryan Jaworski, but it was taking her some time to get that fact through Ryan's thick head. The two of them were jogging, side by side, heading out South Pleasant Street past the Amherst Golf Club. Their pace was relaxed and steady, making talking easy.

"So how'd it go with Lindemann?" Ryan asked.

"She was great. The internship is all set."

"So, you'll still be here over the summer?"

Ryan's attempt to hide the concern in his voice was obvious. Elizabeth suspected that Ryan was disappointed that, with the summer internship, she'd be staying on the East Coast instead of heading back to Minnesota. He clearly had things he wanted to do over the next couple months that did not include her—exactly what, or with whom, she hadn't wormed out of him yet.

"Right," Elizabeth said. "If you want, I could come down to New York on the weekends."

"Of course I want. Are you kidding?" They shifted into single file to get around a woman with a baby stroller. When Elizabeth drew up next to him again, Ryan added, "But Dad says they're going to have me running my ass off at Goldman—weekdays and weekends."

"Uh-huh."

"We could probably do a couple days on the Vineyard in August at the cottage. My aunt will be there, but there are plenty of bedrooms. It's beautiful. The lawn goes all the way down to the water."

Elizabeth didn't say anything. Ryan Jaworski had a capacity for pure sweetness and generosity so extraordinary that it took her breath away. No other guy had ever come close. But she also remembered, as she felt his eyes lingering nervously on her, that for him, there were never any forks in the road. He just went straight ahead, latching onto whatever arose in the moment. This intensity made him very attractive, but she also knew that, if she wanted to keep him, she needed to stay in the center of his field of vision.

"We'll see," she said after a while. Even without looking, she sensed that her slightly distant tone was getting the desired effect. Her boyfriend, with his visit-me-sometime-on-the-Vineyard crapola, was sliding a little off balance. Good.

Ryan Jaworski was the sort of guy Elizabeth Spencer had pictured herself ending up with in her grade-school Prince Charming fantasies—someone handsome and going somewhere, someone, she had to confess, rich and a bit regal, but with a puppy-dog side, too. Someone smart, but she hoped not quite as smart as she was.

She'd met him two years ago at the beginning of her sophomore year, when he was a freshman. Ryan was a midwesterner like her, but growing up in the Hyde Park area of Chicago, he was of a much different pedigree. He'd managed to tell her during their first conversation that the Jaworski house was only two blocks from President Obama's and that his dad was a member of the Chicago Mercantile Board. When she'd revealed that her hometown was Golden Valley, Minnesota, and that her father had worked for General Mills, the company that made Cinnamon Toast Crunch and Lucky Charms, he'd actually started to chuckle, caught himself, and looked embarrassed. That was when Elizabeth decided to make a project of getting him. It hadn't been hard.

Ryan had acquired his touch of preppie charm from attending Choate Rosemary Hall, John F. Kennedy's old private school alma mater, whereas Elizabeth had gone to Hopkins High, a good but distinctly public secondary school. As they got to know each other, Ryan confessed that, being a midwestern Polish Catholic, he'd found it tough to find a place among the offspring of the elite New England families that dominated Choate. For four years, he'd had to endure the nickname "Smote," when a witty upperclassman bent a fragment of *Hamlet* and dubbed him "Smote, the sledded Polack." The vulnerable look that swept over his face when he described this refined bullying was one of the things that had drawn Elizabeth to him.

She let Ryan's eyes keep dodging over at her, not saying anything for a quarter mile or so as they continued their run. Finally, she turned her head and delivered a sly look, a code only the two of them could read. Instantly realizing what this meant, Ryan grinned happily. They'd return to his condo, take a nice cool shower together, and let things unfold from there. Maybe even get their velvet handcuffs out.

Ryan wanted to make a video of Elizabeth to remember her by while he was in Manhattan. If he was good, one day she might just let him. Ryan's dark brown hair, Chopin-pale skin, and especially the single dimple that appeared on his left cheek when he smiled still gave her goose bumps, even after two years with him. Elizabeth had always been a sucker for an asymmetrical dimple.

Ryan turned to a favorite topic. "She say anything about Cranmer?"

"She's worried he's in a lot of trouble."

Ryan laughed. "I love it! Serves him right. Cocky little shit." He picked up the pace.

"Well, I don't love it, Ry." Elizabeth kept up with him easily. She could bust him if she needed to. "This is not a joke. I mean, the FBI and everything . . ."

"He's getting a little embarrassed, Lib. So what? The college will smooth it out."

They ran along for a while, not talking, gradually increasing the pace. The sidewalk petered out, and they continued along the shoulder of the road.

"And there's other stuff." Elizabeth pointed at some broken pavement ahead. "Look out. The cops missed a file of old photographs during the search. Pictures of Dodgson's naked little girls hidden in the drawer with a false bottom. I'm not sure what I should do."

"Does Sid still keep a key under the hose mount? Maybe I'll come by and have another look."

"Forget it, Ryan. Once was enough."

"Fine." He glared straight ahead. "Whatever."

He was being a shit about Professor Cranmer. It made her sick that Sid was being falsely accused like this, especially after all her work to help him get better.

"You weren't there when these guys came through the door. It felt like freaking World War III."

She might just have to invent something important she had to do after the run. Let him twist in the wind for a while. Hoist with his own petard.

Ryan held up a hand. "Stop for a second, okay?"

They halted under a huge sycamore, all mottled bark and bobbing splotches of shade running up and down the trunk. Ryan tilted back to gaze up into the branches.

"I love these big old trees." He breathed a couple times, recovering his wind. "Did you know that Jaworski comes from the Polish word for *sycamore*?"

"I didn't know that." She looked up. "That's actually quite cool."

Ryan held out three fingers. "Three points." He sniffed and puffed out a last, large breath. "First, I love you, Lib. I can be a dick, I know, but you make me happier than anything or anyone ever has or ever will."

"I love you too, Ryan. I'm working on the happy part right now."

"Keep at it, please. Second, in spite of what I said, I am sort of sorry for Cranmer. He's a miserable little fuck, but he probably doesn't deserve what he's going through. The main thing is I know you feel loyal to him and this is hard for you, and I'm really sorry about that, okay? I'm on your side."

"Okay."

"FYI, I was talking to Professor Mattoon about this, and he mentioned that a lot of the faculty have been, like, worried about Cranmer for a while now. Think about it. The guy's never married, just lived with his mother, right? Isn't straight, isn't gay, never even dated? Up and down moods all the time? So, at least to Mattoon, and to some of the other faculty, this kiddie porn stuff is not a titanic surprise."

"He's not like that. If I ever thought he was, Ry, believe me, he'd regret it. I practically raised my little sisters after dad died. Sid's a little odd maybe, but he's—"

"I know. I know. You think he's a sweetie pie, but they know him better than you do, Lib." Ryan started to laugh and stopped himself. "I guess there's even a limerick about him the faculty's passing around now. I saw it, and it's pretty funny."

"A limerick. How creative. So what's the third thing?"

"The third thing is that there is nothing you or I can do about this, right? Cranmer's the one with the kink, or the bad luck, or whatever, and he's the one who has to take the consequences. I'm sorry, but that's life."

Elizabeth looked down at the ground, taking this in. After a few seconds, she lifted her head. "He doesn't have a kink, at least not a kiddie porn kink. I don't know what happened, but this is just bullshit." Ryan was standing with his hands on his hips, still a little out of breath, perspiring, looking very handsome. Most of the time he was incredibly kindhearted. "But you're right that we can't do much, I guess."

"Good." Ryan looked closer at Elizabeth and suddenly grinned. "Why are you gawking at me like that, you sexy thing?"

Elizabeth dropped her eyes and smiled a little sheepishly. He was looking unusually hot, it was true, but there was something else going on with him that she couldn't put her finger on. Was it just that he was talking so much? She could see through him so easily in most places that it bothered her when she hit a spot she couldn't quite penetrate.

"Just enjoying the view." They'd go back to his condo. It was okay. "And you're right about Sid." Elizabeth looked down along the row of trees and wiped her upper lip, bobbing on her toes, ready to resume.

"I know I'm right." Ryan nodded down the sidewalk. "Go."

Elizabeth broke into a strong lope, letting Ryan get a good look at her long legs and making sure he was going to have to work a little to keep up with her.

12

While Claire was finishing her lunch with Darren Mattoon, Judge Norcross was descending an escalator at the Reagan National Airport in Washington, DC. As he stepped off at the bottom, two men in dark suits appeared, presented their Secret Service credentials, and hastily escorted him to a waiting car.

En route to Ray's town house, Norcross managed to convince the driver to pull over and let him grab a pizza. Dinnertime was still a ways off, but he wasn't sure whether he would need to provide something for Lindsay and Jordan to eat. A person *in loco parentis* might have this responsibility, and given what he had to discuss with the two girls, they certainly couldn't go out to a restaurant. He picked something inoffensive and reheatable, pepperoni and green pepper. As they resumed their journey, the comforting aroma of oregano leaked out of the box and filled the car.

The residential side streets of Georgetown reminded Norcross of the Beacon Hill neighborhood of Boston, with overhanging trees, rumpled brick sidewalks, and elegant, historical façades. Both locales emphatically bespoke self-assured privilege. The difference between Boston and Washington, however, was that, underneath this comfortable entitlement, Georgetown projected subjacent muscle. Embassies and official residences appeared on every other block, with black SUVs parked in front. From time to time, Judge Norcross noticed a man in dark glasses standing back in the shadows, finger pressed to his ear, talking into a discreet microphone. The people who lived and worked inside these sedate buildings made things happen.

Ray's mansion was a three-story double town house. He'd bought two, side by side, and with the help of an interior designer, he had broken down the walls between them. Three good-size blue spruces dominated the garden in front. When they slowed to a stop, a man stepped out into the street, spoke quickly to the driver, and opened the wrought-iron security gate. Norcross's cell phone broke into a hum just as they bumped up onto the cobblestone drive that led to a courtyard and carriage house in the back. He could hear a car horn in the background when he connected.

"Hi. David?"

"Claire?" More traffic noise. She had to be walking across campus.

"I'm sorry I missed your calls." She sounded distracted—or maybe irritated.

"It's okay. Listen . . ."

"They tell me I'm in the news."

"What?"

"You mentioned me in court, I guess."

"Oh, cripes! That made the papers?"

"It's okay. It's just . . ."

"That was really dumb. I . . ."

"It's okay, but, you know . . ."

The dashboard phone in the car buzzed, and the agent in the passenger seat grabbed it.

"Totally unnecessary," Norcross continued. He would need to clear this up with Claire, but it would have to be another time. "Listen, the reason I called is I'm in Washington. I may not be back for a day or two."

"What?"

The agent twisted around and held out the car phone, mouthing, "For you."

"Oh, jeez. I've only got a minute." He held one finger up to the agent. "There was a plane crash this morning in Croatia, and it looks as though my—" Norcross broke off. Saying this, especially in front of the agents, made everything painfully real. "My brother, Ray, was badly injured. They think . . ." The agents were looking away, but they could hear, of course. What he was saying, who he was talking to, would probably end up in a report. "They think he . . . He may not make it. His wife was killed. The news will hit the Internet soon if it hasn't already."

"Oh, David."

"Yes, it's really awful." He paused, trying to let his mind settle. "Anyway, I'm down here. I'm about to meet up with Ray's kids and tell them what happened. They're . . ."

The agent spoke two words into the car phone then whispered to Norcross, "They need to talk to you." His tone was apologetic but firm.

"Darn it." Norcross reached for the phone. "I've got another call here."

"David, I'm so sorry."

He wanted to say something brainless like, "Tell me you'll still love me after I foul this up," but of course that wasn't possible. To his left, the face of a little girl—it must be Jordan—was bobbing in one of the house's side windows that looked out onto the courtyard. She was older than he remembered her. Six? Seven? She was partly obscured by a frond of a house plant. It looked like she was chewing as she stared at him.

"I'll . . . I'll call you later."

"Okay. Oh, David, I'm so . . ."

"I know. It's okay. I'll call you later."

Norcross felt almost sick with frustration at having to short-change Claire like this—another layer of cloud over everything—but he had no choice.

The new phone call was from Myra, Ray's chief of staff, with the news that Ray was still alive but critically injured and being rushed to an American air force base in Germany. Sheila's remains would be flown back to the United States in the next two or three days. The office was making the arrangements.

"Has anyone told Lindsay and Jordan what's happened?" Norcross asked.

"No, Judge. At least, no one here. We've been waiting for you." Myra paused, and he heard the murmur of a voice in the background. "But there's been a lot of buzz."

"Okay."

"Main thing I wanted to pass on is that, at first, some of the news organizations—CNN was one—incorrectly reported that both Ray and Sheila had been killed." Myra sighed. "Not just Sheila." This had to be terrible for her. She had been with Ray since he first ran for governor.

"Okay."

"So it's unclear if Lindsay and Jordan know anything, or if what they think they know is correct. Also, intelligence hasn't ruled out sabotage, so you'll be seeing some extra security."

"Right. They're here."

"Sorry, I have to go, Judge. Got a call I have to take. We're all so grateful. I mean it. Good luck!"

The passenger-side agent had exited the car and was standing beside it, sweeping his eyes over the neighboring houses. Judge Norcross got out the back, dragging his overnight bag and the pizza awkwardly behind him.

The driver buzzed down his window. "Need some help?"

"No, I'm fine. Thanks."

A brick walkway led past the bow window, where he'd seen Jordan, around to the front.

Jordan had vanished. As Judge Norcross mounted the granite steps, the front door suddenly swung open, and a handsome woman in her mid-seventies stepped out. Behind her, he saw the live-in nanny, Rosa, standing in the foyer.

"Traffic jam!" The older woman had a surprised but kindly smile. She held out a hand. "I'm Teresa."

Judge Norcross dropped the bag and shook. "David Norcross, Ray's brother."

"Oh, you must be the judge! It's very kind of you to come, David. I didn't see the girls. They're keeping to themselves, I guess. But I brought over a plate of sushi and salade niçoise. I know Jordan likes the California roll. I couldn't think what else to do. Would you please tell them to call me if I can do anything?" Her eyes dropped onto his pizza, and she laughed, "They'll probably appreciate that much more!"

It was only as she stepped into a limo that Norcross realized that the woman he'd been talking to was the wife of the secretary of state.

Rosa was waiting as Norcross stepped through the door.

"Hello, Judge Norcross." She spoke sadly and with a slight South American accent. "Thank you for coming."

"Please call me David."

A passage led from the foyer toward the formal living room, where pillars defined a generous threshold opening into a large, well-furnished area, perfect for cocktail parties. Small, pretty Jordan was peeping at Norcross from around one of the pillars. When she saw him notice her, she stepped hesitantly into the hallway. Her face, a mask of sorrow, instantly told him he wouldn't have to be giving his nieces the news about their parents. They knew.

"Hi, Jordy," he said.

"Hi, Uncle Dave."

Judge Norcross dropped his bag and set the pizza on one end of a marble table positioned along the wall. The table also held a handsome ceramic vase with drooping birds of paradise. Sheila must have put them there before she left. They needed water.

Jordan kept her eyes on Norcross as he made his way toward her down the passage. When he reached her, he squatted down and put his arms around her. It wasn't a great hug, but it was okay. Jordan didn't squirm. Her hair smelled of baby shampoo. After he stood up, he placed his hand on top of her head. It was all he could think to do.

"It's great to see you," he said.

Jordan looked up at him. "My name is Jordan now, okay? Not Jordy." Her tone wasn't unfriendly, but it was clear she wanted him to know.

Perhaps to make sure he realized she wasn't being rude, she nodded back toward the marble table and said, "Thank you for bringing the pizza." She turned toward the living room.

"You're welcome."

"What kind?" Her back was to him. Sheila had trained her to be polite under stress, but her tone was mechanical.

"Pepperoni and green pepper."

"Oh." She looked back at him. "Just so you know, Lindsay's veggie." She crossed into the living room and added, almost to herself, "I don't like green peppers, but I can pick them off."

Lindsay was coming down the stairs to the left as Norcross followed Jordan into the living room. The thick carpeting was a navy blue, vivid in the wash of sunshine pouring in from the tall windows facing the street. Sheila had frequently remarked on how much Lindsay looked like her uncle Dave. Norcross couldn't see it, but it was true that Lindsay was unusually tall, had wiry hair like his, and offered the world a long, earnest face. Her features, hard to read at best, looked at him blankly from the foot of the stairs.

"Hi, Lindsay,"

"Hi."

"Why don't we, uh, sit down."

Lindsay said, "We know."

A silence expanded in the room. Rosa had disappeared.

"I see. Okay." Norcross looked at the two girls. "Can we sit down?"

Lindsay and Jordan silently moved to an enormous white sofa, with Jordan burrowing into Lindsay's side. The little girl's mouth was turned down into a frown so intense it looked like it hurt. Her lip was trembling, and Norcross could see that she was holding herself right on the edge of tears. Lindsay looked straight ahead. She stroked Jordan's hair absently.

Norcross sat in a white upholstered armchair facing the two girls. "When did you learn?" It was all he could think of.

Lindsay looked up at the ceiling, either to calculate how long it had been or to absorb what a useless question this was. "An hour ago. Something like that. One of my friends called."

Judge Norcross leaned forward, resting his elbows on his knees. "Listen. I'm completely awful at this." His eye, he realized, had been bothering him like crazy ever since they'd pulled into the driveway. He paused to rub at it before continuing. "I'm probably more awful than I even realize." Jordan was breathing shakily now, close to going over the edge. Lindsay was facing at an angle, away from him, holding everything in. Maybe she really was like him.

"Why are you here?" Lindsay turned to him abruptly. She covered her eyes, shook her head, and dropped her hands. "That came out wrong. It's nice of you, Uncle Dave. Really. But we're wondering."

"We don't see you that much," Jordan said.

"Not since that time on Thanksgiving," Lindsay added.

"Right. I remember."

"You brought Marlene," Jordan said.

"Right."

The phone on the table next to the sofa rang jarringly, making all three of them jump. Norcross was concerned it might be from his office or from the security detail outside. Lindsay picked up, listened for a few seconds, and put the phone down without saying anything.

"Who was it?" Norcross asked.

Lindsay shrugged, her face frozen.

"I sort of need to know. . . ." Norcross began.

Lindsay turned her head to the side and looked down at the carpeting, her face taut.

"It's just that, it might be . . ."

"It was for Mom, okay? It keeps happening. . . ."

Jordan burrowed into Lindsay's side more deeply. "That's twice already." She craned back to look at Lindsay. "People don't know yet, right? She's not coming back?"

Lindsay pulled Jordan tighter into her side. "That's right."

Norcross could barely keep himself from groaning. "Oh, Lord, I'm sorry! Lindsay, I'm so sorry." It was too awful. A long silence followed, broken by sniffs from Jordan.

Finally, Lindsay pushed her chin at Norcross. "So, not to be rude, Uncle Dave, but why are you here?"

"People were worried. Myra called. She's your dad's . . ."

"We know Myra." A look of annoyance passed over Lindsay's face, and once again, she shook it off. "We've known Myra a very long time." A darker cloud, possibly anger, followed quickly over her face. "Myra should have called us. We shouldn't have to—"

"Are you going . . ." Jordan broke in, her voice raspy. "Are you going to take us away?"

"Gosh, no. I . . . No, definitely not."

"Because we really don't want to go anywhere, okay?" Lindsay gave her little sister another squeeze. "This is our home. We want to stay here."

"Home." Jordan nodded.

"No one's talking about having you go anywhere. Tell the truth, this is all happening really fast for me, too. I guess people thought, because I'm your uncle—"

"We appreciate it," Lindsay interrupted. "We really do."

Norcross recognized Ray's voice. How many times had he heard his brother say something like that—often those exact words—being nice, pushing people back to a manageable distance?

"Thanks." Norcross sighed. "I just want you to know how sorry I am about your mom. She was such a lovely person." He rubbed his upper cheek. "She really was." His voice started to shred. It wasn't so much the thought of Sheila that was cracking him open as it was the tears running along Jordan's nose. The look on the little girl's face was excruciating.

She sniffed and wiped her eyes, blinking at him. "Uh-huh."

"Your mom was. Your mom was a fantastic person. I'll never forget her. And . . ."

Lindsay pressed her hands over her ears, breathed, and then shook her head as though she was angry at herself.

"And Dad, too," Jordan said in a broken voice, continuing to wipe at her face.

"Yes, and your dad. We're hoping his injuries are not going to . . ."

Lindsay's head jerked toward Norcross, her eyes wide. "What? Dad's . . . Dad's dead, right? Like Mom. They're both . . ." As she took in her uncle's expression, she raised her fingers to her mouth. They were trembling.

"No," Norcross said quickly. He shook his head. "He was . . ."

"We thought they were both dead." Lindsay's face flushed, and her eyes began to glisten.

"No," Norcross said. "That was incorrect. Some of the news . . ."

"Dad's not dead?" Jordan asked. She pulled her legs out from under her and sat up.

"No, no. We got a call in the car on the way here, from your dad's office. From Myra. He's being taken to a hospital in Germany. He's badly hurt, but right now, he's alive."

It was a relief to feel a return of focus, to have some objective information to pass on.

Lindsay put a hand on her chest. Her fingers continued to tremble and her breath was coming in shudders.

"Dad's not dead? When's he coming home?" Jordan looked up at Lindsay. "What about Mom?"

"I need to go to the bathroom," Lindsay said in a choking voice. She stood up, looking around as though she wasn't sure where she was. "I need to . . ." She walked quickly toward the far end of the room. In the doorway, she paused, her chest still rising and falling rapidly. She spoke in a hoarse, furious voice, "Jesus, why did it have to be her? Why did it have to be her and not him!" She turned, let out a sobbing cry, and disappeared into the hallway.

13

Western Massachusetts had no federal penal facility, so the U.S. government housed defendants who were detained pending trial at the Hampden County Jail and House of Correction in Ludlow. As his days of confinement stretched out, Sid Cranmer tried a strategy of keeping to himself and staying unnoticed. It wasn't working.

For one thing, the quarters were close. He shared an eight-by-ten-foot cell with a closemouthed white man, forty years his junior, who communicated mostly by scowling and pointing. The cell contained a bunk bed, with Sid allocated the less favorable lower deck, a small table and chair, and a totally exposed stainless-steel sink and toilet unit. At nine p.m. every night, the cell was locked and was not opened again until six a.m. Except for the times when a guard peeped through a six-by-four-inch window to check, what happened inside the cell would be unknown to anyone but Sid and his unfriendly "cellie."

The late spring was growing warmer, and with unreliable air-conditioning, the cell became suffocating at night. Still, Sid's situation wasn't as bad as it could have been. Due to overcrowding, he learned, many cells the same size had a cot squeezed in to permit triple bunking. Screaming and shouts frequently echoed down the cell block. Brawls were common. Most nights, Sid was too frightened to get much sleep.

Mealtimes were a special challenge. To accommodate the crush, dinner started at four p.m. and unfolded in half-hour shifts up until eight p.m., with every table packed through each rotation. People quickly figured out who he was. On his very first day, a man sat down across the table from him and held out a grimy wad of papers that he said was a draft petition for habeas corpus. He asked if Sid would read the thing over and put it into good English. One look at the man's face told Sid he'd better agree, but as he lay on his bunk later, he found the rambling, penciled paragraphs literally incomprehensible. The problem was compounded when his cellie, apparently accidentally, brushed the unnumbered pile onto the floor. It was impossible to reorder the pages in any way that approached sense. Sid couldn't even make out what the man was charged with. Two days later, when the prisoner came up to him, Sid used the excuse that he was still working on the project. The guy did not look happy.

In the food line, big men, and even smaller men about his size, cut in front of him, eyeballing him and daring him to complain. He didn't say anything. At his first breakfast, he got a bowl of Cheerios dumped into his lap. The guy's "Sorry, man" did not sound very sincere.

The day after his court hearing, Sid was sitting at the end of a table in the corner, trying to get his creamed corn down as fast as he could, when a bald-headed black inmate about his age slid in across from him. The man settled himself, then folded his hands and closed his eyes, bowing over his tray. His scalp was so wrinkled it looked as though his skull had been partly deflated.

After finishing his prayer, the man raised his head. "Hey, little brother, what's up?"

At first, Sid hadn't known how to respond to this ritual question, which had never before been put to him. Once, he'd just said, "Fine, thanks," and gotten a puzzled look. Later, he killed time lying in his bunk imagining witty responses, like "the Dow Jones," "your cholesterol," or "my anxiety level."

Now, a couple of days later, he knew the drill. It didn't pay to be clever. "Not much. What's up with you?"

"Not much. Not much."

Their rectangular table accommodated eight chairs, four to a side. The square of four seats on the far end was occupied, leaving the two adjoining Sid and the man across from him empty.

Two young Hispanic inmates, who looked like they might have been brothers or cousins, approached, and one of them slid into the seat next to Sid. The second man, taller and older, hesitated, holding his tray above the last vacant seat. He noticed Sid, and his eyes narrowed. Then he looked at his partner and gave a slight shake of his head. The seated man rose, and the two walked off in search of other spots.

The older black prisoner called after them. "Something we said?"

The retreating men either didn't hear or pretended not to. After a couple bites of his meatloaf, the older black inmate looked up at Sid.

"You the professor dude, right?"

"Yes."

"How long you gonna be in here for?"

"Supposed to be only two or three more days."

"Putting you on the ankle bracelet?" The man jiggled his knees as he talked, keyed up.

"That's what the judge said. Home detention with electronic monitoring."

"Lucky boy." The man stirred some gravy into his mashed potatoes. "Norcross?"

"Yes."

"He's all right. Better than some of them other motherfuckers. Got your own house and so forth you're putting up, too, people saying."

"Guess so."

"Must be nice to have the hard."

The two men ate in silence. Sid concentrated on his tray, hoping the conversation was over.

He'd learned that "hard" meant money. Linda Ames had warned him that prisoners sometimes threatened to beat up a vulnerable inmate unless he arranged regular protection payments to a girlfriend or buddy on the outside. If this happened, she said, Sid should stall as long as possible and get in touch with her right away.

Unfortunately, the man across from him soon resumed speaking. "People call me A.J."

"Uh, Sid."

A.J. raised his eyebrows and smiled almost shyly. "This here is a tough, tough game for old cockadoodlers like you and me, man."

"I know."

"Figured we might help each other out."

Sid had no idea what to say. He had, even in his short time, acquired the instinct to know that if he allied himself with the wrong person, he could make his situation worse, not better. He responded with a shrug.

A.J. continued. "Staties caught me and my old lady body-packing up to Rutland." He sniffed. "Took us in the ladies' room and yanked the shit right out, man. It was ugly." A.J.'s head was bobbing up constantly, scanning the room and then ducking down again. His knees kept jiggling.

It was well known that heroin and cocaine flowed steadily up from Holyoke and Springfield into Vermont, where addicts would pay a 25 or 30 percent premium for their drugs. "Body-packing" was a new term for Sid, but it didn't need much imagination to guess where A.J. and his girlfriend had been carrying their product.

"So now I picked up this trafficking charge, and I can't do the time, you know? The game in here is just, like I say, too tough for me." He slurped his milk and set the glass down with a clack. "So I started talking to them boys about this and that. They open me up and send me out, but I'm taking heat, you know. People in the hood, they think I'm dry snitching, and po-po thinks I'm half stepping, holding back on him. And the pressure, man, it's killing me, so I start using—not too much, just to take the edge off, right? Then I'm pissing in the cup, and the motherfuckers catch me waterloading and throw me in here. Close me the fuck down."

"Okay." Sid understood about half of this.

"But you got the feds on you, I hear. That right?"

"That's right."

"I know shit those feds would just love to hear—good heavy shit, you know? And with the feds, man . . ." He reached over and prodded Sid's shoulder. "You help them, and you get a solid gold credit card, right? Now, you just tell your lawyer— Oh-oh." He was gazing across the room toward the doorway, where two prisoners were talking to one of the guards. "Don't like that." He leaned forward, dropping his voice to a whisper. "Listen up, Professor. One hand washes the other, you know? Lot of guys here have kids. Don't like diddlers. They got plans for you. Soon. Thought it'd be the righteous thing to mention it. You remember A.J., okay?"

"What am I supposed to do? I'm . . ."

"Want my advice? Get in seg."

"Seg?"

"Get yourself put in the hole."

"But how do I . . ."

"Oh my Lord, here it comes. Quicker'n I thought. Get in the hole, friend, get in the hole and stay in the hole."

With a fluid twist, A.J. slid out of his chair, slunk around the adjoining table, and disappeared. At the same time, Sid felt a gathering of shadows behind him, as though a clump of trees had suddenly grown up at his back. When he turned, he found a semicircle of large men creating a screen between him and the rest of the room. The guards who normally kept an eye on things had stepped away.

Sid said, "Hi," but no one smiled.

The four men at the end of his table stood up with their trays.

"Time to bounce," one of them said. All four moved off, not looking in Sid's direction. One of the men, still chewing, wiped his hands on the back of his pants.

"Well, hello again to you, Professor!" It was his cellie. Other people at nearby tables were casually moving off. No guards anywhere. The gang, maybe five or six men of various colors, edged in closer, deepening the privacy and blocking out any witnesses to whatever was about to happen.

His cellie leaned over, put his hand on Sid's shoulder. "These boys asked me to introduce you." He dropped his voice, and his eyes danced back at the group gathered around him. "They thought, since the sheriff bunked us together, I must be in the kindergarten, too. Got to clear that up." He stood and held out both hands. "So here he is, guys—the professor."

Sid's heart was racing. He twisted to the side, facing the men, gripping the edges of his tray. Were they going to kill him?

"Well," he began. "What's the . . . What's the . . ." There really was no way to finish the sentence.

A voice said, "Time to give the perfessor his lesson."

Sid started to get up, still holding his tray, and a heavy hand behind him shoved him down.

He knew then it was real. The normal uproar of voices in the room continued, maybe a little louder, as though nothing was happening, but around him, the pool of silence grew closer.

A ripple rolled over the group, some movement, and then his cellie was holding a steaming mug of coffee in each hand. The mist from the mugs was distorting the man's face.

"Do it," the voice ordered, and his cellie whispered hoarsely, "Coffee break, Teach!"

He stretched out his right hand and began to pour the scalding liquid onto Sid's bald head.

Sid ducked out from under the hand on his shoulder and spun toward his attacker, thrusting up with the tray so it caught his cellie under the tip of his nose. The man's head snapped back, coffee and creamed corn went flying, and a spout of blood shot down his chin. When the inmate beside him lunged forward, Sid jammed the broken remnant of the tray in his face and kicked him hard in the groin. A rush of bodies followed, the table went over with a heavy bang, and Sid saw stars as a punch or club landed on the side of his head and he went down. He could feel a hand grabbing at his testicles, and he crossed his legs and put his hands over the top of his head, pressing his elbows over his face. The initial thumping hurt, but not unbearably—then they rolled him over and began kicking him, which hurt a lot more.

The beating went on for what seemed like a long time until, just as he was losing consciousness, he heard the roar of the guards breaking through, shouting, "Don't kill him! Don't kill him!" There was a tremendous crash, which must have been several people going down over a table. He heard the crack of batons, people crying out in pain, and the voice of the same guard, shouting, very loud, "Goddammit! That's enough!" And then, not so loud, "You'll get us all fired, for

Christ's sake." If the guards had stayed away for another couple of minutes, the mob probably would have finished him off right then and there, which, in Sid's opinion, would have saved everyone, especially him, a lot of trouble.

PART TWO

MOTION PRACTICE

14

It was a humid late-August afternoon in Washington, DC, and Judge Norcross had gotten himself into another serious pickle. Bob Stephenson was smiling over at him, already amused at the imminent disaster.

"Yeah, come on, Your Honor." He gave Norcross a poke. "Show us your stuff!"

The three months since the Dubrovnik plane crash had not been easy. All summer, Judge Norcross had been flying down to Washington every Friday to visit his nieces and give them a weekend in their own home. Lindsay and Jordan spent their weekdays with Bob and June Stephenson—old State Department friends of Ray Norcross. The arrangement was supposed to be a temporary stopgap, but it hadn't worked out that way. Ray's skin grafts were taking longer than expected to heal, and recurring infections continued to bar any move from the hospital in Germany.

This particular Saturday, Norcross and the girls had come to the Stephensons' plush home to enjoy, supposedly, a poolside barbecue. Up until now, the event had not been much fun, for a couple reasons.

First, there were the Stephensons' twin eleven-year-olds, Lloyd and Curtis. Typical of boys their age, they had been spending the afternoon trying to outdo each other with cannonballs that basically prevented anyone else from getting into the pool or even near it.

One of them—Curtis, probably—was standing at the end of Norcross's deck chair with his hands on his hips, smelling of chlorine and backing up his father's challenge.

"Yeah, Mr. Judge," he said. "Put up or shut up." The kid wasn't smiling. In the background, the second twin crashed into the pool, screaming "Cowabunga!"

The second problem was the girls. Lindsay was lying in a recliner well off to the side, alternately submerged in her phone or pretending to doze, waiting out the time until they could go home. Twice, she'd turned down, with no expression of thanks, Bob Stephenson's hearty offer of a cheeseburger with all the fixin's. Jordan, in a green swimsuit with pink rosettes on the shoulder straps, mostly stuck close to her uncle's side, looking lost and visibly wincing at the nonstop hoots from Lloyd and Curtis to come on into the water. When their calls lured her near the pool, she was promptly drenched by a vigorous and deliberately timed cannonball.

Like most kind parents, Bob and June Stephenson were ambivalent about discipline and gave their boys a long leash. Bob's murmured, "Hey, watch it now," had little effect.

Norcross tried to comfort Jordan as she skittered back to him, saying, "It's okay, Jordan. Cannonballs are for amateurs. I bet they couldn't do a can opener."

Curtis immediately jumped on this.

"What's a can opener?"

"It's a kind of dive," Norcross said dismissively. "It's harder to do and much more exciting than a cannonball."

"Show us."

The other twin chimed in, yelling from the diving board, "Yeah, show us. Show us!"

Which was when Bob leaned toward him with a glint in his eye and threw down the gauntlet. Bob was not a mean-spirited man, but he had a quality Norcross had never liked, the tendency to use teasing as a form of aggression he didn't have to own up to. Everybody was supposed to be a good sport. His boys, unfortunately, seemed to have acquired this trait from him.

"Yeah, come on, Your Honor. Show us your stuff." Bob was wearing trendy black frame glasses, a tan silk sport shirt over his black trunks, and a wolfish grin.

Back in Wisconsin, Norcross had been a good athlete, lettering in ice hockey and cross-country skiing. Over the years, he'd stayed trim. Even in his forties, he did not disgrace himself in swimming trunks. But he hadn't been off a diving board in more than twenty years.

"Okay, I will."

The girls' eyes tracked Norcross as he stood and stripped off his Boston Red Sox T-shirt. Folding his arms behind his head, he stretched, and glared down at Curtis. "Watch and learn."

"Oh God," Lindsay said. She rose from her recliner and began pacing toward the far edge of the yard, examining the grass.

Generally speaking, Judge Norcross had less concern than most people about looking like a blockhead. There were worse things a person could do. But on this occasion, he really dreaded making a fool of himself in front of the girls.

All summer, he had been getting regular advice about how to handle them from his old Peace Corps sweetheart, a woman named Susan O'Leary, who was a child psychiatrist, divorced now and living in a big house on Beacon Hill in Boston. She'd emailed him several helpful articles outlining things to do—and not do—with a grieving child, and they'd followed up with three in-person dinner tutorials. These evenings featured almost as much romantic nostalgia about their two years in the Highlands of Kenya as they did pointers about how to manage Lindsay and Jordan. Their meals so far had stayed within bounds—only an extralong hug at the end—but Norcross felt guilty anyway. Susan was very sweet, and Claire, he had to admit, had so far not been nearly as much help as she was.

Even with Susan's advice, his weekends with the girls were often hard. The littlest things sent Jordan into uncontrollable fits of sobbing, and Lindsay rarely emerged from behind her iron mask. Nevertheless, as he walked toward the diving board, Norcross was comforted to think that he might have done one or two things right with them. He'd promised Jordan that someone would always be there to take care of her. He'd shared with her his own belief that while people died, love didn't. He'd told her that her love for her mother would never go away. Bedtimes were especially difficult, and sometimes this consolation would stop Jordan crying and send her off to sleep.

Then, one evening after Jordan had gone to bed, Lindsay noticed a vase of purple irises he'd brought and mentioned how her mother liked flowers. Acting on a suggestion from Susan, Norcross plucked up his courage and spoke.

"What would you say to your mom?" he asked. "If you could tell her just one thing?" When Lindsay closed her eyes and shook her head, Norcross blundered on. "If I could say anything to Faye, I'd tell her that I'll always remember her, that in some way she'll always be with me."

To his surprise Lindsay hadn't fled the room. She'd stayed and finally said in a soft voice, "I'd tell Mom I'm sorry about our fight." She'd looked down and scrubbed at the carpet with her toe. "That I didn't mean the things I said."

She'd quickly gone off to her bedroom after that, but she came to the foot of the stairs a while later and, without making eye contact, said, "Thank you." It was like a gift from heaven.

Why all this should provoke Norcross into trying to do a can opener, and probably making an ass of himself, was not clear. The concrete skirt around the pool felt very hot, almost scorching, on his bare feet. He noticed that Bob was getting out of his deck chair and, still grinning, was joining his boys nearer the pool to enjoy the spectacle. June was shouting some cheery encouragement from the kitchen window. Lindsay was at the far end of the yard, her back mostly turned to him. Jordan had both hands over her mouth, her eyes wide.

As he mounted the step, Norcross hastily reviewed the three essential components of a decent can opener.

First, it was essential to get maximum loft from the board. He must not—must *not*—be shy about taking a good high leap on the very end. He had to remember, when he came down, to keep his knees fairly stiff to maximize the impact, so that the board would fling him as high as possible straight up into the air.

Second, as he reached the apogee of his liftoff, he needed to remember to tip backward at a slightly oblique angle, as though he were leaning onto a pillow of air behind him. If he tipped too far back, he'd risk braining himself on the board, or coming unraveled and doing a kind of backward belly flop—very painful and ridiculous. If he stayed too vertical, he'd hit the water wrong, and the result would be a swishy fizzle.

Third, just as he reached the top, keeping his torso as erect as possible, he had to grab his right knee and then yank it fiercely against his chest in the split second before he hit the water. The result, if it worked, would be a respectable initial splash, but, much more important, a booming recoil that would send a spout of water twenty or twenty-five feet into the air.

In a kind of dream, Norcross took four quick steps down the board and leaped up as high as he could, coming down clean and hard on the end. Everything after that was pretty much blurry instinct. It occurred to him somewhere along the way that the Stephensons' deep end was only ten feet and he was over six feet tall. The blow to his left ankle as it cut through the water and struck the bottom was sharp, but it didn't feel as though he'd fractured anything.

As Norcross's head broke the surface, the first thing he saw, to his immense satisfaction, was Bob's astonished face, cracked open in a hoot of laughter. The man could evidently take a joke as well as dish one out.

"Bravo, Your Honor!" Most of his tan silk sport shirt was now dark brown. He took off his glasses and rubbed his eyes with the back of his hand, muttering to one of the twins, "Go grab me a towel there, will you?"

Jordan came dancing up to the edge of the pool. "Oh my God, Uncle Dave. Oh my God! That was awesome!"

From the end of the yard, Lindsay gave her uncle a half smile and a silent clap of applause that only the two of them could see.

The Norcross family's Saturday victory somehow made the imminent return to the weekday routine harder to bear, especially for Jordan. Sunday afternoon, as the time for the handoff back to the Stephensons drew closer, she slipped into something as near to rebellion as her shy character permitted. When it was time to pack up, she plopped herself in the big chair in her room and pretended to be lost in a magazine.

Judge Norcross was standing in the doorway, admiring the little girl's stiff, queenly posture, profiled against her bow window. June Stephenson would be arriving in ten minutes or so, and he'd asked Jordan three times to pull her backpack together. A cab was already on its way to hustle him to the airport.

"Well, look at you." Norcross pulled on the end of his nose and sniffed.

Jordan, leaning over her magazine, pretended not to hear him. Her short blond hair fell across the side of her face, blocking him out. The child's feigned preoccupation gave Norcross a pang. The façade of aplomb was impressive, and sad, in a six-year-old.

After a few seconds, without looking up, Jordan responded, a little distantly, "God bless you." She was wearing a yellow T-shirt, green shorts, and red sandals. Her pale-white little-girl legs barely reached the hassock. Her ankles were neatly crossed.

"Well," Norcross hesitated. "Thank you, I . . ."

Jordan peeked around her hair, turning her face to him. "You sneezed."

Behind her attempt at composure, she looked very unhappy. How would he have felt at her age confronting the prospect of five days with Lloyd and Curtis? Horrible.

"I did? That's funny. I usually notice when I sneeze."

"You said, 'luh-katchoo." She drew out the words and raised her eyebrows, trying to press her joke into his brain. "Get it?"

"Yes. Look at you. You look like a princess."

Jordan rolled her eyes and went back to her magazine.

Lindsay thumped down the hall with a duffel bag over one shoulder. "Come on, Jordan. Move it. Uncle Dave's throwing us out again."

"I'm not throwing you out."

"Okay, move it, Jord. Uncle Dave's abandoning us again."

"I'm not . . ."

"Just kidding."

"Wait." Norcross broke into a smile. "Luh-katchoo. I get it!"

Jordan put down her magazine and shook her head resignedly. "Never mind."

When June Stephenson pulled into the back courtyard, she was outwardly cheerful. The boys, she said, couldn't stop talking about the can opener and trying to do it themselves. Norcross thought he could sense shadows underneath this sunny cellophane. June's determined profile as she drove off with Lindsay and Jordan told him that their extended sojourn was getting as difficult for the Stephensons as it was for the girls.

In the cab on the way to Washington National, Norcross wrestled once more with the possibility of bringing his nieces to Amherst. It had occurred to him many times that he ought to have Lindsay and Jordan up, at least for a week or two. He had room for them, physically, but he'd always told himself that they'd hate the idea. What would they do in a strange town where they knew no one? Equally important, what would he do with them under foot all week?

For most of the summer, Judge Norcross had had a defensible rationalization for his avoidance in the form of an interminable patent trial. The disputed patent covered a highly technical process for placing an oxide coating on raw aluminum, and it had massive implications for everything from lawn furniture to airplane bodies. Hundreds of millions of dollars were at stake. Putting another major project, like his nieces, on his plate had been unthinkable. Now the patent trial was over, and he had to confront what would happen if the Stephensons ran out of gas.

As he was inching his way through the security line at the airport, he noticed that he was favoring his left ankle, which was still recovering from the blow on the pool bottom. The thought of having a good story to regale Claire with nudged aside his worries about the girls. She'd been away most of the summer on a teaching gig at Dalhousie University in Halifax, Nova Scotia, and she was returning to Amherst that very day. When he closed his eyes, he could almost smell the faint coconut aroma of her hair conditioner.

After clearing security, Norcross was making his way to the crowded gate area, when a deep voice close to him suddenly said, "Good afternoon, Judge."

Norcross had been so preoccupied he hadn't noticed FBI agent Mike Patterson, sitting four feet in front of him. Patterson stood up, shook hands, and gestured to a slim woman with short gray hair.

"Let me introduce my wife." Patterson nodded at her. "Fran, this is Judge Norcross."

As Fran Patterson stood and shook hands with Norcross, her face broke into an easy smile, and she leaned back to take the judge in. "Well," she chuckled. "This is a pleasant surprise. I've been getting an earful about you."

Patterson glanced at his wife nervously, and she added, "Don't worry, Mike, I'm not going to give away any of your secrets." As with so many married couples, it appeared Fran was the more engaging, sympathetic partner. She smiled again and spoke with a relaxed warmth. "These are our kids." She looked down at two teenagers who were sitting next to them. "Stand up, please."

They were a year or two apart, each quite tall—the older one, the girl, nearly six feet. Both of them had been engrossed in their phones and now stood self-consciously, glancing at each other for support. Their mother continued, "This is Margaret, and our younger one here is James."

Margaret glanced at her mother, then held out her hand to shake with the judge. The boy followed suit, and Norcross was impressed at the firmness of their grips and their forthright eye contact. After a nod from their mother, they both sat down again.

Fran's smile faded, and she took a deep breath. "Looks like we're going to be residing up your way for a bit." It was not clear if she was pleased about this move.

"Really?" Norcross was distracted by some announcement from the gate. Flights out of National were often delayed.

Patterson broke in. "We've rented a house in Amherst Woods. The kids will be starting at the high school in a couple weeks." In response to this comment, Margaret looked up at her father disapprovingly and muttered, "Senior year." James, who looked about fourteen, was preoccupied with some message on his phone.

"It's a nice area," Norcross said. "Amherst Woods is just a stone's throw from my house."

Fran laughed and poked Patterson on the shoulder. "Don't be tempting my husband. He has a strong pitching arm."

Mike Patterson looked at her, uncomfortable, but suppressing a smile.

Norcross needed to break this off without being rude. Things were getting too chummy. Fortunately, Patterson felt the same way.

"Well," he said. "We better get the kids ready to board. Nice to see you."

"Very nice." Norcross nodded to Fran. "I hope you all enjoy western Massachusetts. It will be a change from Washington, DC."

"It certainly will be." Fran looked down. "Jimmy, finish up on your phone there, please."

Later, as he settled into his seat on the plane, Norcross wondered what it would be like for the Pattersons to relocate to mostly white Amherst, Massachusetts, after mostly black Washington, DC. Like the thought of the girls, however, this reflection soon evaporated in the anticipation of seeing Claire again. She wasn't expecting him until tomorrow, and he was hoping to surprise her.

When Claire had made her commitment to the summer sabbatical in Nova Scotia—early in the year, way before the plane crash and Sid Cranmer's indictment—the plan had been for David to fly to Halifax in June, before the patent trial, so he and Claire could take two weeks to drive through Nova Scotia, up to Cape Breton, and on to Prince Edward Island. They'd even hoped that, later in the summer, David would be able to run up for an occasional weekend. An easy nonstop flight shuttled between Boston and Halifax.

After the mess with Sid Cranmer broke in May, the promised Canada trip became even more important. They needed it to talk through how they would manage the situation with Claire's friend, who was now also David's defendant. In the days immediately after the dean's garden party, they had worked out a temporary *modus vivendi*, or what Claire called a *modus amandi*, but it was too fragile for comfort. The time on their own would give them space to do some healthy arguing and remember their priorities. Then Ray's protracted convalescence in Germany, full of promised returns and last-minute cancellations, destroyed all their plans.

Claire's long absence opened up a hollow space inside Norcross that he felt every time the press of external demands lifted. Whenever he had a quiet moment, there she was—or, actually, there she wasn't. The collapse of their vacation together, and a summer of unsatisfying FaceTime calls, made him especially anxious to get fall off to a good start. *United States v. Cranmer* had mostly been asleep over July and August while the attorneys fought over evidence and handled other cases. It would soon be moving to the center ring again, and Judge Norcross wanted Claire and him to have their feet solidly under them.

Norcross got back to Amherst in time to collect Marlene from the kennel, take her for a walk, and grab a quick shower. He hummed to himself as he put on a new black silk shirt he'd bought in DC. He'd never owned a black silk shirt before, and he liked it. He'd stashed a bottle of better-than-average champagne and a dozen red and yellow roses in the refrigerator before he'd left that Friday. The flowers still looked fresh, and Mission Cantina had their crispy fish tacos, Claire's favorite, ready when he swung by on his way to the center of town. He kept picturing how Claire's face would look when she opened the door.

As he approached her threshold, awkwardly balancing his offering of food, drink, and roses, a burst of Claire's irresistible laugh erupted from the screened porch around the back of her house. It was the cracking-up gush that bubbled out of Claire when she was amused at something she knew should not really be funny—something a little mean perhaps, slightly crude, or sexy. Her bad-girl laugh.

Clunking her door with the butt of the champagne bottle, David found himself grinning. He wondered what could be tickling Claire so much. Some book she was reading? Some video clip on her laptop? In a few minutes, she would be showing it to him, or reading it to him, and they would be enjoying it together. After the weekend with his nieces, he badly needed a heavy dose of uninhibited adult fun.

When Claire opened the door, she looked startled. "David!"

"Hello, my dear!" David held up the champagne and waved it merrily. "Welcome home." A smell of cooking wafted through the doorway.

"I wasn't expecting you."

"I know. . . ."

"You weren't coming until tomorrow."

"Right, but I . . ."

As David absorbed the confused look on Claire's face, he felt his painstakingly choreographed surprise begin to curl up at the edges and turn brown. It collapsed into ashes when he saw a tall, blond, athletic-looking man emerge through the doorway from the porch area with a glass of wine in his hand. It was Darren Mattoon.

"Well, hello there, Your Honor." Darren spoke with an ironical jocularity.

Claire glanced quickly back at Darren and then turned to David looking distressed. "He happened to be in Boston and gave me a lift from the airport."

"Ah. Uh-huh." David's arms were getting tired from holding all the stuff, but he wasn't going to put it down.

"It saved me waiting for the shuttle."

"Uh-huh."

"You weren't around."

"I know. Exactly. I wasn't around, and your friend there gave you a lift."

"Come in. Come in. We can . . ."

"No, listen, I think I'd rather save all this for another time."

"It's okay. I was just leaving," Darren said.

This was an obvious lie. His wineglass was three-quarters full. The guy had a lopsided smile, and he seemed unfazed, maybe even enjoying the situation.

"Nope, nope, nope." All David wanted to do now was get the heck out of there. As he hurried back down the sidewalk, he called over his shoulder. "Just shoot me a text later. Let me know what's a good time for you."

"You're limping. How did you . . . ?"

"Long story." Somehow, he managed to add, as he stepped back into his car, "This is not a problem. Really."

One of the roses had fallen on the sidewalk, but he didn't bother to retrieve it.

15

"Can I ask you about something, Elizabeth?"

Elizabeth Spencer and Professor Cranmer had been sharing slices of warm coffee cake while she took him through her latest work on Charles Dodgson's bank records. Elizabeth had developed a Florence Nightingale concern about Sid after all their months together, and these periodic oral reports allowed her to keep an eye on him. She knew that Sid's baked offerings were his way of showing how much her visits meant to him. The judge's pretrial home confinement order meant that Sid was enduring many long hours with only Mick and Keith for company. The chats with Elizabeth and the news that, so far, no hard evidence suggested payoffs by Charles Dodgson to any mysterious blackmailer always seemed to give him a boost.

"Sure. Of course." Elizabeth was sitting opposite Sid at his kitchen table. She'd pulled her Dodgson file together and was gearing up mentally for the looming prospect of seeing Ryan, who had just returned from his summer in New York.

"This is awkward." Professor Cranmer shifted in his chair and gazed out the window onto his side yard.

The long process of recovering from his beating had somehow pulled Sid together. This morning he was showered, shaved, and respectably dressed in blue jeans and a starched yellow dress shirt with the sleeves rolled up to his elbows. His face had been gruesome, really hard to look at, after the attack that past spring, but now the bruises were fading into green-and-yellow blotches, and he could get around fairly well if he took it slow.

Despite his improvement, Sid's obsession with ordering junk off the Internet persisted, and the deliveries kept trickling in. An unopened UPS box with a return address in Mexico was sitting at the end of the counter. Still, it wasn't as bad as before. He was really depressed, but he was sane.

The sound of a table saw broke out from the second floor. The professor's tattooed handyman was up there again. He'd finished Doreen's bedroom and was installing a set of bookcases along the upstairs hallway. Elizabeth had run into him once or twice, and he'd given her the typical boring, wriggly-eyebrow look she usually got from guys. He was always popping in at odd times, working around other projects, he said. After ten or fifteen seconds, the saw's screaming died out.

"You remember how I was this spring." Sid blew out a sigh and turned to Elizabeth. "I'm sorry that I put you through that. I was . . . I was pretty flattened."

"It's okay."

"I'm not even sure what was going on with me exactly." His mouth drooped wearily. "My headshrinker says it's all about my mother, of course." He paused and sighed again. "Surprise, surprise."

"Families," Elizabeth said. "I know how that can be." She was going to add, *They can mess you up*, but another howl from the saw drowned her out. Sid looked up at the ceiling and waited for some quiet. When it came, Sid continued.

"So, now, we haven't talked about this, but I need to ask you something. Some kind of hearing, or conference, or whatever, is coming up in my case. I don't plan to go, but my lawyer keeps pushing me to run some questions by you." Professor Cranmer sat up straighter and pulled on the weedy hair at the back of his head.

"Linda's given me some pictures and videos to look over." He hesitated and cleared his throat. "The government—you probably know—says it found some ugly stuff on my computer, and they've turned copies over to her."

Up to now, Professor Cranmer hadn't tried to talk to Elizabeth about his case. They'd always stuck to Dodgson or Amherst College gossip. She tried hard not to remember the glimpse she'd gotten of the little girl on the DVD sleeve or to imagine what she would think if it turned out that Professor Cranmer really was into child porn. It was too awful to contemplate.

"Right," Elizabeth said. "I know what they're saying. It's in the papers."

"I haven't looked at all of it yet. I can only bear it in dribs and drabs." Professor Cranmer pulled again at the hair on the back of his head. "As I told you, pornography of any kind has never really been my thing."

"Well, you know, lots of guys are into it. Some girls, too."

"Yes, but not me. At least, not all that much. I've seen it, of course, mostly while I was in the service." He flicked a worried glance at Elizabeth.

"It's normal in a way, I guess. It's out there everywhere, and people—a lot of people, anyway—decide to look at it."

"Maybe so, but this stuff they say they found on my computer? I can't believe I'd ever look at it, no matter how screwed up I was. What I wondered, Elizabeth, was whether you remember seeing any, I don't know, any disturbing material when you were using the computer, say last March or April? Anything distasteful popping up or left on the screen?"

"Honestly, no. It would have totally grossed me out. I still can't forget the picture on the DVD, and I only saw that for, like, three seconds."

There was a sudden bumping, and Sid's cleaner, Jonathan, banged in through the side door. Like Elizabeth, Jonathan knew where the professor's outdoor key was. He looked a little surprised to see them at the kitchen table.

Professor Cranmer and Elizabeth spoke in unison. "Hi, Jonathan."

"Hi." Jonathan nodded, avoiding eye contact. "Thought you would be taking another nap, Professor, so I, you know, let myself in.

Hope it's okay." He came into the room to collect his supplies. The Comet, the toilet bowl scrubber, the bucket, and so forth were stored under the sink.

Jonathan wasn't actually deformed, but his movements were always off kilter. He had a very high forehead—it seemed to take up half his face—and, whenever Elizabeth turned toward him, he pursed his lips, as though he found it painful to be looked at. When he heard the saw, Jonathan's face fell into a more extreme version of this pinched look. He and the handyman did not get along for some reason. Maybe it was just because all the sawdust made his cleaning job harder. As Jonathan headed up the stairs to do the bathrooms, Keith and Mick padded at his heels. They adored him.

"Yeah. Well, if you think of anything . . ." Professor Cranmer stood and began carrying the plates to the sink.

"Absolutely."

A few minutes later, as Elizabeth walked out to her car, any concerns she had about Professor Cranmer evaporated in the broiling memory of what she had suffered the evening before. The talk of pornography had been more painful for her than Professor Cranmer could ever have imagined.

Her catastrophe was so stupidly predictable it was embarrassing. Elizabeth had been out at The Pub, an Amherst institution close to campus, having a beer with some of her girlfriends. Classes were starting in a few days, and it was fun to connect with the early birds and see what they'd been up to over the summer. When she'd gotten up to go to the ladies' room, another senior, Rachel D'Angelo, someone she only sort of knew, jumped up and followed her from the table. Rachel was an outspoken feminist, and Elizabeth's flirtiness had always kept a certain distance between them.

The ladies' room was empty when they entered, and Rachel immediately said something like, "Wait a second, Libby," and pulled her cell phone out of her back pocket. Glancing over her shoulder at the door, she said, "You have a right to see this." Rachel's face managed to look both apologetic and angry. She pushed a couple buttons and handed the phone over.

Elizabeth was puzzled at first, but, when she looked down, a scene she immediately recognized flashed onto the screen, and the world stopped. It was her "Hot Summer" video, the one intended for Ryan's eyes only.

She saw herself, in her red bra and panties, swaying slowly to some faint music. As she watched, a wave of something Elizabeth still had no word for—something beyond humiliation and betrayal, beyond, but certainly including, rage and heartbreak—poured in a torrent through her. The downpour was so intense it darkened the edges of her vision, as though her brain were trying to shut out what she was seeing.

On the small, sharply focused screen, Elizabeth watched, despite herself, as she reached around with both hands, unhooked her bra, and playfully tossed it onto a chair. She heard Ryan's voice growling, "Yeah!," and then her own voice emerging from the phone, over the music, in a sexy drawl: "Hello there, babe. Remember me?" She was placing her hands on top of her head. The pink vibrator was visible in the background on the nightstand.

Elizabeth had jammed the phone back into Rachel's hand, taken three quick steps into an empty stall, slammed the door, and vomited. Later, after she'd cleaned up and Rachel had left, she returned to the stall, sat down on the seat, and began to sob. Never in her life, not even when her father died, had she cried so hard. It took her forty-five minutes to come out of that bathroom.

Over the past eighteen hours, it was as though whatever had poured through her had congealed into something metallic at the bottom of her stomach—cold and hard and about the size of a golf-ball. She'd tried to eat some cereal that morning but had thrown up again. It was as though she was weirdly pregnant. She felt it constantly—a clammy, nauseous spot inside her. How could Ryan do this to her?

She already knew, of course, what his excuse would be. He'd say he only sent the clip to one buddy—probably Ridgeway, his shithead classmate from Choate whom Ryan was always trying to impress—and Ridge, or whoever, had promised not to share it with anyone else. Now, according to Rachel, Elizabeth's performance was the hottest thing on everyone's iPhone. The whole campus was checking her out. Whenever anyone looked at her, she never knew if they were secretly smirking.

It would take Elizabeth a long time to forgive herself for her stupid, stupid trust in Ryan, but someday she would, maybe. She'd loved Ryan, truly loved him, and with all his flaws, she'd been certain he loved her back. The night they took the video, they'd had three shots of Jack Daniels and a joint. He'd started goofing around with this new app. That's how it always happened. She'd known that, known it and done it anyway—ten minutes of feeling wild and bad, wanting to show off, wanting him not to forget her. But, while she might someday forgive herself, she knew that she would never forgive Ryan, even though, in some screwed-up way, she still loved him. No matter what she accomplished—she could be head of Mass General, she could become secretary of health and human services—that video would always be out there. Her children and her grandchildren might look at it someday. It was in the cloud.

Maybe she'd have to kill Ryan. As she turned her key in the ignition, Elizabeth flushed warmly at the thought, then paused to pull a tissue out of her purse and dab away tears. She backed out of Professor Cranmer's driveway and accelerated, passing through the center of town, going faster than necessary. Yes. She remembered the paper she'd done for Professor Lindemann on the Renaissance corpses. If she did murder Ryan, she would definitely think up some slick way to pull it off. He and Ridge were the computer science majors, and they'd had their day. Now it was biochemistry's turn.

The landscape opened up as she sped out of the center of Amherst and headed south. She couldn't report Ryan to the police—what he'd done wasn't a crime—and she didn't trust the college's complicated process for reporting harassment. Something was bound to leak out. The fact was, she'd been drunk and high, and she'd let him take the video. How would that look when she applied to med school?

She'd handle this herself. Killing Ryan wouldn't be all that hard, with the right chemicals. She shot around a slow-moving van and got a horn blast from an oncoming car. Come to think of it, she might kill Ridge, too, if she could finagle a way to get them together. Simple justice. More tears gathered at the corners of her eyes, and she scrubbed them away. Yes.

Even as Elizabeth savored these thoughts, she knew they were silly. For one thing, she couldn't murder Ryan without risking a huge mess for herself, and she wasn't about to put her mom and her sisters through that. For another thing, she knew that a tiny corner of herself still hoped that she and Ryan could somehow make it back from this, that this wasn't really the end.

By the time she was pulling up the curving drive into Ryan's condo complex, the storm in her mind had quieted a little. She didn't know what she was going to do or what she was going to say. Maybe she would wait to confront him, but for what? There would never be a good time. She wanted to scream and throw things—and she wanted to kill him. What was it one of those Renaissance dramatists had said? "Revenge is a dish best served cold."

In a parking spot fronting on the sidewalk leading up to Ryan's door, Elizabeth noticed a very cute girl with dark, curly hair stepping into a powder-blue Mercedes two-seater. The car had orange-and-black New York plates. The Empire State. She watched uneasily as the girl leaned to the side and refreshed her lipstick in the rearview mirror before backing out and pulling away. Elizabeth pressed her hand to her forehead, breathed, and waited for her heart to slow down.

Over the summer, she and Ryan had enjoyed two long weekends at his family's place on Martha's Vineyard. It had been very pretty, very upscale. They'd had some good long runs, including a 10K in Menemsha for charity, but that was all. No visits down to Manhattan. He was way, way too busy at Goldman Sachs, he said.

Elizabeth's last shred of hope that the girl in the Mercedes hadn't been visiting Ryan flew away when he opened the door, shot a glance at the empty spot where the car had been, and said, "Whoa, hi! You're early."

"No, right on time."

"What's up? You don't look too good."

"I'm fine. Maybe getting a cold or something."

He gave her a quick kiss. "Man, I'm, like, totally wasted."

"Poor thing, I bet you are." She closed the door behind her, stepped up close, and let her hand slide down toward his crotch. "How's Big Jocko? Has he missed me?"

Ryan practically leaped backward.

"Hey, wow! Right. You want some coffee? Mom bought me a Keurig."

Elizabeth felt herself slide into a dead composure, which surprised her and made her feel strangely relieved. There was no need, she realized, to say anything to Ryan right away. She could choose her own time. Maybe she'd just fuck him to death.

His big, squishy sofa was like a comforting friend, and she flopped down onto it, propping her legs up. "Sure." She eyed Ryan as he bustled off to the kitchen for the coffee, clearly pleased to have something to do that got him away from her. "I just got back from seeing Professor Cranmer."

"Sid the Squid?" Ryan called out.

"He says they found some—what he called some—ugly stuff on his computer."

"Newman's Own or Gevalia Signature Blend?" Ryan was rattling around, opening and closing cabinets.

"Whatever."

Ryan poked his head out of the kitchen. "Ugly stuff, huh? Probably like the stuff in his hidey-hole the cops missed." He disappeared back into the kitchen. "They'd love to get their hands on that, I bet." After an interval of busy clattering, he emerged from the kitchen carrying two mugs. "I wouldn't mind taking a peek myself."

"No way, Ry." Elizabeth looked down as she took her coffee. "You forgot I don't take cream."

"Shit, no, here. I mixed up the mugs."

"I thought you liked it black, too."

"Switched over the summer." He spoke quickly. "Everyone at Goldman takes cream because they coffee it up so much. Better than taking pills like some of them do. Anyway, I got to like it this way." He took a hasty gulp and put the mug down, licking his lips. "So, Sid's worried, is he? Too bad. But guess what?" He pointed at her. "I know you like him, Lib, but I can't shake the idea that he's into little kids. When I think about that flyer? I mean, there were like ten or twelve titles, all really disgusting. One of them was called 'Tight Squeeze.'" He took another quick sip of coffee and made a face. "Hard for me to feel much sympathy for the Sidster."

Elizabeth sat up on the sofa and swung her feet around onto the floor. Ryan had come with her once to Professor Cranmer's. He was interested, he said, in the Dodgson material and curious to see the inside of Cranmer's house. They'd made a point of coming in when Sid was away, of course, and as she recalled now, Ryan had been on his own for a few minutes while she used the bathroom.

Elizabeth kept her voice level, placing her mug on his glass-top coffee table carefully. "You, um, you said you never saw the flyer, Ry."

Ryan looked at her, took another sip of his coffee, and swallowed. "I said I saw it, but I didn't touch it." She could see his brain spinning to come up with the words.

"You told me you never saw it."

"I didn't say I didn't see it, Lib." An edge came into his voice. "I was careful not to say anything one way or the other about that. I only said I didn't touch it."

This wasn't true. He'd either said that he hadn't seen the flyer or he'd managed to deceive her without lying outright. It amounted to the same thing. He'd wanted her to think he hadn't seen the flyer when he had. Now it was the video, Curlylocks in the Mercedes—who Elizabeth didn't give a shit about right now—and this lie, whatever it signified. The spot in her stomach twisted as it struck her again, hard, that she'd loved and trusted Ryan far too much. There was no way, almost certainly no way, to go back. If she felt herself starting to cry, she would tell him she had to go to the bathroom.

Elizabeth slid down into the sofa cushions and held out her arms. "Come here, babe." As she watched Ryan, her drift toward tears suddenly changed course, and she almost burst out laughing. Was she going crazy? His hopelessly confused expression of anxiety (he was too drained for sex) and relief (she was dropping the flyer issue) collided on his face like opposing waves smacking into each other. Whatever was going on, she could still, sometimes, read him like a book.

"I don't know, Lib. I know we're just getting back together and all, but I've got judo in a couple hours, and I'm kind of . . ."

"I know you're tired, Ry. I get that." She stretched out her hand and twiddled her fingers at him, urging him to come to her. "Believe me, Ryan." She nodded toward where the Mercedes had been parked. "I totally understand. And, you know, it's okay. Things happen. Just come over here and hold me. That's all I'm looking for right now."

The waves in Ryan's face overlapped, swirled, and resolved themselves into an expression of pure relief and liberation.

"Jesus, Libby," Ryan said. "I love you so much." He lay down next to her, and Elizabeth put her head on his shoulder.

"Ry," she began.

"Listen." Ryan bent back to look into her face. "I want you to know something, something really important. You must have seen this girl I met in New York, Jackie, leaving just now."

"It's okay, I don't care if . . ."

"My parents set me up with her. I, you know, left my car here in Massachusetts, so she drove me up. She lives out on Long Island." A cloud passed over Ryan's face. "Everyone's been pushing me and pushing me about her, my dad especially."

"She's very cute." Ryan's dad had told Elizabeth many times how much he liked her, how good he thought she was for Ryan, and how happy he was that Ryan and Elizabeth were together.

"She *is* very cute, and she's rich as shit, but she's not you, Lib."

"You're sweet, Ry." She kissed his nose. "You really are."

"She's not you." Ryan dropped his head and curled up around Elizabeth. "She's not you, and that's that."

Elizabeth produced a smile for Ryan's benefit, knowing he couldn't see it. His love was real, as real as things got for him. She did truly make him happy. Her mistake was in thinking that this feeling of his, so intense in the moment, would keep him from fucking her over. She wasn't going to bring up the video, not now anyway, and maybe not ever. She wanted that edge. Somehow, she'd get over him, and someday, if she got the chance, she'd even the score. She counted three breaths. She still loved him. Time to change the subject.

"Let's talk birthdays." This was one of their reliably happy topics. Elizabeth's birthday was just a few weeks off now, Ryan's in February, and a big fuss over these events had become a sort of tradition with them. Elizabeth spoke coyly, drawing her finger down his nose. "What I'm wondering, sweetie, is just how you plan to top last year?"

The previous year, Ryan's parents had given them two nights in a five-star hotel in Manhattan with tickets to the play of their choice. They'd picked *Hamilton*. It had cost a fortune.

Ryan stroked Elizabeth's hair. "Oh, don't worry about that, Lib. I'm totally on top of that. What I'm wondering is: What are you cooking up for me, babe? It's my twenty-first, you know. It has to be volcanic."

Elizabeth didn't have Ryan's money, so she had to use her brains and imagination to keep up with him. Last year, she'd given him their velvet-covered handcuffs and the vibrator. When he'd opened the box, it had taken him a full thirty seconds to close his mouth.

She nestled up to Ryan's ear and whispered. "I'm hard at work on yours too, Ry." She bit his earlobe lightly. "A friend of mine—someone with designs on you—and I are planning a private performance that I guarantee will blow your socks off." She tapped his nose, counting out the last three words: "Among. Other. Things."

There was no friend, of course, but the false promise of a threesome lit up Ryan's face. There was no birthday plan, either. Not yet. But there would be.

16

Judge Norcross ascended the three stairs to the bench, and his existence fell into order. For the next little while, he'd have only one thing to occupy his mind: *United States v. Cranmer*, the run-of-the-mill child porn case that had knocked his life sideways.

The view from the bench offered the usual landscape. To his left, Linda Ames was at counsel table without her client, which was typical. Defendants not in custody rarely appeared for routine status conferences. The opposite was true for defendants who were locked up. For them, a few hours out of jail for any reason—even if it was mostly spent sitting in court—was like a weekend on Cape Cod, a welcome break from a numbing prison routine.

To his right, Assistant U.S. Attorney Paul Campanella was accompanied at his table by FBI agent Mike Patterson. The courtroom was nearly empty except for the *Republican* reporter in the rear right and a very pretty young woman, probably some college student doing an assignment, who was sitting in the front row of the gallery on the end nearest the door. She held a wire-rim notebook on her lap and a pen in one hand.

As the judge took in the attorneys' facial expressions and body language, he noted with pleasure that this was going to be a hearing with some gristle. Linda Ames looked ready to punch somebody, and Campanella looked like he hoped she might try. They were both wearing red. Ames was sporting a scarlet blouse under her charcoal jacket, and Campanella was wearing a blazing Chinese-red tie. Classic battle dress.

All this was fine with Norcross. A nice criminal case with a little melodrama felt like heaven after the incredibly dull patent trial.

In contrast to the lawyers, Patterson looked like he couldn't care less about what happened in *United States v. Cranmer*. Nothing in his face sought to remind the judge of their encounter at the airport. It might as well never have happened. His elegant Lincoln-green suit made him better dressed than either of the attorneys. His tie was brown.

Norcross opened his file and began. "Okay. We are here today to take up some preliminary matters and get squared away for trial. The first item on the agenda is the psychologist's report, which I assume you have reviewed." This element of the case had been slowing things down. It had taken ages to locate a properly qualified forensic clinician and to give Cranmer enough time to recover from his brutal thumping to allow a consultation.

In response to the judge's words, Ames and Campanella both nodded and then glanced sideways, checking each other out. The two-second exchange revealed that the lawyers hadn't conferred before coming into court, which meant that they would be feeling out each other's positions for the first time now. This was not good. If Ames and Campanella couldn't talk informally outside the courtroom, it would make in-court proceedings snarlier than necessary. A slugfest over something meaningful was fun; foolish arguments over nothing were a waste of time.

"I'll begin with you, Ms. Ames. Frankly, I find the report ambiguous and confusing. Will you be seeking funds to hire your own psychologist?"

Ames stood, shaking her head. "No need. My client has instructed me not to raise the issue of his competency. We're not arguing that he committed the crime but was crazy when he did it. We're saying that he never committed any crime, period—at least not any crime the government can prove."

"Well, I'm reading from Dr. Katzenbach's findings here, where she refers to 'significant memory loss due to severe depression and anxiety extending over several months.' Later on, she refers to 'profound grief, complicated by alcohol dependence and insomnia.'"

"Right. I've gone over the report with Professor Cranmer."

Campanella hopped to his feet. "I would just note that in her conclusion, the doctor also finds, quote, 'scant evidence' of any disability sufficient to render Professor Cranmer incompetent to commit the crime or assist in his own defense at trial."

Norcross broke in. "Sounds to me like she's saying he was off his rocker, but he probably more or less knew what he was doing—sort of, kind of."

"That's it." Campanella shrugged. "In a nutshell."

"That doesn't help me a whole lot." Norcross flipped a page of the report. "She also says that for about three critical months, he can't remember much of anything."

"Well," Campanella began. "She also says—"

Ames waved a hand at Campanella, riding over him. "This is a nonissue, Judge. My client is adamant. He was going through a very difficult stretch, but he was competent, and he committed no provable offense."

"How can he assist you when he can't remember most of what he was doing when he supposedly committed the crime he's charged with here?"

"We're working on that, Judge."

Norcross pulled his robe up over his knees and resettled himself. "And how about the risk that Professor Cranmer might do himself harm? However bad this all might be, it's not a death-penalty case."

Out of the corner of his eye, Judge Norcross saw the young woman in the front row stiffen and stop jotting notes. She uncrossed her legs and set the notebook to one side, her eyes widening. Was she a relative of the defendant? A grown-up child from one of the videos?

The judge's concern about Cranmer had made Campanella impatient. "He's home, Judge. Agent Patterson tells me he has cats. He's doing fine."

Ames gave Campanella a scornful look and turned to Norcross. "The doctor you appointed has agreed to keep seeing Professor Cranmer. We're monitoring his condition."

Judge Norcross poured himself a cup of water and set it to the side, using the time to think. He didn't want to be sandbagged down the line for not pushing the competency issue. If Cranmer got convicted, which he probably would, he might get a new attorney for his appeal, and then it would be open season on all his rulings.

Norcross leaned forward and spoke with deliberate clarity, being extra sure the stenographer got every word. "If I don't hear something further from you, Ms. Ames—unless you raise the issue explicitly—I'm going to assume that you have waived any claim regarding competency, either at the time of the alleged crime or at the time of trial. Those issues will be out of the case. Do we agree on that?"

"We agree. They're waived."

This exchange—Norcross and Ames both knew—was a message to the court of appeals. Campanella knew this as well. He gave a satisfied nod, sat down, and made a check mark on his yellow pad. With this exchange in the transcript, no appeal would be possible based on any insufficient consideration of Cranmer's psychological condition, past or present.

Norcross's mind touched once more on the strange nature of his world. It was a universe like the land beyond Lewis Carroll's looking glass, with its own independent past, present, and future. Facts found on the record defined the judicial past, no matter what had occurred in the actual world. The tappity-tap of the stenographer's fingers created the present, in the form of a transcript, no matter what was actually being said or intended. And the court's legal rulings, relying on the absence of objections or tossing them aside, outlined the landscape of the future. If the record were not properly preserved, things would simply vanish from the reality of the case forever. It no longer mattered now whether the professor was, in fact, mentally impaired. That possibility had disappeared from the world of the courtroom, like the Cheshire cat, without leaving even a smile behind.

"Okay, what else have we got?"

Ames put her hands on her hips. "Big problems is what we've got, Judge."

"Let's hear."

The reference to big problems made the judge think of Claire, and he quickly jotted *Pick up wine* on his yellow pad. It had taken him most of a week to recover from the collapse of his surprise welcome-home party. In several phone exchanges, Claire insisted that the cozy scene with Darren Mattoon had been no more than a simple act of courtesy to a colleague who'd given her a lift.

This might be what Claire actually thought, but in Norcross's eyes, it was nonsense. He could see clearly that Mattoon had plenty more than collegiality in mind. The situation reminded him of his college hockey days. He wanted to smear Darren Mattoon into the boards. At the dinner Claire was preparing for him that evening, they would talk more about this. On the other hand, perhaps they wouldn't need to talk. It had been a very long time.

Ames was going on. "There's a pig pile of little stuff that's accumulated, but the basic issues come down to two."

Campanella leaned back and tossed his pencil on the table. He and Patterson exchanged looks.

"First of all, Mr. Campanella wants to put some remarks my client supposedly made during the raid into evidence before the jury. He can't deny that these statements were elicited before any *Miranda* warnings were given. I'm going to ask you to keep all those statements out of the trial, and I need an evidentiary hearing to build a record to support your ruling. My brother here"—she pointed over at Campanella, who was staring straight forward, refusing to look at her—"thinks we don't need one—no witnesses, no testimony—which makes no sense. I need you to hear from a number of people, including at least Special Agent Patterson and a young undergraduate intern named Elizabeth Spencer, who happened to be present at the time of the raid. Possibly Professor Cranmer himself, too. I also may call some of the three or four hundred law enforcement personnel who invaded Professor Cranmer's home that day. So, we need to set that up."

At the mention of Elizabeth Spencer, Agent Patterson turned slowly around and nodded at the pretty college student. She stiffened, not responding, and Patterson turned back.

Norcross took a closer look at the young woman who must be Elizabeth Spencer. What was she doing here? Potential witnesses normally didn't bother attending status conferences. After a moment's speculation, he focused back on Ames. "Three or four hundred?"

"Slight exaggeration."

Campanella stood. "May I be heard?"

"Not yet." Norcross waved, and Campanella sat. "Okay, a suppression hearing. What else?"

How nice it was to be able just to tell people to shut up when you didn't feel like hearing from them.

"The 'what else' is that the government is refusing to provide essential discovery. I keep asking for it, and I keep getting stonewalled. We have the supposed chat-room transcripts that my brother thinks are in some way admissible. I don't know why he thinks that. Saying something vomit-worthy is not a crime. We also have the still photos and videos the government says constitute child pornography downloaded and stored on my client's computer by somebody. But we don't have the metadata regarding any of this Internet traffic. We just have the material itself, and the absence of the metadata is handcuffing my expert."

"Metadata?"

"This is not my field, but my expert tells me that metadata is data that describes other data." Ames immediately picked up on the judge's confused frown. "I know, it sounds like gobbledygook, but it isn't. Metadata tells you things like the author of a file, the date it was created, the date it was modified, the file size, things like that. I've told Mr. Campanella like fifty times now that my expert can't do his job without this disclosure. And once we have the metadata, we're going to need time to work through it. There's some interesting law on this out of the Second Circuit, and I'm prepared to submit a formal memo if we can't work this out."

It was the usual collision of opposing agendas, the routine exchange of kidney punches. As he jotted a few notes on his yellow pad, Judge Norcross enjoyed knowing that a few sensible directives from him would tidy all this up. He wasn't sure what these directives would be yet, but he knew they would come to him shortly.

When Campanella got his turn, he complained, as Ames had predicted, that an evidentiary hearing on the *Miranda* issue was a waste of time. In a sense, he was right. If Norcross denied Ames's motion, there was an 80 percent chance that his ruling would be upheld on appeal with or without a hearing. In a more important sense, however, Campanella was wrong. Norcross had acquired enough experience to know that the record needed to be protected, and that squeezing Ames on this point was dumb. If he erred by refusing to hear testimony, and Cranmer was eventually convicted, there was a one in five chance that the court of appeals would send the case back for a retrial. If he erred in the opposite direction, by hearing the testimony of Ames's witnesses, all he lost was a couple days in court listening to what they had to say. If he denied the motion after a full hearing, and made findings based on the testimony, his chance of being affirmed was close to 100 percent.

Besides, Norcross was intrigued by the prospect of hearing from Elizabeth Spencer. She looked smart, and she might give him a helpful perspective on what had really happened during the raid. Her decision to come to court and check things out was interesting. Exactly who was this young lady?

As for the metadata, it eventually emerged that Campanella's real problem was that he'd put in many hours getting the documentary material onto CDs that did not include the level of detail Ames wanted. It would be still more work for Campanella and his investigators to go back to the original records and dig up the additional data. *Boo hoo.* When Norcross was practicing, he'd had many a weekend wiped out by some judge's unexpected demands. You had to accept this kind of turbulence if you wanted to play in the big leagues. Norcross gave Campanella thirty days to turn the metadata over, and he instructed Ruby Johnson to set up the suppression hearing for some time in October, as soon as he had a big enough opening in his calendar to fit it in.

He wrapped up with what was, for him, the most important point.

"Now." He nodded, pausing to make eye contact with each of the lawyers. "I want the two of you to get together and start working constructively to get yourselves on track. I'm blessed in this case with two excellent lawyers." This was mostly true. "I know Ms. Ames will not play games, and I know Mr. Campanella is aware of the government's obligations. Set up a time to discuss the case and go over the documents, face-to-face. When I see you for the suppression hearing, I'll be looking for a progress report. That's enough for today."

His last thought as Ruby called out, "All rise," and he stepped off the bench was that it was beginning to look as though he and Claire might be in limbo for longer than he'd thought.

17

2Kool: u left so fast last time it made me sad :(

LS: i had a pir

2Kool: ? u had to p?

LS: u r so funny!!! :) u dont know pir???

2Kool: i told u i was weird and nerdy

LS: its parent alert like pir is parent in room mos is mom over shoulder kpc is keep parents clueless dont yr mom and dad bug u about chatting??

2Kool: u r so kool u know everything no my parents kind of dont pay that much attention now that im a senior its like so what

LS: my mom loves me i guess but she can be such a b****
about chatting

2Kool : same 4 me when i was yr age now its different i may get my own place this fall maybe u cld come visit???

LS: omg that wld make me sooooo happy and hot!!!!

2Kool: u cld send me some pics if u felt comfterble u don't have 2 but it wld mean everything 2 me.

He waited. Come on, sweetheart. . . .

LS: i cld send a pic now but what do u wanna see?
2Kool: whatever u want me 2 see but i wld luv to see a full nude one :):):)
LS: im kinda shy to do a full nude cuz im kinda big :(
2Kool: come on for me pleez or u cld send me just certain parts i bet u no what i wanna see

He waited. Maybe he was pushing too hard. As the minutes passed, he imagined her in her room, in shorts and a T-shirt. Did she wear a bra yet? He was breathing hard and rubbing himself. This was better than meth. Three or four minutes passed. The night was warm. It was hard to be patient.

LS: there! did u get it? i did a selfie of my u-no-what. did u get it? Am I pretty do u still like me?
2Kool: No!!!! Nothing came thru! im dying!!!!! :(:(:(:(
LS: shitshitshitshit im such a klutz do u hate me???

The little twat. She was doing this on purpose to play him.

2Kool: no i don't hate u i luv u!! do u have skype? we cld skype.
LS: fuckfuckfuckfuck P911!! Stay there!!!

He waited. Time to pull the line in. If she was hooked, fine. If not, there were others. School would be starting soon, and everything would get tougher. He was sick of this shit. He picked up the clicker and switched on the television.

LS: its ok now.

He waited. Fuck her.

LS: r u there?

He waited, breathed, and switched off the TV. Here goes.

2Kool: i dont know how to say this but i think u dont like me.
LS: nonononono i like u so much!!!
2Kool: why cant u send me a pic then i want 2 c u.
LS: i tried but it didn't work
2Kool: yur not telling me the truth i thought we were being honest

Longer pause.

LS: yur right im just shy cuz i think u wont like me cuz im a tub :(:(:(dont hate me pleeze!!!
2Kool: i need u to show me how much u luv me chats r easy i want 2 see all of u.
LS: im too shy for pics or skype i have an idea but u might think im a slut
2Kool: i wld never think that but i do think its easy to talk and not really mean it
LS: ok here goes my 14th is in five weeks do u want to meet irl to celebrate?

He tipped up the rod, lifted her right out of the water, wet and slippery, and dropped her in the net. Li'l Sis's parents, it turned out, were going up to Maine for the Columbus Day weekend, and she'd be staying at her aunt's house. That Saturday, she'd learned, her aunt would be going out with friends and leaving her by herself with Chinese and a video. There was a Howard Johnson's motel walking distance from her aunt's house. If he could get a room and text her the number . . .

They took turns talking about all the things they wanted to do, would do, when they were alone in that room. He could not remember the last time he felt this alive. He'd get his nephew to join the fun again. The kid was screwed up in a lot of ways, but he liked to party, and he'd help if Li'l Sis got too frisky. Afterward, they'd take her for a little swim.

Columbus Day. It wasn't so far off. Open the Happy Meal, dip your head down, and breathe in the salty smell.

18

Claire dipped a wooden spoon into her beef bourguignon and gave it a stir, listening for the sound of David's car. She wasn't certain what the concoction would taste like, but the aroma had her kitchen smelling like dinnertime in heaven. Marlene was dancing around her feet, whimpering for scraps and drooling on the floor.

The weeks in Nova Scotia without David had been really hard. Once, during a FaceTime call, he'd bobbed onto the screen with a big clump of hair sticking out from the side of his head. The sight of him looking so awkward and sweet triggered a memory of the scent of his pajamas that was almost unbearable. Even more painful was having to watch, week after week, how his trips to Washington and the impossible task of comforting his nieces were wearing him down. Her attempts to convey support seemed to help sometimes, but too often they were frustrated by how bulbous and discolored the video camera made them both look. Most of the time, in the silence following a call, she'd find herself feeling useless and stupid.

One thing the break did was give her some clarity about the Sid Cranmer situation. She'd tried to see Sid before she left for Nova Scotia, but visits were forbidden while he was in the ICU. Then, a week before she flew north, when he was finally home, he sent her an email, asking her to hold off coming around. His face, he said, was a fucking mess, and he couldn't bear anyone looking at him except his intern. She was premed, so he figured seeing him would be educational for her.

Claire was still very upset that her friend was getting screwed so unfairly, and fair or unfair, she was still pissed at David for not recusing himself from Sid's case. His decision made her feel second fiddle to his judgy world, and she couldn't help resenting that, even if he was going through a hard time.

On the other hand, she was practical, and the bottom line was that, for better or worse, she loved David and wanted to make it work with him if at all possible. The two of them were obviously at a fragile moment, and the semicomic kerfuffle with Darren Mattoon hadn't helped things. David was being silly about Darren, of course, but she couldn't help enjoying his jealousy a little. Earlier that evening, she'd changed the sheets on her bed. She knew where she wanted things to go, but they'd been apart a long time, and they had issues. The evening would have to find its own track.

The meal preparations, at least, had gone pretty well so far. The beef had been marinating all day, and during a tricky passage in the recipe, she'd practiced lighting the cognac without singeing her eyelashes. Now in its final stage, her masterpiece, which included an entire bottle of côtes du rhône, had been bubbling away for an hour. Claire couldn't help feeling a little proud of herself. David would be touched—he'd better be, anyway—and she would have leftovers for her book group's potluck the following evening. She had set the table and was tossing the salad when she heard David's knock.

"It's open," she called out.

Four things then happened in rapid succession. First, Claire lifted the heavy Dutch oven off the burner, intending to shift it to the counter where the plates and bowls were waiting. Second, the front door thumped closed and David called out, "Hello?" Third, Marlene, who was going deaf, realized her beloved master had arrived and scrambled around Claire in a frenzy to greet him. Fourth, Claire, knocked off balance, dropped the big pot onto the kitchen floor with a crash. Some of the contents leaped up and scalded her ankles, but most of it burst out in all directions across the tile floor, splattering like a huge brown bug.

"Oh, son of bitch!" Claire called out.

Staring down at the lumpy puddle, she heard David hurrying across the dining room.

In a matter of seconds, he stood gaping in the kitchen doorway, while Marlene, ignorant of the disaster she'd caused, nibbled at his fingers for attention.

David looked down at the remains of their meal and then up at Claire. Something about his painfully empathic expression was irresistible. He knew exactly how she felt, and he wasn't going to try to say anything clever. He didn't think she was stupid or clumsy. He was her friend, and he loved her. How could she not love him back?

"I made it for you especially." She looked down at the glop on the floor, feeling foolish at how stricken her voice sounded. "Now it's ruined."

David tossed his suit jacket on a chair, came over, and gave her a long hug. They stood for a while together in the pool of gravy, holding each other, wordless. Before long, they became aware of the sound of Marlene, down at their shoes, slurping away at the massive treat.

In a way, it wasn't a bad start to the evening.

Dinner ended up being grilled cheese sandwiches, the undamaged salad, and the two bottles of zinfandel David had brought.

As they sat down, David looked at Claire, "Aren't we supposed to be drinking something blanc with grilled cheese?"

"Ha ha. Let me pour."

David smiled and took his tie off, tossing it onto the far end of the table. He was wearing a pale-blue dress shirt that Claire was especially fond of, and it struck her, with a wave of sweetness, that he must have put it on to please her.

They kept the conversation easy and general at first. David asked Claire about her classes, and she described a knee-buckler she'd picked up that fall called "Monster Novels," where she had to flog the students through *Brothers Karamazov*, *Moby Dick*, *Ulysses*, and *Infinite Jest*, all in one semester. She deliberately omitted mentioning that the class had been Sid's and that she'd inherited it following his suspension.

"I've read all the others more than once, but I'm still only halfway through *Infinite Jest*," Claire said, sipping her wine.

"Other than English professors, who actually reads *Infinite Jest*?"

"About a quarter of the people who claim to," Claire said. "But tell me about Lindsay and Jordan."

"We Skyped with Ray and one of his doctors in Germany last weekend, trying to get the girls ready for when he returns." David tossed a piece of crust to Marlene, who'd been staring up at him, panting. "Which I hope will be soon. Go lie down." He pointed to the corner.

"You're encouraging bad habits."

"Yeah, well." David sighed. "Typical me."

"How did the call go?"

"The child psychiatrist told me it would be a good idea, but it didn't go very well, actually. Ray's looking better, but—this really shocked me—he started to cry when he was talking to the girls." David chewed a bite of his grilled cheese and swallowed. "Not just sniffling, either—sobs. I've never seen that before. Ray didn't even cry when he was nine and broke both his wrists falling off the combine. It really upset Jordan. I was up half the night with her." He rubbed at the area under his eye. "It got to me, too, to tell the truth. Jord and I kind of comforted each other."

Claire reached out and touched David's hand. "Honestly, David? I don't know how you do this. You're amazing." He clasped her hand in return, intertwining their fingers. They meshed perfectly.

David shook his head. "I don't feel amazing. I feel like a total dope."

"You shouldn't. You know that, don't you? There's just no easy way to do this. No one could handle this better. Really."

David picked up Claire's hand and kissed the knuckle at the base of her middle finger. It was a courtly gesture so unlike David that she had to smile.

"I missed you like crazy," David said. "Talking to you made all the difference."

"Now it's my turn to say I felt like a dope." Claire smiled. "Most of the time there was not a single helpful thing I could think of to say."

"It's just hard. Turns out there's no right way to do this."

Marlene, impatient for another crust, whimpered and shifted her feet back and forth, clicking on the hardwood floor. David made a face and looked down at her. "Shut up, Marlene, please. We're trying to be romantic here."

Claire laughed, let go of David's hand, and stood up.

"You're not doing too badly, big guy. Let's go out on the porch. Should I get us coffee?"

"I'll stick with a little more of this." David refilled his wineglass and lifted the bottle to Claire, raising his eyebrows to ask if she'd join him.

"Please. In fact, bring the bottle."

The daylight was easing away, and when Claire flipped on the ceiling globe, it created an amber nest on her screened porch. Unlike David, she had neighbors close by, and faint voices were floating out of the shadows through the hemlocks at the side of her house. David settled into the recliner. Claire sat on the sofa facing him, pulling her legs up. She'd hoped David would join her on the sofa—things seemed to be going well—but he was leaning forward stiffly with his hands on his knees.

"It's probably not very smart of me to bring this up, but it's on my mind, and I wanted to get it out of the way."

"It's okay. If it's about Sid, we can wait if you want."

"Well, I just want to say one quick thing, and then we can, as somebody used to say, move to the entertainment part of our evening."

"Can't wait."

"Right, so here it is. Professor Cranmer's attorney is a woman named Linda Ames. She's the real McCoy. I've been watching her, and I'm confident your friend is getting the best possible representation." He huffed out a breath and nodded to himself. "She's doing everything for him that can be done. That's"—he paused and looked her—"that's pretty much all I wanted to say, if it's any consolation."

"It is. I appreciate that. Thanks."

David looked relieved, blew out another breath, and began, "Now that we've—"

"Can I just ask you something about this sort of case?" Claire couldn't resist. "Not about Sid, just about this kind of case?"

"I guess." David leaned back and put his hands on the armrests.

The movement doubled the distance between them. On the other side of the evergreens, the voices got louder. The party was breaking up. There was the sound of a door opening and someone calling out, "Don't let the bugs in!"

"How often do juries find people in these cases not guilty?"

"I'm not sure. I've never had one go to trial. Everyone's always pleaded out."

"I see. And what sort of sentences do they generally get?"

David cleared his throat, took a sip of wine, and set the glass on the end table, as though he wanted to be sure not to knock it over. He sighed, gathering himself.

"The minimum for receipt of child pornography is five years, but usually the sentences are longer than that."

"Can a person get—what's it called? Probation? Parole?"

"There's no parole in the federal system, and probation is not permitted for this crime." He looked to the side, weighing his words, then turned back to her. "The lowest sentence he could get—I mean, that a defendant like Professor Cranmer could get—would be five years, minus fifty-four days a year for what's called 'good time,' if he has a decent institutional record."

"My God."

"I have to tell you—I mean, you probably ought to know, Claire—the government in Professor Cranmer's case will be looking for a sentence of over fifteen years."

He'd mentioned Sid explicitly now, so Claire felt free to follow up.

"Do you think . . ." She hesitated. "Do you think he'll be found guilty?"

"My guess is, like most of these defendants, he'll end up pleading guilty."

"But Sid's innocent, David."

"Well . . ."

"Doesn't that matter?" She was pushing, she knew, but she couldn't help it. "He could die in prison."

David glanced back over his shoulder at the noise next door, frowned, and turned to Claire. "Of course it matters." He raised his voice and spoke quickly. "Do you really think I don't care? It matters a lot, in general and to me personally." He put his hand on top of his head and scratched, reining himself in. His tone turned softer. "But my job, Claire, is to give both sides a fair trial. I know this sounds starchy, but my job is to give the government its chance to prove beyond a reasonable doubt that your friend has committed this crime. If they can't do it, he goes free. If they do, or if he admits to the crime, then I try to figure out what a fair sentence is." David shook his head. "I shouldn't have . . ."

"It's okay. Let's drop it."

"It was my fault. I shouldn't . . ."

"It's okay. I shouldn't have either."

A burst of voices broke out next door. People were walking down the front lawn apparently, and an older woman was calling to them from the stoop. Something about Montana, or maybe bananas, and everyone laughed.

"I'm sorry." David nodded at the spot next to her and said abruptly, "Can I come over there?"

"You've been waiting for permission? I was hoping we'd start out here."

"Well, it's been a while. I didn't . . ."

"Please." Claire shifted around. "Make yourself at home."

As David stood, he twitched and looked toward the kitchen. Something had happened. "Oh, cripes, it's my cell. I left it in my jacket."

"Really?" Claire cocked her ear and caught a barely audible buzz in the distance. "Just leave it." She patted the sofa next to her.

"I can't. Sorry. I'll just be a second."

He wasn't a second. Fifteen minutes later, she could still hear his deep voice two rooms away. Claire finished her wine, listening to the night sounds. Two cars drove off next door, and the voices inside the house grew fainter and eventually died out. As the lights over there went off, the area around the porch got darker and felt more enclosed. A quietness settled into Claire that drifted into sadness, like a cloud slowly changing shape. Eventually, she got up, went into the dining room, and began clearing the dishes off the table.

David was still in the kitchen.

"It's okay," he was saying. "We can talk about it when you—" The person on the other end interrupted him. "Ray, we don't—" Another interruption. "Ray, what the heck time is it over there? You're supposed to be—"

When Claire entered the kitchen carrying the plates and salad bowls, David glanced over at her and grimaced. She tried to look sympathetic. After another five minutes, as she was bending over the pans, the gooey Dutch oven slipped out of her fingers and banged down into the stainless steel sink. It hadn't been on purpose, but she didn't regret it.

David said, "Yes." There was another pause. "I'm at a friend's house." David closed his eyes and looked impatient. "She dropped a pan. We're finishing up dinner, okay?" Claire made an "I'm sorry" face, and David shook his head and waved his hand at her not to worry.

"Okay," David continued. "I have to go now, Ray. We'll talk about it this weekend." He paused. "I'm going now, Ray. I'm going, okay? Good-bye." Ray's voice was coming out of the phone, louder. Claire could almost make out some words. "Right. Good-bye, Ray. Talk to you this weekend. Okay? Bye."

David, looking weary, walked to where his jacket hung over the chair and slipped the cell phone into an inside pocket.

"I'm really sorry," he said. "I couldn't—"

"It's okay." Claire rinsed the plate in her hands, set it in the dishwasher, and turned away to pick up another one.

"He's all over the place. Wants to come home but doesn't know if he can manage. Hates the acting guy who's taken his job at Commerce." David closed his eyes and scrubbed his hands over his face. "Now he's cranked up about crying in front of the girls. Sometimes he's just a . . ." He shook his head, looking angry. "He's always been this way."

Claire put another plate into the dishwasher. She felt herself moving with special care, which probably meant she was feeling hurt. He was a good guy. He was doing his best, probably better than she'd do in his position. She ought to be sympathetic.

"What's the best thing to do here, do you think? Is there any way I can help? Sounds like you're pretty . . ."

"I don't know." David's cell phone began to buzz again. "Oh, for heaven's sake!" When he pulled the phone out of his jacket and looked at the caller, he shook his head despairingly. "Oh, Lord." He stared at the phone for a while and put it back in his jacket. "This time I'm letting it take a message. Should have done that last time."

"Who is it?"

"It's Lindsay. My guess is she's gotten into another beef with the Stephensons, the family she's staying with. They've been pretty strict about her curfews since she came home smelling of beer and knocked over a lamp. She thinks I'm the court of appeals." He had his hands on the sides of his head and swiveled to look at Claire. "It's awful. She's sixteen. She promises them anything, then does whatever she wants and hopes she won't get caught."

The phone eventually stopped, but after a short pause, it began buzzing again. David started toward the dining room to help clear the rest of the dishes.

"Just leave them, David. It's okay."

"I'm really sorry." He looked up at the ceiling—a man searching for help from heaven and not finding it. "It's a pressure cooker down there. Lindsay had a big fight with her mother the night before Sheila and Ray left for Europe. Called Sheila a bad name, Jordan said. Now Sheila's dead, and Lindsay never got a chance to work it out. Lindsay's so angry most of the time, you can barely get a word out of her. We talked about it once, and it helped for a little while, but she goes through times when everything, everything, makes her angry. I shouldn't let this get to me, I know, especially tonight, but . . ."

"Jesus, David, how can you not let it get to you?" Claire came over, put her arms around him, and spoke into his ear. "I'm so sorry you have to go through all this. I'm sorry for all of us." He put both hands in the middle of her back, and they stood quietly, holding each other.

Within a few seconds, the phone began buzzing again. David dropped his arms and said, "I better go." He pulled out the phone and looked at it. "Yep. I'll call her from home."

He took out a tissue and pressed it to his left eye.

"Are you going to be okay driving?"

"I'll be fine. It just tears up sometimes and begins to hurt a little."

Claire stepped back and held up a finger. "We'll manage, okay?"

"I'm really . . ." He sniffed and stuffed the tissue back in his pocket.

"We'll get through this. There will be other nights."

When they parted, they hugged again, briefly, and David kissed Claire on the cheek, which would have felt almost insulting if it weren't so obvious that his mind was miles away.

"I'm really sorry about all this," he said over his shoulder. Marlene trotted obliviously after him into the night.

"I love you, David." It wasn't clear he'd heard her.

After David left, Claire put on her corduroy jacket, poured herself another glass of wine, and took it back out onto the porch. The darkness had changed—it was thicker—and the sound of the insects had gotten louder. In her backyard, there were fireflies now.

David was a good man. She could see how hard it was for him, but she was also very disappointed and hurt. Was she being a jerk?

After fifteen minutes, just as she was finishing her wine, there was a tentative knocking at the front door, and Claire, flooded with joy, bounced up quickly. People really could come back. She almost danced to the front door, congratulating herself about the fresh sheets.

To her astonishment, when she opened the door, she found Elizabeth Spencer standing there, holding a large brown accordion file against her chest with both hands.

"Libby?" It was almost midnight.

"I'm sorry, Professor . . ." Elizabeth hesitated, gathering her courage. "I'm sorry, Claire. I know it's late, but I really had to see you."

"You had to see me." This was not the brightest response, but Claire was fairly buzzed and still grieving over her lost evening.

Elizabeth was wearing dark purple Amherst College sweatpants and a gray hooded sweatshirt, and she had her hair tied back in a stubby ponytail. Her face bore the resolute look of someone who has decided to do something, whatever the cost, come what may.

"I need to give you this." Elizabeth held out the file. "I can't keep it in my dorm. I thought of just tossing it into a Dumpster, but someone might find it, and parts of the file may be irreplaceable. I mean, some of the pictures may be originals. I'm not sure."

Claire looked down at the file. "What is it?"

"It's the file of unpublished Dodgson photographs that the cops didn't find at Professor Cranmer's house. I stole it."

"You stole it?" She needed to pull herself together. "When?"

"Just now. I sneaked into his house after he was asleep."

"Oh, Jesus, Libby . . ."

"I don't think he'll notice." Elizabeth looked over her shoulder in the direction of Sid's house, a few blocks south. "At least not right away."

"I'm having trouble following all this. What exactly is going on?"

"Can I come in?"

Claire shook her head. She didn't mean that Elizabeth couldn't come in. She meant that the situation was getting way too crazy. But Elizabeth took this as a refusal, and it made her even more determined to push ahead.

"It's my fault, so I have to deal with it. I trusted Ryan about the pictures, which I shouldn't have, and now I'm worried he'll rat Professor Cranmer out."

"Ryan Jaworski?"

"Right."

"Your boyfriend."

"He hates Professor Cranmer. He thinks he deserves whatever he gets, and there's other stuff happening you need to know. Can I please come in for just five minutes?" When Claire didn't respond, Libby looked up pleadingly. "I really need some help here, Claire. I don't know what to do. I don't have anywhere else to go."

19

By a lucky coincidence, Ethan's piano teacher's house, Sid's house, and Linda Ames's office were all within a few blocks of one another in the center of Amherst. This allowed Ames to organize one of her favorite after-school projects: a walk with her son. The grass on the lower common below South Pleasant Street was yellow at the edges, toasted by the long, dry summer and bleached by the increasingly chilly nights. The maples on the upper common by City Hall were dabbed with orange and rustled against the sky. As Ames and Ethan crossed the grass out in the sunlight, the breeze was still warm, but when they entered a shady side street, it turned cooler instantly. School was under way now, and soon, they'd be having their first hard frost.

Ethan was a quiet boy, and as far as Ames was concerned, they didn't have to say anything. Just feeling Ethan next to her, looking at the top of his head, seeing him down there with his satchel over his shoulder noticing things—there had never been anything happier for her in the whole insane world, ever.

The positioning of her destination and Ethan's allowed Ames to knock off two birds with one stone: walk with Ethan and put in some billable time on the Cranmer case. Following Norcross's order, Ames would be meeting with Campanella in a week or so to discuss where the case was going. It was time to talk turkey with Sid. Because of his home confinement, he could not come to her office, so she had to go to him.

In front of Sid's house, Ames stooped to give Ethan his final instructions.

"Okay, it's just two blocks down." Ames pointed. "It's the dark red house on the—"

"Mom, I know where Mrs. Bass's house is. I've been there, like—"

"So, when you're done with your piano lesson, just come back here, and—"

"I know, Mom."

Ethan had turned ten in July and was starting the fifth grade, something Ames still had trouble bending her mind around. Three weeks ago, they'd gone to the optometrist and picked up his new glasses. Ethan insisted on wire rims for some reason, which was probably not practical—they were bound to end up bent—and Ames was still getting accustomed to Ethan's new blooming-intellectual look. He'd gobbled up the Harry Potter books a year ago and moved on. Now he was halfway through the second volume of the *Lord of the Rings* trilogy, a big fan of Legolas.

"Okay." She leaned toward him, holding out her arms for a good-bye hug. Ethan stepped back.

"No touching in public. Remember?"

"But there's nobody around." Ames straightened up and looked down the street. "No one will ever . . ."

"Bye, Mom." Ethan looked at his watch and called over his shoulder. "See you in one hour and nine minutes." There was a trundling bounce to his walk these days that was almost manly. It amazed her.

As she approached the front door of Sid's house, Ames noticed that the hydrangea had not recovered from its encounter with the postal inspector's Ford Explorer back in May. It was still twisted to one side with a chunk missing.

Sid must have been watching, because the door opened before Ames had time to knock.

The living room, per usual, was impressively neat and had a flowery aroma, mixed with the cozy smell of recent baking. As Ames stepped inside, the two cocoa-colored cats dashed across the carpeting and disappeared up the stairs.

After they'd exchanged hellos, Sid said, "Have a seat. I made blueberry muffins." Walking stiffly, he headed off toward the kitchen. His monitoring bracelet was visible below his pants cuff.

"Damn," Ames muttered, lowering herself onto the sofa. She quickly calculated the Weight Watchers points, then called out to Sid. "Why do you keep doing this to me?"

She'd permitted herself a slice of whole-grain toast with her eggs that morning—eggs without toast were just too grim—as well as half a glass of Ethan's pulpy orange juice, which she'd gulped down when he hadn't finished it. The points were mounting.

Sid's voice came from the kitchen. "I used a sugar substitute."

"I'll have a half. And no butter."

Despite this, when Sid returned, he set a silver tray on the table with two cups of black coffee and an elegant China plate with three muffins. He took a seat in a small rocker at an angle to her and picked up one of the cups. "No sugar in yours."

"Okay, Sid." Ames picked up a muffin. "Wow, this smells incredible." She began peeling back the foil wrapper. "It's crunch time. Like I told you, I slowed the preliminaries down, but summer's over now, and we need to decide what you want me to do. At the status conference, Norcross told me to get together with Campanella . . ."

"That dipshit." Sid put his coffee down and sat up straight. "That was such crap, that ignorant garbage about Charles Dodgson."

"Jesus, Sid, I thought I was going to have to stuff my shoe in your mouth."

"Well, I'll say it again: Enjoying pictures of naked children doesn't make you a pedophile."

"Please, for Christ's sake!" It was ridiculous, but the statement was so unspeakable Ames found herself looking up into the corners of the room for hidden microphones. "Don't say that, even here. We do not, repeat, do not want the judge, the jury, the prosecutor, or the fat lady next door hearing you say that."

"But it's true."

"I don't fucking care."

"But . . ."

"Truth takes a funny shape in courtrooms, Sid. Sometimes you don't want it within a country mile."

Sid shook his head, looking disgusted, and a silence fell over them. Ames nibbled her muffin. It was the moment of truth, or at least a critical moment leading up to the moment of truth. One of the cats crept back down the stairs, slipped across the room, and hopped up into Sid's lap. As he stroked it, Ames could see her client begin to calm down and drift away.

"Listen, Sid." Ames reached out and touched his knee. "Sid?" He looked up. "Please listen to me now. I'm going to say again what I told you when we first met, okay? But now you really have to zoom in." She leaned closer. "If you want to go to trial, I promise, I *promise* I will fight like hell for you, right? Whether you're guilty or not guilty, I don't care. You hear me? Sid?"

"I hear you, Linda." He placed the palms of his hands behind his head, grimaced, and stretched back, trying to work out some soreness. A smear of bruise lingered on the side of his face. "I know you will. I appreciate that."

"Fine." She took another bite of muffin. The warmth, the sugary crust, and the tart blueberry were delicious. "But this is the thing, okay? If we're going to plead guilty, now is when I can get you the best deal. If you do it at the last minute, Norcross will be pissed, and it won't help you as much. We can . . ."

At this point, Ames was startled by the presence of a tall, slouching figure standing in the entry to the dining room. It was a man around thirty. He was staring down at the carpeting.

"I'm done for today," he said dully. He twisted his head to one side, revealing a copper ear stud.

"Okay, Jonathan." Sid nodded in his direction. "See you next week."

"Okay." The man walked toward the door.

Before he reached it, there was a loud clack from the knocker outside that startled everyone. Jonathan jumped back and seemed almost frightened. Sid hurried over to see who it was. As he passed, he put a hand on Jonathan's shoulder and said, "It's all right."

When he opened the door, Sid looked down and spoke in a friendly voice. "Well, hello there, my friend! Who might you be?"

Ames's view of the front stoop was blocked, but she recognized the voice that responded. "I'm Ethan Ames. Is my mom here?"

Ames was instantly on her feet, pushing into the doorway next to Sid. "Ethan. What about your piano lesson?"

"There was a note on the door. Mrs. Bass had an emergency. I didn't know . . ."

"Come in, come in," Sid was waving.

"Just for a minute." Ames did not like this. Her family and her work lives ran on strictly separate tracks, and especially in this case, she did not want a hair of overlap with Ethan.

But the boy was curious. She could see, as he stepped through the doorway, that he was already looking from side to side, taking everything in.

"This is Professor Cranmer, Ethan." Ames gestured to Sid. "He's the man I told you I was meeting."

Ethan nodded.

Sid held out his hand. "Very nice to meet you, Ethan." Ethan hesitated and then shook Sid's hand. Sid continued. "And this is a man who works for me. His name's Jonathan."

"Hey, man." Jonathan inched half a step forward and held his hand way out, as though he wanted to keep as far away as possible.

"Okay." Ethan shook hands with him, too.

The second cat came down and joined its brother. Ethan's eyes lit up.

"You like cats?" Jonathan asked. He let go of Ethan's hand.

"Uh-huh." Ethan flipped his shoulder up in a quick half shrug. "But we can't have one."

"Allergies." Ames pointed to her nose.

"That one there is pretty amazing." Jonathan's voice was flat. "Watch this."

"Well, we shouldn't . . ." Ames began.

"It's real quick," Jonathan said. "And it's really cool." He reached into his pocket and pulled out a ball of paper, made a *fissst* noise at the cat who'd just arrived, and tossed the ball on a line about four feet over its head. The cat jumped straight up and batted the paper out of the air.

"Whoa!" Ethan said, grinning. "That *is* cool!"

"You'd better run along now, Jonathan," Sid said. "We'll see you next time."

By the time the door closed behind Jonathan, Ethan was squatting down on the floor, and the cats were gathering around him, mewing happily.

"You want a muffin?" Sid was smiling down.

"We shouldn't . . ." Ames shook her head.

"I love muffins," Ethan said. "Mom doesn't make them anymore." One of the cats was rubbing its head against Ethan's knee as he stroked it. "These cats are really soft." He looked at Ames. "And friendly."

Sid, catching Ames's look, pointed toward the end of the house. "I'll just get him a couple muffins, and we can set him and the cats up in the music room. The harpsichord is in there."

"I have my iPad." Ethan was trying to be helpful. One of the cats was on its hind legs, propped up against Ethan, purring.

"We can finish up our chat," Sid said. "And you guys can be on your way. Bingety-bing."

"All right, I guess." Ames looked down at Ethan, feeling guilty that she couldn't get him a pet. Her allergies were really bad. They couldn't even have a parakeet.

As Sid headed for the kitchen to fetch Ethan his muffins, Ethan stood up. "What's a harpsichord?"

Sid called over his shoulder. "It's like a piano, only more fun."

A minute later, when Sid returned with another plate, Ethan asked, "What's that thing on your ankle?"

Ames broke in. "Professor Cranmer and I need to talk for a few minutes, Ethan."

"It helps people know where I am," Sid peered down at his plastic bracelet and looked up at Ethan. "I have to wear it for a while." He made a face to let Ethan know it was no big deal. "The music room's on the other side of the kitchen." He pointed toward the back of the house.

Ethan nodded, took the plate, and walked off with his bobbing step. The cats, trotting behind him, looked up eagerly at the food.

Ames started to call out, "Close the—" but the sound of a door shutting cut her off. She turned to Sid, dropping her voice and pointing at the front door. "So who the hell is this Jonathan character?"

"He's a guy from the college's drop-in center. He cleans my

house to earn a little money." Sid raised his eyebrows and managed a grim smile. "Usually, I have to go back and clean up his cleaning up."

"Does he have access to your computer?"

"He wouldn't have the faintest idea how to use it."

Ames spoke a little sternly. "Next time, please tell me if you have somebody floating around, will you? I don't like eavesdroppers."

"He's okay." Sid sat back down on the rocker. "He hasn't had an easy time. Showing Ethan that trick with Keith was a big deal for him." He hesitated. "There is another guy, a carpenter, who comes by now and then. He's doing some work upstairs."

Ames looked up at the ceiling, unhappy. "Is he here now?"

"Oh no. No. He's just here once in a while."

Ames returned to the sofa. "Okay, back to business then." She folded her hands on her knees, a formal posture for a formal moment. "You're facing a very, very tough call, Sid. I know that. But the decision won't get any easier if you drag it out. And you can miss your chance. Do you hear what I'm saying?"

"I hear you." Sid stroked the bruised area along his cheek, opened his mouth, and worked his jaw back and forth. From the far end of the house, two notes from the harpsichord, very soft, rose into the air and died. Sid turned in the direction of the music and smiled. "He's checking it out."

"His piano teacher tells me he's a natural. I never have to bug him to practice." A couple more notes drifted in, then a melancholy chord. She took a sip of her coffee. "Want me to have him stop?"

"No, no. It's fine. You can tell by his touch he won't damage anything."

The silence drew out, and Ames realized they were both waiting to see if Ethan was going to keep playing. Soon, it was clear he'd settled down with his iPad.

"Listen, Sid—"

"You know, Linda," Sid broke in. He hesitated, then plunged. "I'm beginning to think, maybe, I just wanted to see something horrendous, something truly monstrous. I might have. I'm not sure."

"What are you telling me?"

"I'm telling you that this shrink of ours is good, Linda. Some of what's coming back are things I'd rather . . ." He hesitated. "Stuff I'd rather forget."

"Ah."

"I don't remember sending the flyer in, but, to be honest, I do remember thinking about sending it. Just wondering. You know?"

"Uh-huh."

"I was such a fucking disaster last spring after Mom up and died. She was . . ." He took a sip of coffee to steady himself. "She was in the bathtub."

"Oh, Sid. God. That must have been . . ."

"After they hauled her off, I was alone here in the house with the smell of her underwear and her bathroom and all her crap." He waved toward the upstairs. "Her clothes in the closet and her drawers. I couldn't bring myself to touch any of it. Pretty soon, I don't know, I just hated the world and everybody in it, especially myself. I started sitting all day at the computer. Dr. Katzenbach thinks I wanted to see something that was as ugly as I was feeling." Sid took a swallow of coffee and set his cup back down. "It sounds like psychobabble, but it may be true. Maybe I was just bored. I could have done anything. So, it could be I'm, you know . . ." He opened his hands out, palms up. "Maybe I'm guilty. I don't know."

"You went through a tough time," Ames said.

"Yeah, very tough. Problem is . . ." Sid scrubbed at his temples with his fingers, trying to rouse his brain. "While I remember looking at a lot of repulsive stuff, late at night, and visiting some incredibly disgusting chat rooms, I don't remember mailing that goddamn flyer." Sid picked up his coffee cup, raised it to his mouth, and set it down. "The coffee's getting cold." He nodded at Ames's cup. "Want me to give it a shot in the micro?"

"I'm fine." The key thing was to keep Sid talking.

"I can't see myself pleading guilty to that."

"You don't need to plead to anything, Sid. But there are risks."

"Exactly. What chance do I have at a trial?" He gaped at her for a few seconds, then slumped back. "I'm up shit creek whatever I do."

"Well, that's why—"

"I mean, isn't my life basically over?" Sid counted out the points on his fingers. "I mean, first of all, look at me. One: The bruises will get better, but I'll still look like a laboratory rat. Two: I never got married, so I'm a kook. Three: I lived with my mom. That's even worse. Four: There's tons of gossip about me at the college. That I'm gay and hitting on students or that I'm gay but too uptight to admit it."

"They can't put that into evidence."

"Maybe not, but it shows you how people react. I mean, look at me!" He tapped himself on the chest. "I'm the child molester from central casting. Five minutes in the courtroom with me, and the jury will be ordering out for tar and feathers." He paused and continued more quietly. "I'm not gay, as a matter of fact. I sort of wish I was. It might make things easier. And I'm not into kids exactly. I'm just . . ." He hesitated. "I'm odd. I do weird shit."

"You have a right to be odd, Sid. It's in the Constitution."

"Um, excuse me, Mom?" Ethan was standing in the doorway. "Is there more butter?"

"In the kitchen, next to the toaster." Sid rocked forward, pointing. "In the dish with the little pig on top."

"Thanks." Ethan turned out of the room.

Sid looked after him. "If he's interested in the harpsichord, I could teach him a little."

"Uh, no, Sid. That won't be happening." Ames shook her head and repeated. "That will not be happening."

"I see." Sid looked down gloomily. "Of course."

It was obvious what he was thinking. "Nothing to do with the charges, Sid. I just keep home and work very separate. You have to understand. Today is a total fluke."

"I understand." He clearly didn't believe her, and he was right. It was true that Ames kept the parts of her life separate, but it was also true that the nature of the charge against Sid meant that an especially broad, dark, and deep line marked the boundary here.

"Okay, back to business. Listen to me now, okay? You may be up the creek, Sid, like you say. But how far up the creek? A little history." She sipped her tepid coffee. "Child pornography became a growth industry at the Department of Justice once it hit the Internet. The DOJ has this initiative called Project Safe Childhood, and they are on the hunt, big-time. Right now, you're facing a minimum sentence of five years and a potential maximum that's in the stratosphere, a real life-killer. If you plead, I might be able to talk Campanella—"

"That fuckhead."

"Right, but he could save your butt. I might be able to talk him into recommending something below the minimum, something you can survive. If you're thinking of pleading, now's the time to do it. Don't pass up the chance to help yourself, okay?"

Sid looked at Ames with a numb expression. "So, let's play this out. If I stand up in front of the world and say I did all this—I chatted, I downloaded, I ordered the DVD—I'll still go to prison."

"'Fraid so. But for less time."

"How much less?"

"I don't know. Maybe a lot less."

"And they'll still revoke my tenure and fire me, and I'll still have to register as a sex offender for the rest of my life, and all my friends will think I'm a glob of snot."

"I don't know about Amherst or your friends, but you will have to register, yes."

"All because I might have wanted to look at something really, really ugly."

"In a way, yes."

A long silence followed. Sid closed his eyes and placed his hands in his lap, as though he were trying to pull his mind away. This was certainly peculiar, but Ames was glad to see that at least he was not going to start crying. Some clients did. Sid just looked like he was preparing himself to step through the looking glass and drift off into an alternate world.

Finally, he opened his eyes and spoke. "So, like I say, my life is over. God gives some people pancreatic cancer. I get this."

"It's not over, Sid."

"So you say." After another silence, Sid nodded at the plate. "Should I bring more?" Ames realized that she had eaten the remaining half of the original muffin, then the second, entire muffin, and finally, somehow, the third and last muffin after that. How could this have happened? The plate held only a few crumbs. She'd be on short rations for a week.

"No thanks. I hate myself enough already."

"'Frailty, thy name is woman.'"

"Stuff it, Sid."

"I was just quoting Hamlet."

"Yeah, well, look what happened to him."

Sid closed his eyes again, taking long, deep breaths. He seemed to be preparing himself to take the big dive and agree to plead. Getting this out of the way would put Ames in a better position to negotiate with Campanella. After a long thirty seconds, he said, "Can I tell you a story?"

"Sure." Ames leaned back, doing her best to look relaxed. "I love stories."

"When I was in Vietnam, I was a medic, right?"

"I know. We'll be bringing that out at your trial or sentencing, depending on where things go."

Sid opened eyes. "No, we won't." He looked fierce.

"You're the boss."

"The only heroes were the ones who came back in wooden houses. Some of them were my friends. They're still my friends. I talk to them." He looked around the room. "They're here right now."

"Whatever you say."

Sid closed his eyes for a moment and opened them again. "February 1971. The South Vietnamese Army was trying to cut the Ho Chi Minh Trail again. The operation was called Lam Son 719—I forget why—and it was a total fucking disaster. Intelligence was so bad by then, the PAVN knew exactly when they were coming, and where."

"PAVN?"

"People's Army of Vietnam. The bad guys, supposedly. They were waiting, dug in. The ARVNs—the good guys, supposedly—were outnumbered about two to one. We went in after things fell apart, trying to save a few lives. Our door gunner, Jimmy Cameron, sitting right next to me in the helicopter, got killed. His brains were all over me." Sid rubbed his shoulder as though he was trying to wipe something off. "I took over the 60." Ames must have looked puzzled again. "M60. Heavy machine gun on the bird." Sid took another deep breath, looked to the side, and swallowed. "I don't even know how many people I killed that day." He paused, as though he were trying to remember the exact number.

"It doesn't matter. On a bad night, I kill hundreds and hundreds." He leaned forward, elbows on his knees, tapping the tips of his fingers together and looking at the carpet. "Anyway, we were trying to get the fuck out of there. We'd hauled so many people on board we could barely lift off, and two ARVN soldiers were still hanging onto the skids. About a hundred feet up, one fell off on his own." Sid paused and looked at Ames. "I kicked the other one off. The pilot was screaming that we were going to go over. Kicked him right in the face." He paused again, tipped his head to one side, and shrugged. "It was the only place I could kick him, really. I remember how his eyes looked at me just before I gave him the boot, a young kid, scared out of his mind. I watched him fall all the way down, flapping his arms as though he were trying to fly. He bounced maybe eight, ten feet when he hit. I can still see those eyes, like yesterday."

"My God, Sid."

"Yeah." He sniffed. "Things come around."

"Is that how you got your Silver Star?"

"That was for something else."

The harpsichord started up again a little louder now, more confident. As they listened, a tune hesitantly formed and gathered momentum: "Twinkle, Twinkle, Little Star." Sid broke into a broad grin.

"Some boy you got there."

"Sid, listen to me. I know this is tough. It's always tough."

"You know something I'm grateful for? Mother's gone." Sid snorted. "If she weren't dead already, this would fucking kill her."

"Do me a favor and knock off the death stuff, okay? This is a big bump in the road, I know. But don't start thinking about doing anything stupid."

Sid said nothing.

Ames stood up. "Time for me and Ethan to hit the road. Think about what I said. We need to strike while the iron is hot. I'll call you after I get together with Campanella."

"That shithead."

"Yeah, but, like I said, he could be your guardian angel if we play this right." Ames turned toward the kitchen and shouted. "Ethan!"

In a minute or two, Ethan appeared, holding one of the cats against his chest. Ames was distracted and hardly heard Sid say, half to himself, "Believe me, if I do something, it won't be stupid."

20

Darren Mattoon had been keeping his antennae trained on Claire, and when he spotted her one morning, he could tell it was a good time for another move. Claire was hurrying across campus, looking preoccupied. Her shoulders were pulled up under her ears, hunched against the tingling early autumn damp. A touch at this moment might succeed, but more importantly, if it failed, it would not be resented. He had nothing to lose.

Darren shifted direction to put himself on a line heading toward her. By good luck, with the cooler days, he had put on his leather bombardier jacket, his current favorite garment. He loved the way he looked in it, but Claire didn't notice him at first.

"Hey there, Professor Lindemann." He spoke jauntily, but he had to tip down and sideways to get into her field of vision. "Are we on planet Earth?"

Claire looked up and smiled wanly. "Orbiting nearby."

"Ah. Everything all right?"

"Fine. Just things on my mind."

"I was hoping to run into you, actually, to ask a favor."

"Okay."

She looked neutral, which was an improvement. So often, when he tried to talk to her, she'd be giving off this wary, skeptical vibe.

"Harlan Graves's granddaughter Samantha is giving a concert this Sunday at Buckley Recital Hall. I've met her, and she's a sweet kid—a little shy and vulnerable, the way people are at that age." He was encouraged to see Claire nod. "Apparently, she's quite a decent pianist. She'll be trying some of Chopin's dreamier études and nocturnes." He lifted his hands up and twiddled his fingers. "Maybe a mazurka or two if things get really crazy." The last remark brought a mild light into Claire's face. Even in her gray mood, she was very pretty. "Problem is, only a few tickets have sold, and people are afraid Samantha's feelings will be hurt if she gets a thin house. I was wondering if you had time to attend. The program's just an hour or so."

Claire looked at the ground and thought for a moment. "I guess. David won't be back from Washington until late. I'm not doing anything." She nodded, looking up. "Why not?"

"Good. I'll come by your house about seven thirty, and we can walk over together." Darren took a quick look at his watch. "Yikes—I have to scamper. See you Sunday."

He wasn't really in a hurry—class was not for another half hour—but he didn't want to give Claire time to reconsider what she'd done.

As Claire sailed off for her office hours, David was at a coffee shop a short walk away in the center of town, consulting again with his old sweetheart, Dr. Susan O'Leary. Susan's professional training and sympathetic smile were making these occasions a welcome time-out.

"Here's what, I guess, scares me and makes me feel guilty." David rubbed at his eye. "I should probably offer to bring Lindsay and Jordan up here, but I honestly don't know if I can handle that."

"Problems with the Stephensons?"

"They're very nice people, but I'm afraid they're getting burned out. No one thought this setup would go on for so long."

"Hmm. Okay. What can I tell you? If the girls do come for any length of time, a couple things will probably be essential." Susan propped her chin on her hand and looked to the side, sticking her lower lip out to concentrate. The pose made David smile.

"What's so funny?" Susan asked.

"Still the lip thing." He pushed his own lip out to imitate her.

"I haven't changed all that much, David." She stuck her lip out even farther. "And, let's be honest, neither have you."

"Why mess with perfection?"

"See what I mean? Still the same old happy actor."

Susan took a sip of her latte and broke her muffin in half, giving David a look he recalled very well—not hostile, but not about to be taken in by him. In Africa, her dark brown hair had hung down to her shoulders. Now it was short and starting to go gray.

"Sorry," David said. "Shouldn't have distracted us. A couple things?"

"First, you'll want a predictable routine, and second, you'll need to bring on some good help. If your nieces come for more than a week, and you're trying to work, a smart, warmhearted nanny or housekeeper will be essential. Also a coolheaded friend to talk to." She smiled into his eyes and patted his hand. "Maybe we'll get to see each other more often, *bwana*."

Susan's daughter, Allison, had entered Williston Academy, a nearby boarding school, that fall. Now that classes had begun, she would have a good reason to start making regular trips to western Massachusetts.

During their two years in Kenya, David had taught at a civil-service training institute in Kabete, in the Highlands outside Nairobi, while Susan worked twenty minutes away at a university extension in a little village called Kikuyu. A couple times a week, he'd motor through the coffee fields on his Vespa to pay Susan a visit. Their love affair faded after they returned from Africa, but gently. No big blowup, just a slow drift off to graduate schools and new relationships.

"You're a real friend to help me out here. I appreciate it." He thanked her in Swahili. "*Asante sana, memsahib*."

"You're going to have to accept that you can't fix this, David. It's not fixable. You just have to listen and take things as they come. And you'll have to accept that you need help."

"Yeah, but, it just . . . It's like . . ."

She reached over and touched him again, putting her hand on his shoulder and leaning closer. "It's the two things you've always hated:

not being able to wrap something up quick and tidy and having to rely on others." She backed away and held her hands up, spreading her fingers, another familiar gesture. "But that's what children do, David. They make you confront things you spent your whole life avoiding. If you embrace this situation, it can be a terrific opportunity to grow."

"Oh bosh, who wants to grow? They drive me crazy. They go up and down so much, especially the little one, Jordan. And Lindsay is off in her own world ninety percent of the time. I never know what they want."

"Ask them." Susan looked briefly impatient. "It's not rocket science. Every child grieves differently. Remember the basics: Be truthful, acknowledge that their sadness will never completely go away, and let them talk if they want to." Her impatience faded, and she looked at him affectionately. "Then, just hang on for dear life, and let time do its work."

Susan was noticeably older than Claire, and she wasn't the knockout Claire was. Her climb to professional prominence and her divorce had toughened her up. Still, she swam for an hour every morning, and it showed. They weren't in the Eden of East Africa, where they'd held hands under the jacaranda trees, smelling the wood fires in the long evenings before slipping back to her narrow bed. But, as she looked at him, he saw she still had that way of smiling with her eyes that felt almost like being kissed.

Sid Cranmer, alone in his house, was still recovering from his talk with Ames. Some years back, he'd read an article in the *New York Times Magazine* about a woman with Alzheimer's who'd decided to take her own life before the disease cored out her mind entirely. The article described how she'd gotten what she needed from a source in Mexico. After that, it was just a matter of saying good-bye to her family and moving painlessly on. With a little effort, Sid dug up the article, found an address in Mexico on the Internet, and sent off for the things he might need.

He was aware, of course, that he could make his quietus any time he wanted with the help of the .45 upstairs. Apart from taking the clip out, the search team had left the gun alone, which surprised him. When he'd asked, Patterson had just shrugged. "You've got a permit. The warrant doesn't authorize seizure of firearms. But I'd start making arrangements to get rid of it soon." Once Sid was convicted—something Patterson obviously considered inevitable—further possession of the gun would be a felony.

At first, Sid was comfortable reserving the gun as his escape hatch if there was no hope. This exit strategy had occupied his mind a lot in the early days after his arrest—he'd even picked up an extra .45 clip online—sometimes calming him and offering relief, sometimes lowering him into a blank despair. Who, really, would give a shit if he blew his brains out? The world would just be relieved.

The problem was that he hated the mess the gun would make. He knew very well what a high-caliber bullet did to a person's skull. He kept thinking of his beige carpeting—the blood, bone, and globs of flesh spattered all over it—not to mention the shock in store for whoever found him, which would probably be poor Jonathan or, God forbid, Elizabeth.

The tidier medical alternative attracted him. Ironically, though, when the supplies from Mexico promptly arrived, Sid was mildly outraged. Bending over the box, he whispered to himself: "Order a fucking out-of-print book, and you wait for weeks, but if you want to knock yourself off . . ." The key ingredient was something called pentobarbital, and he now had two hundred-milliliter vials of it. Enough to kill himself twice.

As Darren was making his way to his office, he unzipped his leather jacket most of the way down. The sun was beginning to sift through the mist, and the prospect of the concert with Claire, and perhaps drinks somewhere afterward, was lifting him off the sidewalk. He was smitten, that was for sure, and it was time for him to settle down. He and Claire had similar interests and values, they were both at the college, and she was beautiful, in every way. They could take sabbaticals together. Travel. Make love often. Have kids.

Darren knew he would be better for Claire than that shovelful of sod, Norcross. The guy might be decent and hardworking, but really. He looked like a man with a broom handle up his butt who figured, if he just maintained a thoughtful expression, no one would notice.

A puff of breeze inflated the sides of his jacket, making it bubble out, an apt metaphor for how he was feeling. Then he heard someone calling his name, and the sight of Ryan Jaworski hurrying toward him punctured his cheerful mood. The kid was clearly agitated about something. He was trotting along with his hands in fists.

Ryan quickly drew up and got right to the point. "Libby knows I saw the flyer."

Darren kept walking. "So?"

Ryan put his hand on Darren's arm, stopping him. "So? What do you mean, so? She could tell somebody—Lindemann or one of her friends, and I'd be—"

Darren broke in, using his classroom voice. "I'm curious to know, Ryan, how she happened to learn about this." Darren looked around. It didn't seem as though anyone was within earshot, but it wasn't impossible. One of the college patrol cars was parked at the side of Converse Hall.

"It just sort of came out." Ryan grabbed at Darren's arm harder to stop him from walking off. "Listen, I can't get in trouble, okay? My dad would cut my balls off."

"This is a fix you put yourself in, Ryan."

"Bullshit! You put me in it! You told me you thought it would be funny."

"That's not true, Ryan. I said it would be funny, yes, but I never told you to do anything. I never put you anywhere." He resumed walking, with Ryan in pursuit.

"You did. I never would've—"

"Hey!" Darren put his hand on Ryan's shoulder. "Just calm down, okay?"

They walked together for a few tense steps, Ryan muttering and shaking his head. Darren zipped up his jacket. Finally, he stopped and turned to Ryan, keeping his voice steady. "We're just going to have to agree to disagree about what I said or didn't say. All right?" He looked at Ryan, drawing out one of his well-practiced icy stares. Ryan glared back at him; he was not quailed. After a few more steps, Darren continued, in a more relaxed tone. "This does not have to be a problem, you know."

Ryan burst out. "Jesus Christ on a crutch, if I'd ever thought the FBI would get involved . . ." Ryan breathed in, pressing a hand against his chest. "But you had this cute idea." The boy was more upset than Darren had realized. "Jesus, my dad! I can't even think about it."

"Hey, listen to me," Darren repeated. "This really does not have to be a problem, okay?" He pointed a finger at Ryan. "All you have to do is make sure your lady friend keeps her lip buttoned. You can do that, can't you? Contain yourself, and contain the situation. As long as she is as silent as a tomb, neither of us will have a thing to worry about."

21

Paul Campanella was anxious about his meeting with Linda Ames, so he put in a call to Mike Patterson and asked if he would sit in.

"You need a bad cop?"

Campanella could hear traffic in the background. Patterson must be out in the field.

"Sorry?"

"I'm happy to sit in, Paul. Hold on a minute." There was a sound of distant voices and a tractor-trailer accelerating. "Have to pay a toll." A minute or two of grunting and rustling followed before Patterson's voice resumed. "Okay. You be the good cop. I'll be the bad cop. We can have some fun with la-la-lovely Linda."

A few days later, Campanella was waiting in his office on the second floor of the courthouse. Both Ames and Patterson were late. After checking his watch, Campanella hurried down the hall into the bathroom, hoping that one of them might arrive while he was gone and find his office empty. It wouldn't hurt to make them wait for once.

Linda Ames showed up accompanied by his secretary, Bonnie, just as he was returning. Ames apologized for being late, and Bonnie told him that Patterson had been held up.

"I can wait if you want," Ames said. She was wearing black jeans, running shoes, and a gray silk blouse. In court, she'd worn makeup and earrings, which she hadn't troubled with today. Female charm apparently wasn't her forte, which was a relief to Campanella. On the other hand, Ames's offer to wait for Mike Patterson might imply that she didn't think he had the chops to handle this situation on his own.

"We can start." Campanella pulled some papers from a file on his desk. "I can lay out what we've got here."

"Got your power tie on, I see." Ames nodded at him slyly. This was true. He was wearing the lucky red paisley number Denise had gotten him for Valentine's Day.

"It's just because you scare the hell out of me, Linda." This happened to be true, sort of, but it worked as a fake joke and got a smile from Ames.

"I don't bite."

Campanella placed a pile of photocopies in the center of his desk. Boston had decided that this would be an "open file" case, meaning the U.S. attorney's office was basically giving Ames every piece of paper the investigation had generated. Except in rare, particularly sensitive cases, this was a common practice. It had several advantages.

First, criminal defendants often held back information from their attorneys or just plain lied. The prosecution file very often provided a better picture of the crime than the half truths or flat-out malarkey the lawyer was getting from his or her client. Lots of times, the defense lawyer would end up using the documents received from the U.S. attorney's office—photographs, witness statements, wire intercepts, and so forth—to persuade a reluctant defendant that his situation was hopeless if he went to trial. Since a guilty plea would usually get the client a lower sentence, nine times out of ten, the result would be no trial and a lot of effort saved for everybody. Campanella didn't have any problem with this. Guilty people ought to plead guilty.

Another advantage to the "open file" policy was that it protected a prosecutor from accusations that he or she had withheld evidence improperly. The law gave defendants the right to examine any evidence the government had that might be exculpatory, meaning evidence that tended to show that the defendant was innocent or that the case against him had holes. The consequences for a prosecutor who negligently or deliberately concealed this sort of material could be horrendous. Revelations of improperly hidden evidence could lead to mistrials and even outright dismissals. Worst of all, a touchy judge could go ballistic at a prosecutor and report him to the Board of Bar Overseers, get him fired, and destroy his career. With a guilty client shoveling out money, an aggressive defense lawyer would be on the lookout for some way to attack the AUSA and get a dismissal for prosecutorial misconduct where he could never get an acquittal before a jury.

Campanella was determined to avoid this trap. He cleared his throat and launched into his summary for Ames.

"The case originally came out of a child-exploitation task force in the Chicago division of the FBI. They received a tip from the NCMEC that—"

"What's that?"

"Sorry. National Center for Missing and Exploited Children." Campanella handed Ames a copy of the FBI form opening the case eight months earlier. "The tip related to the posting of child pornography images on something called 'Yahoo Groups.' It's a free service for people—"

"I know what a Yahoo group is. For people with the same hobby, right? Like stamp collectors."

"Maybe, but not in this case. A task force officer using an undercover ID got access to a Yahoo Group called 'Candyman' and discovered that forty-three individuals were using it to discuss their mutual interest in child sexual abuse and to swap images of underage pornography. One of the individuals, who used the ID 'Luv2look,' shared child pornographic images with his chat buddies, including this one."

Campanella passed a black-and-white photocopy to Ames. It showed a naked girl, who looked about five years old, with her arms tied over her head and her vagina exposed. Something that looked like a clamp device was fixed on one of her nipples.

"Ugh," Ames said. She turned the photograph over, closed her eyes, and shook her head.

"It wasn't hard to trace 'Luv2look' back to your client."

"Well," Ames said. "We'll see."

"Sure." Campanella pushed another document toward her. "On April 23, the U.S. Customs Cyber Crimes Center in Fairfax, Virginia, issued this administrative subpoena to Yahoo, Inc. requesting subscriber information for 'Luv2look.'"

"I never heard of any Cyber Crimes Center."

"They're pretty new, a division of Immigration and Customs Enforcement—ICE. The return on the subpoena disclosed the IP address used by Luv2look." Campanella pointed at a line at the top of a new document. "You can see it listed there: 67.31.142.44, okay? They could tell, for example, that this IP address was online on April 18 at 23:46:22 EST, a little before midnight. You'll see it in the log when you go through it."

Campanella pulled another sheet out of his file. "ICE served a subpoena on Comcast on May 4. The return identified the user of this particular IP address as belonging to your client Sidney Cranmer, with a particular Amherst street number." He slid the sheet of paper over to Ames, who leaned back in her chair without looking at it.

"The images your client posted were forwarded to an FBI intelligence analyst named Brittany Gomez, who compared them to known victims contained in the CVIP—"

"Got to translate for me again, Paul."

"Child Victim Identification Program. Gomez looked for matches to known child victims. Her analysis disclosed positive hits, including six from one particularly notorious group called the Bauchwalder series, where the father was the abuser. Here's Gomez's report."

"I saw some of the Bauchwalder stuff in a case last year before you came to Springfield." Ames sighed. "Not pretty."

"Right, it's been floating around for more than ten years now. Thanks to the Internet, it will never disappear. Somebody's probably looking at it right now." Campanella glanced up at Ames and hazarded a dart. "Very popular with people like your client."

"Ease up, Paul. You don't have him convicted yet."

The Bauchwalder series was heartbreaking and especially infuriating to Campanella. Typical images of child pornography showed the child victim frozen and terrified, usually in severe physical pain, which was unforgettably appalling in itself. Occasionally, though, the child had been coached, or physically coerced, into pretending she was enjoying the things being done to him or her. This fake eagerness, the glimpses of the degraded child looking up anxiously at the videographer in hope of approval—Was she being a good girl? Would he get another beating?—were somehow even worse than the images of pure torture.

The notion of an adult doing this to a child was the moral bottom, in Campanella's opinion, the lowest a member of the human species could go. The popularity of this kind of child pornography derived from the perceived absolution it gave the viewer. "See," the video seemed to say, "she isn't being injured—she's having fun. She likes it!" But the frightened glances and frozen smiles of the Bauchwalder girl made the truth obvious. A child's life was being destroyed. Elise Bauchwalder had died of a heroin overdose at age seventeen, and the fact that the girl's father was serving a seventy-year sentence in a federal prison in Beaumont, Texas, was slim consolation.

At this point, the door opened, and Patterson stepped in.

"Sorry I'm late. I-91 was bad." He hauled a chair from the corner of the room and positioned it across the desk from Campanella, next to Ames. His large body seemed to take up a lot of space.

"Show and tell?" He gestured down at the pile of papers, then turned to Ames, holding out a hand. The two shook, both with their game faces on, expressionless. Campanella sensed immediately that Ames might think of Patterson as her real adversary. He'd have to watch that.

"Just wrapping up," Campanella said to Patterson, then turned to Ames. "Based on your client's street address, the investigation was transferred to the postal inspector here in Massachusetts, which coordinated with our local FBI office. Postal Inspector Tom Levine sent a flyer to Professor Cranmer, inviting him to become a customer of Tiger Entertainment, a company purporting to specialize, as the flyer said, in 'taboo, hard-to-find, forbidden material.' The flyer had a list of DVDs with titles and short descriptions that left no room for doubt about their contents. Three days later, your client mailed back the flyer, with his credit card information, ordering the DVD called 'Playing Doctor.' The description says that it involves a prepubescent girl supposedly being examined by a doctor. According to the flyer, she is quote 'spread-eagled on a table while the doctor'—"

"I read the flyer, Paul."

"Hot stuff," Patterson said, with a disgusted look.

"You've got no confirmed handwriting," Ames said. "You can't even . . ."

"Block capitals." Patterson's face turned impatient. "Probably using his nondominant hand. A typical dodge. Shows your professor knew he had to be—"

"If it was my professor," Ames broke in.

A short, pregnant silence followed, until Campanella continued. "Fine, Linda. As you know, we got an anticipatory search warrant from Judge Norcross, authorizing Mike's team to enter your client's house as soon as the DVD was delivered. Professor Cranmer admitted to the agent posing as the UPS driver that he was expecting the DVD, and he told Agent Patterson that he recognized it as something he ordered."

"More or less," Patterson interjected.

"My client denies ever saying or implying any such thing." Ames's voice had an edge.

Campanella made a mental note of this. Was Ames actually thinking of putting Cranmer on the stand? He prayed she would. He would roast the guy alive on cross-examination.

After another pause, Campanella continued. "Well, that may be up to the jury to decide, Linda. It will be his word against two federal agents."

"Three actually," Patterson held up his fingers. "Maybe more, if I ask around. But who's counting?"

"And then there's all this junk." Campanella shoved a fat subfile across the desk to Ames, who eyed it suspiciously. "A search of your client's computer disclosed three separate files, all with code names to disguise their contents, containing nearly one hundred still images of child pornography and three videos he'd downloaded."

Patterson looked over at Ames. "Our cyber guys also pulled up the contents of Luv2look's chat-room conversations. One of Cranmer's chat buddies used the ID 'loves_infant_pussy.' Real hard to figure that one out. LIP and Sid got up close and personal, talking about yanking diapers off and so forth." Patterson leaned back and folded his arms. "My bet is, one or two of the jurors will actually throw up. I've seen that happen twice now."

"So that's it. These are all copies of originals." Campanella gestured at the pile of papers. "You can take them with you, Linda. Just let me know if anything's missing, and I'll get it to you."

"Have a ball," Patterson added.

Linda Ames did not look a bit bothered, which Campanella certainly would be if he were her. With an indifferent expression, she gathered the papers together and dumped them into her briefcase, then looked at the two of them.

"I'll get together with my client, then maybe we can talk again."

"Not a whole lot to talk about," Patterson said.

Campanella watched as Ames gave the FBI agent an appraising look.

"You may be right," she said. "But you've been pretty open with me, so I'll reciprocate."

Patterson reached into the pocket of his gray linen jacket. It impressed Campanella how sharp Patterson always looked. Campanella could try for the rest of his life, and for two lives after that, and he'd never look half as cool as Special Agent Michael Patterson.

"Want a pistachio?" Patterson asked.

Ames smiled and nodded her head. "You bet. I'm starving."

Patterson dumped a generous pile onto the desk in front of Ames. "Help yourself."

"Okay, I've got two things for you to think about," Ames said. Campanella noticed that Ames took the approach of methodically opening half a dozen shells first, then eating them in a group, fast and greedily. Patterson always went one by one. He tried to think if this was telling him something about Ames but came up empty.

"First," Ames said, "something sort of unusual has happened I think you ought to know about."

"Okay." Campanella looked carefully at his adversary across the desk. She was still busily shelling pistachios with her eyes down. Patterson had a half smile creeping over the far side of his face where Ames couldn't see. Did Patterson think Ames was funny? Attractive?

"I've never done this before," Ames said. She popped another handful of pistachios into her mouth.

"First time for everything," Patterson said.

"Right, here goes. Norcross's girlfriend . . ."

"Oh, God." Campanella put his hand on his stomach and looked slightly ill. "Now what?"

"Some English professor who also happens to know Cranmer—"

Campanella broke in. "The very close friend he mentioned at the—"

"Right, at the initial appearance. Claire Lindemann." Ames chewed and swallowed. "Called me out of the blue. Except for the mention in court, I never heard of her. She didn't sound like a nut job, and she gave me the name of a kid at Amherst College, someone who might have a grudge against Cranmer, who she thinks might know something about how all this garbage got onto my client's computer."

"You're kidding me." Patterson broke in gruffly. "Norcross's girlfriend is doing investigative work for you?"

"Oh, Lord." Campanella dropped his face into his hands. This case was supposed to be a layup.

"I know, it's loony tunes. But here's the kid's name. I'll be talking to Sid about this, naturally. Maybe give the kid a call." Ames shoved a sheet of yellow paper, folded in half, across the desk toward Campanella, blank side up. "Up to you if you want to do anything with him. Just letting you know."

"Do you plan to let Norcross know about Lindemann's phone call?" Campanella knew this was a Hail Mary, trying to fob a nasty job off onto the defense attorney.

Ames snorted. "Oh yeah, like I'm going to touch that with a ten-foot pole." She leaned back and folded her arms. "Anyway, why would I do it? Lindemann's not a witness herself, just a middle man."

"Middle woman." Patterson reached across the desk and shoved the slip of paper back toward Ames. "We don't work for you, Linda. Do your own interviewing."

"Fine. It's your decision. But if it comes up later, I can say I told you. I'll probably give the kid a call, like I say, but my bet is he won't want anything to do with me. You might have better luck, Mike, flashing that shiny badge of yours." Patterson had poured out more pistachios. Ames gave him a grateful look and went back to shelling. "Anyway, now you know."

Campanella's brain was reeling. He stared down at the sheet of paper. Should he submit something ex parte—for the judge's eyes only—to make sure Norcross knew that this Lindemann person was sticking her oar in? Ames was right, though. She wasn't a witness. If she'd only passed a name along, Campanella might look like a tattletale going to the judge, as though he wanted to zing Norcross for not recusing himself. On the other hand, had the judge put Lindemann up to this? The possibilities were mind-boggling. Ames was going on.

"There's another thing you ought to know. It turns out that Sid Cranmer got a Silver Star from when he was a medic in Vietnam."

"I thought it was a Purple Heart," Patterson said.

"Silver Star. Much bigger deal. He won't talk about it, but I did some research. Sid was involved in some horrific battle called Lam Son 719 in 1971."

Even inside his mental dust storm, Campanella sensed a sudden change in the feel of the room. Patterson's body tensed. He sat up, then seemed to notice and make himself relax. Taking his time, he gathered a pile of shells into a heap on the desk and shoved them over the edge into the wastebasket before speaking.

Patterson's tone was casual. "Your guy was in Lam Son 719?"

"Right. I never heard of it, but I checked Wikipedia, and my God . . ."

"I know about Lam Son 719."

Patterson was a military history buff. He'd talked to Campanella about his library of books on the post-WWII military, especially Vietnam.

Patterson continued. "So that's where Cranmer got his star?"

"Something like that," Ames said. "And I thought, with you getting wounded in Afghanistan . . ."

"Who told you that?"

"Little birdie."

Campanella watched Patterson, who had fallen silent and was drumming absently on the desk with his fingers. One of the deputy marshals must have mentioned Patterson's combat record to Ames. Hadn't he been rescued by a medic? Two or three of the deputies had been on deployments to the Middle East, and Ames had probably managed to wheedle this information out of one of them.

Ames lifted her chin at Patterson. "Any more pistachios?"

"You've eaten them all." Patterson tossed the empty bag into the wastebasket.

"My bad. If there's no more food, I'll be heading out." Ames picked up her briefcase and stood. "I'll go over this stuff with Sid and get back to you."

The folded piece of paper was still sitting on the desk when she left.

22

Claire Lindemann steered up her driveway, stopped with a jerk, and cranked the hand brake. She'd drunk three large glasses of some sort of delicious red wine—exactly what vintage, she couldn't recall—and she was happy to be home without attracting the attention of the Amherst constabulary. All she needed at this point was a DUI. David would go ape shit.

The evening with Darren Mattoon had turned out frighteningly well. Darren made her laugh, really laugh, which was something she needed to do more of. She was flattered at how obviously he was interested in her and impressed at how tactfully he was letting her know. His careful, self-assured approach was awakening something in her that felt free and sexy. The kiss on her cheek at the end of the evening was affectionate to just the right degree, and he offered no more snarky comments about Sid Cranmer.

Somehow, out of her giddy and intoxicated mind, the thought emerged that something dramatic needed to be done about David. Unless she took forceful action, she was going to wake up in Darren Mattoon's bed fairly soon, probably in the next month. Some headlong evening, she'd let herself be convinced that it was just recreational, just a romp in the hay, and it would be, literally, a fucking disaster. As she sat in her drive, listening to the faint whistle of her own breathing and the ticking of the car's engine as it cooled, her need to take some wild and extravagant action grew in intensity.

Before long, it was obvious exactly what had to happen. Claire needed to go to David's house. Right then. It was after ten p.m., but he'd be back from DC. It was possible he'd still be up, and if she got him out of bed, then what the hell. They needed a large bucket of ice water thrown over their heads. Exactly what this meant as a practical matter and not as a metaphor, she wasn't sure, but now was the time, and she was the person to do it, whatever it might be. She shifted into reverse, backed quickly out of her driveway, and sped off on her quest.

A few minutes later, Claire felt uncertainty gnawing at the edges of her brave impulse. She'd been determined, for once in her overintellectualized life, just to do something without thinking it to death, but it was not coming easy. Her dwindling confidence took a big hit when she oversteered a turn, bumped up onto a neighbor's lawn, and missed taking out a mailbox by a whisker.

By the time she was making her way up David's shadowy driveway, she was in a losing battle with a strong sense of impending doom. It was very possible that she was about to screw up badly again. Would David mistake her for a burglar? An outraged litigant? Did he own a gun?

The nights had gotten frosty, and the trees bending over David's house had dropped some of their leaves. They made a deafening racket as she waded through them toward his front door. The house was dark except for a glow from the right-hand upstairs window, David's bedroom. When she stopped walking and stood in front of his door, the leaves mostly settled down, and except for a soft fluttering, all was quiet. Her breath came in silvery puffs against the moonlight.

Apparently, he hadn't heard her. He must be in bed, probably reading. The cool air was dissolving the fog in her head, revealing what a truly borderline idea this whole thing was. Nevertheless, she reached up, took hold of the knocker, and gave it a tentative clack. Four woofs, the first one softly uncertain and the final three good and hearty, immediately broke the silence. A sound of footsteps followed. Rubicon.

When he answered the door, David was in his painfully familiar burgundy bathrobe and slippers. Marlene, standing behind him, looked ready to resume barking at first, but when she picked up that it was Claire, she began hopping around, trying to wriggle past David.

"Claire?" David's face didn't give much away.

She plunged. "When I started on my way out here, I thought we needed to have an immediate and serious conversation." She struggled with the tricky phrase "serious conversation," but then, by a miracle, what needed to happen—what she really wanted to have happen—and why she had made her dangerous journey—suddenly became clear to her. It helped that under his robe David was wearing the cranberry silk pajamas she'd given him, an outfit that belonged, in her opinion, as much to her as to him.

David tipped his head. "Okay." A smile, very faint, was forming at the edges of his eyes. "A serious conversation."

Marlene nosed forward, and Claire patted her head.

"But now that I'm here, all I want to do is . . ." She was trying to find a phrase that would get her point across without being too coarse.

David put his finger on her lips. "For once, let's not talk."

She bit his finger, not too hard, and he pulled it back.

"See that?" He touched his finger to her mouth again and then held it up. "Now I need you to make it better."

David swept his arm across the threshold and toward the staircase, an ironical, showy gesture, like a concierge at a fancy hotel giving a lavish welcome to a favorite guest. With a glance up at David as she passed, Claire proceeded straight up the stairs, unbuttoning her blouse as she went. David followed, putting his hand on her right hip.

In David's bedroom—their bedroom—Claire found the blankets folded back in a neat triangle where he had gotten up. The lamp on his side of the bed was on, and two piles of First Circuit appellate decisions, one faceup, one facedown, were sitting in the space Claire usually occupied. David threw back the bedspread, shooting the papers onto the carpet in a swirling shower. Very soon, it was clear that, whatever else was going haywire with them, one part of their relationship was working as beautifully as ever.

23

Buddy liked that the new girl was chubby.

"The roly-polies are my favorite," he drawled. "Remember . . . what was her name?"

He'd managed, after several tries, to reach Buddy on his cell. His nephew needed a lot of lead time, and a lot of reminders, to get his head into the game. Right now, he could tell from the background noise that Buddy was trawling the mall—probably the one in Holyoke, which he called his Fishin' Hole. He'd be playing his usual game of selling pot to the middle schoolers. When a girl—or a boy if he was young and pretty enough—didn't have the cash, Buddy would sometimes swap half an ounce for a blow job in the back of his pickup.

He guessed Buddy was at his hangout spot near the entrance. A burst of engine noise in the background, some dickhead teenager showing off, drowned out the piped-in pop music and the gabble of voices. He couldn't remember the porky girl's name either. Something Jewish-sounding, just a few months ago. He was getting fuzzy in his middle age.

"We're going to need you to book the room, Buddy, but not until that morning, okay? Buddy?" As usual, the kid was pissing him off. "Buddy,

are you there?" He could hear some kind of conversation in the background and waited. After a little while, Buddy came back on.

"Sorry, man. The fish are biting."

"Listen to me, okay?"

"I'm listening. I book the room, like last time."

"But not until that morning, Buddy. And don't forget your outfit. We don't . . ."

"Hey, man, you know how I like dressing up. No way the girl at the desk will ever pick me out." He spoke off to the side, fainter. "Hello, sweetheart. Can I help you with something?"

"Buddy, listen, are you there?"

"Right. What day was it again?"

"The Saturday before Columbus Day. Jesus Christ, we talked about this. At the Ho Jo's."

"What? Oh right. I got it on my phone."

"And, Buddy, tell them—"

"I know. Tell them we need a quiet room, away from—"

"Because I have trouble sleeping. Something at the back."

"Got it. And pay cash. But call me that morning, okay? I lose track sometimes." More voices to the side. Business must be good. He couldn't help being a little envious.

Buddy suddenly laughed. "Hey, listen to this. I'll hold the phone up." There was some pop song in the background. He couldn't make out the lyrics.

"Come on, Buddy. Stay focused here."

"Gotta run. Sorry." And the line went dead.

Fucking idiot.

24

Despite his reluctance, Patterson had picked up Linda Ames's slip of paper after their meeting and put it in his pocket. This had bugged Campanella. He'd asked, nervously, what Patterson was planning to do. Patterson had told him he didn't know.

"I wish you wouldn't poke around, Mike. It's just going to complicate things."

"I probably won't."

Campanella had looked suspicious. He was no dummy.

"If you do talk to someone, for God's sake, don't put anything in writing, okay? I'll have to turn any new witness statements over to Linda, and she'll try to stuff them down my throat at the trial." He'd watched Patterson carefully. "Can we at least agree on that?"

Patterson thought for a while, then said, "It's a deal, Paul. Nothing in writing."

"It would be better not to contact this kid at all. It's just giving Ames a stick to beat me with. If she lists him as a witness, you can talk to him then."

"Got it. I probably won't do anything. I don't know."

Campanella grimaced. "And for heaven's sake, don't tell anyone

I told you not to follow up on this." He stroked his goatee nervously. "I had a hard enough time convincing Boston to let me take this case on my own, okay? I don't need any red herrings complicating the trial."

Campanella's boss, U.S. Attorney Buddy Hogan, had been blunt. He'd let Campanella take his first solo flight, he said, but if Campanella crashed such an easy case, he'd be back sorting documents in the subbasement of the Worcester courthouse for the next decade.

"Those herrings," Patterson said. "They'll swim right up your butt." They both laughed, and Patterson stood. He patted Campanella's arm and smiled down at him. "Don't worry, Paul. This conversation never happened."

Patterson's statement that he didn't know what he was going to do with Ames's note was not quite true. In fact, Patterson did know. He owed it to Cranmer—not to the moth-eaten little professor of today, but to the scared, gutsy kid up in the chopper forty years ago—to check out this Jaworski character. The interview probably wouldn't go anywhere, but he'd feel better.

As he merged into the traffic on I-91 heading north from the courthouse toward Amherst, Patterson ran over the handful of facts he knew about Jaworski. He was a junior, a computer science major, and he came from Chicago, where his dad was a big shot. His girlfriend—Lizzy Spencer? Libby Spencer?—was the girl they'd run into at the arrest scene. She was Cranmer's research assistant and probably would have been happy to sneak Jaworski into the professor's house. According to what Claire Lindemann had told Ames, Jaworski had a beef with Cranmer over some class he'd taken. Patterson had trouble imagining a mediocre grade provoking all this, but with some of these kids nowadays—especially the rich, entitled ones—you never knew.

The visit to Jaworski was prompted partly by convenience. The kid's condo was located on his route home from Springfield to Amherst Woods. It was coming on toward sunset as he passed Holyoke driving north, and the slanting light deepened the lingering greens and contrasting oranges and reds lining the Connecticut River. Columbus Day was coming up, the peak of the foliage. Now and then, on a rise, he'd catch a glimpse of the smoky Berkshires off in the distance to the west. He was getting a soft spot for this area. The rented house was very comfortable, and Margaret and James were starting to make friends at the high school. A year here wasn't the end of the world.

When Patterson knocked on Jaworski's door, he heard hip-hop music and a male voice inside, not too happy, shouting "Just a sec!" The condo complex was swank, with neatly trimmed lawns, lush shrubbery around the Colonial-style buildings, and big pots of yellow mums on the brick landings.

The kid's family definitely had the cash. Did he bother with a roommate?

Jaworski was wearing baggy cargo shorts and a black-and-gold Chicago Bulls T-shirt when he answered the door. His hair was wet, and he was scrubbing the sides of his head with a big orange towel.

"Uh, hullo?"

"Ryan Jaworski?"

"Yeah?"

"My name's Mike Patterson. I'm a special agent for the FBI. I wonder if I could talk to you for a couple minutes." He held out his badge.

Jaworski squinted down at the badge and then blinked up at him. "I don't know. Do I have to?"

"No. But I could sure use your help."

"What kind of help?"

"Can I come in?"

"Gee. Boy, I don't know. What's your name again?"

"Mike Patterson. I only need a couple minutes." Jaworski was taking his time looking him over. Was he scared or just trying to figure out if Patterson was real? A black FBI agent?

Patterson ran into this situation regularly. The number of African American FBI agents these days must have that old racist J. Edgar Hoover spinning in his grave—assuming his pantyhose didn't get in a twist.

"Well . . ." Jaworski glanced behind him and ran his fingers back through his hair.

Ryan Jaworski was real nervous. Interesting. Patterson was glad he'd stopped.

Patterson shrugged and started to turn away. "Hey, man, if you don't want to talk to me . . ." The "man" was deliberate. Sometimes a touch of street talk, or what a white kid like Ryan might take for street talk, could crack things open. It worked.

"Nah, nah, it's okay, I guess. Just a couple minutes, right?"

"All I need, Ryan. Two or three minor details we're looking into. Just happened to be in the neighborhood. No biggie. My dinner's waiting."

"Okay." Jaworski threw the towel onto a sofa. "Place is a little messy." The kid was working hard to act casual.

"I'm used to messes." Patterson gave him a smile, patted him on the shoulder, and stepped in. Whatever happened after this, he could testify that Jaworski had voluntarily given him consent to enter. "Got a roommate? Anyone else on the premises?"

"No. It's just me." Jaworski looked around vaguely as they crossed into the living room. "Um, I'm not sure where we should sit."

Patterson picked up a chair from the dining area and swung it around so it was facing the couch. "Why don't I take this, and you can shove some of that stuff over and sit there?" Patterson nodded at a heavy canvas robe with a black belt on top of it. "Judogi?"

"Just got back from a workout."

"Good for you."

Patterson started his questioning as he always did, with things he already knew, jotting on a pad as he went: Ryan's full name and birth date, his class, his major, and easy basics to get the kid comfortable responding. He got Jaworski talking about the fact that he was a Bulls fan.

"Sorry." Patterson tapped himself on the chest. "Wizards. I'm a glutton for punishment."

"Bulls stunk, too." Ryan made a face. "Next season may be better."

"Listen." Patterson put the pad aside and leaned forward. "You probably read about the problems one of your professors is having. Sidney Cranmer. Can you give me some background? Did you ever take any classes with him?"

"No." Jaworski sniffed, looked to the side, and wiped his hand across his mouth. "Like I said, I'm a computer science major."

"Any contact with him at all?"

"Not really."

Patterson made a point of looking bored. He'd been right. This was getting interesting.

"Well, I doubt you can help me then. Let me see. I wrote a couple things down so I wouldn't forget. Where did I put that piece of paper?" No law required a person to answer questions from an FBI agent, but if you did answer, it was a crime to lie. Jaworski's fib about not taking a class with Cranmer was a five-year felony, something that might come in handy if they needed his cooperation. "Ah, here it is." He unfolded Ames's note and pretended to read it over. "Do you know anyone named, um, Lizzie Spencer?"

"Libby." Jaworski supplied the correction quickly, flushed, then put on the brakes. "Not all that . . . Not . . . Well, we've dated. She was, for a while she was, sort of my girlfriend."

"You still seeing her?"

"Sometimes. I'm mostly dating someone else now. Not from around here."

"Uh-huh." Patterson looked down at the paper again, putting on his confused face. "Says here she worked with Professor Cranmer, or something like that. Were you aware of that?"

"I think she said something about it, yeah."

"Uh-huh."

"Actually, now I'm remembering, it's stupid. I forgot. I guess I'm . . ." Jaworski scrubbed his head, putting on a show.

"People forget things all the time, Ryan. You'd be amazed."

"I-I did take a class with Cranmer."

"Oh, that's terrific." Patterson picked up his pad and jotted a note. "What was it like?"

"Dull as dirt." They both laughed. "I have to take a certain number of classes outside my major. I kept, like, falling asleep in Cranmer's class. I guess that's why it slipped my mind." Jaworski chuckled again, trying to get something back from Patterson, who obliged by smiling and waving a hand dismissively.

"Remember it well. How'd you do?"

"Pretty good. B-plus or A-minus, something like that."

"Any chance you've ever been to Cranmer's house?"

"Why are you asking me that? I mean, it's kind of weird. . . . I can't even . . ."

Stepped on the kid's toe. Sometimes his job was more fun than beer and Super Bowl commercials. "No particular reason. Says here something about Ms. Spencer working out of his house sometimes. Thought maybe you might have dropped by or something and could help me out with what his place is like."

"Let me think." Jaworski actually grasped his chin and did such a crude pantomime of brain work that Patterson had to bite the inside of his cheek to keep from breaking into a grin. "Yeah. Yeah. I . . . actually, I do think I might have dropped by there once. I don't remember when. I think Libby and I were going out, and I was picking her up—something like that."

"Uh-huh. Great. Happen to go inside?"

"Maybe for, like, twenty seconds."

"Excellent. What was it like?"

"Little old lady's house. Prissy. Smelled like my grandmother."

"Really? That doesn't surprise me." Patterson tossed the pad on the coffee table, as though the interview were basically over. "One quickie. This is a long shot. Did you happen to see a flyer, a piece of paper, anywhere in the house, a kind of advertisement from some company selling pornographic DVDs? Anywhere in his house? Doorstep? Mailbox? Anything like that?"

Jaworski's mouth dropped open, and he actually went pale. Generally, Patterson didn't consider himself a particularly good judge of when someone was lying. He'd been fooled many times. But this poor worm had a flashing light over his head.

"No, no, no way. Nothing like that." Jaworski breathed and settled himself down a little. "Like I said, it was, like, thirty seconds I was in the house."

"Got it. Just so I'm clear, you never saw, say, a brochure or flyer or anything like that advertising child pornography, or any kind of pornography, in his house. I know I'm pushing here, but my supervisor says I have to run through this with everybody. Part of the drill." He chuckled and shook his head. "Almost forgot."

"No," Jaworski said, relaxing a little. "Nothing like that. I mean, I barely stuck my nose in the place."

"Okay, that'll do it." Patterson retrieved the pad, stuck it in his pocket, and stood up. As they walked toward the door, he put a hand on Jaworski's arm and said, "I'm getting absentminded in my middle age. Just a wrap-up question. Anything further you can think of about Cranmer that might give me a better picture of him? Anyone else you think I should talk to?"

After a pause, Jaworski responded casually. "Well, I know there's more child porn at his house, that's for sure."

"I bet there is."

Did Jaworski actually think this information was not important? Or had he just made the decision to croak Cranmer to cover himself?

"And there's this one professor I know who kind of hates Cranmer, a guy named Harlan Graves. You might want to talk with him."

"Good. Thanks. Maybe I will." Patterson stopped inside the front door, looked down, and scratched his head. "Maybe." He sighed and made a show of hesitating. "This is probably not going to make any difference, but could I have, maybe, just two more minutes of your time?"

25

Claire, sitting in her office, eyed the phone, trying to decide whether to take a shot at calling Sid again. Would it be kinder just to let him alone? After five or six messages, it was clear he was avoiding her. She knew, of course, that he must be crawling into his cave out of sheer humiliation. The college was certainly dropping him off a cliff. Students who'd been victims of childhood abuse had made their views known—which took tremendous courage—and rumor had it that the administration might be reprinting the course catalog to expunge Professor Cranmer's name.

But Sid was her friend, and Claire had no intention of being maneuvered out of his life just because things were tough. She also badly wanted to fill Sid in on a couple things that, for better or worse, she'd been up to. Time was flying. The Columbus Day holiday was next week; the sugar maple below her office window was already a red-and-orange bonfire.

Claire's safe-deposit box at the Amherst Savings Bank now held the folder Libby Spencer had given her, containing a sheaf of black-and-white photographs taken by Charles Dodgson in the 1860s of partly or entirely naked little girls. The prints were originals, made by Dodgson himself. Many had never been published, and from an academic point of view, they were priceless. Claire hadn't been able to resist taking a look at them. While they weren't quite pornographic by contemporary standards, they were certainly erotic and creepy—the kind of preteen cheesecake that might very well get a pedophile sweating. She had stored the file with relief (a) that it was out of Sid's house and (b) that she wouldn't be needing to look inside it for a long time, if ever.

She hadn't made up her mind whether to tell Sid about Libby's theft of the folder. He might be better off not knowing it was gone or where it went. On the other hand, the photographs, for better or worse, belonged to him. Claire hoped talking to Sid would help her feel her way toward a decision about what to do.

Then, there was the phone call she'd made to Linda Ames about Ryan Jaworski. Claire badly needed to let Sid know about that. She had done it on an impulse the morning after the upsetting grilled cheese dinner with David. She kept telling herself that she'd acted with the best of intentions, suspicious of Ryan and inspired by David's description of what a good lawyer Ames was. But now, no matter how often she recalled her good motives, the sheer brass of what she'd done almost gave her vertigo. If David found out, his Boy Scout sense of betrayal would probably end their relationship for good. It would be proof positive that they just couldn't navigate as a couple. After their recent overnight, which had improved things between them tremendously, a heartbreak like that would be unbearable, especially since it would be her own stupid fault.

But it was done, and she couldn't go back. She needed, at least, to let Sid know before Ames told him first, so he'd have a fair opportunity to call Claire an interfering asshole to her face, instead of just hating her on his own, on the other side of his big high wall.

Problem was, he wouldn't pick up his goddamned phone. She decided to make one last attempt. Punching in his number, Claire told herself that, if she got his answering machine again, she was going to shout, curse, and threaten to pitch a rock through his window. If that didn't get him to call her back, she'd go stand on his front lawn and scream.

She'd worked herself into such a lather of enraged determination that she was caught off guard when Sid actually picked up. His voice sounded thin but healthy, and they quickly decided that if she wanted to come over and see him there was no time like the present. Just at the moment, he said, he could really use some company.

When Sid opened the door, Claire was shocked at how haggard he looked and the way he seemed to be sagging to one side.

"Still healing up?"

"Yeah. It's nothing." Sid was shorter than Claire, and when they hugged, he leaned his head into the side of her neck. "God, it's good to see you, dearie." He waved her inside. "Come in, come in. Sorry about the hide-and-seek." He closed the door. "What can I say? I'm a fucking basket case."

"Don't worry about it."

"My friends are few these days, Claire, and I've decided to stop walling them out." The house was as well ordered as ever, and there was the usual lovely aroma coming from the kitchen. "From now on, drop by any time. You don't even need to call." He held up a finger and spoke as though he were lecturing. "The wonderful thing about home confinement is that you're always home."

They spent the next half hour eating warm three-berry pie and catching up on college gossip. Claire was reassured to see that her friend, though pale and moving slowly, had not lost his edge. When she told him that Darren Mattoon had taken over one of his fall classes, and overhauled the syllabus substantially, Sid shot back, "Darren doesn't need a syllabus. Every class he teaches is the same thing: Mattoon 101, Mattoon 202, Mattoon . . ."

"Now, now."

Sid leaned back in his chair. "It's okay. Let him have his fun ruining Western literature. Adversity is making me stoic. I'm a regular Socrates without the hemlock."

This seemed like a reasonable opening to inquire about the case. When Claire asked how it was going, Sid got quiet for a while, dabbing at his pie and then turning to stare at the row of African violets he kept on the sill of his bow window.

Finally, he looked back at her. "Don't ever get indicted, Claire. It sucks."

"I'll bet."

Claire waited while Sid gathered himself, poking at a piece of crust. "I'm going to say something that may surprise you. I hope it will anyway." He spoke quietly, and his eyes when he lifted his face to her were moist. He took a deep breath, cleared his throat, and spoke a little louder. "I'm beginning to wonder if I might be better off pleading guilty." He swallowed and flicked the corner of his eye. "Nothing to cry about. A lot of people in this world have it worse."

The suggestion took Claire's breath away. "How can you plead guilty?"

"Because, basically, there seems to be a ton of evidence that I am guilty, Claire. I don't think I've done everything they say, but I have done some stuff, and it turns out there are parts of me . . ."

"Everybody has parts, Sid. Everybody's done stuff . . ."

"My lawyer says if I plead, she can maybe work the sentence down to three or four years."

"Three or four years!" Claire fell back in her chair. After a few seconds, she realized her mouth was open, and she closed it. "Three or four years? My God!"

"She says if I go to trial, and the jury finds me guilty, I'll get at least five, and the judge could give me eight or ten. I doubt I could survive that."

Claire's wave of shock and anguish slapped up against a concrete wall as she remembered that the judge he was talking about was the man whose furry chest she had recently laid her cheek against. She couldn't believe that Sid had actually voluntarily downloaded and looked at child porn—it was too revolting, too impossible—but she also couldn't endure the thought of what might happen to him if he admitted he had. She pictured him in some remote federal prison, in a cell, sitting there in the shadows for years. He'd nearly been killed during only a few days in the local jail. She could barely find words.

"Couldn't you . . . Can't you . . . ?"

"No, Claire, I couldn't, and I can't." Sid placed his fork down on his plate carefully. "My lawyer's more or less telling me that if I go to trial, I don't stand a chance. She says it's my decision, and she'll fight for me no matter what and all that. She's trying to be, I don't know, diplomatic or something, but . . ."

"There's always a chance." She knew she was babbling.

"No, dearie, there isn't. Linda Ames is one of the nicest, smartest, and toughest people I've ever known. If anyone could pull my ass out of this, it would be her." He hesitated and shifted uncomfortably in his chair. "I've been looking over samples of the stuff they took off my computer, and it's just fucking horrible."

"God."

"Some of it." Sid wavered. "Some of it seemed familiar."

"Oh, Sid." She reached over and took his hand. "Do you honestly think you could stand up in public and . . . ?" She couldn't finish the question.

"That part is hard to imagine, I admit. I go back and forth." He squeezed her hand and dropped it. "But I'm like Nixon." He held up his arms and flashed V signs. "I have a secret plan for peace with honor."

"What's that supposed to mean?"

"Just bravado. More pie?"

"No thanks. I'm fine." Was he talking about suicide? It was probably only Sid-style melodrama. She'd have to find a way to push him on that, but there was something else she needed to get out first, before she lost her nerve. "Sid, I have to tell you something. I'm kind of embarrassed by it. Truth is, wow." She put her hand on her chest. She hadn't realized how hard this would be. "Truth is, I called your lawyer, Linda Ames, to pass on some thoughts I had about your case. I'm afraid I stuck my nose in, where I—"

"Really?" Sid seemed more bemused than annoyed. "What'd you do that for? I mean, you're a sweetheart, but—" The sound of the knocker interrupted him. Sid frowned and stood up. "Oh, for God's sake." He strode across the room. "You know, for a guy who's supposed to be in home confinement, it seems like every five minutes someone is banging on my . . ."

Claire stayed in her seat and was surprised to overhear Sid saying, "Well, my goodness, Agent Patterson! Back again?"

Claire could hear the deep voice of the agent. "Sorry to bother you, Professor, but we've got another warrant to search your house."

Outside, car doors were slamming.

26

Judge Norcross brought Chitra and Erik into court for the hearing on the motion to suppress in *Cranmer*. The issues were classic, he said, and the lawyers were pretty good. The show would definitely be worth the price of admission.

Chitra appreciated the fact that the judge liked to do this. After a hearing, he would often spend half an hour with them, pointing out what had impressed him and what hadn't—what, as he said, went "ping!" and what went "clunk." This kind of mentoring was invaluable, of course, but it was also terrific fun.

In the courtroom, Campanella—known affectionately to Chitra and Erik as "Campy"—led off with an oral summary of the government's argument. The issue was whether the statements made by Professor Cranmer at his arrest were admissible against him at his trial. Campanella predicted that the evidence would show they "clearly" were. His first witness was Special Agent Mike Patterson.

Chitra leaned back in her chair and took the scene in. She loved the courtroom. Norcross was a profile in black up on the bench, bent forward to jot a note. Linda Ames and the defendant were sitting at counsel table, Ames now and then leaning to whisper to Cranmer.

At the podium, Campanella had his hands in his pockets and was putting questions to Patterson as though they were two guys having a comfy chat about some ordinary morning five months ago. It was all very measured and under control. Even the branch of the sugar maple, visible through the high courtroom windows, bobbed in the breeze as though it were conducting music.

Chitra was suspicious of Patterson's testimony. He was trying to make the FBI raid sound no more remarkable than a visit from the Girl Scouts during cookie season.

"After you introduced yourself, what did you say to the defendant?"

"I asked him if he would have a seat on the sofa."

"And what did he do in response to your request?"

"He sat."

"What tone of voice did you use when speaking to him?"

"Same tone I'm using now."

Professor Cranmer, Patterson said, was unfazed during his arrest, heard and understood his *Miranda* rights, and spoke freely in the comfort of his living room. No one shouted, threatened him, or brandished a firearm. Everything Professor Cranmer did, and everything he said, was entirely voluntary.

When Campanella asked Agent Patterson whether anyone else, other than Cranmer and the search team, was on the premises at the time of the search, Patterson nodded at a young woman in the gallery wearing a dark gray skirt and white blouse.

An Amherst College undergraduate, Elizabeth Spencer, was present, he said, at the time of the team's entry and during the early stages of the search.

At this point, Erik shoved a note over to Chitra. It read: *An interesting morning for Ms. S.!* Chitra added two exclamation marks.

Patterson described, step-by-step, his administration of the required *Miranda* warnings to Cranmer, and Cranmer's response that he understood them and that they sounded "just like TV." This prompted a long-suffering look from Ames over at her client. Patterson's performance began to get a little monotonous, which was probably Campanella's goal here. It was all straightforward, no big deal.

After Campanella finished up with Patterson, Linda Ames had her turn. She started out easy, with simple questions: the time of day, what Cranmer was wearing, what he was up to when the agents burst into his house, and how many agents were at the scene.

Then things got interesting.

"Now, Agent Patterson, you've described how you informed my client of his *Miranda* rights at the time you confronted him, correct?"

"Yes, I read them to him, actually, off a card I keep in my wallet."

"Right, and the last question in the standard *Miranda* protocol is: 'Having understood these rights, are you willing to give them up and speak to me at this time?' Isn't that true?"

"Yes, that's usually the last question."

"Okay, and you never asked him that question, did you?"

"No, because I was interrupted by Agent—"

"That's fine." Ames held up a hand. "And you even have a written form you use to confirm a defendant's waiver of rights. Isn't that true?"

"Yes."

"And you had that form with you the morning of the search, isn't that true?"

"It was probably in my car."

"But you never used that form to obtain any written waiver of *Miranda* rights from my client, did you?"

"No."

"No written or oral waiver, correct?"

"Correct."

Erik pushed another piece of paper over to Chitra. *Big hole in Campy's case. Check out J.*

The judge was writing quickly on his yellow pad. Not a good sign for the government.

After this, Ames's voice got increasingly sharp as she moved into a new area.

"Now, just recently, you conducted a second search of my client's house, isn't that true?"

Campanella was immediately on his feet. "Objection. Irrelevant."

"Overruled."

Campanella looked stricken. "Judge, respectfully, I can't see how this second search has any relevance to the question of whether this defendant's statements at the first search are admissible."

Still writing, Norcross spoke without looking up. "Events at the second search may bear on credibility." He put his pen down. "There's no jury here. I can sort out what's relevant, don't you think?"

Erik slipped another note to Chitra: *Go, J!*

The two clerks wanted to hear about the futile second search, regardless of its relevance. They were dying to learn the identity of the mystery confidential informant whose false information had lured the government into such an embarrassing quagmire.

Ames led Patterson through his arrival and search of Sid's house the second time. Patterson described how the agents went room by room, looking into every nook and cranny, and found none of the alleged child porn described in the CI's affidavit. Then the testimony took another interesting twist.

"By the way, Agent Patterson, was there anyone else on the premises other than Professor Cranmer when you conducted your search this time?"

"Yes."

"Really? And who was that?"

"A colleague of Professor Cranmer's from Amherst College." Patterson hesitated. It may have been Chitra's imagination, but he seemed to be working very hard not to look up at Judge Norcross. "Professor Claire Lindemann."

Now it was Chitra's turn to scribble a note: *Yikes!!!*

Without changing expression, Judge Norcross leaned over, took a tissue from the box under the lip of the bench, and began cleaning his glasses.

Things got even more entertaining after this, when Linda Ames asked Patterson who the CI was whose bogus information provided probable cause for the second search. Campanella leaped up again, objecting. This time he added emphasis by slapping his yellow pad on the table. Judge Norcross was leaning partway over, retying his shoe.

He sat up. "Objection sustained. No need to get into this now." He nodded at Campanella. "Be aware, however, that I may reconsider this ruling prior to trial. We'll have to see."

Following a short redirect by Campanella, the government rested, arguing that although the administration of the *Miranda* rights was truncated, Patterson wasn't obliged to obtain the waiver since Cranmer wasn't formally in custody at the time he made his statements. To Chitra at least, this argument was a loser. Patterson had him pinned to the sofa. They never would have let him leave freely, and they took him away in cuffs a half hour after their initial entry.

Ames, however, wasn't taking any chances. When the judge asked her if she would be calling any witnesses, she nodded back at the young woman in the front row of the gallery.

"Yes, Your Honor. The defense will call Elizabeth Spencer."

Judge Norcross glanced over at her.

"This is the undergraduate that Agent Patterson testified was present at the time of defendant's arrest?"

"Not the formal arrest, Judge, but in the time leading up to it. She will testify that my client was effectively in custody from the moment Agent Patterson entered his house. Absent a knowing waiver of his *Miranda* rights, any statements he made after that point are inadmissible."

Two days later, Patterson got a copy of Norcross's written ruling on the motion to suppress. The statements Professor Cranmer made to the agent posing as the UPS driver were admissible at his trial. Cranmer was not in custody then, and *Miranda* warnings were not required. However, anything he said after Patterson entered his house was out. Based largely on Elizabeth Spencer's testimony, Norcross ruled that the defendant was effectively in custody from the moment Patterson confronted him. The absence of a proper waiver of rights made any statements after that inadmissible.

Patterson flung Norcross's memo into the wastebasket and went downstairs to the marshals' exercise room to work off his bad mood. This was just the latest in a string of problems they were encountering in *Cranmer*.

The exercise room, located in the marshals' area in the basement of the courthouse, didn't turn out to be much of a haven. One of the deputy marshals had come in early and was on a stationary bicycle reading that morning's *Republican*.

"Hey, Mike," he said. "Who threw the monkey wrench?" He held up the headline, which read: "Porn Prof's Case Hits Headwind."

"Give me a break, okay?"

"Says here this Spencer girl made you guys sound like the Mongol horde." The deputy, an Asian American man named Jacob Lee, grinned over at Patterson and tapped the paper.

"Yeah, I know," Patterson said. "And I was Genghis Khan." He settled himself on the weight bench to begin his daily set of presses. "Pisses me off. A diddly-squat case like this shouldn't be such a pain in the butt."

"You got screwed by your informant. Happens to all of us."

"When I told Campanella the news about the hidden porn stash, he about jumped out of his socks. It meant our professor was violating his conditions of release, and he'd get to stick the guy back in Ludlow. I let myself get stampeded. Dumb."

The strain on his arms and upper body felt good. He'd move through his weight routine and do a half hour on the treadmill. Then he'd shower and get back to work.

"Like the bumper sticker says, Mike, shit happens."

"Yeah, you should have been there when I told Campanella we came up dry on the second search. Guy threw a paperweight and wiped out his coffeepot."

Lee, pedaling furiously, broke into a delighted smile. "I love it, man."

"Then, after that, I had to listen to Linda Ames lecture me for half an hour over the phone about her client's rights. Practically called me a Nazi." He nested the weight bar and sat up. "Right after that, I got a call from my very unreliable informant, freaked out because he's afraid the judge will release his identity."

Lee began to slow down, moving into the cool-off segment of his ride.

"What do you think will happen?"

Patterson looked around the room. "Keep this under your hat, okay? Our death-or-glory U.S. attorney has decided that Campanella needs adult supervision. He's jumped into the case with his size sixteen galoshes. Campanella has his marching orders: Do whatever he has to do to sweep the whole dog bowl under the rug and out of the papers."

"What are you going to do?"

"Well, at first, I thought my CI had made up the tall tale about the porn stash. I was ready to pull the kid's head off. Now I'm wondering if someone grabbed the pictures before we got there. I'm going to head up to Amherst College. Do a little independent research."

27

Patterson decided he might have the best luck approaching Elizabeth Spencer after class. That afternoon, he waited on a bench outside Converse Hall until he spotted her coming down the long steps. Even from a distance, she was a strikingly poised young woman—curvy but not flaunting it too much, with medium-length light-brown hair framing an intelligent, heart-shaped face. She was wearing a bright-red fleece and, fortunately, she was on her own. A couple of the boys hurrying into the building smiled at her as they passed. Her quick return twinkle told them she was friendly but happened to be in a hurry to get somewhere. The young lady had already mastered the art of the gracious brush-off.

"Ms. Spencer?" He approached from the side, and she had to stop to turn and see him.

"Uh-huh." Her eyes, widening slightly, marked him as an enemy. She looked around to make sure there were other people in the vicinity, on her guard.

"I'm sure you remember me. I'm Mike Patterson from the FBI." He held out his badge. "You did a terrific job at the hearing the other day. We're trying to straighten a few things out, and I was wondering if I could ask you a couple quick questions?"

"I remember you. What do you want to talk about?"

"This isn't the best spot." He smiled. "Maybe we could find an empty classroom." He nodded up at the building she'd just left.

"No, this is fine." Her eyes narrowed, and she shifted a strap of her backpack. "I'm in kind of a hurry."

"Let me just get some basic information. Your family's from Minnesota, right?"

"You know all that. Come on."

"Well . . ."

"Listen. I know you are doing your job, Mr. Patterson, and I don't want to be a problem. But my uncle always told me never to speak to the police—or the FBI, or whatever—without having a lawyer. If you want to talk to me, then I want to talk to a lawyer first, and you can contact him. Or her. You're a nice person, I guess, but I really don't want to talk to you like this, coming up to me out of the blue and all. I'm sorry."

She started to turn away.

"Fair enough. Can I just leave you my card?"

"Sure." She took the card and gave him a slightly apologetic smile. "Usually, I'm not such a crab."

"Well . . ."

"Bye."

She walked off, increasing her speed a little and not looking back. Without suggesting panic, her posture underlined her decision to have nothing to do with him. It was exactly the way he'd want his daughter to handle a situation like this if some cop ever approached her. The young lady had left him with absolutely no idea whether she had anything to hide.

The attempted contact with Harlan Graves, a half hour later, produced something approaching outright fireworks. In response to Patterson's knock, Graves opened his door halfway and peeped out at him suspiciously. The professor was wearing a threadbare olive cardigan, a pair of wrinkled khakis, and carpet slippers. As soon as Patterson mentioned that he was from the FBI, the guy practically turned purple.

"I don't have anything to say, and I don't appreciate these Gestapo tactics! If you want to talk to me, make an appointment."

"Well, I was just in the area . . ."

"What do you want to talk about, anyway?" The professor was at least curious, and Patterson hoped for a second that this might get him in the door.

"Well, we're checking on some things about your colleague, Professor Cranmer, and—"

"Cranmer! He's a twisted little peacock. Other than that, I have nothing to say." Graves looked over his shoulder, possibly at some noise inside the house, and dropped his voice. "If you want some dirt on Cranmer from someone who would eat Sid's liver on toast, go talk to Professor Mattoon." His eyes glinted with malice. "You might strike oil there."

The indistinct voice of an elderly woman reached Patterson from somewhere in the house. Graves turned and called out, "It's okay, Martha. It's just a man." He turned back to Patterson. "My wife is not well. Now go away."

The door shut hard, and Patterson heard the cluck of the dead bolt. Graves's response didn't especially bother him. It wasn't the first time someone had shut a door in his face. But he couldn't help wondering what this guy's problem was. Tax evasion? Tearing the tag off a mattress?

He wasn't doing anything, so he decided he'd take a shot at talking to this Mattoon character. After a few inquiries, he located the professor's office and arrived just as a student, a tall black kid—probably not an American—was leaving.

Mattoon's reassuring voice came from inside. "Don't break your back, Robert, okay? Next Wednesday will be fine. Let me know if you need another extension."

The tall boy paused in the doorway, looking back. His handsome face was solemn, his skin very black. "Thank you. I appreciate it very much. My family appreciates it. I will submit the paper by Wednesday without fail." The kid had a lovely accent. Nigerian? Haitian?

When the student was down the hall and out of earshot, Patterson leaned into Mattoon's office. The place had a cozy, in-control feeling, without being fussy. Floor-to-ceiling bookshelves occupied the left- and right-hand walls, full but not overstuffed, and a large window looked out over the lawn behind Mattoon's uncluttered desk. A computer table sat at a right angle to the desk, its monitor displaying some electronic document. Mattoon was looking over a sheaf of papers as Patterson entered.

"Excuse me. Professor Mattoon?"

"Yes? Hello? What can I . . . ?"

"I'm Mike Patterson. I'm a special agent with the FBI. I was in the neighborhood and was wondering if I could have two minutes of your time for a couple questions." He held out his badge.

The guy's reaction was calm. "The FBI? Goodness." Mattoon bent his lips into a half frown—puzzled but not scared. "I can't imagine how I could help you." He hesitated. "I hope it's not about Robert?" He reached over to close the screen on his computer. "Because if it is, I'm afraid . . ."

"Nothing to do with him. Immigration's not my area." Patterson guessed from the student's accent that he probably had some battle going on with Immigration and Customs Enforcement. A lot of the foreign students did, especially the Haitians. Mattoon's relieved expression confirmed the nature of Robert's predicament.

"I'm glad to hear that. He's a terrific kid, very smart, and he's in a very unfair, scary situation."

"No, I'm following up on a couple details in the case involving a colleague of yours, Sidney Cranmer. As I said, I was in the—"

"Oh, God, not Sid. What's he done now?"

"Do you know him?"

"Of course. It's a small department. In fact, I've picked up one of his classes, now that he's"—Mattoon raised his eyebrows—"otherwise occupied."

"What's Cranmer like?"

"He's a crackpot."

"Really. Is he—"

"No. Wait, wait." Mattoon scrubbed a hand over his face and sniffed. "That was mean. What I should have said is that he's most of the way over the hill and somewhat eccentric."

"In other words, a crackpot?"

"Well, there's this difference between connotation and denotation that I keep trying to teach my students. Sid's okay. His scholarship is out of date, which does nothing to reduce his arrogance, and he can be a pill." Mattoon shoved the papers he'd been reviewing to one side. "He has meltdowns during department meetings when he more or less tells everyone to go fuck themselves. People take it in stride—just Sid being Sid. I'm probably less patient with him than some people."

"Had you ever, before he was charged, gotten the sense that he might have some sexual fixation on children or collect child pornography?"

"Well, to be honest, his problems were not entirely a shock to most people. The author he specializes in, Lewis Carroll, was what we'd probably call a pedophile nowadays. The guy enjoyed taking pictures of naked little girls, and I guess Sid liked keeping the pictures around."

"Charles Dodgson."

Mattoon raised his eyebrows and bestowed a smile on Patterson that was so condescending that it lifted the hair on the back of Patterson's head.

"Very good. Very good. It's an unusual specialty, but I have the impression that everyone just thought that he was a lovable, or at least mostly lovable, nut. I doubt anyone thought he had any, what you might call, repulsive proclivities."

"Ever been in his house?"

"Nope, never invited."

"How about his office?"

"A few times, mostly just to stick my head in."

"Ever happen to see a flyer or advertisement, sitting on his desk or somewhere, inviting him to send off for any kind of pornographic DVDs?"

Mattoon laughed. "I doubt he'd leave something like that sitting around. The administration would have a purple cow. Not to mention our small army of feminists. No, never."

"Did he or anyone else ever mention anything about such a flyer or advertisement to you?" Now the guy was tightening up, drawing out the smile left over from the cow joke, which wasn't all that funny. Patterson disliked Mattoon, but that didn't mean the man had done anything wrong. Even if he was lying, who knew what about, or why?

"Well, I . . . An advertisement? What kind of advertisement?"

"Yeah, I know, this is kind of a long shot, but I'm asking everyone. One of the pieces of evidence against Professor Cranmer is a DVD with some very graphic child pornography. It was ordered in response to a flyer that advertised a bunch of DVDs all with this same sort of contraband material. Professor Cranmer sent it in, and that's part of the case against him. I was just wondering if you ever heard anything about it."

"About the flyer?"

"Right. I'm asking a lot of people about this."

"What other people?"

"I'm afraid I can't reveal that. My supervisor would kill me."

"Well, I can tell you, Agent Peterson . . ."

"Patterson."

"Sorry. I can tell you that I never saw any advertisement, never heard anything about any flyer. Don't know a thing about it. Afraid I can't help you with that. It came to his house, you say?"

"Well, I didn't say because, to tell the truth, I can't remember. It came to his house or his office or got to him somehow."

"Don't know a thing about it." Patterson's catch about the flyer at the house had Mattoon tightening up more. His face had gone plastic.

"Well, thanks. Here's my card. Would you give me a call if you remember anything related to the charges, particularly anything you might hear about underage material? It might help us a lot."

"Sure. I can give you my cell number in case you have any follow-up."

"It's okay." Patterson threw Mattoon a fastball under the chin. "I already have it."

"Oh."

Patterson allowed himself to leave Mattoon's office entirely before he did his Columbo-style return. He stuck his head back in. "Forgot one thing. Do you know a student named Ryan Jaworski?"

"I do, yes. He took one of my classes."

"Do you know of any reason Jaworski might have a problem with Cranmer?"

"No idea."

"Well, we're doing a handwriting analysis on the flyer. It may help us out."

Mattoon smiled, turned, and flipped the text back up onto his computer, letting Patterson know he was done with him. "Well, good luck!"

Patterson knew very well that the FBI expert's attempt to break down the handwriting on the flyer had gone nowhere. But Mattoon wouldn't know that. It never hurt to give the tree a shake now and then. You never knew what might come tumbling out of the branches.

28

The Friday before the Columbus Day weekend, David filled his briefcase with work and caught a plane down for another weekend in Washington. His first stop was a rehabilitation center in Arlington, Virginia, where Ray, finally back, was gathering strength and learning to walk again. During their Skype calls, David had been disturbed to notice how the skin grafts were giving Ray a leathery, frozen look that erased any element of charm from his face. Ray had also lost most of his hair. David did not look forward to seeing his brother in person. How would he conceal his dismay? Only six months ago, Ray had been a handsome man.

During the long cab ride from the airport to Arlington, David had a conversation with himself, basically trying to stop feeling what he was feeling. The closer he got to Ray, the more he found himself dreading the meeting, and the guiltier he felt about it. His emotions weren't generous—they didn't reflect the sort of person he wanted to be—but they would not go away.

When David walked into Ray's room, Ray was sitting propped up, reading the latest edition of *The Economist.* The room was small but sunny, with a large window on the far side of the bed looking over a park. The only furniture was a table, a chrome visitor's chair, and a large television screen high up on the wall. It was tuned to CNN, muted. A big bouquet of flowers sat on the table.

"Hey, brother. What's up?"

"Hello, David." Ray tossed the magazine aside. David stood inside the door, not knowing what to do. Ray's face was bad, but not as bad as he'd feared it would be. His forehead and cheeks were stiff, like leather that had been wet and overdried. Ray's attempt at a smile looked painful, as though it might crack his skin.

"It's been a while."

"I know," Ray said, still holding the smile. "Aren't you supposed to hug me or something?"

David stepped forward quickly, starting to hold his arms out, but Ray waved him back. "I'm joking." He shrugged. "We've never been huggy types, have we?" He nodded down at the chair. "Have a seat."

Ray was wearing a light-gray warm-up suit, which must have been for his physical therapy. He was in stocking feet, with his walking shoes sitting next to the bed. There was a ragged hole in the heel of one of his white sweat socks. The sheets and blanket were kicked back in a heap at the foot of the bed. All this was, for some reason, very depressing. The room had a medicinal aroma mixed with a smell from the bathroom that evidenced recent use.

"Sorry to drag you back down here again. I know how busy you are." Ray hesitated, squinting at David as though he'd just thought of something. "This must be a real pain for you."

"A little bit, but I'm lucky." David took the chair next to the bed. "In my job, nothing can happen until I show up." He leaned forward and put his hand on the bed, a kind of bearable version of touching Ray himself. "I'm really glad to see you, Ray. It's great to have you back."

"Yeah, well, thanks."

"And I'm, you know, like I said, so sorry about Sheila."

"It's been rough." Ray peered out the window. "Really rough." He turned back to David. "Don't ever, *ever* take your sweetheart for granted, David." He sniffed and raised his eyebrows as though he were disapproving of himself. "Remember that if you don't remember anything else." He took a deep breath and blew it out. "Let's move on."

"I'm— I'm really glad you're back. I mean it. All this has made me realize, I guess, how important you are to me."

Ray sighed again and cleared his throat. "Well, that's fortunate, because . . ." He dropped his head back on the pillow. His voice went shaky. "Listen, we might as well get right to this. Fact is, I . . . I need a big favor."

"Anything."

"Well, wait to hear what it is first, little brother." Ray was suddenly seized by a coughing fit that threw him forward and bent him over. When he pulled his knees up, the magazine slid off onto the floor. The hacking went on for so long that David finally stood up, wondering whether he should pound Ray on the back, call for help, or get him some water. Ray's face had gone almost scarlet. As David turned to step into the hall and look for a nurse, the attack subsided, Ray fell back, breathed in, and gathered himself, exhausted. He smiled grimly. "You can only inhale so much vaporized plastic before it does some damage." He turned again to gaze out the window, his chest rising and falling, apparently thinking of something. The crash? Sheila? After a while, he seemed to remember himself and looked back at David. "Here's the thing, Dave. I need you to take the girls."

David hesitated just a second too long before answering. His voice slipped into a slightly higher octave. "Okay?" The second syllable of the word curled up as though it were a question.

David couldn't control it, but he didn't like himself for it very much.

"Not forever, of course." Ray spoke quickly. "Just for the rest of this fall semester. Things are up and down, and I . . ." David was sickened to hear Ray's voice breaking, see him starting to tear up again. "I just can't manage it. The Stephensons are being posted to Dubai in ten days. I was hoping to get it postponed, but I guess I don't have the clout I used to. The girls have nowhere to go. I know it's a hell of a thing to drop in your lap, but my staff tells me Amherst has good schools, and I honestly don't know what else . . ."

"Ray. Ray, of course. I'd be glad to do it. The girls are great. We have a terrific time together. I'm happy to do it."

"I honestly . . . You don't know. I could handle it physically, maybe, with some help, after a couple more months in rehab, but I'm just . . . I'm just not up to it yet, without Sheila. I think maybe by . . . They tell me maybe by New Year's. Just for the semester. I don't want them to fall behind. I feel so . . ." The words were tumbling out.

David broke in, holding up a hand. "Ray, really. They're wonderful kids. I'd be happy to do it. It's no problem."

He was painfully aware that he was speaking with a tone of certainty now that should have rolled off his tongue as soon as Ray asked. At this point, no verbiage could camouflage his real feeling: Having Jordan and Lindsay under his roof for three or four months was his absolute worst nightmare. Even through his distress, Ray was clearly taking this in, seeing to the essence the way he always did. He knew that David did not relish taking the girls, but he also knew that David couldn't decline. He'd do it. Even through tears, the glint David knew so well shone in his big brother's alert, penetrating eyes: Ray had him. David would do what he'd asked, and that's what mattered.

Ray quickly pulled himself together, and the conversation veered off into the practical arrangements, things like Lindsay's Advanced Placement classes and Jordan's asthma medication.

As he was leaving, David finally managed to touch on the aspect of the situation that had been bothering him the most.

"I don't . . . I'm not sure the girls actually want to come to Amherst."

"Afraid they won't have a choice." Ray shrugged. "I'll have a talk with them." He pointed at the floor. "Would you hand me the . . . ?"

David passed Ray *The Economist*, and Ray flipped back to the article he'd been reading when David arrived. His face had relaxed into another look David knew well—a man who'd put a difficult task behind him and was moving on to other things.

29

It was a good thing Campanella's news arrived by telephone. Linda Ames would never have been able to maintain her cool in person.

After their hellos, Campanella went right to the point. "Okay, Linda, Christmas comes early this year. Here's the offer, straight from Boston. We dismiss the indictment for receipt, and your guy pleads to simple possession. He takes two years' custody of the Bureau of Prisons, with three years of supervised release."

Ames tossed her pen up to the ceiling, threw her head back, and broke into a huge, silent grin.

"Hmmm." She had to say something.

"You win. We all go home."

"I'll need to talk to my client."

"Right. You do that."

"I'll need to . . ."

"Couple conditions. He's got to take the two years. It's a binding agreement on both sides, with a full waiver of any appeal. And he's got to admit he ordered the DVD. We want that on the record. No fooling around."

"Well, like I say . . ."

"And if you want to do this, we need a quick turnaround, okay? So we can set the plea up for some time in the next month. Boston wants this one out of the newspapers. It's now or never."

"We have the Columbus Day weekend here, Paul. I'm not sure Sid's available. I'll need until Tuesday."

"He better be available. He's on home confinement, for crying out loud."

"Well . . ."

"It's an exploding offer, Linda, understand? I'll give you until Tuesday, but then it's gone. This is not up to me. I'm just the messenger. It's a one-time-only deal."

"I hear you." Ames flipped another pen into the air. It fell into her wastebasket with a clang like an exclamation mark. "I'll get back to you."

This was, simply and truly, unbelievable. Ames had never heard of anyone getting a deal in a child pornography case like this, where the evidence was this strong, in any federal court anywhere in the country.

The ironic side to it, of course, was that Campanella's largesse demonstrated just how completely the government controlled child porn cases. Prosecutors could, at their discretion, charge someone either with receipt of child pornography, which carried a five-year minimum mandatory sentence, or with possession of child pornography, which had no minimum mandatory. In a receipt case, the defense attorney was powerless—even the judge was powerless—to avoid the five years. Sid's record of risking his life for his country was irrelevant. The fact that he'd never improperly touched a child, and never would, was irrelevant. He'd get the five years, period. And maybe more.

On the other hand, also at their discretion, prosecutors could charge these defendants with simple possession—not receipt—of exactly the same material, in which case there was no minimum mandatory sentence. The judge could consider the particulars of the charged criminal conduct and the background of the defendant. He would have the power, in appropriate cases, to hand down a prison term above or below the five years, or impose a term in a halfway house, in home confinement, or on probation. In other words, the judge could judge.

As a practical matter, of course, no difference existed between receipt and possession of child pornography—it was hard to possess something without somehow receiving it—but the statutes gave the U.S. attorney's office free rein to determine the sentence simply by choosing which interchangeable statutory provision to invoke.

Sid's case was a rare instance where the power of the prosecutor could, in a way, work in a defendant's favor. Ames had no illusion that this miracle had anything to do with the merits of the case. The failed search, the ruling on the motion to suppress, the pending motion to reveal the CI, and the potential embarrassment to the U.S. attorney's office had bent the prosecutor toward generosity and cracked the case open.

As soon as she hung up from talking to Campanella, Ames contacted Sid and told him she was walking over. She had good news.

The autumn rain gathering in puddles on the common did nothing to dampen Linda's spirits. In fact, the soft, steady tapping on her black umbrella was music to her ears. The cool air smelled of leaf mold and faint wood smoke, and her mind danced forward into the coming weeks. A plea in the Cranmer case would open up time to take Ethan down to Tampa to visit her parents over the holidays. It had been a while since they'd had a real vacation together. They could pop over to Epcot or Universal Studios, or both. She imagined them checking out the rides or looking for some place to eat. Nothing even came close to making her so happy.

When she got to Sid's house, Ames thought at first that his reserved manner was just his default mood of gloom. She had prepared herself to fight off his latest round of pastry, but for the first time he didn't offer. They took their usual seats around the coffee table, him in the rocker, her on the sofa.

As she described Campanella's phone call, Ames felt her balloon deflating. Sid's face grew increasingly remote, with no eye contact. When she finished, Sid was quiet for a painfully long time. She hadn't expected a celebration at her news, but she'd hoped that, even if he wasn't cheered, he might at least be relieved.

Finally, he spoke. "I don't know, Linda."

"Uh-huh."

"I've been thinking a lot about pleading. I really have. I've been going over and over it until I'm almost out of my mind. I mentioned the possibility to Claire Lindemann. She was kind of shocked." He shifted in his seat. "She didn't like the idea."

"Uh-huh. Where did she go to law school?"

"I just . . . I can't imagine getting up and admitting I ordered that DVD."

"I see."

"I can't plead guilty to something I'm not really sure I did."

Linda Ames wanted to slap Sid Cranmer hard. If he turned down the deal, Campanella and his boss, Buddy Hogan, would decide that Sid was spitting in their faces, and they would be merciless. Norcross was fair, but he was not one of the district's easier sentencers. If she had to guess, she'd estimate seven or eight years after a guilty verdict, but something over ten was not impossible.

She folded her hands in her lap. Patience.

"I hear you, Sid, but please think carefully about this, okay? You can survive a two-year sentence. They'll send you to a camp, and with good time, you'll be out in twenty months."

"I hate camping."

"Don't be cute, okay? It's not the Boy Scouts. You'll be in a dorm with mostly white-collar people, and you'll spend a lot of time outdoors."

"Amherst College will revoke my tenure."

"You still have friends at the college. I'm betting they'll be happy to let you retire. You're old enough. A nice, clean break."

"But I'd have to register . . ."

"That's right, but you're far enough from the nearest public school that when you get out, you can move back into your house right here, if you want to. I checked it out. Once you're released, you fill out a form from time to time, and that's it. Nothing changes."

"Except I can't teach anymore."

This was getting ridiculous. "You're almost seventy, for God's sake. Most people have retired by your age. Besides, there are community colleges, adult ed. Who knows?"

"I just don't see how I can plead guilty to something I didn't do, Linda."

"Sid, here's what's happening." Ames stopped herself, realizing she was getting loud. She looked to the side and shook her head. Turning back to Sid, she forced herself to speak softly. "You're lying on the railroad tracks, the train's coming around the bend, and you can stand up and walk away. Do you want to keep lying there?" Sid looked into his lap, not saying anything. "I haven't pressured you before, but I'm telling you now: If you don't take this deal, you're making a huge, *huge* mistake."

Sid cleared his throat and squared himself. He looked up at Ames apologetically. "I can't do it, Linda. I know I can't. I can't physically stand up in court and tell the world I'm that sort of person. That I'd do that sort of disgusting . . . That I'm that . . ." He paused. "That I'm that ugly."

Ames leaned back and nodded. "Fine. So what's our plan then?"

"I guess we go to trial. I'll testify, and maybe they'll believe me. If they don't . . ."

The coffee table had four thick coasters with a floral patterns. Ames arranged three of them in a row and placed the fourth facing them from a few inches away.

"Okay, here you are. Let's play this out. You'll tell the jury that you think you actually did download some of the teen stuff, right? You think you probably did do that."

"Mixed in with the adult. . . ."

"Right, stay with me. And you did go into the chat rooms, and you're pretty sure you did say some of the things on the government transcripts, but most of it you don't remember?"

"I know it sounds . . ."

"Correct. It does. And then, with the DVD, you're pretty sure you didn't order it, but not a hundred percent sure. Right?"

"Right."

"You were thinking about it, and you kept the flyer, but you don't think you mailed it in. That's what you plan to tell the jury?"

"Right, because that's the truth."

Ames leaned back, put her hands over her eyes, and groaned. "Oh, the truth! Give me a break!" She dropped her hands and gaped at Sid, getting loud. "The truth? Really? The truth?"

"Well, if they don't believe me . . ."

Ames waved at him dismissively and dropped her voice. "Sid, don't worry, they definitely won't believe you."

"But how can I go into court, Linda, and admit to all these things I just . . ."

Now, Ames deliberately raised her voice to a shout and slapped her hand down on the lone coaster. "Because if you don't, you'll get five years in federal prison!" She leaned toward Sid. "Probably more. And it will kill you." A long silence froze them—Ames staring at Sid and Sid staring down into his lap again.

Finally, Ames broke off and looked around impatiently. "Okay, fine." She stood abruptly, walked to the dining area, took a high-backed chair, and placed it in the middle of the living room.

"Sit."

"What?"

She pointed. "Just . . . Just sit in the chair, please."

Sid stood uncertainly and had a seat. The chair's position in the center ring of his hooked rug, with nothing within reaching distance, made him look exposed and ridiculous.

Ames walked over to a bookcase, pulled out a book, and tossed it into Sid's lap. "Place your hand on that, please."

"This is *Alice's Adventures in Wonderland*, Linda. The annotated version."

"I know. It's perfect. Just do it."

Sid put his hand on the book.

"Do you solemnly swear that the testimony you give to this court will be the truth, the whole truth, and nothing but the truth, so help you God?"

"Linda . . ."

"Come on, Sid, let's do this. You say you want to testify. Federal judges mostly don't have people swear on bibles anymore, but this will get us in the mood."

Sid put his hand on the book. "By the soul of Charles L. Dodgson, I swear to tell the truth." He tried a weary smile, but Ames was not having it.

"Good." Ames turned and walked several paces away from him. She stood next to the wingback, placed her hand on it as though it were a lectern. "I'm going to be Paul Campanella, and you'll be you, okay?"

"Okay."

"This will be a mild version of what you'll get, because I haven't prepared, and Campanella will have been up half the night for a week polishing his questions, practicing them with the other assistants in his office. But here goes. Now, Professor Cranmer—he's sure to call you 'Professor' as often as possible, since the jury will assume, right off, that anyone who is an academic must have a twist in him. Now, Professor Cranmer, let me take you back to the morning of the DVD delivery."

"Okay."

"There's no question in front of you, Sid. Don't say anything until you have a question. This is not a conversation; it's cross-examination."

Sid did not say anything.

"Ready?"

"I'm not saying anything until you question me."

"Hilarious. Do you recall the morning last spring when a UPS truck arrived at your house?"

"Yes."

"And do you recall the driver coming to your door and asking if you were Professor Sidney Cranmer?"

"Yes, I suppose so."

"You suppose so? Didn't he in fact ask you, Professor, whether you were Professor Sidney Cranmer?"

"I don't exactly remember, but I do remember giving him my name."

"Is it your testimony, Professor, that you might have just given him your name without his asking for it? Did you just open the door and say, 'Hi, I'm Professor Sidney Cranmer,' without him saying a word?"

"No, obviously not."

"*Obviously* is a snotty professor's word, Sid. The jury already dislikes you. So we can agree, can't we, that the driver asked whether you were Professor Sidney Cranmer, or words to that effect, and you said 'yes,' just as Agent Crawford—the agent who we now know was posing as the UPS driver—told us you did when he testified?" She raised her voice. "Isn't that correct?"

"I guess."

"You guess? That's brilliant, Sid. We've taken nearly five minutes to establish a point we should have put behind us in fifteen seconds, and your credibility is now in the very low digits."

"Sorry, I'm new at this."

"It's okay. Now, Professor Cranmer, do you also remember that Agent Crawford, in his role as the UPS driver, asked you whether you were expecting a delivery?"

"Sort of."

"Sort of. That's also brilliant, Sid. And please, please, keep your hand away from your mouth. The pope, or the Dalai Lama, or Mother Teresa come back from heaven, would look like a liar if they kept rubbing their upper lip. Do you remember anything about Agent Crawford asking you, in effect, whether you were expecting a package?"

"I think he did."

"Thank you. Now, assuming he asked you, in substance, whether you were expecting a package—as the jury heard Agent Crawford testify to them that he did—is it not true that you responded that, yes, you were expecting a package?"

"I don't think I said that. I think I said it didn't surprise me that a package was arriving or something like that."

"Oh my God. Okay. Stop scratching yourself, Sid. No one ever died of an itch. So you are drawing a distinction between expecting a package, which you don't *think* you said but maybe might have, and not being surprised that a package was arriving, which you think you probably did say, right?"

"I guess."

"You guess. Hands away from your mouth."

Ames knew she was being cruel, but she also knew that this ordeal was nothing compared to what Sid would face if he took the stand in the actual courtroom. The fact was that, one way or another, he was going to have to reveal himself and probably face humiliation whether he pleaded guilty or went to trial and testified. Going to trial and exercising his Fifth Amendment right to remain silent would, in the face of the government's evidence, be tantamount to a plea of guilty with none of a plea's advantages. That option was out.

Ames shifted to the other side of the wingback, the way Campanella would move from one side of the podium to the other, to keep the jury's attention and mark a transition. "I could play with you for another few minutes about your uncertainty about whether you said you were expecting a package, but let's just focus on what you're telling the jury you probably did say. You think you *probably* said that the arrival of this package didn't surprise you? That's your testimony?"

"Yes, that's what I probably said."

"Now, Professor Cranmer, was there any package on its way to you, other than Exhibit One, the DVD that the jury has seen, that it would not have surprised you to receive that morning?"

"I don't understand."

"Well, was there some other package on its way to you, other than this one? Hand, Sid."

"Maybe. From some colleague, or journal, or professional society or something."

"From who? Can you identify anyone else besides Tiger Entertainment that might have had a package on its way to you that morning that you wouldn't have been surprised to receive? At this point, I walk over and pick up the exhibit and wave it in front of the jury."

"I can't give you any name."

"A package that pretty clearly contained a DVD, wouldn't you agree?"

"Yes, but I can't give you a name."

"But we can agree that you said you weren't surprised to receive the package, correct?"

"Correct."

"Uh-huh. Do your colleagues often send you DVDs?"

"It's mostly drafts, or articles . . ."

"Can I have an answer to my question, please? Do your colleagues often send you DVDs?"

"Not really."

Ames clapped her hands together lightly. "Well, let me put it this way. Can you tell the jury any occasion within, let's say, the last ten years when a colleague, or journal, or professional society has sent you a DVD, Professor?"

"I can't think of any right off the top of my head. Maybe once."

"Who sent you that?"

"I can't remember."

"When was it?"

"Maybe seven or eight years ago."

"I see, but you admit, at least, that you said you weren't surprised when this DVD arrived at your house that morning? You admit that?"

"I've said I wasn't surprised several times now."

"Great, Sid. That condescending answer confirms you're a jerk. Professor Cranmer, isn't it true that, about a week earlier, you had filled out this form—here I pick up Exhibit Two and wave it in front of the jury—ordering this DVD—now I'm holding Exhibit One in this other hand—and that is why you were not at all surprised when it arrived that morning? Isn't that just the simple, and as you would say obvious, truth?"

"No, it's not true."

"But you admit you did get the flyer. You remember that? Campanella might not be lucky enough to ask this question, but let's say he does. You remember getting the flyer, right?"

"Yes, I remember getting it."

"But you don't recall what you did with it, do you?"

"I just can't remember."

"You don't remember throwing it away, for example?"

"I may have, but I'm not sure."

"You might have put it aside somewhere?"

"I'm not sure. I might not have gotten around to throwing it out."

"Really. You didn't do what anyone else in your position would have done and tear the sickening thing up and throw it in the trash? You don't remember doing that, do you? I'd object, and Norcross might sustain my objection, but you know, don't you, Sid, exactly what the jury will be thinking?"

"I just don't remember. I can't say I remember something when I don't."

"Ah, the truth thing again. Okay. Let's try another angle." Ames shifted so she was standing in front of the wingback, a little closer to Sid. "You admit that when Agent Crawford handed you the package with the DVD in it, with the name Tiger Entertainment right on the label, you signed for it, and you took it right away, isn't that correct?"

"Right."

"You didn't say, 'Gosh, there's been some mistake, I didn't order anything from Tiger Entertainment. I didn't order any DVD.' You didn't say that, did you?"

"Well, I didn't . . ."

"Thank you. Don't squirm, Sid, when you give up a damaging answer. It just confirms that I had to dig it out of you. And the reason you didn't indicate that there was any mistake was because you had, in fact, ordered something from Tiger Entertainment, and as you said, weren't surprised when it arrived?"

"No."

"I see. But you took the DVD, without any hesitation or questions for Agent Crawford, just signed for it and took it and went back into your house, isn't that right?"

"That's what happened."

"And you got a pair of scissors, or a knife, or some sharp tool, and you immediately, right away, began to open it, because you couldn't wait to see what UPS had brought you? Isn't that true?"

"I wouldn't say I 'couldn't wait.'"

"Oh, I see. You weren't all that eager. But isn't it true that within one minute, or two minutes at the most, after you had the DVD in your hands, you started to open it? Isn't it true that, in fact, you didn't wait?"

"Yes. I started—"

"Eyes up."

"I started to open it right away."

"And when you get something from a colleague, or a journal, or a professional society, do you always get the scissors out and start opening those packages within a minute? Is that your habit?"

"Sometimes I'm busy."

"But this time you certainly weren't busy. You started opening the package within a minute after it was in your hands, correct?"

"Yes. I already said that."

"Please, Sid, for God's sake. You opened it right away, even though you say you never ordered it, but were not surprised to receive it?"

"Yes."

"Sid, you do realize how dead you are by now, don't you?"

"Yes."

"Campanella could sit down right now, and the jury would convict you in fifteen minutes. Two more areas. When you heard the knock at the door, what was the first thing you did?"

"I don't understand."

"When you heard the knock on the front door, when Agent Patterson and his team arrived within a minute or two after the delivery, and began knocking, the very first thing you did, before you went to the door, was hide the DVD in a drawer, right? Isn't that what you did?"

"I wasn't exactly hiding it."

Ames let her voice dip down into a tone of scorn. "Well, you put it in a drawer, right? And you closed the drawer. And when it was in the drawer, the DVD was out of sight. Can we agree on that?"

"Yes, it was out of sight."

"If this was a DVD from a colleague or a journal or a professional society, would you bother sticking it away when you heard someone at the door?"

"I don't know. I guess I didn't want it out."

"You didn't want it out, right. Because you knew exactly what it was, and you didn't want anyone else, any visitor, seeing it. Isn't that true?"

Sid didn't say anything, and Ames continued.

"Okay, final topic. You enjoy looking at pornography, don't you, Professor?"

"God, Linda."

"Trust me, Sid, this question is coming, and you'll be answering it in a room full of people, including a half-dozen reporters. Isn't it true that you enjoy looking at pornography, Professor?"

"Sometimes, yes. Adult pornography."

"Well, your computer hard drive had quite a bit of pornography on it, and it got there because you had been looking at it, right?"

"Yes, at least some of it."

"Some of it, okay. And some of that pornography included young girls, correct?"

"What do you mean, 'young'?"

"Teen stuff. Teen porn sites, advertising models who were quote unquote barely legal. Stuff like that."

"No one underage."

"Really? Then I show you a series of pictures they pulled off your hard drive of some fairly young girls, maybe eighteen or nineteen, but maybe fifteen or sixteen, and I say, 'Recognize these?' They've been downloaded onto your computer for more than a year."

"They all have breasts and pubic hair, Linda. They're not . . ."

"I'm Campanella, remember? And there are fourteen people, twelve jurors and two alternates, listening to every word you say. So, you do admit that these are young girls you actually did look at, right? No question about that."

"Right."

"And you enjoyed looking at them?"

"Yes, I guess."

"You guess. Well, when you're viewing pornography, you like looking at younger girls, isn't that true?"

"Christ, Linda . . ."

"You're telling me you're up for this. You like to look at younger girls, right?"

"Sometimes."

"Okay, younger girls. So let me show you another picture." Ames walked over to the bookcase again. "Where's the good old Cohen biography? Here we go. Give me a sec." She pulled a book out, checked the index, and found the page she wanted. "Okay. How old would you say this girl is?" She held the volume up to Sid, folded open to a page of photographs.

"That's one of Charles Dodgson's photos of Evelyn Hatch taken around 1867."

"That wasn't my question. My question was, how old would you say this girl is?"

"About seven or eight."

"And then I say, let's just put this up on the document camera. Then I display the photograph on the video monitors around the courtroom, so all the jurors can see it, blown up, and then I ask, she's completely naked, right?"

"That's right. Dodgson—"

"Just answer my question, please. She's entirely naked, right?"

"Right."

"No breasts or pubic hair on her, correct?"

"Correct. Linda . . ."

"Just a little more, Sid. And you can see her vagina, right?"

"Well, it's sort of in a shadow, and . . ."

"Would you care to examine that area of the photograph a little closer, Professor? The document camera has a zoom device, so you and the jury can have a closer look. Her vagina is partially exposed, and you can see the fold of one of her labia, wouldn't you agree?"

"Correct. Linda, this is horrible."

"Just a little more. And this little seven- or eight-year-old girl, who is lying completely naked with her vagina partially exposed, is positioned in what art fanciers call an odalisque pose, stretched all the way out with her head propped on her hand. Am I right about that?"

"Yes, Dodgson sometimes posed his subjects like that."

"*Odalisque.* Am I pronouncing that word correctly, Professor Cranmer? This question pins you as someone the jurors will be sure to dislike."

"Can he really do this?"

"If I object, it will just make it worse. So, am I pronouncing *odalisque* correctly?"

"Yes, perfectly correctly, Mr. Campanella."

"Don't spar with him, Sid. You can't win. And the odalisque pose is designed to show off the subject's body, right?"

"Well, I don't know."

"Okay, that's fine. You don't know. But you enjoyed looking at this photograph, didn't you?"

"Well, enjoyed? I don't . . ."

"You've looked at it often, right?"

"Yes, but . . ."

"How many times?"

"I don't know. I can't estimate."

"More than you can estimate, can we agree on that?"

"I guess."

"You'd seen it often enough that you knew right away who it was and when the picture was taken when I showed it to you a minute ago, right?"

"I know, but I wouldn't say I enjoyed looking at this photograph the same way I enjoyed looking at . . ."

"Finish your sentence, Sid."

"The same way I enjoy looking at adult pornography."

"Ugh. You'll never say that, because I'll kill you if you do. Then Campanella might say, 'Let's try it a different way, Professor. Does this photograph of this little seven- or eight-year-old girl, Evelyn Hatch, disgust you, Professor?"

"No, it doesn't disgust me. It's . . ."

"Leave it, Sid. You'll just make it worse. It will certainly disgust most of the jurors, I can promise you that. Okay, then Campanella will pull some contemporary photo off your computer of some child who looks like, or has the same pose as, the Hatch girl and he'll ask you how old the contemporary girl is."

"I can't answer, Linda. We don't have a picture."

"Believe me, the child in the contemporary photo will be around the Hatch girl's age, so you'll say she's seven or eight, too. And then he'll say, and looking at this more recent photograph we took off your computer of a little girl we've identified as, let's say, Sally from Rochester, just as naked, you don't find this photograph disgusting either, do you? It doesn't bother you, does it?"

"Not exactly. It's sort of . . . I don't know what to say."

"Of course you don't. There isn't anything you can say." She flung the Cohen biography down on the wingback. "And that is why you have to take the deal, Sid."

"But how can I get up in court and admit to something I'm not sure I did?"

"Because you'll die telling what you think is the truth, Sid—die alone and in prison—and you can live with just a little white lie."

30

He liked to buy lottery tickets. Once, he'd won $1,000 on a scratch ticket, and he was sure it was a sign that his luck had turned. He'd spent the whole grand on tickets for the giant Mega-Millions drawing, positive that he was going to cash in. During the forty-eight hours before they pulled the numbers, he was so lost in fantasies about what he'd do with his big payoff that he could barely sleep. In the end, he hadn't won. The loss made him so bullshit he needed a whole afternoon shooting squirrels to work off his frustration. But the happy hours he'd had to dream were still great.

The gradual approach of the Columbus Day weekend had been like that. In fact, the pleasure he took in anticipation was, in a way, even more intense. He'd won this lottery before, and he knew just how sweet the payoff was going to be. He hummed to himself—actually hummed!—as he cleaned out the back of his Jeep. The old buggy had a little rust on her, but the cargo area was nice and big, and they were going to need it.

He and his nephew had been texting all morning, and Buddy was going to meet him at the motel and bring the happy powder and the condoms. With all the cameras they had in the pharmacies these days, he didn't like to be the one to pick up the necessaries. He wasn't worried about the girl getting pregnant, but you never knew what these kids had been up to, and he certainly wasn't taking any chances if he played second fiddle behind Buddy.

His nephew had booked the reservation per his instructions, using a false name and a disposable phone—telling the clerk that he had trouble sleeping and needed a room around back, as far away from the other guests as possible. Buddy also had the job of putting down the cash for the room and picking up the key. It was something Buddy always enjoyed because it allowed him to play the sleuth and use one of his outfits.

The plan was to wait until Li'l Sis texted them that she was on her way before giving her the room number. Once she got inside, they'd be sure she didn't make too much noise, just enough for fun.

It was going on eight p.m. and almost dark when he slid into the parking spot below Room 305, at the back of the Ho Jo's. As he made his way up the outdoor stairs to the third floor, he counted only a handful of cars in the lot below. The traffic noise was muffled, and he could make out the chirr of a red-winged blackbird in the ragged field beyond the asphalt. Birds and little girls. He stood for a while on the third-floor balcony, listening. Dusk. It was perfect.

When he got to the room, he found something he didn't like: a folded scrap of paper taped to the door with a note in Buddy's scrawl: "Meeting a Guy. Be Right Back. Rooms Open."

What the hell? Li'l Sis could be texting him any time now, letting him know she was close. This was Buddy to a T. He always put things off too long, and then if there was some hitch, they'd be up the creek. It didn't matter, of course. He could stall Li'l Sis if he needed to. By this time, he could tell her anything, and she'd believe him.

He pushed open the door and went inside. The room was nice and neat, with a big queen-size bed and the smell of some artificial perfume. Was it supposed to be roses? Behind the flower aroma was the scent of a cigarette. Buddy. A sign in the room clearly said NO SMOKING. *He must have stood in the doorway, thinking the smell wouldn't enter the room, the stupid shit. There was a big mirror at the foot of the bed; he liked that.*

The canvas tool kit always went on the floor on the far side of the bed, where it couldn't be seen from the door. He took out the tubes of Vaseline. Then he snipped off three swatches of duct tape—wrists, ankles, and mouth—and hung them on the far side of the nightstand within easy reach. In plain sight at the head of the bed, leaning against the pillows, he placed the large pink teddy bear with the I LOVE YOU!! *T-shirt. Pinkie Bear always got a smile.*

He walked into the bathroom, turned the water on good and hot, soaked a washcloth, and held it over his face to calm himself. His girls had all been different. Each one, after she figured out what was up, had been scared out of her little mind, of course—the blind, helpless terror in their eyes was the biggest turn-on—but each had had her own way of acting her part. One just froze, could hardly open her mouth or make a sound. Another, a smarter one, tried to talk her way out of it by negotiating. If I let you do this, then you'll let me do that, her eyes all the time darting toward the door. Sure thing. His favorite one put up a fight, trying to yell, flinging her arms around, and kicking. Gave him a bloody lip. By the end, she wasn't saying much.

He breathed and examined himself in the mirror. The years were piling up. His face didn't look like he was nineteen, but he'd fixed that. He'd told Li'l Sis he was really twenty-seven and looked a little older. He admitted that he'd lied to her and had sent her a fake picture, but he told her he'd only done it because he loved her so much, couldn't stand to lose her, and after all, he reminded her, she had lied to him, too. It had taken a while, but she'd forgiven him, and now she loved him more than ever. When she saw him "irl," she'd hesitate just long enough for them to get her into the room. After that, they'd keep her quiet, pretty much, and how old he looked wouldn't matter anymore.

The time crawled. He thought about watching TV but decided not to. He sat in the armchair, read a pamphlet about local businesses, drank a glass of water, dabbed up his shirt where he spilled, and paced the floor. He nearly jumped out of his shoes when his cell phone beeped. It was a text from Li'l Sis: "aunt finally left, finally, finally, finally!!! im coming dont hate me r u in the room? i cant wait!!! xxxxxxx ;)"

He quickly texted back: "of course i luv u! its ok im in 305. Cant wait to give you tons of XXXX come quick!!!"

Ten never-ending minutes later, there was a knock on the door. He peeked through the curtain and saw a tall shadow—Buddy, the dick, skidding in at the very last minute. One of these days, he was going to kick that kid's rear end up around his eyelashes.

But when he opened the door, it wasn't Buddy. It was a black guy who obviously had the wrong room. He wasn't scared, just pissed. He didn't need any interruptions at the moment, especially not from some black asshole.

"You got the wrong room, pal."

The man didn't say anything, just limped forward, put out a big hand, and shoved him hard, backward into the room. Trying to get his balance, he tangled himself up in the chair and fell onto the carpet. He hurt his wrist catching himself. As he tried to get up, the black guy shoved him back down so hard his head popped on the floor. What the fuck? Was this a rip-off? Did Buddy set him up?

The black guy was squatting over him now with a knee on his chest, holding out some kind of metal thing that caught the light. Other people were crowding into the room.

"Hello there, 2Kool," the guy was saying. "My name is Li'l Sis. Pleased to meet you in real life." Hands were flipping him over, slamming him onto his stomach, and yanking his arms around his back. "Been looking forward to this." The steel of the handcuffs was icy and bit into his wrists. His heart was slamming away. He couldn't think. He could barely even breathe.

A voice behind him with a Puerto Rican accent. "Hola! Trick or treat bag over here by the nightstand." A disgusted snort. "And some tape, Mike. Nice and handy."

"Get a good shot of it."

"Should I smile?"

The black guy was bending down now, close, an inch from his ear. His breath smelled like steak. "Welcome to our world, punk. Your life is officially over." The voice was deep, very angry. They were going to kill him.

The Puerto Rican man off to the side broke in. "Want to stand him up, Mike?" He could see the tips of the guy's high-tops. Black jeans.

"Don't bother," the deep voice continued. "Just grab his legs there, Jimmy, and we'll throw the son of a bitch off the balcony." He felt hands slipping down under his shoulders, strong fingers hooking into his armpits. "We'll say he was trying to escape."

A man with a Marine crew cut began to pick up him up by his feet. His heart kept banging away like a pile driver, and he heard a high-pitched moan. Was that him? A fart bubbled out of him as he rose into the air.

"Jesus, Henry!" The crew-cut guy was struggling to keep his grip on him. "The fuck you have for dinner?"

Another, shorter man helped out, grabbing his right leg, and the two of them hoisted his lower end together. His top end rose up smoothly, head jammed against the black guy's stomach.

"Upsy-daisy."

"You're going to make an awful mess on the blacktop."

A new voice, higher, "Christ's sake, don't drop him on my van. I just had it detailed."

The two men holding his legs set his feet on their shoulders. They staggered as they moved forward. The black guy shifted him easily, strong fingers digging into him painfully, no problem with the weight.

"Hey!" He barely recognized his own voice, begging, "Come on!"

They cleared the doorway, stepped out onto the balcony, and began to swing up him up over the railing. Somebody said, "One . . . Two!"

The black guy's face, hovering over him, looked evil. They were going to kill him. He managed a scream, not as loud as he wanted.

"H-Help!" He couldn't breathe. His throat was clogged. He could barely move his lips.

"What's the matter, Henry?" Crew-cut, down by his legs, was looking at him with an expression he'd never seen before. A killer's eyes. "Aren't scared, are you?"

"It'll be over in a second. Quick splat, and you're done."

"M-My name's not Henry."

The black guy spoke down to him. "You're all named Henry."

They dropped him abruptly inside the railing. The landing hurt and produced a gray puff of air that smelled like concrete dust. The shorter guy was wiping his hands on the back of his jeans, making a face as though he had touched something filthy.

"What's the matter, Henry? Can't take a joke?"

A shadow fell across his face, and he saw the black cop on one knee looking down at him. The others were standing in the background, hands on their hips.

A blue light was bouncing off the side of the building. In the pale flashes, the faces appeared and vanished, like devils out of some nightmare. He could see they were all still hoping to kill him. What was going to happen? He couldn't stop making little squeaks. Was it him or someone else? The cuffs, mashed between the concrete and the middle of his spine, cut into him.

The deep voice slid into his ear again. "My name is Mike Patterson. I'm a special agent with the FBI. You have certain rights, and I want to be sure you understand them. You have a right to remain silent. Anything you say . . ."

Out of the corner of his eye, in the six inches under the bottom rung of the railing, he could just make out a pickup truck down in the parking lot, rounding the corner of the building. It was Buddy, with his right-front headlight still out. For once in his godforsaken life, the fact that Buddy could never get anywhere on time was working out for him. One of the plainclothes guys was leaning over the balcony, keeping an eye on the lot. Buddy never hesitated, just drove slowly right past the squad cars and the milling cops and on around the far corner, as though he didn't have a thing in the world to worry about.

A glimmer of last-laugh satisfaction flickered across his mind. Buddy was not the brightest bulb on the tree, but he had a fuck-you-all vicious streak that ran deep. He wouldn't appreciate being cheated out of his little fun. Some of these bastards must have kids, and somebody besides him was going to rue this day.

PART THREE

DIRECT AND CROSS

31

You mean, you just let Patterson come in your living room and start asking questions?" Elizabeth couldn't believe it. "And you waited all this time to tell me?"

Elizabeth and Ryan were heading to class, squeezed under a dented umbrella, which protected them hardly at all from the stinging rain. The air was sharp and carried a tang of distant charcoal. The Thanksgiving break was a week away.

When Ryan didn't say anything, she continued, a notch louder.

"And your dad's supposedly a big-shot lawyer? Good grief, Ry, my dad made Cinnamon Toast Crunch, and I know better than that."

"He was only there for, like, two minutes."

"Yeah, but you answered his questions, right?" When Ryan didn't say anything, she went on, increasingly angry. "I gave him the polite kiss-off, Ryan, to protect you. I didn't tell him you'd been at Professor Cranmer's house. I didn't tell him that you saw the flyer, okay? Because I just didn't talk to him."

"I know, and I love you for that, Lib. I really do." Ryan's eyes brimmed with sincerity.

It was true that Ryan did love her, in his way. Elizabeth's birthday had been a good example. He'd arranged a catered dinner at his condo, complete with candelabra, lobster, and two bottles of sparkling wine in an ice bucket. At the end of the meal, he'd blindfolded her, and when he'd slipped off the blindfold, there was her birthday cake, candles ablaze, with a Tiffany-blue box sitting next to it. Inside the box was the most beautiful piece of jewelry Elizabeth had ever seen, a diamond-and-emerald pendant on a delicate silver rope. The pendant was in the shape of a sycamore leaf—the Jaworski tree.

So it was true, yes, that Ryan did love her, sort of. But his version of love hadn't stopped him from showing Ridge the video or snuggling up with his little friend Jackie when he had the chance or lying about the flyer. He'd do anything for her, except be honest.

They walked along in silence under the rain. Most of the trees were bare now, and the sidewalks across campus were a sodden mat of brown and yellow leaves. Elizabeth had been right to grab Sid's pictures. Ryan had obviously ratted the professor out. It was such a shithead thing to do she could hardly believe it.

Ryan stopped, keeping the umbrella over Elizabeth. "Wait a sec, okay?" He looked at the ground, getting himself ready to give one of his speeches. "I'm sorry. I'm really, really sorry." He stared at her, letting the rain trickle down his face. "You're right. I shouldn't have spoken to the FBI guy. I'm just not as smart as you are, Lib. I don't know how to do that thing you do." He scraped a wad of leaves off the walkway with the side of his shoe. "I get freaked out, and I worry about my dad and everything. You saved my ass by not talking to Patterson."

"I did."

"But let's not fight, okay? We fight too much these days. I just . . ." Ryan wiped a hand over his face. "I just want to be like we were."

"Let me think about that." They continued on their way to class, saying hello to an occasional friend. By good luck, no one was going their way. The rain was beginning to let up as they parted for separate classes.

"You keep the umbrella," Ryan said, offering it to her.

"I was planning to, since it's mine." Elizabeth smiled and let her face soften as she gave Ryan a quick kiss.

"Okay, no fighting." She held a finger up under his nose. "But behave yourself, buddy boy. Remember you've got a birthday coming up. We have big plans for you if you're good."

Ryan's face eased into a lopsided smile. "What do you mean 'we'?"

"Just be good, Ry, and you'll find out."

"You know I'm always good, Lib. Really good." His smile broadened, deepening the dimple in his right cheek.

Ryan's birthday, February 12, was still almost three months way, which was fortunate, because Elizabeth needed the time to operationalize her plan to settle up with him. Her scheme might teach Ryan a useful lesson; if it didn't, it would at least get her justice.

The plan had three parts: chemical, logistical, and psychological. She could manage the first two, no problem. The third was tricky, and potentially dangerous, since that portion of the program required Ryan's cooperation, and he had to be kept totally in the dark right up to the big moment.

For the chemical part, Elizabeth would have her lab partner, Chase Bergstrom. Chase was a fellow midwesterner, a brilliant chemist, and a complete nerd. He regularly experimented with various drugs to help with his social awkwardness, and he was the go-to guy for party meds, which he either concocted himself or ordered over the Internet. Chase's transparent crush on Elizabeth made it natural to ask him for help, and she could be sure he'd keep quiet afterward.

To carry out her plan, Elizabeth needed three chemicals. The first, Chase simply "borrowed" from the lab: sixty milliliters of pure alcohol. She might not need it all. Ryan's tolerance for booze was so low that two large glasses of red wine typically had him slurring his speech and making loud, stupid jokes. A flavorless boost, slipped into his merlot while he wasn't looking, would give him three or four glasses in one.

The other two intoxicants, roofies and liquid X, would take more work. Roofies were sold by prescription as Rohypnol, but Elizabeth and Chase referred to them by their chemical name, flunitrazepam, a class of benzodiazepine and the primary ingredient in notorious "rape cocktails." Chase ordered the roofies from Thailand, where they were still available in two-milligram, tasteless, easily dissolvable white tablets, which were illegal in the United States and Europe. Their effect, Chase said, was to induce a kind of pliant automatism and what he called "anterograde amnesia"—meaning that if you popped a couple roofies, you would have trouble, the next day, remembering exactly what had happened.

"Liquid X" was a party drug, sometimes known as "GHB," for gamma hydroxybutyrate, very effective in generating a lust-crazed, anything-goes state of mind. Elizabeth and Ryan had tried a dose once, and the resulting marathon sex had given Elizabeth a urinary tract infection that took two rounds of antibiotics to snuff out.

If the chemical aspect of Elizabeth's plan went right, the overall effect on Ryan would be to reduce him to an extremely horny zombie.

Part two, the logistical element, involved finding a large, high-ceilinged trysting spot, very private, where no one would hear Ryan if he made noise. With some poking around, Elizabeth located an auxiliary garage on the edge of campus, fifty yards down a twisting dirt and gravel road. The Amherst College snowplows were parked on the ground floor, but the second floor was empty except for some equipment covered by a tarp in one corner. The upstairs room had no ceiling, only bare beams exposing the underside of the roof. Best of all, by plan or fluke, the college kept the garage heated, and the rising air made the empty room on the second floor nice and toasty, which was important to Elizabeth's plan.

That left only the challenge of getting her boyfriend's unknowing cooperation. At first, Elizabeth was concerned that she would have only Ryan's impaired judgment and her own resourcefulness to count on. Then, with a lift from whatever gods watch over abused girlfriends, Ryan's handling of her birthday celebration, including the blindfold and the necklace, provided the perfect setup. Now Elizabeth had her own version of Ryan's scenario in mind. With any luck, his twenty-first birthday would be something he would remember for the rest of his pathetic life.

32

As Judge Norcross looked down from the bench at the cast of *United States v. Cranmer*, he became aware of a sensation of relief that he didn't like. In the wake of two continuances requested by the defendant, and a postponement necessitated by a paralyzing sleet storm, Professor Cranmer was finally making it to court to offer his guilty plea.

This feeling of something approaching pleasure was not good. Judges often experienced satisfaction when some contentious piece of litigation resolved, but this case was different. Norcross knew that Professor Cranmer's admission that he had, in fact, ordered the contraband DVD would be gratifying to him personally, and this fact was making him distinctly uncomfortable.

A big part of the judge's ambivalence had to do with how things were going at home. Moving Lindsay and Jordan to Amherst had been a pistol. He didn't know what Ray had said during his "talk" with them, but all through the flight from Washington, Jordan hardly spoke more than three sentences, just stared out the window with her mouth open. And Lindsay didn't utter a single syllable, barely even looked at him. It was as though they were being taken off to be executed. In the coming weeks, Norcross would need to give more of his attention to his nieces, and the removal of the *Cranmer* distraction, he had to admit, would be a big help in that department.

Then there was Claire. She'd responded to the girls' arrival by being incredibly generous and helpful. She'd located an Amherst College freshman to act as an after-school nanny for Jordan, and she'd joined the three of them for several of their awkward dinners. Once, when he and Claire were alone for a few minutes, he'd briefly broken their ban on discussions about *Cranmer* and asked her how on earth she happened to be at the defendant's house during the second search. She'd told him, a little breezily, that it was just a fluke, just one of her occasional visits—Sid was still her friend, after all, and he deserved support—but Norcross had a terrible inkling that something more might be going on. Getting Cranmer's case closed was the only way out of this briar patch.

The judge opened his plea folder and exhaled to allow this tangle of emotions to slide past. In the microgap before his mind shifted entirely to the courtroom, his memory of Claire changed shape and warmed him like a passing burst of sun. She'd stayed at his house over Thanksgiving when Lindsay and Jordan had a trial visit to Washington. This visit hadn't gone well—Ray was rehospitalized shortly after they departed—but it had been a heavenly interlude for Claire and him. They had a lot to be thankful for.

Judge Norcross took a sip of water and moved into his standard plea colloquy.

"Professor Cranmer, we are here this afternoon, as I understand it, to take your plea of guilty to the charge of possessing child pornography. There are some questions I need to ask you and some things I need to be sure you understand."

As he focused more carefully on the professor, Norcross noticed that Cranmer was looking odd, even for him. He'd lost a lot of weight, which was not unusual for a criminal defendant, and his shirt collar was drooping sadly, but what struck Norcross most was the man's posture. Cranmer was sitting, frozen, on the front three inches of his chair, his short body stiffly upright and angled forward. The fingers of his right hand were resting on his upper lip, as though he'd just heard something upsetting or was trying to conceal a burp.

His only moving parts were his two eyes, enlarged by his glasses, which kept flickering up to the bench and then dropping down into the well of the court. His unkempt hair hung over his collar. He looked distinctly creepy and possibly on the verge of a meltdown.

Norcross checked defense counsel for a hint about what might be up with her client, but Linda Ames, her arms comfortably folded, looked unconcerned. From time to time, she glanced without expression over at Cranmer. As Norcross watched, Ames's lips moved, and Cranmer's hand dropped from his mouth into his lap.

To the right, Assistant U.S. Attorney Campanella seemed irritated, or anxious, or both. He was drumming faintly on the table and stroking his goatee. Next to him, Special Agent Patterson exuded boredom, as though he hoped the proceeding would be over quickly so he could go do something more important.

Norcross shoved forward, bringing himself an inch or two closer to the defendant. He tugged his robe back over his knees, so the hem would not snag in the casters of his big leather chair.

"I want you to know that as we go through this process, Professor, you should feel free to speak up if you're not following me. I'll be happy to repeat or explain myself at any time, okay?"

A murmur from Linda Ames prompted a jerky nod from Cranmer. "Okay."

The *Republican* reporter had moved from her usual perch at the right-hand side of the back row of the gallery to the front, directly behind Cranmer. The defendant tended to mumble, and she clearly didn't want to miss anything. A sketch artist sat next to her, working quickly. Once in a while, these drawings would include a depressing likeness of Judge Norcross in the background, making him look older than he felt and grimly pompous. The coverage of Cranmer's plea would definitely be above the fold in tomorrow's paper.

"Same goes if you need to talk to your lawyer. You can confer with Ms. Ames at any time. Just let me know, okay?"

"Okay." Cranmer's voice was a little croaky. Had he been crying? Yelling?

"Now, let me tell you how I go about taking a plea. In a couple minutes, I'm going to ask you to step up into the witness box, over there." Norcross pointed to his left. "Ms. Johnson will place you under oath, and I will have a series of questions for you. A guilty plea generally takes me about half an hour, but we'll take as long as you need, to be sure you know exactly what you're doing. Do you have any questions before we get started?"

"No." Cranmer cleared his throat into his fist. "Nothing so far."

The inflection of Cranmer's answer—the suggestion that he might have questions later—prompted a smothered stiffening in Ames and a twitch from Campanella.

Was Cranmer going to have trouble getting through this? Norcross knew from reading the plea agreement that the government was giving this guy a very, very sweet deal. Was there really any chance that Cranmer would throw a gift like this away, in return for a hopeless trial?

The temptation Norcross sometimes felt in these situations was to hustle the defendant through the guilty plea as quickly as possible to rescue him from his own disastrous reluctance. He generally resisted this urge, and he certainly wasn't going to give in to it today. His written plea script, an outline of reminders he always used in taking guilty pleas, sat squarely in front of him, and he intended to follow it, question by question. Cranmer was going to have to cough everything up, or go to trial, with no special help from him.

"All right, sir, at this stage, I'll ask you to step up into the witness box, please. Raise your right hand. Ms. Johnson will place you under oath."

Cranmer stood mechanically and made his way around the counsel table toward the witness box. Norcross used the time to top off his water, setting the small paper cup to the right of the pretrial services report. It pleased him that the report confirmed Cranmer's good behavior during his home confinement. For all of Campanella's dire predictions at the initial appearance, the decision not to lock him up had been correct.

Ruby Johnson stood and raised her right hand, pronouncing the oath in her elegantly tinted Jamaican accent.

"Raise your right hand, please. Do you solemnly swear that the testimony you will give to this court will be the truth, the whole truth, and nothing but the truth, so help you God?"

"I do."

As Cranmer took his seat and Ruby returned to her desk in front of the bench, the door to the courtroom swung open, and a gaggle of teenagers blundered in, supervised by a stocky, dark-haired woman. Presumably a teacher, she gave an apologetic grimace toward Norcross's end of the courtroom and began shooing the kids onto the pews. Everyone turned to look.

Norcross leaned down and whispered to Ruby. "What do we have here?"

Ruby swiveled in her chair. "Students from Amherst Regional High. Forgot to tell you. Sorry."

"Ah." Then he spoke louder, nodding in the direction of the students. "Welcome." He paused to give them a chance to get settled.

The kids were gawking around, checking out the courtroom. One boy on the end, taller and handsomer than the others, smirked and muttered something to the boy sliding in next to him, who covered his mouth to keep from cracking up. The kid's squinty-eyed amusement was so contagious Norcross felt himself starting to smile, which irritated him. The teacher glared down the row, and both boys stopped fooling around. Norcross pulled out a tissue and began cleaning his glasses.

Kids.

Lindsay and Jordan were basically driving him nuts. Jordan had made a friend at Crocker Farm Elementary, and her stomachaches were less frequent, but she wanted the same thing for dinner every night—spaghetti, nothing but spaghetti. She was going to end up with scurvy if he couldn't get some fruits and vegetables into her. Out of the blue, it occurred to Norcross that she might tolerate spinach ravioli, and he jotted a note to himself on his yellow pad.

Lindsay, most of the time, was a force of gloom that hung over everything. She appeared to hate Amherst High and barely talked to him. He'd had to negotiate a rule about using her phone when they were eating dinner. No more than two texts. The judge was concerned, at first, that the group of students in his courtroom might include Lindsay, but she was not there. Some of them might know her, though, and presumably, they'd be reporting back on his performance.

"My first question for you, Professor, has to do with the fact that you have just sworn to tell the truth. Do you understand, sir, that if you deliberately lie to me in response to one of my questions, you can be prosecuted for perjury?"

Cranmer's hand began to float toward his mouth, but he caught himself and lowered his fingers to the top of the witness box.

"Yes, I understand." Cranmer cleared his throat again. "I certainly have no intention . . ." He looked over at Ames. "I certainly understand that I have to be completely truthful."

"Good. Now I want to move on to what you will be giving up if you do plead guilty. You have certain rights at this moment that will be gone in twenty minutes or so, if you carry on with your intention to plead. I'm going to spell these rights out for you now."

"Okay."

"First of all, you have a right to a trial. If you choose to exercise that right, your trial will take place in the courtroom we're in now. It will be prompt and public. Your jury will sit over there. . . ." Norcross gestured toward the oak-veneered jury box to his right. "And the witnesses will testify from the witness box where you are sitting now."

"Okay."

Cranmer seemed to be relaxing a little—probably experiencing the usual transition from the hairy prospect of doing something to actually beginning to do it.

It occurred to Norcross that, once Cranmer's plea was in, he might give Claire a call and invite her out to dinner after work. They wouldn't mention the case, of course, but she'd probably know what had happened through the Amherst College grapevine. The thought of this very pleasant possibility hit a bump when he remembered he'd have to come up with some last-minute arrangement for Jordan and Lindsay if he wanted to get away. Lindsay could manage on her own, but she resented babysitting Jordan, and he hated the thought of dealing with her mood of grievance. His brief, happy dream fluttered off.

"At this trial you'd have the right to be present, and to see and hear all the witnesses against you. Do you understand this?"

"Yes."

As he ran down the first page of his notes, the judge wondered fleetingly whether Professor Cranmer enjoyed the same consolation and release from looking at his grotesque videos that he and Claire did from their times together. Of course, it couldn't be remotely the same. He dismissed the idea and turned the page.

"You'd have the right to the assistance of your attorney throughout the trial and the right to have your attorney question all the witnesses offered by the government." He raised his voice. "Everybody okay back there?"

The clique of students farthest from the teacher had been elbowing one another and passing a note, provoking faint titters. The kid on the far end gave Norcross a smart-aleck grin and held a thumbs-up, letting the judge know that, at least for him, everything was peachy.

Norcross turned to the teacher. "After this proceeding, my clerk can bring you all back to chambers for a few minutes, if you have time. I'd be happy to answer questions if your students have any."

Ames, Campanella, Patterson, the reporter, the sketch artist, and even the two or three spectators in the courtroom all turned, following Norcross's look, and stared at the students. They'd heard the giggling as well, and like Norcross, they didn't seem to appreciate it.

Patterson's eyes stayed on the kid at the end of the row for a few extra seconds. The silence in the courtroom deepened.

The teacher, Norcross noted now, had a stripe of pearl gray in the part of her dark brown hair. She stood with a slight grimace, pulling herself up on the pew in front of her. She must have been pretty once.

"Thank you, Your Honor." The expression in her large eyes was grateful but tired. "That is very generous of you. Unfortunately, we may have to slip away. Our van is . . ."

"No problem," Norcross said. "If you have to go, please make your exit as quietly as possible."

Is this what being around kids did to you? Made you secondary? An aging facilitator of their pushy lives? After the death of his wife, the possibility of children seemed unjustifiably risky. Now it struck Norcross that, even at its best, parenthood must be dreary and exhausting a lot of the time. And this is what Claire wanted, soon, as a condition to marriage? These thoughts, once more, flew by swiftly—sparrows shooting past a murky window.

He turned to Cranmer, who'd also been looking at the students.

"All right." Norcross hiked himself up. "Let's resume. As I was saying . . ."

The standard language of the plea colloquy unfolded smoothly: the defendant's right to choose whether he would, or would not, testify; the fact that the jury would be instructed not to hold it against him if he remained silent; the burden on the government to convince twelve jurors unanimously, beyond a reasonable doubt, in order to secure a conviction.

"Do you understand, sir, that if you plead guilty, you will be waiving, meaning giving up—"

Cranmer broke in with something Norcross did not catch.

"Excuse me?"

"I understand what *waiving* means."

"Fine. Do you understand that if you plead guilty you will be waiving all the rights I just described?"

"Yes."

"Do you understand that if you plead guilty, there will be no trial, no witnesses, and no burden on the government to prove you guilty?"

"Yes."

"Have you had sufficient time to discuss this plea with your attorney, Ms. Ames?"

"More than enough. Time hasn't been the problem."

"And are you satisfied with the representation Attorney Ames has given you?"

Cranmer looked over at his lawyer, then returned to the judge and nodded. "Yes, she's been very patient. She's been super."

Cranmer was continuing to defrost. This was good. Judge Norcross moved forward, maintaining the steady pace, keeping the questions and answers rolling.

"Have you been seeing a doctor for any reason?"

Cranmer hesitated, glancing over at the reporter. "Yes, uh . . ." He sighed. "I see a psychiatrist once a week. Nothing other than that."

"Has this psychiatrist prescribed any medication for you?"

"At first, yes, something for . . . I forget. I haven't needed it for the past couple months."

"Do you feel okay at this moment? Are you having any trouble understanding what is going on here?"

"No, I'm fine." Cranmer twitched and snorted out something like a pained laugh. "I mean, I'm not all that fine, to tell the truth. I'd prefer to be just about anywhere else. But I'm physically and mentally okay, more or less."

"It's natural to be nervous. We'll take our time to make sure you're following everything." Norcross turned over another page. The kids in the back of the courtroom had settled down. The one on the end was looking up at the clock. The plea colloquy was about a fourth of the way through.

"Has anyone threatened you, or any member of your family, in order to pressure you into pleading guilty?"

It was a standard question, straight from the outline, but it seemed to buffalo Cranmer. He started to answer, stopped, and stared blankly at the judge for a few seconds. Then he looked down, peering at a spot inside the witness box next to his right foot, as though he might find an answer to Norcross's question there. The judge let the silence draw out for fifteen or twenty seconds—a long time in a hushed courtroom—and was just about to repeat his question when Cranmer looked up.

"I don't exactly know what you mean by 'pressure.'"

"Has someone tried to force you to plead guilty against your will by using threats of any kind?"

"My lawyer and I . . ." Cranmer glanced over at Ames, who maintained her poker face. "We discussed the consequences, you know, of my *not* pleading guilty. They looked really bad. I don't know if that counts as pressure."

Cranmer's uncertainty was plausible, but picky. Too much formal education and too little common sense sometimes gave a defendant like Cranmer problems entering into the alternate universe of the courtroom. Pressure in the context of a plea proceeding didn't mean the same thing as pressure in the real world. Most defendants, even those who'd never graduated from high school, knew this instinctively. Norcross brought an edge into his voice, his no-playing-games tone.

"Every defendant, Professor, has to choose whether to plead guilty or to put the government to its proof at a trial. As with most decisions, there are pluses and minuses depending on which alternative you opt for. The process of making this particular choice is bound to be difficult. That's not the kind of pressure I'm talking about."

The atmosphere in the courtroom had tightened. The reporter was writing, quickly but soundlessly. None of the kids was squirming.

"When I say *pressure*, I'm referring to some external physical threat, or economic threat, or threat to your reputation perhaps, or a threat to harm someone dear to you. What I'm talking about is some effort to put you in fear in order to compel you to do something you wouldn't otherwise do. Have you been threatened in that way?"

There was another pause while Cranmer checked on his shoe again. Finally, he looked up. "No, I guess, not that kind of threat. No."

It was impossible to tell whether this answer meant that Cranmer truly didn't feel pressured or was merely giving up and accepting the meanings that words took on in the world of the courtroom. Whatever intent was behind his answer, the words on the transcript would suffice to satisfy the court of appeals that Cranmer's guilty plea was not the result of any improper arm-twisting, physical or psychological—at least not the type that might prompt a reversal and remand. That hurdle was behind them, and they could move on.

"I guess my next question sums it up, Professor. Is your plea of guilty here this morning entirely free and voluntary?"

Cranmer was staring again, and another long pause ensued. "May I talk to my attorney?"

Judge Norcross peered down at Linda Ames, who did not look remotely bothered. "Ms. Ames, would you like a short recess?"

Ames stood and shook her head. "I don't think we'll need one. If I could approach the witness box?"

After getting permission, Ames walked over to Cranmer. Norcross tapped a corner of the display on his video monitor to turn on the white noise—his clerks called it his "whoosher"—to allow Ames and Cranmer some privacy. Trying not to stare, the judge busied himself reordering his sentencing script and tearing a page off his bench calendar. AUSA Campanella sighed, looked up at the ceiling, and shook his head.

As far as Norcross could tell out of the corner of his eye, Cranmer was doing most of the talking, leaning to the side and partially turning his back to Norcross. Behind the gush of the audio camouflage, indistinguishable murmurs floated up to the bench. Ames, after listening without expression for about thirty seconds, put her hand on Cranmer's shoulder, dropped her head, and said something back to him. Cranmer spoke more briefly and nodded.

Ames nodded back, turned to the bench, and raised her hand. Norcross switched off the white noise.

"We're all set," Ames said.

"Very good." Norcross let Ames return to her seat and relaunched. "For the record, the defendant has consulted privately with counsel for approximately a minute. Professor Cranmer, are you satisfied that you've had a sufficient time to speak with your attorney?"

"Yes. Thanks. Thank you."

"And are you ready to resume?"

"I am now. Thanks."

"Is your plea of guilty here this morning entirely free and voluntary?"

"Yes. What I'm doing is entirely free and voluntary."

Another check in the box for the court of appeals.

"Okay. We'll move now to the next portion of this proceeding. I'm going to be asking you, Professor Cranmer, whether you did, in fact, commit the crime that you propose to plead guilty to. I do this in every case, because I would not want a defendant to plead guilty to a crime he did not commit. Do you understand?"

Cranmer took a deep breath and let it out. "Okay."

Norcross slipped a document out of his file and prepared to read from it. "The superseding information against you, as I mentioned before, charges knowing and intentional possession of child pornography. We will be going over your plea agreement in a moment, but my understanding is that, if you plead guilty to this charge and agree to the imposition of the sentence described in the agreement, the government, in return, will dismiss all the other charges contained in the original indictment. Is that your understanding, Professor?"

"Yes. My lawyer has been over that with me many times now." He glanced at Linda Ames, who cocked her head to one side without changing expression.

"Okay. So the substituted charge against you is as follows." Norcross nodded down at Cranmer, careful to make eye contact. "It's a little long, so stay with me, okay?"

"I'll try." The judge could see Cranmer start to hazard a smile and stop himself.

"Okay. On or about May 17, of this year, in Amherst, within the district of Massachusetts, you did knowingly and intentionally possess one or more matters containing visual depictions that had been transported in interstate commerce"—Norcross paused, looked sharply at Cranmer, and continued—"the production of which involved the use of a minor engaging in sexually explicit conduct, all in violation of 18 United States Code Section 2252(a)(4)(b)."

A shuffling in the back of the courtroom told him the students were preparing to leave.

As requested, they were moving discreetly. When he glanced up, he saw the kid on the end, whose antics had been so annoying, lingering in the doorway with an intrigued expression. The situation had gotten his attention. Law school in his future maybe?

Norcross returned to the text. "The material knowingly and intentionally possessed by you portrayed sadistic and masochistic conduct and other depictions of violence and involved a prepubescent minor under the age of twelve years. The charged material you knowingly and intentionally possessed included, among other material, an approximately twenty-seven-minute DVD, entitled 'Playing Doctor,' which you had knowingly and intentionally obtained by placing a written order into the United States mail approximately one week earlier, on or about May 10."

Norcross lifted his head from the document and faced Cranmer, deliberately looking into his eyes to make sure that the defendant understood exactly what he was asking. "Now, Professor Cranmer. Are you pleading guilty because you did, in fact, commit this crime?" It was a simple question, but it was the critical point for the record.

The kid was still standing just inside the doorway, looking over at Cranmer. The teacher had the door propped open with her foot and was waiting for him with a long-suffering expression.

After a short pause, Cranmer nodded. "The DVD came to my house, yes. And I possessed it, knowingly and intentionally. I put it in a drawer, which is where they found it."

Campanella swiveled his head sharply and gave a hard look at Ames, half angry, half inquiring. Ames ignored him, keeping her eyes on her client, but Norcross noticed a pale shadow bobbing along her jaw. Attorney Ames was grinding her teeth. The kid in the doorway turned and held his pointer finger up to the teacher.

"Right, Professor." Norcross spoke with calculated patience. "You're saying that you knowingly and intentionally possessed the physical object, the DVD. But for you to be guilty of this crime, you must have knowingly and intentionally possessed the child pornography. You must have known that the DVD contained the contraband, prior to, or at, the time it was seized. You must have knowingly possessed the illicit material itself."

"Well, Your Honor, I didn't, you know, actually have time to look at it before . . . you know . . ." Cranmer's tone, to Norcross, seemed to be verging on the sarcastic. Time to take control.

"I'm aware of that. The government charges, however, that you knew the contents of the DVD because you had ordered it. You knew when it arrived that it contained child pornography, and you intentionally possessed that child pornography, knowing what it was."

"Well, I guess there could have been something else on the DVD. What I'm saying, Your Honor . . ."

"There was also, according to the record, considerable additional child pornography on the hard drive of your computer, clearly evidencing—"

"What I'm saying, Your Honor," Cranmer interrupted the judge, something Norcross always resented, and then compounded this sin by speaking slowly, as though the judge was a student who needed to be led by the hand, "is I knowingly and intentionally possessed the DVD. I did that." He put his hand up to his mouth for a moment, then dropped it. "What happened before that, I'd been going through a tough time, and my memory is not that . . . you know." Cranmer trailed off, apparently seeing something in the judge's face.

Judge Norcross prided himself on never getting angry in the courtroom, or at least never showing it. In nearly five years, he had avoided losing his temper. But he could feel the inkling of fury starting at the back of his head and beginning to sweep up over the top of his skull. This man, this college professor who took pleasure in watching a small child being raped and tortured, who'd been ready to pay money to support the people who'd made the video, this man who was getting the deal of a lifetime, was actually trying to bandy words with him.

Norcross felt his face growing warm and was on the point of speaking when Ames eased up onto her feet.

"May I request a recess, a short recess?" She spoke without any trace of annoyance. "My client is a little confused. It's definitely my fault, Judge, and I apologize. If I could just have a few minutes, I know we can straighten this out."

AUSA Campanella leaned back in his chair and folded his arms across his stomach in disgust. The door to the courtroom closed. The kid was gone.

Norcross did not bother to hide the irritation in his voice. "The court will be in recess. Let Ms. Johnson know when, and if, your client is ready to resume."

33

Lindsay Norcross sat in an Adirondack chair on the stone terrace behind her uncle's house, feet propped up on a small bench. A boy sitting next to her, a skinny classmate named Bobby, handed her a joint, and she took a hit. The third member of their group, Bobby's friend Candace, was pacing around the terrace, peering in through the big French doors.

"Nice house." Candace leaned against the glass, shading her eyes to get a better look.

The day was overcast, like most of December, but the clouds had thinned and the afternoon air had lost its bite. Lindsay was comfortable sitting with her parka open. Marlene, Lindsay's sidekick and confidante, was haunch-down in her perennial spot next to Lindsay's chair, keeping an eye out for squirrels. Lindsay stroked the dog's thick neck, took another drag, and blew the smoke out. Jordan was away at her little pal's house, the nanny had the day off, and Uncle Dave would not be home until dinnertime.

Lindsay passed the joint back to Bobby. He spoke over his shoulder. "Don't be nosy, Candace. Come over here and sit down. Be a courteous guest or we won't get invited back."

The breeze came in soft, wet licks, doing little to carry away the smoke. If the aroma lingered, and Uncle Dave asked what the smell was when he came home, Lindsay would just lie. He probably wouldn't notice. A lot of things went past him, such as Lindsay's habit of cutting school in the afternoon now and then. Candace had a car and was happy to give people rides. This was the first time Lindsay had asked them to stick around.

"So how'd you meet this guy?" Bobby started to hand the joint back to Candace. She was a very petite black girl, barely five feet tall. Her father taught Italian at Smith College.

Candace waved the joint away. "Stopped smoking last summer." She plopped into the chair on the other side of Bobby. "It was stunting my growth."

Lindsay smiled. It felt good to relax a little, even if it was just the punch of the weed loosening her bolts. If she got caught, she'd tell Uncle Dave that she wasn't getting high; she was self-medicating.

"So how'd you meet this guy?" Bobby asked again.

Lindsay looked up at the cottony sky. "Met him in the 'Party Time' chat room."

"Oh wow." Candace twisted to look over at Lindsay. "Drop that dude." She put her hand on Lindsay's arm. "Seriously, Linds. P.T. is bad shit."

"The guy seems okay." Lindsay sounded tired and distant even to herself, and she made an effort to perk up. "He has this old pickup, and he wants to show me around some afternoon." She scratched the top of Marlene's head absently. "He sent me a picture. Him and his cute little truck. Now he wants me to send him one."

Bobby snuffed out the joint on the wet terrace and popped the roach into his mouth. "Bad idea." He chewed and ran his tongue around his teeth. "Really bad idea, Lindsay."

"Sometimes bad ideas feel good." Lindsay reached inside her parka and kneaded the skin under her arm. "I doubt I'll do it."

"I wouldn't," Candace said.

Bobby sighed. "At least for me, most of the time a bad idea is just a bad idea."

For a while, nobody spoke. They sat, tilted backward by the angle of the chairs, looking at the tops of the trees at the far edge of the lawn. Blue jays were making a racket somewhere off in the woods.

Finally, Bobby brought up a new topic. "It sucks they suspended Mr. Scanlon."

Candace squirmed forward in her Adirondack chair. She had to bend her toes down to reach the ground. "It totally stinks. I love Latin."

"Me too," Lindsay said. "I like how it fits together."

"Now they'll have to get a substitute."

Bobby shrugged. "Nothing they can do. Somebody said he was up to something. Once that happens, they have to investigate. It's the law."

"Do they know who complained?"

Bobby looked at Lindsay and raised his eyebrows. He knew, but he wasn't telling.

"It's like that case your uncle has," Candace said. "The porn professor. It's in the paper all the time. Ms. Cooper took her class to watch."

"Yeah," Lindsay said. "I heard."

"I wouldn't want to be a judge." Bobby shook his head. "Couldn't do that."

Marlene had been making muffled squeaks and shifting her front feet back and forth as a squirrel crept farther into the backyard. Now she suddenly bolted across the lawn. The squirrel took off into the brush and Marlene crashed in afterward.

"You go, girl!" Candace laughed, clapping her hands. She grinned over at Lindsay. "Awesome dog!"

"Very cool." Lindsay looked at Bobby, who was slapping his pockets and squirming around. "What are you hunting for there?"

"Trying to find my other joint." Bobby was getting frustrated. "Problem is, you have all these stupid pockets in the wintertime." He shook his head and sat back. "I give up."

"Where do you buy?" Lindsay asked.

"Don't buy at school," Candace said. "They'll kick your butt out."

Bobby laughed. "There's this sort of totally insane wacko sinister dude at the Holyoke Mall who has amazing product."

Candace broke in. "You have to come with us sometime. He's . . ."

At that moment, they heard a car door slam, and they all jumped. Marlene's performance with the squirrel must have masked the sound of the car's approach. They also heard crying.

Lindsay sat up with a worried expression. "It's Jordan. Crap. She's home early."

At that moment, Claire walked around the back of the house, cradling a bag of groceries in one hand and resting the other on Jordan's shoulder. Lindsay, Bobby, and Candace just froze, and Claire stopped, pulling her chin in, as astonished as they were. Marlene pranced down the lawn, wagging her tail ecstatically.

Lindsay stood. "Hey. What's up, Jord?" She kept one hand on the Adirondack chair to steady herself.

Claire's face was not friendly. "Jordan's having a tough afternoon." She shoved the dog back with her foot. "Okay, Marlene."

"We're supposed to have costumes," Jordan said. Her face was streaked with tears, and her voice was scratchy. "For the holiday pageant. Brianna's aunt is making her one. Mom always . . ."

Lindsay felt like a complete asshole. She could see all this stuff moving back and forth across Claire's face. Claire was struggling about Jordan—trying hard to figure out what to do—and now she was also getting really pissed about the weed. The smell of it was strong. You could see she knew exactly what they'd been up to, and it was just too much for her.

Lindsay walked over, stooped, and gave Jordan a hug.

"Hey, it's okay." She pointed toward the house. "There's raisin cookies."

Jordan shook her head, angry. "I just want to read my book." Her voice rose. "I don't want to talk to anybody." She turned abruptly, sniffling, and stalked into the house. Over her shoulder, she called out, almost yelling, "And you smell funny!"

Bobby and Candace said their good-byes and took off pretty quickly. As they hurried around front, they called out "nice to meet you," trying to sound all friendly, but in a way, that showed they knew Claire had picked up on everything. Lindsay wasn't sure how horrible all this was going to get, but it seemed like it might be bad.

"So," Claire said as Lindsay followed her into the house. She clunked the bag of groceries onto the counter. "Cutting school for a little pot break."

Lindsay didn't say anything, just stood watching Claire while she unpacked the bag. In the silence, the sound of the boxes and bottles hitting the counter—the different drawers and the door to the refrigerator banging open and closed—seemed especially loud. Lindsay thought about taking off to her room, but somehow she couldn't bring herself to do it. It would look as though she didn't care what Claire thought, and she did.

After she unloaded everything, Claire took her time carefully folding up the brown paper shopping bag and putting it in the recycling tub under the sink. When that was all over, she stood bracing her arms against the counter. She blew a strand of hair out of her eyes.

"Whew."

"Sorry about Jordan. Mom always made the costumes. It was, like, a thing."

"Uh-huh. It wasn't just the costume. Something else happened at Brianna's that got Jordan upset."

"What?"

"I don't know." Claire's mouth turned down. She pointed with her thumb at the backyard. "But we sure didn't need to come home to that." She paused and then hurried on, a little louder. "You know, Lindsay, I have no idea what I'm supposed to do here. Should I tell your uncle? What would you do if you were in my position?"

Lindsay rubbed under her armpit again. It ached. "I don't know."

"How stoned are you?"

Lindsay shrugged. "Not too."

"I need to go upstairs to check on Jordan. Can I trust you to chop salad?"

The atmosphere lightened a bit. Claire was probably not going to start screaming at her or anything. Lindsay nodded and took a chance at a half smile. "I can give it a try."

Claire switched on the oven to preheat. Lindsay got out a knife. A cucumber and a red pepper sat on the counter. It helped to have something to do.

"The lettuce is in the fridge," Claire said.

Lindsay felt like she ought to say something. As Claire started upstairs, she called out, "So what's for dinner?" She did her best to sound normal.

Claire called back over her shoulder. "Still working on that. I can tell you one thing. It sure as hell isn't going to be spaghetti."

34

Henry's real name turned out to be George Underwood. Within a few days of Underwood's arrest, Assistant U.S. Attorney Paul Campanella had Mike Patterson on the witness stand before the Springfield Grand Jury, recounting under oath his impersonation of Li'l Sis and the takedown of Underwood at the Ho Jo's. Campanella was pleased to see that Patterson's testimony about the duct tape and lubricant had the grand jurors looking sick, scared, enraged, or some combination of all three. After a very short deliberation, they returned a four-count indictment charging Underwood with attempted interstate travel for the purpose of engaging in illicit sexual conduct with a minor, attempted use of a facility of interstate commerce to entice a minor to engage in criminal sexual activity, attempted sexual exploitation of a minor, and possession of material involving the attempted sexual exploitation of a minor. In addition to the chat-room transcripts and the evidence found at the motel, a search of Underwood's lakefront home in Vermont uncovered a load of child pornography on his laptop and other encrypted material on thumb drives that the FBI's tech staff was still trying to crack into.

A week after the grand jury returned the indictment, Underwood appeared for his initial appearance before Judge Norcross with his attorney, a Greenfield lawyer named Alan Spade. Campanella wasn't surprised when Spade did not contest the government's motion for pretrial detention. Underwood faced a minimum mandatory prison term of ten years and a sentencing guideline range of 324 to 405 months. Spade was no Linda Ames, but he could add two and two. The judge's body language during Campanella's summary of the evidence against the defendant made it clear that any effort to get Underwood released now would be a waste of Spade's credibility. Daniel Webster himself, come down from heaven with the tongue of an angel, wouldn't be able to talk Norcross into letting Underwood out for five minutes.

After the hearing, as the deputy marshals were taking Underwood away in cuffs, Campanella was pleased to find Spade coming up to him.

"If you've got a second, I thought we might chat." Spade was a pleasant-looking man with wire-rim glasses and thinning red hair who'd picked up his dad's small-town law practice and had done well in the twenty years since. Reputation in the western Massachusetts legal community counted for a lot, and the word on Spade was basically good. He might not have Ames's fire, but he was a hard-working, decent guy who was known to use his spare time raising money for the United Way and the local women's shelter.

Campanella shrugged. "Sure." He glanced back at Patterson. "Got a couple minutes, Mike?"

"Fine."

"I was thinking." Spade turned to watch as the marshals escorted his client from the courtroom down to the basement lockup. He dropped his voice. "I was thinking, since George is here, we might have him join us to talk about a possible proffer. We can't commit to anything, but, you know . . ."

Patterson sniffed. "Better be a hell of a proffer."

Spade gave a short laugh and scratched the back of his head. "He's up the creek, Mike. I admit that. I'd like him to hear what you might do for him." He gave another nervous laugh. "Or *to* him."

Campanella broke in sharply. "I'm happy to talk, Alan, but you need to know that this is not a case where we're going to be generous."

"I understand. But I think George may have some information you might be interested in. He could help himself out here and make life easier for all of us. Problem is, he's not listening to me much right now."

Patterson began to say something, but Campanella broke in. "Fine. Like I say, we're happy to talk." Campanella snapped his briefcase closed. "I'll ask the marshals to bring your guy up once they've booked and fingerprinted him."

While they waited in the U.S. attorney's conference room on the third floor, Campanella used the time to probe just how spongy Spade's position was. Patterson sat in as a resource, in case Campanella needed reminders about details of the investigation.

After the usual chitchat—an imminent snowstorm and the distraction of the upcoming holidays—Campanella got to the point he was most interested in.

"We know George had an accomplice, Alan." He leaned back and folded his arms. "Somehow he slipped away. What was the vehicle, Mike?"

"Dark Chevy or Ford pickup." Patterson was wearing an especially ominous version of his game face.

"If your client wants to help himself, the best thing he could do is tell us who this other character was." When Spade hesitated and looked confused, Campanella pursued. "Look. You've got kids. My little guy just turned three." He tipped his head toward Patterson. "Mike's got teenagers, heaven help him." This got a very brief smile from Spade, but no change of expression from Patterson. "Somebody is out there, Alan, somebody local, and he's still on the prowl. We need to get him off the street."

Spade looked lost. "This is news to me, Paul. George tells me he was acting alone." Patterson rolled his eyes at the ceiling, broadcasting his "tell-me-another-one" look. Spade's voice went up a notch. "I'm not kidding. That's what he said. I mean I can—"

Patterson blew out a breath. "Well, then, he's a damn—"

Campanella broke in. "Then he's not telling the truth, Alan." He leaned forward, folding his hands on the table. "We know he was working with someone else. Mike's guys found his note in the wastebasket."

"It wasn't the cleaning lady." Patterson glared at Spade. "Your guy's bullshitting you."

"And somebody else picked up the key," Campanella added.

Spade responded a little aggressively. "You check the desk clerk?"

"Yeah," Patterson said. "And she remembered some guy with a bushy beard, obviously false, and dark glasses. Big help."

As Patterson spoke, the door opened, and one of the agents from the raid team brought Underwood inside, holding him by his upper arm. It took a minute for the cuffs to be removed and for Underwood to take a seat next to his attorney. He rubbed his wrists and looked nervously around the table.

"Hi." His eyes struck Patterson and bounced over at Spade. "You didn't tell me he was going to be here." He nodded at Patterson. "Last time I saw him . . ."

"Calm down, George. We're just here to talk."

The escort agent said, "Jack and I will be outside if you need anything." He stepped from the room and closed the door.

The truly scary thing about George Underwood was how ordinary he looked. He had a large head, with a prominent slightly hooked nose, and his black hair was slicked straight back. Old fashioned, Clark Kent–style black frame glasses, slightly askew, perched on his nose. About Campanella's age, he had a moist, flabby mouth like an oyster.

As Campanella stared at him, trying not to imagine the things this guy had been up to, Underwood seemed to notice. He ran a pink tongue around his lips, pushed his glasses up, and looked around. "Well, here we are, I guess."

Spade put his hand on Underwood's shoulder, squeezed it, and left it there while he spoke. "George, I don't want you to do any talking, okay? Like I told you, you're in a hell of a mess here. You know it, I know it, and they know it." Spade pulled a pen from his suit jacket pocket and scribbled something on his yellow pad. "I want you to listen to Mr. Campanella. After he talks, I may have some questions, but we'll need to work out some formalities—okay?—some paperwork, before you start saying anything. So just listen. Understand?" Spade dropped his hand and turned to Campanella and Patterson.

"I got it." Underwood rubbed his hands together and peered over his glasses at Patterson, still nervous. "At least I'm alive, right? Which is more than he—"

"Okay, George." Spade gave his client a sharp look. "Enough."

"Refuse to lose." Underwood spoke under his breath, half laughing.

"Excuse me?" Patterson sat up and leaned forward.

"Well, okay." Underwood sighed. "Refuse to lose any more than I have to."

"George, just listen, okay?" Spade was getting annoyed.

"Sorry." Underwood pushed his glasses up again, licked his lips, and drew a finger across his mouth. "I'll zip it."

Patterson had gone dead still. His face was blank, but Campanella could sense the surge coming off him, expanding into the room. Even Spade caught the vibration and looked with a puzzled expression at Patterson, who seemed to be getting larger. Only Underwood appeared oblivious, darting his head around anxiously and squirming in his chair.

"Okay, Mr. Underwood. As I was just telling your lawyer, the first thing we're interested in is the identity of the man, or possibly men, who . . ."

Patterson spoke in a growl, hardly moving his lips. "Taisha Steptoe." Underwood's head twitched over to Patterson. His mouth dropped open and sagged.

Neither the name, nor what Mike might be up to, made much sense to Campanella, and he couldn't help resenting the intrusion. They could make some progress here if there were no distractions. Was Patterson trying out some hard-ass interview technique they'd taught him at the academy?

Campanella pushed on. "Now we know from this note"—he pulled the document, which was stored in a plastic sleeve, out of his file and slid it into the middle of the table where Underwood and Spade would be able to see it—"that someone was with you, George. We know that, okay?"

Patterson spoke again, raising his voice only slightly and staring intently at Underwood.

"Allison Wozniak."

Underwood's mouth quivered. He tilted toward his lawyer, on the point of speaking, but Spade ignored him and spoke to Patterson.

"What's going on here, Mike?"

Patterson did not turn his head away from Underwood, still speaking in a low tone, but now with a distinct edge of menace.

"Amber Cohen."

Patterson was leaning halfway across the conference table toward Underwood. He looked as though he were about to reach out and grab the man around the throat.

"Get me out of here," Underwood said, jamming his chair back against the wall to stay out of Patterson's reach.

To Campanella's amazement, Patterson leaned farther toward Underwood, slammed his open hand down on the table, and shouted, "Where are they, you piece of shit?"

Spade stuck a protective arm in front of Underwood and shouted, nearly as loud as Patterson, "Hey, back off!"

The door opened and the escort agent poked his head in, looking worried.

"Did you throw them in the lake?" Patterson said savagely, gesturing at the north wall. "We'll drag the lake. Where are they? I've got six parents who—"

Underwood clutched at his attorney's arm. "Get me out of here, Alan."

Spade stood up. "This conference is over." He turned to Campanella. "I came here in good faith. I didn't—"

"Look at his face!" Patterson stood, gigantic, jamming his finger down at Underwood, who was struggling up out of his chair. "Look at him sitting there! It's written right on his goddamn face. Three girls. Three, at least!"

"We're done." Spade grabbed his client under the shoulder, pulled him up, and began hauling him toward the door. Underwood raised two hands up to the side of his face, blocking out the sight of Patterson, muttering, "He's going to kill me. He's going to kill me."

The escort agent glanced at Patterson and reached around to retrieve the cuffs from his belt.

Campanella now suddenly recalled the phrase "refuse to lose," and said, "Okay, Mike, I get it. Take it easy!"

But Patterson was scrambling around the table, snatching chairs out of the way, chasing after Spade and Underwood as they retreated toward the door. One chair banged against the wall and fell over. It actually looked as though he was about to lunge at Underwood.

Now it was Campanella's turn to shout. "Mike! Come on!" He lowered his voice and spoke to where Spade stood in the doorway. "Your pal's hiding a lot more than the name of some accomplice, Alan." He pointed to Underwood. "Talk to this guy and tell him to cut the crap, then get back to me if he wants to do anything." He dropped his hand and looked Underwood up and down with contempt. "He knows what we know." He pointed his chin at Underwood, almost snarling. "And we know what he did." The ferocity of his anger was making his hands shake. He kept picturing his son.

Spade didn't bother to hide his disgust. "I can't believe this, Paul. I came here . . ." He turned to his client. "Come on."

"Just get me out of here." Underwood twisted away from the escort agent and pressed his hands behind his back to make it easy to apply the cuffs. His eyes were locked on Patterson. "He's going to kill me. I know it. He's going to kill me."

"I won't have to dirty my hands." Patterson, subsiding a little, bent over to pick up a chair.

"Is that a threat?" Spade asked.

"No," Campanella said.

Patterson glared at Underwood. He spoke in a low growl, stepping toward him. "Watch your back, Henry. Every second of every day."

35

For David, the worst part of having the girls with him was confronting what a crotchety old fussbudget he'd become.

He liked to think of himself as fairly relaxed and easygoing, but now the smallest things bugged him inordinately. Lindsay, for example, always left a dusting of grounds around the coffeemaker. Jordan, although she was dainty in most ways, found it impossible to sprinkle sugar on her cereal without scattering a quarter teaspoon next to her bowl. David found himself muttering each morning after the girls took off for school, when he was left to wipe the counters. It was such a little thing, but he'd asked them three times, and they'd promised, and it still made no difference. Had he always been such a crab?

He reminded himself that they were good about putting their dishes in the dishwasher and their shoes in the mudroom most of the time. Still, it pained him when he came home and found clothes and books dumped on the sofa and Lindsay's softball equipment and Jordan's My Little Ponies scattered everywhere. The constant noise of television or discordant pop music left him edgy and off balance.

Both girls made amazingly frequent use of the toilet facilities. On one disastrous occasion, the girls' bathroom ran out of paper, and

David had to promise to close his eyes while he threw a borrowed wad from the roll in his bathroom to Jordan, who was stranded with her bare bottom on the seat, very concerned that he might get a peek at her.

One incident where his lack of equilibrium reached life-threatening proportions was emblematic. Jordan's new friend Brianna was teaching Jordan how to play jacks, and Jordan had been practicing on David's bathroom floor, the bounciest locale for her little red ball. Jordan picked up afterward but overlooked one jack, which David of course stepped on with his full weight the next morning as he emerged from the shower. It hurt like blazes, and as he hopped around on one foot, he lost his balance and crashed over sideways into the bathtub.

By some miracle he didn't seriously injure himself, but as he was floundering back up—jarred, naked, and soaking wet—Lindsay banged on the door asking if he was okay. He had an idiotic moment of panic that she would open the door and catch him in the altogether. As he snatched at a towel, he drove her off by shouting out that he was okay and everything was all right. She wouldn't go away at first, trying to interrogate him through the door about what had happened. He told her to never mind. He was fine. Really.

Things like this kept happening. He felt as though he was losing command of his life.

Worse than the physical disruption was the constant sense of being in the dark about what was going on with the girls. David learned from Jordan that Brianna was being raised by a single dad, a carpenter named Hank who encouraged his daughter, and Jordan, to call him by his first name. A quiet word with one of the deputy marshals got him a records check on Hank that turned up a twenty-year-old possession of marijuana conviction as well as an arrest for DUI, later dismissed. This could mean anything. When he briefly met Hank as he was dropping Jordan off, he noticed that the guy had garish tattoos on his arms and the side of his neck. He suggested to Jordan that she might like to invite Brianna over to their house more often. She replied that Brianna's dad had built an awesome playroom in their basement. Sheila Norcross, he imagined, must have worked out some way to manage these situations, but he was lost.

The problems with Lindsay were even more acute. He wanted to know as much as possible about what was up with her, and she for some reason seemed to want him to know hardly anything. She "needed her space." One weekend night, she told him she was meeting new friends at a hockey game and going out for pizza afterward, which seemed an unobjectionable, even positive, development. But, after he dropped her off at the rink, it struck him that she was perfectly capable of heading off anywhere once his car was out of sight. They'd agreed, with minimal eye-rolling on her part, that she would be home no later than midnight. When she didn't make it back until 12:20, he had to restrain his fury while she trolled through an explanation that never would have passed muster in his courtroom.

Then, one day when he came home early from work, he found a pickup truck on its way down the driveway, with some weedy twentysomething behind the wheel. Later, Lindsay told him he was the older brother of one of her friends, giving her a lift home when she'd had to stay late after school for some vaguely described project. It sounded plausible, but he had no idea whether it was true, and it seemed pushy and mistrustful to ask exactly whose brother this fellow was. He never saw the guy again, but whether this meant Weedhead had disappeared or merely that Lindsay had gotten more careful, he had no idea.

In this wilderness, Claire was a godsend. She came over once, sometimes twice, a week to make something special for dinner. At meals, she was so much better at thinking up things to talk about with the girls than he was. Still, these oases were only occasional and left him on his own most of the week.

The most serious crisis occurred one morning when both kids had taken off for school and he was allowing himself a second cup of coffee. He had a so-called Markman hearing facing him that afternoon, a highly technical proceeding in which he would be taking evidence on the proper scope of a patent involving a laser device used to shrink the prostate. Two years earlier, reeling from his first patent trial, he had stuffed a folder up onto a shelf in the closet of what was now Lindsay's room summarizing how the appellate courts wanted a Markman hearing to be conducted. On the morning of the hearing, he decided to make a quick foray into the room, retrieve the article, and escape with as much of his sanity as possible.

As he crossed to the closet, Marlene, who typically slept with Lindsay, stood guard in the doorway, eyeing him suspiciously. He quickly retrieved the file and then noticed a square Amazon box wedged way back into the corner. Puzzled, David took the box down and opened it. Inside was a flattened Ziploc bag of what the DEA liked to call "green, leafy material." David sniffed it, and from long experience in the courtroom, recognized it immediately as marijuana, about half an ounce, with a street value of between fifty and a hundred dollars.

Holding the contraband, David felt a surge of disgusted anger combined with despair. This was a stupid, stupid thing for Lindsay to be doing, especially knowing his position, and she was smart enough to realize that. At the same time, he suspected that if Lindsay learned he'd been snooping around in "her" room, his transgression might far outweigh, in her mind, any drug felony she might have committed. What on earth was he supposed to do?

He eventually decided on two things. First, he wouldn't say anything to Lindsay. Ray was improving, and the tentative plan was that she and Jordan would go home to Washington for Christmas vacation. If the holidays went well, the girls would just stay on after New Year's, picking up with their old schools for the next semester. In that case, a confrontation with Lindsay would be neither necessary nor helpful. Second, he'd confiscate the marijuana and dispose of it without saying anything. Even Lindsay wouldn't dare complain, and the evidence would be gone.

David retreated from the bedroom, making sure that the empty Amazon box was tucked back in its corner and that nothing looked disturbed. He felt like a housebreaker.

Leaving the room, he looked down at Marlene. "No snitching, okay?"

A short time later, when he was departing for the courthouse, he popped the baggie in his glove compartment. He'd dispose of it at some handy Dumpster on the way to work. Of course, with the Markman hearing bearing down on him, he immediately forgot all about it.

36

Ryan Jaworski was totally in the dark. He had no idea when, or even whether, the judge was going to reveal that he was the mysterious "confidential informant" who'd told the feds that Sid Cranmer had more porn in his house. Sid's woman lawyer was pushing for disclosure, arguing to Norcross that she had a right to call what she referred to as the "lying CI" as a witness at Sid's trial. The black cop, Patterson, had stopped taking Ryan's calls, probably blaming him for the blown search and the howling load of crap the newspapers had poured onto the government afterward. If Ryan's name came out, Libby would go crazy. Nine chances out of ten, she'd tell Patterson that Ryan had seen the flyer while they were at Sid's house, and Patterson would realize he had lied about that.

In half an hour on the Internet, Ryan learned that lying to an FBI agent was a serious crime. He couldn't believe how—without really doing anything wrong—he'd ended up in such an unfair, fucking horrible mess.

As the days passed, the situation ate away at him. With "The Dog That Didn't Bark, and the Porn That Wasn't There" in and out of the front pages, the news that the "CI" was an Amherst undergrad would be banner news locally. Jackie might hear about it way out on Long Island, not to mention Jackie's mom—who hated him already—and eventually his dad back in Chicago, which made Ryan sick to his stomach. His entire life was wobbling toward the toilet. No one could blame him if he couldn't just stand by, doing nothing.

The linchpin was Lib. She was the only one who could connect him to the flyer. As Professor Mattoon said, if he could keep Lib's lip buttoned, they could ride this out. Mattoon was texting him every other day now, asking whether he'd "had his little chat" with Libby. But just having a chat with her wasn't going to do it; she'd talk rings around him. Wasn't there a case in New York where some girl died during "rough sex"? And hadn't the guy gotten off? Ryan wasn't going to go that far, obviously—though it would be easy to slip up during one of their games, especially if they were shit-faced. His judo experience made him an expert on choke holds, which he and Libby sometimes played around with to jack things up. The holidays were coming up soon, which would give him a timely escape and the space to think. When the new semester began, his birthday wouldn't be far off. The celebration was bound to be wild. Accidents happened all the time.

37

The botched plea proceeding was the last straw for Sid Cranmer. During the recess, he'd told Linda that he just couldn't swallow owning up to the DVD, not in public and not in the way the judge wanted him to. He couldn't remember ordering the DVD or knowing its contents, and he wasn't going to lie.

Now he was facing a trial. Jury selection would commence as soon as the judge's schedule opened up, in a month or two at the most. Assistant U.S. Attorney Campanella was probably sharpening his instruments of torture at that very moment.

Judge Norcross must certainly despise Sid now, and after the inevitable guilty verdict, he was bound to clobber him. Hardly surprising. Linda Ames must think he was an asshole, too, and she was certainly right. What needed to happen was no longer a tough question. He was all out of options, but for the one elegant solution.

Sitting at his kitchen table, Sid wrote out a short note to Claire Lindemann, apologizing and asking her to look after Mick and Keith. Claire was sweet, and she would be upset, but she'd get past 90 percent of her sadness in a week at the most. After that, she'd remember him and maybe feel a twinge now and then, which was nice. No one else would even pretend to miss him. Linda Ames would move on to other clients, relieved to be rid of him. Just another pebble in the pond, a barely noticeable plop.

It was quiet in the kitchen, only the muffled bump of the heat kicking on and the grandfather clock ticking back in the music room. A snowstorm the night before had dropped eight inches. Jonathan had come early, shoveled the walk and driveway, collected his twenty dollars, and departed. The cats were curled up on the guest room bed upstairs, as they always were at this time of day. The tattooed carpenter's tools lingered in the spare room. He still hadn't quite finished his work—he was taking forever—but he wouldn't be coming by today. The snow had dropped a silence over everything.

Sid opened the fridge and took out one of the two vials of pentobarbital. He hadn't been sure whether it needed to be refrigerated, so he'd stashed the vials in the fridge's crisper to be on the safe side. His gardening scissors were in what he liked to call his "miscellaneous device" cabinet. He snipped around the collar of the container, removed the plug, and poured the liquid into a juice glass. It was clear, like springwater.

In the living room, he sat down on the sofa and set the glass on the coffee table. This was as good a place as any for them to find him. He didn't like the idea of being discovered stretched out on his bed like an invalid. Here, he could get comfortable without disturbing the cats and maybe reread the first paragraphs of *Alice's Adventures in Wonderland* while he waited for the big black door to swing open.

Then he remembered that the *New York Times* article had mentioned that pentobarbital had an unpleasant taste. A glass of wine apparently hid the bitter flavor and helped smooth the liftoff. As he sat staring at the glass, he pondered what kind of wine might go best with an entrée like this. Sid wasn't a connoisseur, but he didn't want to go out drinking the equivalent of Boone's Farm, for Christ's sake. This was not an occasion for some of his bargain-bin, two-for-twelve-dollars plonk. Also, as he thought about it, he wasn't sure whether he'd want red or white, or maybe some sparkling wine. It was a big decision, maybe the last he would make.

Sid pulled himself up and started toward the kitchen to look over his very limited wine selection. Halfway across the room, he changed his mind and decided he would make one last attempt to find the file of Dodgson photographs, his old unpublished treasure trove, which had mysteriously disappeared. Suddenly, of all things, he wanted most to see the images of those sweet children one last time.

The renewed search of his house by Patterson and his myrmidons a couple months back had been a near-death experience for Sid. It shouldn't have been that big a deal. Sid was familiar with the drill now, and he knew to get out of the way and let the agents go to it, yanking doors open, shouting to one another, running up and down the stairs, and terrifying the cats.

After the initial whirlwind, he and Patterson had taken their familiar seats on the sofa and wingback, with Claire shooed into the background. This time, though, when Patterson started asking him questions, Claire had shouted, "Sid! Don't be a dope. Call Linda Ames!" Agent Patterson had given Claire a weary look, and that was the end of that.

The awful part—the true, two-handed head squeezer—came afterward, when Patterson had walked straight through the house, into Sid's study, and up to the antique oak credenza behind his desk. With the bottom dropping out of his stomach, Sid had realized that Patterson must be looking for the drawer with the false compartment, where Sid kept Dodgson's clandestine pictures of Alice Liddell, Beatrice Hatch, and his other naked little cherubs.

Sid drifted from the living room, where the glass of poison stood waiting, toward his study, hoping the file might have magically reappeared in its old hiding place. He stood in the doorway, hesitating. He knew it wouldn't be there. He was stalling. He'd always been a terrible procrastinator.

On the morning of the second search, Sid had been forced to watch from this very spot, not saying anything or even looking concerned, as Patterson pulled out the drawers of the credenza and ran his fingers along their tightly crafted seams. Soon, he was lifting the false panel out of the oversize lower right-hand drawer and reaching his big paws inside.

Sid had assumed at this point that he was a dead duck. The rebarbative AUSA Campanella would tell Judge Norcross that Sid had flouted the court's no-porn order, and the judge would stick him back in jail again. Sid's fellow inmates would be waiting to finish him off, if he didn't die of natural causes first.

To Sid's astonishment, when Patterson groped into the secret compartment, he'd only run his hands around inside briefly and moved on to other drawers. Even today, Sid had no idea what the fuck had happened.

Over the years, Sid had regularly taken the Dodgson file out and examined the photographs it contained, one by one, trying to imagine the real-life scenes the photos captured. It was true, he had to admit, that these innocent, naked little bodies did something for him, as they no doubt had done for Dodgson. Looking at them would send Sid off to bed, in a pleasant hum, to sweet dreams. Did this mean he was as evil as Campanella said he was?

Sid floated across the study for one last, hopeless look into the credenza, but the secret compartment was still empty and the file was still nowhere to be seen. There was no other place he could imagine having put the goddamn thing.

Beyond the Dodgson photographs, Sid knew he had looked, from time to time, at what was probably, technically, child pornography mixed in with other garbage he found on the Internet. The confusing thing was that the government had found so much of this crap, and so much that he not only couldn't remember seeing, but couldn't imagine himself ever wanting to see. It made him sick, and hardly any of it seemed familiar. Had he been that crazy?

The psychiatrist Ames sent him to kept hinting that his post-funeral porn binges may have been an expression, somehow, of his anger at his mother. Mom had ruined his life, supposedly, and then abandoned him by dying. This seemed like psychologistic horseshit, but who knew? Who, in the end, had more than the slimmest grasp on what was really going on inside him? Certainly not him. Soon it wouldn't matter.

Back in the kitchen, Sid noticed a half bottle of decent pinot noir, left over from yesterday's dinner and still sitting on the counter. It would do. He got out a wineglass, filled it right up to the top, and took a couple long swallows, more for anesthesia than enjoyment. Back in the living room, the juice glass was still waiting for him with its clear, placid contents.

Sid set the wineglass down and lifted the glass of pentobarbital. He may have been on the verge of drinking, or he may have simply been contemplating his version of Socrates's hemlock, but whatever he was up to was interrupted by a hesitant but clear tap on the front door.

Of course, the easiest thing, if he was so determined to off himself, would have been to ignore the interruption and down the cocktail. But Sid was curious, and then surprised, when he peeked through the sidelight to see that it was Linda Ames's son, Ethan.

"Just a second!" Sid hurried back to the coffee table, picked up the two glasses, walked into the kitchen, and dumped them into the sink. He still had the other vial.

A smile broke onto his face when he opened the door. He couldn't help it.

"Ethan, my lad. What brings you here?"

After the overnight storm, the clouds were still heavy. The overcast muffled everything, and undulating shadows stretched across the snow in his front yard. Ethan's breath came in short puffs.

"Mom says I'm not supposed to bother you, but I wanted to just say hi to the cats." He pointed over at Sid's Volkswagen, half buried in snow. Given Sid's home confinement, Jonathan hadn't bothered to shovel it out. "Plus, I could help with your car. Mom says you're going to court soon."

"Come on in." Sid stepped back and opened the door. As Ethan entered, Sid added, "I have some leftover cupcakes. Do you prefer chocolate or yellow?"

"It's only for a minute. Mom says—"

"Don't worry about that." Sid put a hand on Ethan's shoulder and bent down, dropping his voice and speaking conspiratorially. "We don't need to tell her about this. It can just be our little secret."

PART FOUR

DISPOSITIONS

38

On the Saturday before jury selection in *United States v. Cranmer*, Chitra and Erik were in chambers banging out memos on late-filed pretrial motions. Chitra's topic was a provision of the child pornography law that made an exception for materials, otherwise illegal, that had, in the words of the statute, "serious literary, artistic, political, or scientific value." Judge Norcross had Chitra looking into whether Dodgson's published photographs of children—ones that appeared in the academic biographies and articles found in Cranmer's library—fell into this protected category, and, if they did, whether the government could put them into evidence anyway, not as proof of a crime but to show Cranmer's so-called "criminal state of mind."

Erik was bent over his desk in a jumbled nest of books, hammering away on an even thornier assignment: the wording of an instruction that would guide the jury in determining whether Cranmer's pornographic stills and videos depicted real, or only virtual, children. Possession of the charged material was a crime only if the images featured actual, flesh-and-blood kids—not cyber creations—and advancing technology made it hard to tell the difference.

The lengthening winter had hit bottom, congealing into the shortest days of the year, with temperatures dropping below zero at night. By late afternoon, the weak January sun, reduced to an apricot smudge on the western horizon, barely penetrated the overcast. The atmosphere in the Norcross chambers was murky.

Chitra didn't notice. The last-minute research was giving her an interesting slant on the whole area of child pornography law and a new opportunity to wrestle with Erik in their ongoing debate. Her co-clerk had been distant lately, which was making Chitra uncomfortable. A little argument would be both good fun and a chance to pry Erik out of his shell. She was standing in her usual position in his doorway, gesticulating as she spoke.

"The plain words of the literary escape hatch seem to cover Dodgson's pictures, but that bothers me because . . ."

Erik gestured at Chitra with his coffee cup, not bothering to look up at her. His voice was flat. "Because they're protected only because Dodgson took the pictures, right?" He glanced at her and quickly dropped his head, continuing to grind away on his own project. "You are so predictable, Chitra."

They were in weekend attire. Chitra was wearing bleached jeans and a navy blue Yale jersey. Erik had on khakis and a plaid lumberjack shirt. Chitra's thick black braid fell almost to her waist, brushing the small of her back as she lifted her chin to respond.

"Sorry, Erik, I am who I am." Her voice was a little sharper than she intended. "And what I'm wondering—"

"You're wondering why it's the person who's taken the pictures that protects them and not the content of the pictures themselves." Erik set his coffee down, put his hands behind his head, and stretched. His face was unhappy, and he didn't try to hide his impatience.

"Exactly," Chitra said. "If someone enjoys drooling over dirty pictures taken by a famous writer or artist, then the pictures have literary merit, and he's safe. But if the same photographs were taken by Joe Nobody, then we lock the drooler up for five years, minimum."

Erik shrugged. "The law has boundaries, Chitra. A lot of the time, they're arbitrary. Too bad for the porno fans."

The new baby had to be wearing Erik out. His fatigue was making him short-tempered, and Chitra realized it was time for a tactical retreat. She stepped away from Erik's door, then ducked her head back. "How's little Miss Becky? How old is she now?"

"Four months and doing great." Erik smiled, rallying a little. "Just a great little girl. Her brother and sisters adore her."

"I keep asking you for pictures, but you don't bring me any." Erik had his head down, withdrawing. Chitra couldn't resist the push to keep talking. "By the way, I may have to leave early. Tom's coming out from Boston tonight."

Erik looked up with a muted twinkle. "Things going well with that guy, eh?"

"Yes, I'm blessed that Tom is a sapiosexual."

"What's that?"

"A deviant who finds intelligence in women sexually attractive."

"There's more to you than gray matter, Chitra."

Chitra rattled on. "I think our judge has the same proclivity. His professor girlfriend seems really smart." Claire had dropped by the chambers during the week between Christmas and New Year's to take the judge out to lunch, and he'd introduced her to the clerks. "I worry about him, though, with those two kids. What do you think it's like, having them this long?"

"Hard. Extending their stay through the end of the school year must have been a wallop. You can see it in his face."

"I still can't figure out how that happened. Why are they still here?"

Erik tipped his cup up and finished his coffee. "Brother Ray supposedly had a relapse. Lucille tells me that the Christmas visit was"—Erik held up his fingers to make quotes—"'too much' for Ray."

"How'd she find that out?"

"Lucille knows everything. She's not sympathetic with old Ray, and neither am I. His job is to be a good dad, and he doesn't seem in a hurry to do it." Erik dropped his head and began writing something on his yellow pad to signal the end of the conversation. "Anyway, that's the story."

Back in her office, Chitra's happy nature did not allow her to be oppressed by Erik's mood for long. She was soon immersed in a brilliant opinion by Judge Jack Weinstein in the Eastern District of New York. Entitled *United States v. R. V.*, it offered a comprehensive overview of the evolution of child pornography law. Chitra was surprised to learn that up until the 1880s, most state laws set the age of consent for girls at ten years. Images and accounts of adult-child sex were common throughout the nineteenth century. Even in the twenty-first century, the evidence that people who looked at child pornography presented a risk to actual children remained surprisingly thin. Some did, but most didn't.

R. V. described how, in the 1960s, when President Lyndon Johnson's Commission on Pornography recommended repeal of laws banning "obscene" material, child pornography became available in a few grubby, but not illegal, commercial outlets. Outrage at this eventually shut down the small network of bookstores and mail-order services that specialized in this material. By the early 1980s, the battle against child pornography was basically won. Then, the Internet hit.

Chitra was glued to the Weinstein opinion for most of an hour. When she heard Erik get up to hit the coffeepot in the copier room, she realized she was ready for her own refill.

As they bumped around in the cramped space, she started in. "Did you know that the child porn industry is almost entirely a product of the Internet?"

"Doesn't surprise me." Erik was bent over the minifridge, fishing out the cream. "Depressing if you think about it." His coffee cup rested on a messy stack of old ABA journals, dangerously near his elbow. "Human beings invent painkilling drugs, which revolutionize medicine, and then immediately start sticking needles in themselves and ruining their lives. They invent the Internet, this glorious new way to communicate, and they bulldoze it full of manure. Makes you want to move to another planet."

Chitra began, "But it's—"

"Anyway, most of the time, the government is not going to go after people who just take a sip out of the cesspool."

"That's true, but it's up to the prosecutors. If they want you, they've got you, or they've got your kid or your husband. Then it's five years in prison, at least, and a lifetime registering as a sex offender. Is it really worth it?"

At this point, Erik flushed and took a deep, fed-up breath, as though he was about to yell. Chitra leaned back to tip away from the blow, but before Erik could speak, he bumped the stack of journals, and his coffee cup tumbled onto the floor.

"Dammit!"

"Oh dear," Chitra said. "Here, let me help." She began grabbing paper towels.

To her surprise, Erik spoke almost harshly. "Just leave it. Just leave it, okay?" He took the towels out of her hand, squatted, and began mopping up the floor. "Just let me handle this, will you, please?"

Chitra felt as though she'd been slapped. Watching him down on the floor, she tried to think of something witty to say, but she came up dry. She wanted to retreat to her office, but Erik was blocking the doorway to the small room, finishing his cleanup.

Eventually, he stood and tossed the soggy wad of paper towels into the wastebasket. He put his hands on his forehead, closed his eyes, and took a deep breath.

"I should have shared something with you a while back, Chitra. But I didn't want to make a big deal about it." He looked down at the floor and then up at her. "Becky has Down syndrome."

"Oh, Erik, I didn't . . ."

"It's okay. We love her like crazy. We're not sorry, and we don't want people thinking we're sorry or feeling bad for us. She's a sweet, cheerful little thing, and we love her."

"Of course she is. Of course you . . ."

"But it's been hard, naturally. It caught everybody by surprise a little."

Chitra got up, came around her desk, and held out her arms.

"Is it okay? Would you mind?"

"Don't overdo it." He breathed in shakily as Chitra hugged him. It started out stiff, but after a few seconds, Erik put his arms around her and gave her a good squeeze in return. The top of her head came up to his third button. "Sorry I sort of lost it there."

"You're entitled. I'm the one who should be apologizing. I . . ."

"It's just that she's such a happy girl. Sleeps well. Makes no trouble. The easiest baby we've had. A gift from heaven." His voice wavered. "But people in stores look at her, you know? And you can see in their faces what they're thinking. Becky's in for a rough time, and I won't always be there to protect her. Sometimes it just kills me."

39

The following Monday morning, Linda Ames, on three hours of sleep, sat at counsel table in Judge Norcross's courtroom, waiting to commence jury selection in *United States v. Cranmer*. She felt totally alive. Even her fury at Sid for blowing the "Plea Bargain of the Century," and embarrassing her in front of Judge Norcross in the process, had evaporated. This morning, she was going to trial—her favorite thing in life, next to Ethan—and every neuron in her body was firing.

Part of the source of her energy spike may have been the French toast she'd had for breakfast—real Vermont maple syrup and lots of butter. No diets while on trial was her rule. The carbo-loading had the tips of her fingers tingling.

Behind her, ninety or so randomly selected citizens of the four counties of western Massachusetts sat in the gallery, murmuring like bees, uncertain whether they'd be picked. Ruby Johnson, the courtroom deputy, had already diverted a dozen of them into the jury box for preliminary questioning when the judge came in, which would be any second. At least four of this first batch were giving Sid menacing looks, evidence that they'd seen the newspaper reports about the notorious local porn professor. One, an enormous Mafioso-looking guy, had been glaring at Sid, arms folded, for a steady three minutes. In the unlikely event that he made it onto the final panel, one of Ames's ten peremptory strikes would definitely be going to knock this leg-breaker off.

The headlong rush of preparation in the last twenty-four hours had been, as always, like going over Niagara Falls on a tea tray. The court's electronic docketing system, which permitted attorneys to file motions any time of the day or night, allowed almost no letup. At one a.m. that morning, hoping Campanella would be asleep, Ames had made two last-minute filings: an emergency motion to postpone the trial and a motion to exclude certain evidence. At two a.m., Campanella had filed his oppositions, along with a motion of his own, probably thinking that she'd be in bed. At three a.m., she'd opposed his motion with a six-page memorandum. Life just didn't get any better than this.

To her chagrin, Judge Norcross had once more denied Ames's motion to release the name of the confidential informant whose supposedly "reliable" information had provided the basis for the futile second search of Sid's house. The judge had noted that the denial was still "without prejudice," which meant she could resubmit the motion if she discovered new grounds. For now, he said, the sealed information was irrelevant, since no evidence against Sid had been uncovered at the second search. Ames had confidence she could come up with something new to justify resubmitting the motion, if only to jerk Campanella's chain. Something was going on there. Campanella was trying way too hard to keep this information away from her.

Ames placed her hand on Sid's shoulder and spoke into his ear. "How you doing?"

"I'm okay." Sid kept looking down at his hands, which were clasped in front of him. "Like going into combat." He gave her a resigned look. "The waiting's over, finally."

It was okay if Sid was miserable. Given the charges, Ames certainly didn't want the jury seeing him looking cocky. The situation, in fact, seemed to be making Sid unusually calm, which was a relief. His student intern, Libby, had trimmed his hair, and his blazer and tie looked okay. The tie/no-tie decision was always tough, but as she looked at him now, Ames felt good about having him stick one on. He was a professor, after all, and some of the jurors might see it as a gesture of respect. In the courtroom, every detail mattered.

AUSA Campanella sat to Ames's right at the neighboring table, two arm's lengths away.

Now, he leaned over and said in a low voice, "I'm going to want to play an excerpt from the government's proposed Exhibit One, the DVD, before we begin formal selection. It's just a thirty-second snippet, so they'll know what they'll be dealing with. I assume you have no objection?"

Campanella's timing was such a transparent ploy that Ames would have laughed if she weren't so disgusted. She'd noticed Campanella keeping an eye on Ruby Johnson and suspected he was up to something. It was only when Ruby picked up her phone and nodded—a sure sign Norcross was on his way in—that Campanella made his move and dumped his crafty little plan on her. Now he'd be able to tell the judge he'd conferred with her, without actually giving her time to think. If he'd hoped to rattle her with this bush-league move, he was wrong.

"Of course I object, Paul. Are you out of your skull?" She wasn't sure why she was objecting yet, but if Paulsie wanted to do it, she was opposed.

"Sorry I didn't mention it earlier. Just thought of it now."

"Uh-huh. Bullshit."

"Well, the DVD is going to be—"

"We don't even know if it's coming into evidence yet. I can't believe you're—" The door behind the bench opened, and Ruby's strong voice broke in: "All rise!"

Everyone stood while Norcross strode up the three stairs to his perch, bent forward, as usual, peering down at the fringe of his robe as though he was concerned he might stumble.

He slid into his chair with a relieved smile and said, "Please be seated." A soft rumble followed while everyone tried to get comfortable. A backpack or purse hit the floor with a thud, then silence.

Seeing Norcross up there, Ames took comfort in the fact that he was basically a good guy and a fairly decent judge. He might make a lousy call, or get impatient, but he was not a jerk, and that, on the whole, was what mattered.

The judge squared up a slim folder in front of him, and they were off.

"Welcome! My name is David Norcross, and you're in the United States District Court for the District of Massachusetts, Western Division. I want to begin by thanking you all for being here this morning, especially on such a cold day."

The assemblage deserved the judge's thanks. Temperatures had dropped down into double digits below zero the night before. Everyone was deep in the New England winter freezer, and some of the potential jurors had come from as far away as North Adams, a two-hour drive through an arctic landscape, to fulfill their civic responsibility.

"Let me begin by telling you what we're up to this morning, what your role might be, and how long we might need you for."

The usual stuff followed: jury service as the duty of every citizen including judges—Norcross had never gotten onto a jury, he told them, but he'd sat around several times over in state court before being excused—his commitment to use their time efficiently, and his hope that, if chosen to sit, they would find their jury service rewarding.

As they moved toward the more substantive part of this introduction, Ames leaned forward to get on her feet and ask for a side bar. Norcross noticed her immediately, made eye contact, and nodded her back down.

"Now, I'm going to impose on your patience here for just a minute while I take up a couple of last-minute things with counsel. They'll be coming up to the side of the bench over here, and I'll be using this whoosher thing"—he turned it quickly on and off—"to give us some privacy. I'm going to ask that you not talk while we're conferring. It will distract us. We won't be long, I promise you. Okay, Counsel, please approach." He turned on his white noise, stood up, and stepped to the right-hand side of the bench.

Ames and Campanella walked around their tables and crossed the well to where Norcross was waiting. The court reporter, Maureen, a tall woman with striking red hair, joined them, planting herself and her machine close by.

"All right." Norcross leaned over them and spoke in a low voice. Both Ames and Campanella squirmed forward to be sure to hear him. "I've got three motions you guys dropped on me last night. All of them could have been filed earlier, but we won't get into that. First, Ms. Ames, your motion to postpone the trial is denied."

"May I be heard?"

"No. I'll give you a chance to put your reasons on the record later. But I've read your memo, and I know your expert says he needs more time. I'm not convinced. Your rights are saved."

"Very good, Your Honor." It was a Hail Mary motion anyway. No point in annoying him.

"Your second motion to exclude evidence is allowed, for now." Norcross turned and spoke to Campanella directly. "I'm barring you from referring to the defendant's academic specialty, Charles Dodgson, Dodgson's practice of photographing children, or the defendant's possession of these published photos. As you know, Mr. Campanella, these photographs fall outside the definition of child pornography based on the exception protecting material of serious literary or artistic value. I don't want you mentioning any of this without a further order from me."

"But, Your Honor, it's . . ." Campanella, to Ames's satisfaction, looked shocked and was starting to splutter.

"It's out, okay? I'll give you a chance to be heard on this issue later, if necessary."

Campanella wouldn't give up, a mistake on his part. "But it's not being offered substantively, Your Honor, merely to show state of mind."

The judge's tone went dangerously acid. "I'm aware of your argument, but it's out. Understand?" Then his voice softened. "I may reconsider later, depending on how the evidence develops. Okay, finally, Mr. Campanella, you've added another proposed voir dire question you'd like me to put to the jurors."

Like most federal judges, Norcross did not allow lawyers to question jurors directly about their biases, exposure to pretrial publicity, general fitness to serve, and so forth. Rather, he invited lawyers to submit, in writing, proposed questions that he would put to the potential panel himself, if he felt they were proper.

"So, Mr. Campanella, you really want me to inquire of those folks over there"—the judge tipped his head toward the jury box—"whether any of them has ever looked at pornography of any kind, legal or illegal? You really want me to ask them that?"

"Yes, Your Honor, it's important to know whether . . ."

"Have you ever looked at pornography, Mr. Campanella?"

"Excuse me?"

"Have you ever looked at pornography?"

"Well . . . I . . . When I was . . . It's been a long time, and . . ."

"I'll withdraw my question, but I note for the record that you looked darned uncomfortable just now, which is exactly how the jurors over there would feel facing that question. Prying into this topic will either humiliate them or turn them into liars."

"Very good, Your Honor, but there's one other thing."

"Besides, how am I supposed to define pornography? The Supreme Court gave up trying forty years ago. My advice? Just assume that everyone has, at some time, looked at or read something that someone somewhere would call pornographic. Very good. We'll resume."

Norcross reached to turn off the white noise, but Campanella still wouldn't give up. "I understand, Your Honor, but there's just one other thing."

Norcross made a face. "There's always one more thing."

Campanella moved closer to the bench. Without knowing exactly what she was going to say, Ames prepared herself to indignantly oppose whatever Campanella wanted.

Campanella leaned forward, dialing up the intensity of his voice. The other issues clearly didn't matter as much to him as this one. "Many jurors, when they first see child pornography, find the experience very upsetting."

Norcross sighed. "Okay. What am I supposed to do about that?"

Ames broke in. "I'd object to this strenuously."

Campanella pushed on, talking more quickly. "I want to play a short excerpt from the DVD, Judge, before we start formal selection. If the jurors don't see this material until they've already been picked, we could have some of them wanting to bail out after they're sworn. It would be a mess, maybe even cause a mistrial. We need to sift out the people who can't tolerate looking at this material now and pick our jurors from the remainder that can handle it."

"When do you want to do this?"

Norcross's question meant trouble. When a judge stopped asking whether something would happen and moved on to how or when, it was not good.

"Judge," Ames began, but Campanella plowed forward.

"As soon as you've reviewed the charges here, I'd like to play approximately thirty seconds of the DVD to the jurors, just to give them an idea of what they'll be in for."

Ames pushed her shoulder against Campanella, nudging him to the side. "I object, Judge. It will contaminate the jury from the get-go. We can't even be sure at this point that the DVD is admissible. No foundation has been laid."

Norcross looked at Ames sharply. "You've never moved to suppress the DVD. It was legally seized pursuant to my warrant. The jurors are bound to see it some time."

"Your Honor, I . . ." Ames was rummaging for a persuasive argument but coming up empty.

Norcross shook his head. "It's a sensible idea. I know how shocking this stuff can be. We'll do it."

Campanella said, "Thank you, Your Honor."

"Wait until I tell you it's time." Norcross switched off the white noise and returned back to his chair. The moment was gone.

If some way had existed for Ames to head this off, she simply hadn't been able to come up with the words fast enough. All she could do now was shake her head, feigning disbelief more than anger. She turned to the court reporter to be sure she was on the record and said in a fierce tone, "Please note my strenuous objection."

Actually, Ames reflected as she returned to counsel table, there might be advantages to Campanella's suggestion. And at least she'd made a record of a possible error that could come in handy on appeal if Sid got convicted. It was a good thing to plant as many of these appellate hand grenades in the trial as possible.

The mumble and rustle of the jurors died as soon as Norcross resumed speaking.

"Let me move now to the topic that is probably foremost on all your minds: How long are we going to have to be here? The good news is that, for most of you, the torture will be over by lunchtime. Let me lay out our schedule for you."

As Ames resumed her seat, she patted Sid on the shoulder reflexively and turned her mind to the jurors. Their patience always amazed her. This random, voluntary gathering of the community, a miracle of civic commitment, was one of the things that drew her to trial work in the first place. As she shifted toward the gallery to observe the pool, Ames noticed only one or two with sour expressions. Just about everyone was listening to Norcross with open, attentive faces, willing to do their job if called upon—even if it was inconvenient, even if they'd had a long drive, and even in the dead of winter. It was hokey to admit this, but the scene was real, practical democracy in action, the United States of America actually working. Being a part of this always made Ames, basically a cynical person, proud.

After his overview of the time schedule, Norcross moved to the darker topic.

"The next thing I'm going to do is describe to you the charge against the defendant here, Sidney Cranmer. But, before I do this, I need to make three very important points." He leaned forward and surveyed the room, pulling everyone into his gaze. "First, by describing the charge, I am only informing you of what the government here says the defendant did. I am not suggesting that he in fact did it or committed any crime at all. Please understand this clearly. I'm only informing you of the charge so that you will know what the government says, the *government* says, and what this trial will be about—in order to orient you.

"Second, you must understand that the defendant, Sidney Cranmer, the gentleman sitting right there"—Norcross nodded at Sid—"is presumed innocent. This presumption of innocence is not a technicality. Mr. Cranmer is presumed to be as innocent as any of you, or me, or anyone. He comes here with a clean slate. The fact that I will be describing the charge against him, which is only a charge, does not alter that fact one bit."

This was always a difficult passage for a lawyer. On the one hand, Ames wanted to eyeball every single juror, to dig right into their brains to see how deeply this key point was penetrating. On the other hand, it was critical that she look relaxed, confident, and, above all, utterly trustful of the jurors' intelligence and good faith. As her eyes moved over the assembled men and women, she was harnessing all her intuitions and already identifying or discarding certain candidates, all the while doing her best to appear cool as a cucumber.

Norcross was winding up. "Third, and finally, you must understand that this presumption of innocence—the same innocence that cloaks us all—can only be overcome if the government carries its burden of proving Mr. Cranmer guilty"—and now Norcross emphasized each word by tapping his forefinger heavily on the bench—"beyond a reasonable doubt." He repeated, tapping even harder, "Beyond a reasonable doubt. Mr. Cranmer has denied the charge I am about to describe to you, and he cannot be found guilty of anything unless and until the government proves its charge beyond a reasonable doubt. Now, here's the charge."

In a few sentences, Norcross laid out the statutory language and the elements of the charge of knowingly and intentionally receiving child pornography. He promised that at the conclusion of the trial, he would be defining some of the terms he used in more detail, adding that if there was any inconsistency, they should be guided by his final instructions and not by the summary he was giving now.

At the conclusion of this segment of his remarks, Norcross closed his folder and pushed it to one side. Ames could feel Campanella over at his table, shifting around, slipping his copy of the DVD out of his file, getting ready for his show-and-tell. The prospect of what everyone was about to see was making Ames feel slightly sick to her stomach.

"Before we go any further into jury selection, I'm going to ask Mr. Campanella, who is here representing the government, to show you a short segment of one of the pieces of evidence you may be called upon to examine if you are selected as a juror. I have a special reason for doing this, and I want everyone to understand me clearly."

Norcross folded his hands in front of him and dropped his tone slightly, as though he were having a fireside chat.

"The heart of a juror's task, in the end, is the careful, objective assessment of the evidence. A juror must be neutral. He or she must be able to examine the evidence dispassionately, meaning without being overwhelmed by, for example, biases or powerful emotions. Everyone has issues that hit us especially hard. I do, you do, everyone does. Cases where the government brings a charge relating to child pornography may be especially difficult for some people. That is very understandable.

"Now, I'm going to permit the government to show you a portion of the child pornography it will be offering in this trial. My purpose in doing this is to give you an idea of the evidence you may be asked to look at and weigh. When you've seen it, I'm going to be asking whether, given the nature of the charge and the evidence, any of you has doubts about his or her ability to act as a neutral and impartial juror and weigh the evidence objectively in a case of this sort. Mr. Campanella, when you're ready."

The courtroom's presenter sat on a table next to the podium, between and a couple feet in front of the two counsel tables. It could be used to display evidence in various forms: still pictures, diagrams and drawings, downloads from a laptop, even items from the Internet. Campanella walked up to the presenter, slipped the DVD into the player, and began pushing buttons.

He spoke half to himself. "Still getting used to this thing." Watching, several jurors chuckled sympathetically.

A grainy, indecipherable patch jumped up onto the two large video monitors on either side of the courtroom and on the smaller monitors set up in the jury box, at counsel table, and up on the bench. Then the scene, one of the worst, came into focus in full color, and the audio kicked on. In the center of the tableau, a blond girl no more than three years old lay on a table screaming. The inky shadow of the videographer fell across the lower half of her naked body. Then the camera trained in for a close-up of her terrified face, lingered, and began trolling down her skinny torso.

Many jurors closed their eyes or turned away. Others went further, bending forward and covering their faces with their hands. As the scene unfolded, the naked back of a heavy male form approached the child, and the soundless throb of horror coming from the gallery thickened and became almost palpable. One or two groans, and a murmured "Jesus Christ!" floated up. A woman rose hurriedly, stumbled, and left the courtroom. A man, then two more women, followed soon afterward. The courtroom door swished and thumped repeatedly.

Ames kept her eye on the gallery as discreetly as she could, searching for faces she might trust. There weren't many. Nearly all the jurors exhibited pure pain and disgust, but, disturbingly, a few faces shone with avid interest. Research about child pornography trials suggested that as much as 10 percent of jurors in these cases actually took pleasure in looking at scenes like this. Afterward, this minority would go home and search for similar material on the Internet. The terrible irony was that high-profile trials like this one could serve as effective marketing tools for the child pornography business. It was possible that they did almost as much to encourage it as to deter it.

For Ames, of course, the important question was: Who among this cohort of jurors had the fiber to give her client a halfway fair trial, and who would want to crucify him before the first witness testified?

Norcross's voice broke in. "That's enough, Mr. Campanella. We have the idea."

Campanella turned off the presenter, and the screen went blank. The atmosphere in the room seemed to sag. Even Norcross had a haggard expression. He turned his face to the side, looked out the windows over the jury box at the gray winter sky, and breathed in deeply. Two of the escapees peeped into the courtroom and slipped back into their seats.

"Okay." Norcross turned to the jurors. "The evidence in this case may include a twenty-seven-minute version of what you have just seen. I want to emphasize again that the defendant Sidney Cranmer is presumed innocent." Norcross nodded down at Sid. "He has pleaded not guilty, and he denies ever knowingly and intentionally receiving this or any child pornography. As I've told you, he may only be found guilty if the government convinces you of his guilt beyond a reasonable doubt."

The judge leaned forward and steepled his fingers in front of him.

"Jurors have a difficult job. They must be able to consider evidence without losing the balance of their dispassionate neutrality. In this case, you must be able to give both sides, the government and the defendant, a fair trial. If any one of you, based on what you have just seen, feels that it would be impossible, or very difficult, for you to act as a neutral and impartial juror in this sort of case, please raise your hand."

A forest of hands shot up—nearly half the pool, including the thuggish man who'd caught Ames's attention earlier. He was raising his right hand so far in the air that his shoulder was mashed up under his ear.

Norcross leaned forward and said quietly to Ruby Johnson, "We're going to need to summon in more jurors. This may take a while."

40

In the upstairs room of the unused storage shed, the long-awaited, very private celebration of Ryan Jaworski's twenty-first birthday was finally getting started. Elizabeth, wearing her green thong and push-up bra, led Ryan, blindfolded, into the room. Apart from the bandanna over his eyes, he wore only flower-patterned boxer shorts. Blow-up palm trees and cardboard hula girls were in the room's entryway and Hawaiian music was playing in the background.

As they approached the center of the room, Elizabeth whispered over her shoulder, just loud enough for Ryan to hear, "Not yet. Stay there until I call you."

Chase Bergstrom's chemical smorgasbord had hit Ryan like a Mack truck, which was good, because if he'd been able to think clearly, he would have wondered what was going on. The room was empty of people except Elizabeth and him. A hangman's noose hung down from a beam in the center of the ceiling, and a throne-size wooden armchair stood under the noose. Behind the chair, almost out of sight, was a short stepladder for Elizabeth to use at the critical moment. The building's old heating system was overreacting to the February chill, and the place was very warm.

Ryan, barefoot and guided by Elizabeth, wobbled blindly toward the noose. One hand grasped Elizabeth's shoulder; the other, holding a bottle of red wine, waved back and forth checking for obstacles.

"Sheesus Chrise, Lib." Ryan paused to take a long swig from the bottle. "Iss just. I don't think I've ever been so whacked." He swiveled his head blindly around the room. "So, come on, who've we got here?" He waved the bottle. "Hey, whoever you are, say something, okay? I'm, like, dying of . . ." He wiped his mouth on the back of his arm and coughed out a laugh. "Dying of horniness and cold toenails."

Apart from getting the chemicals into him, Elizabeth had done a thorough job preparing Ryan on the landing. Wearing his favorite fantasy outfit, she got him down to his shorts and fooled around with him until he was right on the edge of the sexual precipice. The drugs had him so pumped that at one point he'd slobbered, "Just do me here, Lib, please. Forget the surprise." Instead, not long after that, she tied the blindfold in place, good and snug, and drew him into the room.

"Okay, darlin', onto your throne." She put her hand into his armpit and started to hoist him up onto the chair. "One big step here."

Ryan rocked back and batted at the air with his bottle. "Whoa! What the hell?"

Elizabeth whispered to the side, "Wait a second, Sofie. Hold your horses." Then to Ryan, louder. "It's just a chair here, Ry, for you to stand on. We're going to want Big Jake right at mouth height."

"Sofie's here? Sofie Martinez? I didn't . . ." He put one foot on the chair. "I didn't think she even liked me."

"Up you go. Give me this." Elizabeth took the wine bottle out and set it behind her.

Ryan teetered to the side and then took his foot off the chair, shaking his head. "I'm sorry, Lib. This is too crazy. I'm feeling, like, really . . . Wow. Less jus' . . ."

"Oh, come on, babe." Elizabeth spoke plaintively. "You're going to spoil my surprise. It took me all semester to set this up."

Ryan turned in Elizabeth's direction, waved a finger, and slurred out, "Come on now, Libby Spencer, no means no." He laughed and replaced one foot up on the big chair, then looked over his shoulder. "Who's here? Seriously."

"One more step." Elizabeth pulled at his arm. "Then we take the blindfold off, and you'll see. You're going to love it, I promise."

"I don't know." Ryan still hesitated. "This time, Lib, you've really blown the end off my weirdo-meter." With a grunt, he heaved himself up so that he was standing on the chair. "Whoa, shit." He wobbled and steadied himself.

"There you are, babe. Turn toward me. Perfect." Elizabeth dropped her voice again and muttered. "Isn't he gorgeous? I'm so lucky." More loudly, she added, "And we have to get you properly undressed for the occasion!"

She jerked his boxers down. Ryan bent his knees and grabbed at them but began to lose his balance and had to stand up quickly, flapping backward with his arms to steady himself.

"Come on, Ry, don't be a party pooper."

With an obedient sigh, Ryan untangled his ankles from the shorts and kicked them to the side. His penis was standing up like the high end of a teeter-totter.

Elizabeth raised her voice, almost squealing. "Damn, Ryan, you look gorgeous! Doesn't he look awesome?"

Ryan grinned stupidly, put his hands over his head, and gave a drunken Chippendale wriggle. "Everybody happy now?"

"You bet, and we're almost ready for the grand finale." Elizabeth singsonged: "Open our mouths, and close your eyes, and you shall get a big surprise." She fondled him, keeping his battery charged.

"Sheesus, come on!" Ryan gasped. "Just keep . . ."

Elizabeth stepped quickly across the room, pulled the silk bag containing their handcuffs out of a duffel over by the wall, then skipped back and mounted the stepladder behind him.

"Okay. Put one hand here." Speaking in a baby-doll voice, Elizabeth took his right hand and set it on his right buttock. "And the other little hand . . ." She took Ryan's left hand and placed it on his left buttock. "Right here."

Ryan leaned slightly forward, mouth open, hands firmly on his behind. "Ah, okay. Can somebody please tell me what this is for?"

"Follow instructions, Ry. Don't move a muscle." Then she whispered. "Everybody gather around." To Elizabeth's relief, Ryan's hands stayed in place.

"This isn't gonna hurt, is it? I'm not . . ." A worried tone crept into Ryan's voice. When he wobbled backward, his head brushed against the noose. "The hell's that?"

"Just a decoration. Keep your hands right there." She snapped the handcuffs around his wrists and hastily slipped the noose over his head.

"What's with the collar thing? For Christ's sake, Lib . . ." Ryan was just about to get fed up, but it was too late now.

"Your necklace." Elizabeth adjusted the noose around Ryan's throat, snug but not tight enough to choke him. Ryan's body stiffened and he knit his brows, trying to figure out what was happening. Then, Elizabeth whipped off the blindfold and stepped down from the ladder.

She'd done it. It was a miracle. Standing in front of him, she gave him a big smile.

"Well, la-dee-dah!"

Ryan started to smile back, then looked around, and pulled at his hands. "What the fuck, Lib?" He twisted his head to look back at the cuffs. Then he cast his eyes around the room. "Where is everybody?"

Elizabeth gazed up. "You look so darn cute."

"Come on. Where'd everybody go?" He kept peering around, as if someone might be in a corner he'd overlooked, all the time absently tugging at the handcuffs. He'd never get loose. The cuffs were old, reliable friends.

Elizabeth turned her back and walked over to a paint-spattered bench along the wall. She pulled a towel out of her duffel and began wiping off her arms and the back of her neck, like an athlete after a good workout. Ryan's penis, she noticed, was beginning to lose heart.

"What's. Whass going on, Libby? Really!" Ryan kept darting his head back over one shoulder then the other.

Elizabeth pulled a fresh bra and panties out of the duffel—plain white and practical—and peeled off the uncomfortable thong and push-up bra Ryan loved so much. He stopped squirming to take in her nakedness, and she could see the look of disappointment falling over his face. She was just a piece of anatomy now, nothing especially sexy about her.

"You want me to do you some more, Ry? I will if you ask nicely."

"Fuck, Lib. What is this? Are you pissed or something?"

She slipped on the new bra and reached around to hook it in back. "No. Not pissed." She adjusted the shoulder straps.

"Honestly. I don't get this." He twisted the handcuffs. "What the hell." He was starting to sober up, which was good. Chase told her the drug combo hit with a big punch at first but might wear off quickly with a guy Ryan's size. "I'm feeling really weird up here." Then, in a sharper voice: "Take the cuffs off, Lib. I mean it."

"I lost the key." Elizabeth was buttoning her blouse. "I honestly don't know where it is."

Ryan tipped his chin down and worked it from side to side, trying to see if he could squirm free of the noose.

"I wouldn't do that, Ry." Elizabeth pulled on a pair of jeans and zipped up the fly. "You'll just make it tighter."

She could see Ryan grasping the extent of his predicament and beginning to get angry. He twisted his hands harder behind his back to test if he could snap the chain that held the cuffs together. It wasn't going to work. He shifted tacks.

"This is dangerous, you know, Lib. I'm drunk as shit up here, to tell the truth, and my feet are getting sweaty. I could slip."

"You're right. And it's a bad way to go." Elizabeth was tucking her blouse in. "Usually, when somebody gets hanged, the scaffold thing is rigged to break their neck, and they go quick. We don't have that, so you'd strangle, which is a lot slower. People bicycle their legs to keep a little blood going and stay alive for a few more seconds." She sat down on the bench and began putting on her sneakers. "The longest recorded time for someone to die like that is supposedly seventeen minutes. Usually, though, it's less than two minutes." She was leaning down, working on her shoelaces. "I got that off the Internet, so I'm not positive about the data. Could be crap."

The Hawaiian-theme music stopped, and the noise from a dorm party in the distance either got louder or became more noticeable. The falsetto voice of some singer, repeating a phrase over and over, wailed in on top of the bass. Elizabeth looked up and saw Ryan staring at her with an expression she'd never seen before. Good.

"You're kidding right? You really want to play this game?" He twisted around, presenting his hands. "Come on, this is bullshit.

Take the fucking cuffs off." His voice became threatening. "I mean it, Libby. Knock it off." When Elizabeth didn't respond, Ryan pushed on, raising his voice. "Whatever's going on, if there's some kind of accident, you'd be in deep shit, too. It's not worth . . ."

"I didn't force you up there, Ryan. I'm a girl, and you're a lot stronger than I am." She finished tying her shoes and stood up. "We were drunk, playing around—just two stupid kids in a fantasy sex game that went wrong. I'd be, you know, totally distraught." She shrugged. "In the end, I doubt very much would happen to me."

"Fuck this. I'm going to start yelling if you don't get me down from here."

"Go ahead. No one will hear you."

Ryan breathed in, opened his mouth, and then closed it. He was an asshole, but he wasn't an idiot, and now he was just a piece of anatomy, too, pasty and flaccid. His penis looked like a child's punctured toy.

Libby got her purse off the bench. "Okay. I'm all dressed now, and you're all naked." She pulled out her cell phone. "It's time to make our movie."

Ryan looked confused at first. Then, it was like a cloud lifted off his face.

"Oh, Jesus Christ, Libby!" He spoke in a tone of impatience verging on disgust. "Is that what this is all about? The vid?"

"That's part of it."

"You're doing this because of that? Give me a fucking break!" His tone softened slightly. "It wasn't supposed to go anywhere. Ridge promised."

"I figured it was him."

"Look, I'm really sorry, okay? It was a fuckhead thing to do, I admit it." He sighed again, scornful but resigned. "Okay, go ahead and take the video. We'll be even. Then, get me down from here. After that, we're gonna have a little talk." When Elizabeth didn't say anything, he added, "I mean it. You and I have big problems."

"The video's only part of it."

"Oh, for God's sake, what else? Jackie?"

"I want you to tell me what you did when you saw the flyer at Professor Cranmer's house."

Ryan answered too fast. "I didn't do shit. I saw it. I thought it was sick, and that was that." He was pretending to get even more frustrated.

"Time for me to be going." Elizabeth picked up her purse and slipped the strap up over her arm. "Be careful up there."

"I'm telling you the truth, Libby. I never touched the fucking thing. Now take the . . ."

"Good-bye, Ryan." She picked up the duffel bag and walked toward the door. Then she paused and turned back into the room. Ryan must have thought she'd been bluffing.

"Oh, Jesus." He twisted his behind toward her. "Just help me with . . ."

But Elizabeth only went as far as the bench, where she'd tossed Ryan's pants, and pulled his cell phone out of the hip pocket.

"If you ever get down from there, you're going to need a new cell. This thing's going into the river."

As she was leaving the room, Ryan completely lost it and yelled after her. "Come back here, dammit! I mean it. Hey!" Elizabeth was halfway down the stairs when his tone changed, and his voice got louder. "Okay!" His voice pursued her. "You're right!" Then, even louder, screaming the syllables out, "Lib-beeee! Goddammit!"

Elizabeth took a seat on the bottom stair. Listening to Ryan howl was a pleasure, in a way, and she let him go at it for a while.

A few minutes later, back in the room, she approached him, keeping some distance between them. He was still pretty drunk, and his face was red from all the yelling. She didn't want to tempt him to take a kick at her.

"It wasn't just me," he said sulkily. "It was mostly Mattoon."

Elizabeth looked at him. "Okay. Let's hear."

"Let me down first. That's fair." Ryan shot her his sincere look. "Then, I promise, I'll tell you the whole thing."

Elizabeth turned to leave.

"Okay, okay," Ryan said. "I saw the flyer, sitting, like, on top of the wastebasket, okay? It was so gross. I couldn't imagine even a creep like Cranmer being into that kind of puke."

"Uh-huh. What then?"

"You were in the bathroom. I took it. Later, I showed it to Mattoon. I wasn't going to do anything with it, except maybe give it to you, but he talked me into mailing it in. He said it would be a joke." He twisted his head. "This rope is getting tight, Lib. I could slip, and it would be hard for you to get me down in time."

Elizabeth shrugged. "I might not bother." When Ryan gaped at her, Elizabeth added, "Professor Cranmer could die in prison."

"We didn't know that."

"But you didn't say anything after you did know. You didn't, and Mattoon didn't."

Ryan looked to the side, started to say something, but then thought better of it.

Elizabeth looked him over for a few more seconds, then punched in the code on her phone. "You also took his credit card information, Ry. You weren't all that innocent."

"He kept it sitting right out on a sticky on the side of his computer, okay? So I wrote it down. I admit that." He looked at his feet and shifted from side to side. "Can we do the video now? Then you'll get me down, right? Honestly, I'm getting scared up here." He swayed a little, either because he really was losing it, or because he wanted her to think so.

"First, we rehearse. Then the video. Then I call campus security. They'll come get you."

"That's fucking stupid, Lib. What you've done here is, like, a crime. What are they gonna think? Don't be dumb."

"As I said, it was a sex game that got out of hand, Ry. You were drunk and pissed, and I got scared you'd hurt me, so I did the responsible thing: I called the police."

"Such bullshit."

"Right. So, you and Professor Mattoon . . ."

"When we heard about the FBI coming to Sid's house and everything, believe me, we were like—" He was talking fast. Elizabeth slowed him down.

"Details, Ry. I need to know you're not feeding me a line just to get off that chair." Elizabeth folded her arms. "Tell me something you can't deny tomorrow. Then we'll do our recording. After that, we'll see."

The noose had gotten tighter, and Ryan, she could tell, really was getting a little scared. She felt a nudge of sympathy. He wasn't an evil person, just a shit. Maybe this whole project of hers could still bring him around. Maybe he'd learn something.

"Okay, but don't forget my *Miranda* warnings, babe." He made his dimple, recalling a legal studies course they'd taken together, *The American Constitutional System.*

"The *Miranda* warnings?"

"I have a right not to incriminate myself, you know."

Elizabeth turned toward the far wall and shook her head, as though she were sharing this bit of brainlessness with their invisible professor. What had she seen in this loser? She lifted her chin up at him. "The Bill of Rights only protects people from improper state action, Ry—things cops and officials do—not from private parties like me. Don't you *ever* listen in class?"

41

Jordan Norcross woke up in the strange house, more scared than she had been in her whole life. A fading memory of some nightmare—fire, a huge red mouth with teeth, and everybody screaming—was still crowding her chest, making her heart pound. Her cheeks and eyelashes were damp, and the feeling in her throat told her that more tears would be rushing in soon. When they did, they would never stop.

Jordan slipped out of bed, keeping her head turned away from the horrible smiley-clown nightlight Uncle Dave had bought for her. Halfway down the hall, she passed the room where Lindsay was sleeping and slowed from running to a fast walk. She did not want to wake up her sister, who might get mad and say something mean. Her heart was still hammering.

She continued down the hall past the bathroom—she didn't need to go—and right up to the open door of Uncle Dave's room. A warm smell was coming from inside that reminded her of her dad. As she stood there, catching her breath, her heart began to slow down a little.

Jordan very carefully entered Uncle Dave's bedroom, barefoot on the carpet, like an Indian.

Uncle Dave was in his big bed snoring. Not loud. Sort of like breathing-snoring.

She did this with her father, when he was home and they had bad thunderstorms. The two of them would snuggle up. He was big and squishy, like the Saggy Baggy Elephant. Uncle Dave's room had a safe smell. After waiting a little while, listening to the house creaking, Jordan pulled back the covers and slipped into the big bed. Her side was cool, but she could reach a hand to where Uncle Dave's long lumpy shadow lay. Over there it was warm.

Uncle Dave moved in his sleep, rolling toward the window and pulling most of the covers off her. His movement was kind of a jiggle-bounce. He was skinnier than her dad, more like the Very Hungry Caterpillar.

Jordan whispered, "Uncle Dave?"

Uncle Dave made a jumpy move and said something like "Whuh?" and sat up very quickly, which made Jordan feel like laughing. He was wearing a piece of tape over his nose, and his wiry hair was all over the place. She'd never seen Uncle Dave, who was always so serious, looking silly like this. He had his hand on his chest and was peeping around in the dark. He hadn't seen her yet.

Jordan reached over and took one of his pillows. Uncle Dave looked down at her, as though he wasn't sure what she was or where she'd come from. The pillow was extralarge, big enough to put her head on and hug at the same time.

"Don't be a cover hog," Jordan said.

"I'm sorry?"

"Don't be a cover hog."

Uncle Dave looked at her for a while—would he kick her out?—then flapped some covers over toward her. The flap made a puff of air that smelled exactly, *exactly* like Dad. "There you go," he said.

After a while, Uncle Dave lay back down and rolled away again, but without yanking the covers this time.

"You're stinky," Jordan said.

"So are you."

Soon after that she must have fallen asleep.

* * *

The next morning, after another bad night, Lindsay woke feeling like she had a truck parked on her chest. Today was, or would have been, her mother's birthday, and Lindsay realized she was possibly the only one on Earth now who remembered it. Jordan was too young to keep the date in her head, and it was a family joke that her father always forgot. Her mom would put on a determined face and arrange her own party, with some kind of crazy cake—a cake in the shape of the Washington Monument or whatever—and pictures and videos of things that had happened during the year. Presents she'd bought for herself would be wrapped up so she could act surprised. It sounded lame, but it was fun actually.

The pain of this memory was so overwhelming that Lindsay had to bury it in anger at her prick of a father. Her feeling of rage swelled in her chest as the daylight grew and the outline of the room came into focus. Her mom had confided to Lindsay that she did not want to take the Croatia trip, and Lindsay had tried to convince her to stand up to Dad for once and just not go. She'd been totally furious at her mother for caving in again and leaving Jordan and her at home with the nanny. At the end of their talk, Lindsay blew up and stomped out of the kitchen, deliberately muttering that her mother was a stupid cow, loud enough for her to hear. Now, the very last image she had of her mother was her standing next to the island looking really hurt.

During one of their trips back to DC, she'd tried to confront her dad about him dragging Mom along on the stupid Croatia trip, and they'd both lost it. The next day, after she and Jordan were on their way back to Massachusetts, he'd supposedly nearly died or something. She almost wished he had.

Plus, her weed had disappeared, which was the only thing that evened her out these days. Had Uncle Dave been sneaking around in her room? He didn't seem like that kind, but what else could have happened? On top of all that, she'd forgotten to dump her clothes in the laundry, and now she didn't have anything to wear except the jeans and sweatshirt she'd slept in.

All this had her dreading the idea of going to school, sure she'd start crying if someone said something nice to her—or even something mean to her or talked to her at all—when a knock on her door startled her.

It was Uncle Dave. Great.

"Hustle up, okay? Bus is coming in fifteen minutes."

She kept very quiet. Maybe he would think she was asleep and go away.

He knocked again. "There's a bagel on the counter and some cream cheese." He wouldn't leave. "Okay?" A pause. "Lindsay? Are you awake in there?" It was incredibly annoying.

She called out, "I'm not going today." A longer pause.

"Are you sick?"

It was ridiculous talking back and forth through the door. She got up and opened it a crack. Uncle Dave was standing there in his navy pinstripe looking hassled. He was just like her dad, always in his suit and tie and in a rush.

"No, I'm not sick. I'm just not going in today, okay?"

He looked at her, then looked down and scratched the back of his head. "You can't just not go to school when you don't feel like it."

"Why can't I?"

He sniffed and looked at her. "We all have our jobs, Lindsay. I have to go to work, you and Jordan have to go to school. We all—"

"I need a mental health day."

"You had two mental health days last week. I'm getting uncomfortable having you hang around the house while I'm—"

"Uncle Dave, I'm really sorry you're uncomfortable, but I can't manage school today, okay?" She opened the door a little wider.

Jordan ran up. "What's going on?"

It was like someone was pumping air into Lindsay, just one thing after another until she'd explode. "Jord, do me a favor and vanish for a second, will you, please? Uncle Dave and I are—"

"Hey." Now Uncle Dave was getting protective. Lindsay knew she was being a bitch, but he was the one who wouldn't leave her alone, and it really bugged her that he was going all Poppa Bear with Jordan.

Plus, he wouldn't shut up.

"Just take it easy now, Lindsay. I put a bagel on the counter, and your bus will be here in ten minutes or so. Staying home isn't going to work out today."

The sense of something pushing up from Lindsay's gut was getting overwhelming. Part of it was that she could see Jordan, with her wet brown eyes, picking up on things and getting stressed, which just made her angrier.

Jordan turned and skipped down the hall, calling over her shoulder. "I'm going to put my Eggo in the toaster."

Lindsay turned to Uncle Dave. "I'm not going to school."

Uncle Dave was shaking his head, about to tell her about how much work he had to do. "Listen, Lindsay. Today is a particularly tough—"

"I heard Jordan running down the hall last night. I suppose she hopped in bed with you?"

Uncle Dave shrugged. "She startled the heck out of me. I guess she was scared."

"I could tell the counselor at school that I'm concerned."

"You're concerned?"

"I could tell the counselor at school that I'm concerned about something maybe going on with you and Jordan."

"She was scared, that's all."

"Yeah, but I'd just have to say I was worried. I wouldn't have to say I knew anything for sure." Uncle Dave was standing there looking at her. Lindsay was hating herself, but hating herself was just making her angrier. "I'd only need to say that Jordan was with you, right? And that afterward, she seemed to be acting sort of strange, and I was worried about what was going on. And they'd have to investigate. That's the law now."

Uncle Dave's face changed. He got it.

"Jordan had a bad dream, Lindsay. You can't . . ."

"Just don't push me, Uncle Dave, okay? I'm, you know, I'm my father's daughter, and I'm not going to school today. That's it." She stepped back and closed the door hard.

A silence on the other side. Then Uncle Dave's footsteps going downstairs. Sounds of Jordan and him talking in the kitchen. Lindsay crawled back into bed and pulled the sheet up to blot out the daylight. She was so, so fucking sick of all this.

She must have dozed off, because she was jerked out of sleep sometime later by a loud rapping on her bedroom door. The door popped partway open as she was pulling herself up onto one elbow, and an empty suitcase came flying in and bounced off the side of her bed.

"Pack up." It was Uncle Dave calling from the hallway.

"What?" She was still foggy.

"Pack up, Lindsay. You're on a ten thirty flight to DC."

"What?"

"You're going home. You dad doesn't like it, but that's too bad."

"He agreed?"

Uncle Dave was standing in her doorway now. He probably hadn't wanted to poke his head in until he was sure she was covered up and everything.

"He didn't have time to agree or disagree, but he'll have someone at Washington National to meet you."

"What . . . ?"

Uncle Dave pointed at her. "You may be your father's daughter, but I'm his brother, okay?" He nodded at the suitcase. "Pack up. We're leaving in half an hour." He walked down the hall. "Your bagel's still on the counter if you want it."

A few minutes later, Norcross was down in the kitchen, his laptop open on the island, emailing his staff to rechoreograph the day. He'd already called Ruby and asked her to contact as many of the Cranmer jurors as possible. Seat Nine was from Great Barrington and was probably already on the Pike, but David couldn't help it. The trial today would be starting at eleven instead of nine in order to give him time to drop Lindsay at Bradley Airport. A sentencing he'd scheduled for late that afternoon would also have to be pushed back, which would inconvenience the marshals, who were already on the road bringing the defendant in from Rhode Island. It was a mess, but he had no choice.

He never should have let Ray talk him into taking the girls in the first place. He wasn't suited for it. The memory of getting manipulated over Christmas into agreeing to the six-month extension made him furious now. He closed the laptop, picked up his coffee, and drank most of it in two long gulps. Out the window, past the garage, the remains of the most recent snowstorm were piled along the sides of the driveway. The traffic would be heavy on I-91, so they'd need to leave plenty of time. Heaven help him if the flight were canceled.

Had he been wrong to make a big deal about Lindsay's not going to school today?

Probably. He really had no idea. But she'd been missing so much school, and the marijuana and the kid in the pickup had given him the jitters. What was she up to all day?

If it hadn't been this, it would have been something else. Who did she think she was, pushing him around with that hooey about talking to a counselor? It was just the sort of stunt Ray would pull. In fact, when he had called Ray and told him what was going on with his daughter, Ray had just chuckled and said, "That's my Lindsay!" By the end of their phone call, he wasn't so jolly.

When he came home from work later, he'd explain to Jordan that Lindsay had gone back to Washington to talk to her dad about something. The two of them would have pizza with carrot sticks and watch *Frozen* for the eighteenth time. In honor of the movie's theme, he'd pick up ice cream bars on the way home for dessert. It actually didn't sound too bad.

Norcross looked up at the ceiling and listened. Jordan had dashed out the door in time for her bus, but aside from a few vague thumps, he hadn't been hearing much from Lindsay. With a feeling of dread he trudged upstairs to find out what the heck was going on.

"You all set in there?" Something moved and a shadow flickered under her door. "We need to push off in about fifteen minutes." There was a noise, like a groan. Something fell over. "Lindsay?"

"Yeah. Yes. I'm coming. I just need . . ." Her voice was odd somehow, and muffled. He opened the door.

Lindsay was sitting on the edge of her unmade bed, elbows on her knees, hands covering her face. Was she sick? The suitcase sat open on the floor next to the bed. There was nothing in it except a bra and her catcher's mitt.

Lindsay looked up and then quickly turned and stared over her shoulder into the far corner of the room. She said something he didn't catch.

"Pardon me?"

"I just need a minute." Then she spoke a little louder, still facing the corner. "I have nowhere."

"You have nowhere?"

"My dad doesn't like me. You don't want me. And Mom's . . ."

To David's astonishment, Lindsay raised both her hands in the air, then pulled them into her sides, and bent over with a rending groan so loud it brought Marlene bustling into the room and jamming her nose into Lindsay's stomach, wagging her tail for all she was worth.

Lindsay just sat there crying and making these horrible noises while Norcross stood paralyzed in the doorway. Fifteen minutes ago, Lindsay was coming across as a tower of arrogant strength, a frightening adversary. Now he had no idea what to do, no idea anything like this had been lurking inside the girl. Marlene was baffled, too, and she looked over her shoulder for guidance. At first, David suspected it might be an act, and he put his hands in his pockets to wait it out.

But Lindsay just kept crying, hands over her face, tears leaking through, as though she didn't care that he was there. It was impossible to cry that hard and be putting it on.

Finally, in a gap while she breathed, Norcross said, "I'm sorry."

"I know." She gave a shudder as she exhaled. "I'm sorry, too. Shit."

Norcross took his hands out of his pockets and flapped them at her uselessly. "Can we talk?"

Lindsay shook her head and sniffed. "Do you really want to?"

42

Later that morning, Judge Norcross was tearing down the interstate, doing 70 in a 65 mph zone. As a rule, he never broke the speed limit, but he hated to make jurors wait. They were his flock, and even from behind the wheel, he felt their confusion and restlessness. It helped that he no longer had to ferry Lindsay to the airport. After a long talk, more tears, and their inaugural hug, he'd phoned Ray back and told him she wouldn't be coming down after all. Ray, still peeved about the earlier call, hadn't bothered to thank him.

When Norcross finally made it to the courthouse and hurried through the glass doors into his chambers, Chitra was waiting in the reception area, with an ominous "thank-heaven-you're-here" expression on her face. She pursued Norcross toward his inner office and started in, talking fast, before he even had time to pull his parka off.

"Attorney Ames filed a motion to dismiss an hour ago, Judge, under seal. She's accusing . . ." Chitra stopped, catching the look in Norcross's eye.

"Whoops!" She stuck out her tongue and bit the end of it to stanch her words. "Okay, I'll pack it in." She pointed through his door. "A copy of the motion is on your desk. I checked some First Circuit cases. Buzz if you need me."

"Thanks."

Chitra had broken a cardinal chambers rule: no bugging Judge Norcross until he had his coat hung up and his coffee poured. He disliked having a law clerk pounce on him the second he arrived almost as much as he hated making jurors wait. The motion Chitra was so worked up about didn't particularly worry him. It was bound to be only some trumped-up act of desperation thrown in by Linda Ames to try to save a doomed client.

Judge Norcross watched with concern as Chitra retreated to her office, worried that he'd hurt her feelings. Her hair, piled on top of her head in a bun, was slumped to one side and her shoulders looked tired. Erik was taking sick time to help out with his new baby, and Chitra had probably been in chambers since who knew when, dealing with incoming artillery and trying to keep everything on track all by herself. He'd need to say something nice to her later on.

The judge and his two law clerks were putting in long hours. Jury selection in *United States v. Cranmer* had eaten up two weeks and a pool of almost a hundred and fifty candidates before they culled out the twelve impartial jurors and two alternates they needed. New England's sugaring season was almost upon them, and Erik pointed out that their pool-to-juror ratio was about the same as the proportion of sap needed to produce a gallon of maple syrup.

Following jury selection, as the government's case took off, Norcross found himself impressed with Campanella's trial skill. During his opening to the jury, Campanella used no podium and no notes. This was the preferred technique and the one that Norcross had used when he tried his own cases way back when. Forgoing notes enhanced a lawyer's engagement with the jury panel, but it was a practice that only the most confident, experienced lawyers had the nerve to employ. For most attorneys, the risk of forgetting something important was too great.

Campanella's entire opening, spooned out in easily absorbed morsels, detailing each item of evidence against Cranmer, took only twenty minutes. When he finished, it was obvious from the jurors' faces that Professor Cranmer was already three-quarters of the way down the tube.

After Campanella sat down, Norcross nodded to Linda Ames, expecting her to take her turn. Instead, to Norcross's surprise, she had informed the court that she would postpone her opening until the government had rested at the close of all its evidence. This was a permissible but rare tactic. Defense attorneys almost always opened right away, to raise immediate doubts about the strength of the evidence. Ames had to be assuming, or hoping, that she could bring out something during the government's case that would give her postponed remarks enough extra force to compensate for the delay.

With no opening from the defense, the trial had moved straight into the government's witnesses. Campanella had stage-managed the presentation persuasively, day by day, along the lines promised in his opening. This morning, after almost two weeks, and the two-hour delay, the government would be calling its last, longest, and most crucial witness, Special Agent Michael Patterson, to deliver the coup de grâce.

When Norcross approached his desk after hanging up his parka, he remembered the memo Chitra had mentioned, sitting in the center of his blotter. Its title, in bolded sixteen-point font, was "Motion to Dismiss Based on Prosecutorial Misconduct." The caption jumped out so dramatically that Norcross had to smile. He picked up the memo and began skimming it without bothering to sit down. As he read, all the distractions of the morning winked out.

One floor down, Patterson was in Paul Campanella's office, leaning over his desk, trying to pound some sense into the AUSA's head.

"We never would have brought this case, Paul, except for the DVD. That was the whole deal."

Paul had been reviewing the final draft of his opposition to Ames's motion to dismiss, and Patterson's interruption was coming at a bad time. He spoke a little impatiently.

"So you're saying I should just bail, dismiss everything?"

"Yes, that's exactly what I'm saying."

"When the case has gone this far? Forget it. Would you sit down, please?" Campanella didn't like Patterson looming over him. After Patterson sat, Campanella continued, trying to sound reasonable. "First, with all due respect, Mike, this is not your decision." Campanella paused to let this sink in, eyeballing Patterson. "It's not even my decision. I'd have to get permission to dismiss from the big guy in Boston, Buddy Hogan, and there's no way in a million years he'll give it."

Patterson eyeballed Campanella right back. "Really. And how many hours have our Boston friends invested in this case?"

Campanella flapped a hand at Patterson, brushing him away. "Not going to happen, Mike, not after all the press. Besides, the material you guys found on Cranmer's computer is plenty to hang him. If we have to, we can go forward just with that."

Patterson looked to the side and sniffed, speaking mostly to himself. "My God." He reached his hands halfway across Campanella's desk. It was his turn to try to sound reasonable. "Come on, Paul. You know it's a chickenshit case now. Without the DVD, we never would have bothered with it."

"I don't know about that. Cranmer's a juicy plum, and if we drop the charges, it looks as though we're running from Ames's motion. It might even seem like I'm admitting some kind of misconduct, on my very first solo trial." Campanella waved his papers. "I need to finish my memo here, okay? We've got good arguments that—"

"You didn't engage in misconduct. We both got smoked by this Jaworski kid."

"We don't even know for sure that this video is legit." Campanella sighed and shook his head. "Dammit. The evidence has been going in like hot fudge. And now, out of the blue, this pain in the—"

Patterson was shaking his head, refusing to give it up. "The confession is the real deal, Paul. It tracks just what we thought. Jaworski filled out the form with block capitals using his left hand, and he wore plastic gloves. Everyone's seen too much *CSI*. But the fold did him in." Patterson leaned back and crossed his arms, dropping his voice. "This Spencer girl reminds me of Margaret. Scary smart. I can't decide whether to arrest her or hire her."

Earlier that morning, they'd watched Elizabeth's short video, forwarded to them by Linda Ames, at least a dozen times. The crucial moment was when Jaworski—naked, handcuffed, and standing on a chair with a noose around his neck—recalled how he had folded the flyer the wrong way, lengthwise, the first time he tried to slip it into the return envelope provided in the mailing. Prodded by Elizabeth Spencer, Jaworski detailed how he had then refolded the flyer horizontally to make it fit properly.

When Campanella and Patterson had slipped the form out of its cellophane sleeve and examined it, they could easily see the faint, vestigial crossways fold that had been Jaworski's first attempt. This killer detail, which only the sender would know, was irrefutable evidence of the confession's credibility.

"We ought to talk to Jaworski, at least," Campanella said.

"Like I told you, I tried to call him first thing, with no luck. I figured he'd flown the coop and, yep, the airline confirmed he was on a six thirty nonstop to Chicago." Patterson glanced at his watch. "He'll be landing about now, and my bet is his daddy already has him lawyered up to his eyeballs. That boy is not talking to anybody."

Paul Campanella rubbed his face and pulled his hand over his goatee. "What Elizabeth Spencer did was probably a crime, you know."

"Whatever she did is a state court matter, if it's anything. Frankly, I can't imagine the DA going after a smart, good-looking girl who did the right thing. There's a state election coming up this fall, you know."

"Linda Ames says Spencer made a copy of the video and gave it to one of her professors, someone she doesn't identify, who passed it on to Ames."

Patterson nodded. "Uh-huh. And I can guess who that professor was."

Campanella shook his head wearily. "Jesus, what next?"

43

Down in the courtroom, Ames was struggling to translate the storm of incoherent fury and guilt raging inside her into syntax recognizable under the law. It was now obvious that the government had fastened on Sid as the bad guy on day one and then simply switched off its collective brain. No further, even minimal, investigation was pursued. This was inexcusable, but what made the situation truly unbearable was that Ames herself had swallowed their line. She had not believed Sid, her own client, whom she was supposed to protect.

Of course, her emotional state was irrelevant to the here-and-now crisis she was facing. She had to put aside her thermonuclear mood and find words that could make their way into Judge Norcross's head and get him to dismiss these charges. Just thundering wouldn't do it.

Any second now, Norcross would enter the courtroom, and she'd have maybe two minutes, three at the most, to find a path into his brain. If she slipped, he'd simply pick up with the trial and move on to the testimony of Agent Patterson.

Ames had gotten the call from Claire Lindemann at 1:30 a.m. that morning. Half asleep, she was on the verge of hanging up, sure this overagitated professor lady was just a typical academic kook. Then something in Lindemann's voice got to her, and she agreed to meet—as Lindemann insisted—right then. Ames had barely pulled on a sweat suit and splashed some water in her face before Lindemann was at her door, looking even more tousled than she was. By 2:15 a.m., Ames was looking at the video. By 2:45 a.m., Lindemann was making coffee, and Ames was at her computer, fingers trembling, banging out the affidavit in support of her motion to dismiss.

Ames's motion deliberately omitted revealing that it was Norcross's girlfriend who had brought her the video. There was no legal or practical reason to share this information with him. The Amherst coed, Elizabeth Spencer, could testify, if necessary, about the circumstances under which the video was taken. How it got to Ames didn't matter. More important, one more mention of Professor Lindemann might just be enough to push Norcross into recusing himself, and Ames wanted him presiding. He was familiar with the case, and she had her best shot at getting a dismissal from him. What he didn't know wouldn't hurt her.

Besides, screw it, she'd been so jerked around by now that anything was fair.

The dawn was breaking and the blue jays were starting to argue in her backyard before Ames hit the send button on her motion to dismiss, legal memorandum, and sworn affidavit. It was only then that Ames called Sid Cranmer, woke him up, and told him what had happened.

Sid had been incredulous. "Jaworski? That dipshit?" Then after a pause he added, "As they say in Wonderland—curiouser and curiouser!"

"Sid, I'm so sorry, I've been doubting you all this—"

"Forget it." He laughed ruefully. "This is what happens when when you give somebody a C-minus these days."

Now Sid was sitting next to her at the defense table, and neither of them knew what was about to happen. AUSA Campanella hurried into the courtroom and slid into his chair over at the government's table. The jury box was empty. The jurors would be gathered in their deliberation room down a back hallway, out of earshot and ignorant of Ames's motion. Campanella obviously hoped to keep it that way.

"Morning, Linda."

"Fuck you, Paul."

Campanella handed her a memorandum. "Same back at you."

"What's this?"

"Opposition to your motion to dismiss."

"You're giving it to me now?"

He was scribbling something on his yellow pad, not looking at her. "I only printed it five minutes ago."

At that moment, the courtroom door swung open, Norcross entered, and Ruby Johnson called out, "All rise!"

Ames could see that the judge was holding her motion in his hand and that he looked odd. She couldn't say how. One of his law clerks, the South Asian woman, glanced up nervously at Norcross as he took his chair. Problems? She looked intelligent and must have been researching the authorities Ames cited in her memo. What had she been telling the judge?

"Please be seated."

The gallery contained only a couple reporters, the sketch artist, and two or three spectators.

Patterson wasn't in the courtroom yet. He must be off somewhere trying to follow up on this new evidence, the jerk. On the other hand, his absence might mean that the government did not think he'd be going on the stand right away, which might be good. Ames was in a world where anything could happen.

Norcross was giving her a close look. His face was serious but neutral. She still couldn't read him.

"Ms. Ames, I've read your motion, and I must say I'm amazed." Not looking particularly amazed, the judge turned to Campanella. "Do you concede, Mr. Campanella, that the DVD you talked me into playing to the jury might, in fact, never have been ordered by this defendant?"

Campanella lifted himself to his feet with a soft grunt.

"Um, we agree, Judge, that significant evidence now suggests that the DVD was, in fact, ordered by a disgruntled undergraduate as a prank."

"A prank? Significant evidence?" Norcross's face went dark, and he raised his voice. "Don't play games. Yes or no? Are you conceding that the government cannot prove that this defendant sent in the flyer ordering the DVD?"

"We haven't had time yet to investigate thoroughly, so we—"

"Oh, for heaven's sake!" The judge's volume increased on the last two words. "The time to investigate thoroughly was six months ago!" He slapped his hands on the bench and shook his head. "Where does that leave us? More importantly, where does that leave the jury?"

"I agree it's a very unusual situation, Your Honor."

"Unusual? That's what you'd call it?"

Ames's lawyerly side had to give some credit to Campanella. The fact that Norcross was normally so unflappable made his anger now even more intimidating. But Campanella was maintaining his cool—not getting rattled, keeping his voice even.

"Unusual, Your Honor, right, but not entirely unprecedented. I have a memo I'd like to submit laying out the government's suggestions for how to proceed." Campanella picked up a sheaf of papers. "May I approach?" He took a step toward the courtroom deputy, holding the memorandum out.

"You have a memo for me? Now?"

"Well, Judge, I only got Ms. Ames's motion when I arrived at my office this morning at seven a.m. I had no prior notice it was coming." He hesitated. "I'm doing the best I can here, Judge."

"Fine. Summarize your argument for me, please. I'll read your written version later."

"Well, Your Honor, the government proposes either of two courses, both well supported by First Circuit authority. First, we would not oppose a motion to strike the DVD and an instruction from you to the jury telling them to disregard it entirely."

Ames could not suppress a disgusted explosion of breath. Norcross, who usually disliked this kind of display, gave her a quick sympathetic look. No power existed in heaven, hell, or anywhere in between to wipe the memory of that DVD out of the jurors' minds. It was impossible to imagine evidence any more indelible or any more unfairly prejudicial.

Sensing where things stood, Campanella moved quickly on. "Alternatively, the government would assent to a defense motion for a mistrial, based on circumstances outside the government's control—outside the control of anyone, really—and we could immediately reempanel the case with a new jury and without reference to the DVD. It would be a fresh start, perfectly fair to both sides."

Norcross grimaced. "It took us forever to pick this jury. How easy do you think it will be to pick another one after this morning's news hits the papers?" Norcross nodded at the *Republican* reporter. "I see Ms. Crawford writing away with her usual energy." Ames glanced back at the corner of the courtroom to see the reporter—without pausing in her scribbling—dart the judge a quick, professional smile.

Norcross turned to Ames. "Okay. Ms. Ames, what do you say? Have a seat, Mr. Campanella."

Taking care to stay unhurried, Linda Ames walked from her seat up to the podium and arranged her yellow pad and a copy of her memorandum on it. Campanella had stayed back at the counsel table to deliver his remarks, which was almost always a mistake. Best to get right under the judge's nose.

"Circumstances outside the government's control. Really?"

She raised her voice and looked up at the bench. "Let me say, first of all, and loud and clear, that the defense is not, repeat *not*, moving for a mistrial." She pointed back at the government table, where Campanella sat, not bothering to look at her. "Mr. Campanella is fully aware that retrials strongly favor the government, and he's trying to lure me into asking for one.

"He'd like to have another crack at Sid Cranmer, after this practice swing, a do-over where the government could get its act together. But under our Constitution, the government only gets to try a man, or woman, once. I'm asserting that right, Judge. I'm moving for dismissal without possibility of a retrial, based on the horrendous mess the government has made of this case."

She stepped to the side of the podium to mark her transition.

"Let me begin, first, by reviewing what we know for sure about what has been going on here. Then I'll move to things I don't explicitly know, but which I can be pretty sure about. Things that are obvious. Just a second, please."

She stepped back to the government's table and spoke to AUSA Campanella, being sure to keep her voice loud enough for the judge to hear. She pointed at the DVD on the corner of his table. "May I borrow that?" When Campanella shrugged, she said, "Thank you," picked it up, and returned to the podium.

"Okay. First, we now all know that Sid Cranmer never ordered this awful DVD. Mr. Campanella's suggestion that there is only 'significant evidence' suggesting this is a ridiculous understatement. He now knows flat out, or he ought to know, that an Amherst College undergraduate named Ryan Jaworski, not Sid Cramer, ordered this DVD using the flyer he stole out of my client's wastebasket. So much for the government's Exhibit One."

She turned, tossing the DVD on the table so that it clattered and skidded toward Campanella. The gesture confirmed Ames's point: the DVD was now trash. Without missing a beat, she turned her face up to Norcross and pushed on. "Second, we know that the government has been aware of Mr. Jaworski for a very long time. They've known about him since way before this trial started.

"Third, we know that Agent Patterson has actually spoken to Mr. Jaworski. The government provided some vague information about this contact in its pretrial disclosures, even though Mr. Campanella never included Mr. Jaworski on the government's witness list. So, we don't know all the details, but we do know they've talked to him.

"Next, um, jeez, I forget what number I'm at." This was deliberate, keeping the judge with her.

The judge broke in, just as she'd hoped. "I think you're at fourth."

"Thanks. Fourth, I can tell you, Judge, that I tried to contact Mr. Jaworski. I doubt I possessed one-quarter of the information the government had about him, but it seemed clear enough to me that Mr. Jaworski had important information. I left three phone messages for him, and I wrote him a letter, but he never got back to me. Ryan Jaworski has been hovering around the edges of this case, Judge, since the beginning. The government has had full access to him, and I haven't. That's how it is. There can be no debate about that.

"Fifth, the government has known about Elizabeth Spencer, the young lady who obtained by informal means, highly informal means, Mr. Jaworski's confession. In fact"—Ames tapped on the podium with her pointer finger—"they've known about her since the very day this investigation blossomed, the very day"—she tapped again—"of the very first raid at Sid's house nine or ten months ago now."

Ames took a breath to remind herself never to refer to Sid using the unsympathetic "Professor" prefix.

"Ms. Spencer was there, right in Sid's living room, right there, going over some research with him, when the FBI's raid team came charging through his door. The government has had months and months to follow up with their investigation by interviewing her. They've had ample opportunity to find out from either one of these kids all about this so-called prank. Instead, this whole time they sat on their big, fat . . ."

She paused and looked to the side to draw out the tension. "They sat on their hands and did nothing."

At this point, the door to the courtroom swished, and Ames turned to watch Patterson walking across the gallery. He stepped through the small swinging door that marked the entrance to the well of the court, nodded to Ames, and took his seat next to Paul Campanella.

Ames turned back to the judge. "Good. I see Agent Patterson is here. Now, finally, let me tell you something I don't know absolutely for sure, but which I'm ready to put money on. Agent Patterson, who has just joined us, submitted an affidavit a few months back in support of a second search of my client's home, claiming that he had received information about a big cache, supposedly, of hidden child pornography. In that affidavit, Agent Patterson quoted an anonymous, purportedly reliable confidential informant who knew about this hidden mother lode of pornography that Patterson's team had somehow overlooked during the first raid. This supposedly reliable CI had even informed Agent Patterson of where the pornography was hidden.

"As you know, this search came up dry. Nothing was found. Zilch. The pornography never existed. Now, Judge, I haven't so far been permitted to learn who this anonymous—not reliable but actually highly *unreliable*—CI was, but I'll tell you who I think it was. I think it was this same character, Mr. Ryan Jaworski, the same guy who, encouraged by one of Sid Cranmer's jealous colleagues at Amherst College, sent the flyer in using Sid Cranmer's name and credit card information. They thought this whole nightmare would be just hilarious, I guess."

Ames pointed over her shoulder back at Patterson and Campanella. "Have them disclose to you who this CI was, Judge. Right now. Have Mr. Campanella walk up to side bar right now and tell you if it was Mr. Jaworski." She pointed back at her chair. "I'll stay in my seat. You can turn on your white noise, and I promise to stick my fingers in my ears." She was jabbing her finger back at the prosecution table. "I will lay you one dollar to a hundred that the lying CI was Ryan Jaworski, the same guy who we now know sent the flyer in and who was on a crusade all along, with this Professor Mattoon, to have a little jolly fun at my client's expense." She pointed back at Campanella and raised her voice. "They've known this Jaworski guy somehow got inside Sid's house, and they've known he was a liar with a motive to tell stories about Sid for months." She smacked the podium and shouted. "Months!"

Ames paused to let herself settle down. She'd taken a risk by dialing up the intensity, and she could see Norcross shifting uncomfortably. The judge, Ames knew, liked people to make nice. She needed to reassure him that she wasn't going to go ballistic.

She let her voice slip into a conversational tone. "And let me interject something here, Judge, if I might. Something personal." She took a break to look down, a consciously tactical move this time, then looked right up into Norcross's face. "Last month, I pressured Sid Cranmer to plead guilty." She tapped herself on the chest. "I did that. I made sure he knew the decision was his, but, frankly, I hammered him hard to take the two-year deal the government was offering. As a result, I put him through the humiliating plea attempt a few weeks back, and in the process, I'm afraid I irritated you."

Norcross broke in. "These things happen."

"They don't happen to me, Judge. Not like that."

"It's water under the bridge, Ms. Ames. All part of the world we find ourselves in."

"Maybe so." Ames paused and cleared her throat to mark another transition. "Last of all, I'll tell you another thing I don't have to infer, something I know. Ryan Jaworski has flown the coop. I spoke to his girlfriend, or probably ex-girlfriend, Ms. Spencer, this morning, and she's already heard that he's landed in Chicago, where his very well-connected father no doubt has him walled up, two thousand miles from here, behind so many lawyers we couldn't hack our way through with a battle-ax. He's gone, at least for the foreseeable future." She glanced back at the government's table. "Mr. Campanella may be able to drag him back eventually, assuming he wants to, but it's not going to be easy and it's going to take a while."

Ames stepped out from behind the podium again and stood next to it.

"Okay, there's only one thing to do here, and that's to dismiss this utterly, utterly bungled case. Mr. Campanella's suggestion that we might continue forward with this jury is ridiculous. His suggestion that I should somehow join with him in a motion for a mistrial is even sillier. To be blunt, I'm not that dumb. Mr. Campanella knows very well that any request by me for a mistrial would undercut my motion to dismiss, which is why he cleverly suggested it. But no new trial and no new jury can cure the violation of Sid Cranmer's rights." She held her hands out in front of her, cupped, as though she was holding something precious. "The Fifth Amendment to the Bill of Rights protects us all. It says 'nor shall any person be subject for the same offense to be twice put in jeopardy.'" She dropped her hands. "I ask that this indictment be dismissed based on the gross negligence of the government, with prejudice, without possibility of retrial."

Ames returned to her seat.

Campanella immediately stood up. "Your Honor, if I might . . ."

"Just a minute, Counsel." Norcross leaned down to Ruby Johnson and said, "Please tell the jurors they are excused for today. I'll want to see them tomorrow, either to continue the trial or to thank them for their service." Ruby got up and hurried out of the courtroom.

Norcross returned his attention to Campanella. The judge's expression was troubled, and he rubbed at the crinkled skin under his eye. Ames knew that her argument wasn't the clear winner she'd tried so hard to make it look like. A judge, or a court of appeals, might conclude that this was just a hiccup, a crazy fluke that was nobody's fault. Unexpected things happened all the time in this alternate universe—jurors couldn't agree, inadmissible evidence popped out accidentally, a lawyer or judge dropped dead, whatever. If this wasn't the government's fault, they could retry Sid with a new jury, and retrials were almost always deadly for a defendant. The defense had an argument here, but so did the government.

Campanella made his way to the podium. Like Ames, he took care not to appear in the least frazzled. He spoke softly.

"Judge, we can solve this quickly. I can put on a witness right now who will testify that up until this morning, about two hours ago, the government had absolutely no inkling, and more importantly no way of knowing, that it was this Amherst College student who sent the flyer in. We are as astonished as Ms. Ames is, or, I presume, as you are."

"No one is as astonished as I am, Mr. Campanella."

"Fair enough. But this testimony will demonstrate that the responsibility for any mistrial, if that is what you're considering, simply cannot be laid at the feet of the government. If you don't like the option of striking the DVD, we can excuse this jury and resume promptly before a new one. That will be fair all around." He looked back at Ames. "But that's her choice, not ours. We're not moving for a mistrial—I don't think it's necessary—but we would not oppose it if the defense wants one. The reason she's not asking for one is that she doesn't want twelve impartial jurors to hear this case."

"I'm not happy being put in this position, midtrial, Mr. Campanella."

"Your Honor, let me repeat. I can show—can show clearly—that Ryan Jaworski's bizarre confession came entirely out of the blue."

Norcross was beginning to settle down and look thoughtful, which was a bad sign. A quick, emotional response was what Ames was hoping for.

"What's this testimony that you want to offer, Mr. Campanella, that you're so sure will convince me of the government's innocence here?"

Campanella nodded over his shoulder back at Patterson.

"I propose to put on Special Agent Michael Patterson for just a few questions. He'll confirm that this video confession has been as much a surprise to us as it has been to you."

"Well, Mr. Campanella, the court has—"

Picking up on the continued skepticism in Norcross's voice, Campanella hazarded an interruption and lifted his tone. "Judge, we have a *ton* of independent evidence here, seized from Professor Cranmer's computer. This material has no connection whatsoever to the flyer or the DVD." The AUSA lifted his hands up, stretching his fingers out. "If the government is without fault, if we did nothing to create the dilemma about the DVD, we should be permitted, at least, to present this independent evidence to a new jury. It's just not fair, Judge, to deprive the government of this opportunity in a situation where the public interest is so prominent and where the government did nothing wrong."

Ames could see something that Campanella, who was facing the bench and totally focused on Norcross, could not see. Agent Patterson was staring at Campanella with a distinctly unhappy expression, a stormier version of his usual game face. Did Patterson resent being shoved onto the front line like this?

Whatever was going on, Ames needed to protect the record. She stood up. "Your Honor, I strongly object. This is not—"

"Sorry." Norcross shook his head curtly. "I want to hear from Agent Patterson. It is a straightforward question: How did we end up down this rabbit hole? And there are some basic facts I'm looking for."

Norcross's expression made it clear that it was pointless to push this.

"Very good. May I make a personal request then?" Ames gestured down at Sid. "My client and I have been here for some time, and we would like, we actually badly need, a short break, if the court would be so kind." These were the standard polite phrases typically used to request a bathroom break. It was a rare judge who would turn this down. Ames actually had no idea whether her client needed a pit stop. She didn't, but she urgently needed time to absorb where things were going now and to think over the questions she might put to Patterson.

"Fine," Norcross said. "We'll take a fifteen-minute recess. One final matter before we break. I want counsel to speak with Ms. Vaidyanathan"—he nodded down at his law clerk—"and make arrangements with her to get me a video file of Mr. Jaworski's confession. I want to review it myself in chambers before we pick up with the testimony."

Campanella stood up. "Right now, Your Honor?"

"Right now."

Both Ames and Campanella began talking at the same time.

"Judge, it's kind of . . ." Ames said, just as Campanella said, "Your Honor, it's not the usual . . ."

"I don't care," Norcross said gruffly. He stood up. "I want to see it, however unusual it may be. Talk to Ms. Vaidyanathan. The court's in recess."

44

Judge Norcross had a bad habit sometimes of telling his law clerks to do things they had no idea how to do. His brusque assignment to Chitra to get a copy of Jaworski's video confession was a good example. She knew how to download a video file, of course, but this transfer would have to be handled so that it could be preserved for the record and retrievable months or years from now. How could she ensure this? The technical challenge was complicated by the fact that the judge had instructed Chitra to work with counsel to make the download, and the two attorneys were barely speaking.

The defendant disappeared right after the judge left the bench, and within less than a minute, it was clear that neither Campanella nor Ames was going to be any help. Chitra knew more about this kind of technical thing than either of them, which was frightening. In the end, she had Attorney Ames forward the video clip to her at her personal email address as an attachment. In a few seconds, it popped up on her iPhone, and she hurried down the back hallway to chambers.

She found the judge sitting at his desk, reading over Campanella's memo. He looked up when he saw her.

"Got it?"

"I just had them send it to me on my phone. I couldn't think of any other way to . . ."

"Good for you. That's fine."

"I'm worried about preserving the record."

Judge Norcross stood up as she approached.

"We can have the IT staff transfer it to a DVD, and I'll mark it as a sealed exhibit." As Chitra approached, holding the phone out, Norcross said, "Sorry if I've been a bear. You really are doing a great job here, Chitra. I'd be up the creek without you."

The compliment made Chitra so happy she felt herself misting up. "Thank you." She gave a quick smile to hide how she was feeling. "I'm not sure how much help I've been."

"You've been great. Let's see what we've got."

Chitra stood next to Judge Norcross. Her shoulder bumped his elbow, and they each immediately adjusted to maintain a proper space. The judge was much taller, so Chitra had to hold the phone up high so they could both see. She tapped the icon to open the attachment.

Both of them froze when, after a few seconds, the image of Ryan Jaworski appeared, handcuffed, naked, perched on a chair with a noose around his neck

The judge pulled his chin in. "Good Lord!"

Chitra wasn't sure what to do. The scene was certainly bizarre, but her own situation was almost as strange, with the two of them bent close together over the tiny screen, staring like Peeping Toms. She could smell Judge Norcross's aftershave.

She stepped back. "Judge, I could let you handle this on your . . ."

"Nope. Nope. I want your opinion here." He pursed his lips, pulled on his nose, and sniffed. "They weren't kidding. This certainly is unusual."

The two of them watched as Jaworski mumbled the date and time, recited his name, and described his location. Drunk and miserable, he looked like something that had been pulled up out of a clogged toilet. A female voice in the background faded in and out, instructing him to speak up, pushing him through the chronology. Step by step, he laid out how he pilfered the flyer, took it to Professor Mattoon, and ultimately sent in the order for *Playing Doctor* with the defendant's address and credit card information.

He was pressed to repeat himself at various points to make himself clear. The only time his face took on any animation was during the description of his total horror when he realized that he and Mattoon had blundered into an FBI sting.

The video went on for about five minutes. When it was over, and Chitra had closed the screen, Judge Norcross shook his head and spoke disgustedly. "For heaven's sake, a promising young man like that, with all his privileges."

Chitra glanced at the judge. "He's what we ladies in the Asian community would call a classic cad."

"Well, I'd agree with them. He's that and more."

"It's slang, Judge. Short for Cadbury—too tasty for his own good."

The sides of Judge Norcross's mouth turned down, and he spoke impatiently. "Why do kids get into these darn things? I don't understand it."

"It's hard to explain after the fact, I guess," Chitra hesitated. "Sometimes people do foolish things."

"Well, this was a doozy." Norcross cleared his throat. "What did you think of Jaworski?"

Chitra looked up at the ceiling for a moment. "I think he's accurately describing what happened. I believe him."

"If a law enforcement officer ever procured a confession this way, I'd put him in jail."

"Of course."

Judge Norcross shook his head and sighed. "I'm going to want to see that fold."

"Definitely. Amazing how such a small detail can make such a big difference."

Linda Ames's request for a bathroom break may have been a ruse for her, but after an extralarge coffee on the way to court, it was a lifesaver for Sid Cranmer. In the men's room, he sidled up to a urinal and began a process of draining that seemed to start somewhere up around his cerebral cortex and proceed downward organ by organ. He could actually feel the muscles in his calves start to relax.

When he was emptied about halfway, the door thumped open,

and someone entered. It was Patterson. The encounter wasn't as awkward as it might have been—they'd gotten to know each other, in a way, during Patterson's two raids on his house—but it was still very, very strange.

They stood side by side, not talking, taking care of business.

"How you holding up?" Patterson finally asked, shaking off and zipping. Cranmer felt like Alice, encountering the Caterpillar, being asked "Who are *you*?" and not being sure what to say.

"I'm okay." Sid took his turn zipping and stepped over to one of the sinks. "Things keep changing. Sometimes I wake up in the morning and wonder if I'm still the same person."

"Sorry about what happened when you were at Ludlow."

Sid shrugged. "Fun and games."

Patterson stepped over to the neighboring sink. They bumped hands reaching for the soap. "Sorry."

Sid nodded at the dispenser. "Go ahead."

If this got any weirder, Sid thought, he was just going to wipe his hands on his ass and get out of there. They rinsed off in silence.

Patterson pulled a paper towel out and turned to Sid. "I'm not supposed to talk to you, okay, so let's forget we ever had this little coffee break. Paul Campanella would have a screaming bull calf."

"Linda would be fine with it, as long as I peed on you."

Patterson grunted. "Just had these trousers cleaned." He looked to the side, pondering something, then continued. "I did some research on your star."

"Ah."

"Says you pulled two leathernecks out of heavy fire."

Sid took a while to answer, conscious that Patterson was keeping his eyes on him. Finally, he spoke.

"Only one counted. The other guy was a sack of meat by the time I got him back to the line." Sid hesitated, then plunged. "He was a friend, you know, a nice kid. That kind of thing." He looked down at the black-and-white tiled floor. "It was a long time ago."

"Says you got shot up."

"I caught a couple scratches."

Now it was Sid's turn to give Patterson a hard look. The wonderful thing about combat was that the guy who was trying to kill you had nothing against you personally. Maybe even respected you in a crazy way. This was kind of like that.

"I don't have to tell you, right? Once the shit starts flying, the only heroes are the ones who come home in wooden houses. The rest of us are just . . ."

Patterson nodded. "I know."

45

Would you please state your name for the record?"

"Michael Patterson."

"And would you tell the court your profession."

"Special agent, FBI."

The judge broke in. "Let's dispense with the formalities, Mr. Campanella, and get to the central issue, shall we? I know who Agent Patterson is."

Campanella nodded up at the bench. A streamlined approach was okay with him. The facts were simple, and the quicker this went, the better.

"Fine, Judge."

Agent Patterson was sitting in the witness box, at about two o'clock from the podium where Campanella was standing and about fifteen feet away. Judge Norcross was straight in front of him, at noon. Ames was behind him at the defense table at around five o'clock. During the break, Campanella had consulted with the senior assistant U.S. attorney in his office and, in a moment that still warmed him, had received a compliment for his quick and effective response to Ames's motion to dismiss. This short evidentiary hearing would make the record clear and set the trial back on track.

"How long have you been working on the Cranmer case, Agent Patterson?"

"I first learned about it a little over a year ago and was formally assigned to the investigation about eleven months back."

Agent Patterson was the perfect law enforcement witness—a physically impressive, well-dressed, serious-looking man, who radiated competence and reliability. The jurors, when they heard his testimony tomorrow, would be eating out of his hand, and Campanella was fairly confident that even Judge Norcross would find Patterson's charisma magnetic.

"And you participated in the initial search of the defendant's residence, isn't that true?"

"Yes. I was the lead agent. We came in following a controlled delivery of a contraband DVD."

"Now, Agent Patterson, would you please tell the court how it came about that you made the controlled delivery on the morning you seized the DVD?"

"An earlier investigation had picked up Professor Cranmer on a website used by pedophiles. Somewhere down the line, the postal inspector sent him a flyer supposedly advertising DVDs containing pornography with prepubescent subjects. When the flyer came back, my team got involved. We assumed—"

Campanella said, "Please don't tell us what you assumed. Just tell us—"

Ames stood. "Defense has no objection to testimony about the witness's assumptions, Your Honor. That's what this hearing is about—incorrect assumptions."

"Well, we'll see." Norcross nodded at the witness. "Okay, Agent Patterson. What did you assume?"

Campanella was pleased to have the judge getting involved. It was always helpful, when the flow was in the right direction, to have the court get in the canoe and paddle.

"We assumed, Judge, when the flyer came back, that Professor Cranmer had filled it out with his information, including his credit card data, and sent it in. Once we had what we thought was his order,

I organized the team handling the delivery of the DVD." Patterson paused and folded his hands in front of him. "The plan was to conduct the search immediately after the delivery, to ensure we didn't lose control of the contraband. So, as soon as Your Honor approved the warrant, we moved quickly. We wanted that DVD back in our hands ASAP."

Campanella waited while Norcross scribbled down a short note, then continued with his next question. "And would you tell the court if there was anything else that made you assume that this defendant had been the one who sent the flyer in, ordering Exhibit One?"

Patterson shifted in his chair so that he was directly facing Judge Norcross.

"Well, Professor Cranmer immediately accepted the package when it was delivered with no questions, and he started to open it right away. He told the agent posing as the UPS employee something to the effect that he was expecting the package. As I said before . . ." He paused. "Is it still all right to say what I assumed?"

"I believe so." The judge looked at Ames, raising his eyebrows.

Ames half rose, leaning over the table. "No objection."

"We assumed when we saw him through the window that he was hiding the DVD when he saw us coming. Then, when I spoke to him, he never denied ordering the DVD, and he said he wasn't surprised when it showed up."

"Uh-huh, and . . ."

Ames broke in. "Your Honor, I'd object . . ."

Patterson continued. "At least, that was my interpretation of what he said."

"Aha. With that clarification, I withdraw my objection." Ames sat down.

Campanella pressed on. "Now, in the months leading up to this trial, did your assumptions with regard to the defendant's role in sending the flyer in ever begin to change? Did it ever, *ever*, occur to you, even remotely, that someone else might be involved in sending it in?"

"At some point, yes."

This was not quite the answer Campanella was expecting, but he had no trouble clarifying. "And that was when you learned this morning that an Amherst College undergraduate had made some kind of confession, isn't that right?"

Ames's voice piped up again. "Objection, leading."

Patterson's answer came out before Norcross had a chance to rule on Ames's objection. "Well, no, I had some suspicions before then."

Ames popped up. "Objection withdrawn."

Patterson's answer was a thumb-size cloud on the edge of Campanella's clear horizon, a smudge he could wipe away.

"In your work as an investigator, it is part of your job to keep in mind all kinds of hypothetical possibilities, correct?"

"Yes, but this was different. I became concerned some months back that—"

"So, as a conscientious law enforcement officer, you simply—"

Ames was standing again. "Wait a minute now, hold up. Let's let Agent Patterson finish his answer. He was saying something about concerns some months ago."

Judge Norcross folded his hands and leaned toward Patterson. "Yes, please explain your concerns."

"Well, Your Honor," Campanella interrupted. "I'd object to that." Something was happening with Patterson. His eyes had gone hard, and he was looking to the side.

Judge Norcross did not sound happy. "You object to your own witness's testimony?"

"Well, Your Honor, I'd like to conduct the questioning in my own manner."

"I appreciate that, Mr. Campanella. It's true that this is your witness, but this"—Norcross tapped himself on the temple—"this is the brain that will be making the decision here. And I'd like to know what Agent Patterson's concerns were some months ago." He turned to Agent Patterson. "Would you please tell us what these concerns were?"

"Your Honor, I object."

"You're objecting to *my* question now, Mr. Campanella? I think it's an excellent question. Objection overruled." Norcross turned to Patterson again. "Please tell us when you had these concerns and what they were."

Campanella could do nothing but stand there resting his hands on the podium. He'd been abruptly dumped from his pilot seat, and the water was cold.

"Well, like I say, a few months ago, I began thinking there was something funny about this case. Professor Cranmer was certainly eccentric, and it turned out that, like a lot of men, he looked at pornography. But he was quite successful professionally, which is not the usual profile, and I was, frankly, a little surprised to find someone like him interested in really hard-core prepubescent material."

"I see." Norcross jotted something on his pad.

This was agony. If Campanella interrupted again, Norcross was likely to fling a lightning bolt at him. All he could do was fall back on nonverbal advocacy. Campanella began furiously jotting notes, scribbling extra hard to let Norcross know just how many excellent questions he had, praying that his performance would be distracting.

Patterson continued. "Eventually, after I made some inquiries, I found there were a number of other people who might have had access to the defendant's home and computer and possible motives to injure Professor Cranmer."

"Can you give me examples of these other people?"

"There were several. Elizabeth Spencer, his research assistant, was refusing to talk to us. Two colleagues, Professors Harlan Graves and Darren Mattoon, clearly didn't like Professor Cranmer and could possibly have been involved. There was a housecleaner and, I believe, a carpenter on the premises. And then, of course, there was Ms. Spencer's boyfriend, Ryan Jaworski."

"Did you follow up on these leads?"

"Not for quite a while."

"Why not?"

Patterson took a breath and looked at his hands, appearing to struggle. Finally, he spoke. "From the beginning of the investigation, Mr. Campanella led me to believe he didn't want to hear about other suspects."

This was too much. Campanella couldn't restrain himself. "Your Honor . . ."

Norcross didn't raise his voice, but his tone went steely. "Please sit down, Mr. Campanella. You'll have your chance in a moment." The judge pulled on his nose and sniffed. "Mr. Campanella told you this?"

After a pause, Patterson said, "Yes."

"He told you he didn't want to hear about other suspects?"

"Yes, I believe those were his exact words."

"And why didn't he want to hear about them?"

"Well, he was sure that Professor Cranmer was guilty. I was pretty sure, too, in the beginning. And he told me if I broadened the investigation, it might generate written documents, witness statements and so forth, that he would have to turn over to Attorney Ames. It would complicate the case, he said, and make it harder for him to get a conviction."

A clatter told Campanella that Ames had tossed her pencil onto her table in what was probably a gesture of disgust. The hearing was drifting out of his control.

"Anything else?" Norcross asked.

"He said if I broadened the investigation, I would just be manufacturing red herrings that Ms. Ames would use to distract the jury."

"And Ryan Jaworski was one of these possible red herrings?"

"Yes." Patterson looked sadly over at Campanella and then up at Norcross. "Judge, it's not easy for me to go into this. I'd just like to say that—"

Ames quickly stood. "Objection!"

"Overruled. Please continue."

"I have to say that I'm sure Mr. Campanella meant no harm. He was positive Professor Cranmer was guilty, and, like I said, I pretty much agreed with him at first. He was focused on what he thought were the interests of justice and was trying to keep the case simple."

"I understand. Did you at any point pursue the investigation of these other possible suspects?"

"Yes."

"Did you tell Mr. Campanella?"

"I told him about my conversation with Ryan Jaworski."

"And what was his reaction?"

"He seemed pleased initially because . . ." Patterson paused, sighed, and looked up at the bench. "Judge, am I permitted to reveal the name of the confidential informant whose information led to the second search?"

Campanella started to stand, but the judge nodded him down. "No need to be explicit. I think it's now obvious."

"Okay, well, Mr. Campanella was pleased that we had the information to support a second search. But he didn't see any reason to pursue Mr. Jaworski further."

"Did you pursue other leads?"

"Yes."

"And did you tell Mr. Campanella about this?"

"No."

"Why not?"

"He wouldn't have liked it. It was his case. He might have called my superiors."

"What happened when you spoke to the other people on your own initiative?"

"It all started with the interview of Mr. Jaworski at his condo. At first, he said he didn't want to talk to me, which was not surprising, but then, after he agreed to talk, he started volunteering information I knew was false." Patterson hiked his body up, getting more comfortable. "He lied to me at the beginning of our interview about even knowing Professor Cranmer. Then he admitted, when I pressed him, that he'd actually taken a class with him. He also lied about the grade he'd gotten from Professor Cranmer, which I knew was a C-minus, the lowest grade on his transcript by far. He told me he'd gotten a B or B-plus."

This was too much. Campanella clutched the podium to anchor himself. "Your Honor, could I point out that—"

"You'll have your chance in a minute, Mr. Campanella."

"I only want to point out—"

"I've told you several times now, Mr. Campanella. Now I'm instructing you to take your seat." Judge Norcross nodded at Campanella's empty chair and took a moment to complete another note. Campanella stepped away from the podium and sat, tossing his yellow pad on the table a bit harder than necessary. Norcross looked up at him sharply. "I want my questions answered right now, Mr. Campanella. I'll hear what you want to point out in a minute."

Norcross turned again to Patterson. "Did you reach any conclusions as a result of your interview with Mr. Jaworski?"

"I was confident that he was hiding something, that he might somehow be involved."

"Did you tell Assistant U.S. Attorney Campanella about this?"

"I tried to."

"What happened?"

"He asked me to put nothing in writing and not to pursue this any further."

"Did he say anything else?"

"Well . . ." Patterson looked to the side, frowning.

"Did he say anything else?"

"Early on, we talked about the possibility of checking out other suspects. This was before I'd even spoken to Jaworski. Mr. Campanella asked me not to do it. And he also said . . ." Patterson stopped and looked at Campanella.

Norcross pressed the question. "What did he say?"

"He said, if anyone ever asked me, I should be careful not to reveal his instructions to me."

"About not pursuing other suspects?"

"Yes. He said it might get him into trouble. It was kind of a joke, really. We were laughing."

"It was a joke?"

"It was kind of a joke. About red herrings."

"What was the joke?"

"That the red herrings might swim up our behinds."

No one laughed. Campanella made an impatient noise and started to stand, but Norcross waved him down. Then Ames began to get up, but Norcross shook his head.

"No, not yet." The judge's mouth had gone taut. Campanella had not seen this expression before. "Did anything else come out of your further inquiries?"

"I spoke to Professor Graves and also Professor Mattoon. Halfway through the interview with Mattoon, I began to suspect he might be hiding something, too. He made it clear he didn't like Professor Cranmer. He knew Ryan Jaworski. I thought there might be some connection."

"Did you mention this to Mr. Campanella?"

"No. No, I didn't say anything about Mattoon. I wasn't sure about my suspicions, and by that time, I knew Paul would be very unhappy about my even talking to him."

"But you had, as you say, suspicions?"

"Yes."

"And now we know that Professor Mattoon had a role in persuading Ryan Jaworski to send in the flyer?"

"It appears so, yes. That's what Mr. Jaworski says."

Judge Norcross spent some time writing on his yellow pad, probably outlining something that was not going to help the government. The silence in the courtroom drew out for at least thirty seconds before Norcross stopped writing and continued.

"A couple more questions, Agent Patterson. You say Mr. Campanella told you not to reveal his instruction to you not to broaden this investigation, and you told him you'd keep your activities secret. Is that correct?"

"Yes. I told him that."

"Yet you're revealing your conversations with him in court now. Why is that?"

Patterson looked over at Ruby Johnson, who'd placed him under oath. "I've sworn to tell the truth here. The whole truth."

"Thank you."

After this, things from Campanella's viewpoint descended from catastrophe to nightmare. Norcross said that, before he allowed Campanella to take up his questioning of Patterson, he had a few questions for Campanella himself. Campanella, Norcross noted, was not under oath, but as an assistant United States attorney, he was an officer of the court and ethically obligated to respond truthfully.

Campanella returned to the podium, which felt more like a very hot witness box at this point. He had heard that David Norcross, when he'd practiced law, had been a fierce cross-examiner, and now he got painful proof of this. In response to the judge's tightly phrased questions, Campanella was forced to admit that he had, in fact, probably used the phrase, "I don't want to hear about it," when Patterson raised concerns about other possible suspects. He had to concede that he'd told Patterson not to pursue other lines of investigation, and not to draft any reports or witness statements that might have to be turned over to Linda Ames. He confessed that he had said something about not wanting to get in trouble and that he and Patterson had laughed about red herrings.

"And you instructed him not to reveal the fact that you'd restricted his investigation?"

"Well, I thought that—"

"Did you, or did you not, tell him that he was not to disclose your conversation?"

"I told him I'd prefer that."

By the time Norcross concluded his questioning, and Campanella got a chance to try to put his conversations with Patterson in context, it was like blowing bubbles against a granite wall. Half the time, Judge Norcross wasn't even looking at him. He just stared out the windows over the jury box at the black branches of the trees rocking against the winter sky.

When Campanella finished up and sat down, Ames rose to her feet, boiling. But Norcross just waved her down and took the floor himself.

"I will be brief. The motion to dismiss is allowed based on prosecutorial misconduct. The evidence is crystal clear. I commend Agent Patterson on his forthright testimony, which could not have been easy."

By this time, Agent Patterson was back at the counsel table, sitting next to Campanella with his arms folded. Campanella couldn't imagine what he was going to say to Patterson when they left the courtroom. Rage at Patterson's betrayal was finally working its way up through his confusion and shock.

Norcross continued. "Gross negligence on the part of the government has created a situation where this case cannot be fairly tried before the current jury. Retrial, under these circumstances, would be a violation of the defendant's Fifth Amendment rights. I will be issuing a written memorandum shortly, citing the applicable authorities in detail, but my basic rationale will not change. This case is dismissed with prejudice and without possibility of retrial."

Campanella rose. "Your Honor, for the record, the government strongly, very strongly, objects to this ruling. I ask that the court reconsider and, at a minimum, provide the government with an opportunity for a hearing at which its supposed responsibility for this situation can be ventilated properly. I expect another assistant U.S. attorney will take over handling that hearing, since I will be a witness."

"Is that an oral motion?"

"Yes."

"The motion's denied. The record is clear."

"Then I'd ask that our rights be saved to allow us to pursue an appeal."

"Your rights are saved, Mr. Campanella. Your objection is on the record. The indictment is dismissed for the reasons I have already stated in summary, which will be further expanded in my written memorandum. Ms. Ames, would you like to put anything on the record before the court adjourns?"

Ames restricted her response to six words: "Thank you, Your Honor. Nothing else."

As Judge Norcross was making his way out of the courtroom, Campanella overheard Professor Cranmer speaking to his lawyer.

"What do I do now?"

Linda Ames put her hand on his shoulder. "You go home, Sid. You're a free man now."

It was a bush-league thing to do, and something he was embarrassed about afterward, but as he strode toward the courtroom door, Campanella pointed back at Cranmer. "Enjoy your freedom while you've got it, Professor. You won't have it for long."

Then he hurried back to his office to begin drafting his notice of appeal.

46

Two weeks after Sid's trial collapsed, Claire Lindemann was sitting alone in her living room, cross-legged on the rug in front of her fireplace. A vigorous blaze was crackling up the chimney, and on her lap, she held Sid's secret file of Charles Dodgson's published and unpublished prints. She'd decided to burn them.

This was painful to do, of course. But she couldn't return the file to Sid without revealing Elizabeth Spencer's theft and her own connivance in it. Beyond that, she didn't want to expose Sid to the danger he might face by having the photographs around, or maybe just by knowing where he could put his hands on them.

The dismissal of the charges against Sid had provoked a Category 5 shitstorm at the college. Half the community was furious that Sid had been charged, locked up, and nearly beaten to death for a crime he apparently hadn't committed. The other half was outraged that Professor Cranmer had dodged justice on a legal technicality. Throughout the gale, Ryan Jaworski stayed put in Illinois, and Professor Mattoon pushed on with his classes, denying everything. Ryan Jaworski was a liar, Mattoon said, and he was a victim as much as Sid was. Despite these protestations, Professor

Mattoon was rumored to be angling for a new position out west somewhere.

Claire held Dodgson's most famous photograph up to the fire. It was the portrait of Alice Liddell, the inspiration for his fictional Alice, bare shouldered and tricked out as what Dodgson called "The Beggar Child." As Claire prepared to place the image onto the grate, she could see the flames licking up eagerly behind it, visible through the translucent paper. In the photo, Alice was exhibiting herself provocatively, her tattered clothes barely clinging to her. One hand sat on her hip; the other reached out for money. Someone had coaxed a salacious boldness into her eyes. What had really gone on between this child and Dodgson? Probably nothing.

Claire let her hand fall back into her lap, hesitating. Probably nothing, but Dodgson took the photograph in 1858, when Alice was six years old. He saw her frequently, often alone, until 1863, when her parents abruptly cut off contact. After his death in 1898, Dodgson's diaries covering the years 1858 to 1862 were found to be missing.

Claire set the Liddell photograph to one side and spread some of the other prints out on the rug around her. The group included one of the few surviving prints of Evelyn Hatch at about the same age as Alice, lying entirely naked with her arms behind her head. This wasn't Claire's field, but Sid's catastrophe had inspired her to read the basic biographies. She knew that sometime in the 1880s Dodgson had destroyed a number of plates containing other photographs of the Hatch girl, and that these were now permanently lost. He had commented in a letter that he had destroyed them because they "so entirely defy conventional rules."

Most scholars agreed that Dodgson had an intense obsession with little girls but found no convincing evidence of actual abuse. His child models maintained amiable relationships with him well into adulthood; none, including Alice, ever publicly complained of anything improper.

After his case's dismissal, Sid persisted, as profanely as ever, in rejecting the accusations of pedophilia leveled against Dodgson, but he was less generous to himself. Over a long dinner, despite protests from Claire, he described himself as a "disgusting fuckup" and announced that he would be retiring. He needed a quiet year, maybe two years, to recover. He might go to Europe. Of course, any plan depended on the court of appeals affirming Judge Norcross's dismissal of the charges against him. Until then, he didn't know what part of Wonderland he would be living in.

The fire was beginning to die down, and still the photographs lay piled in Claire's lap or scattered around her. Time to do this. She had a nine a.m. class the next morning. She looked over the pictures one last time. The images of these children were so touching, their little lives long vanished now, obliterated by the passing decades.

A sharp double knock at the front door brought Claire back to the present, and she leaped up, grateful to be off the hook even for a minute. A car sat in her driveway, but it was too dark to make out whose it was. Most of the snow had melted. In the murk by her extinguished light pole, only pale scraps remained of the mounds plowed up after the last blizzard.

When she opened the door, she was astonished to see David. He was supposed to be at a judicial conference in New Orleans for at least another day.

"David!" A smile burst onto her face, and as she kissed him, a wave of helium lifted her onto her toes. "You skipped out!"

Standing in the doorway, David gave her a truant's grin. "They're doing an entire morning tomorrow on the Employee Retirement Income Security Act." He shook his head. "I just couldn't take it."

"Wow!"

"May I come in?" He peered around her into the house. "Or is Professor Mattoon here?" He lifted his nose and sniffed. "Do I smell expensive Italian cologne?"

A thin rain was misting the tops of Claire's rhododendrons and baptizing the shoulders of David's London Fog. The weather sites were predicting a 50 percent chance of a thunderstorm, possibly the first of the spring.

Claire was so happy. She gestured with her thumb over her shoulder. "Poor Darren's escaping through the backyard at this very moment, hauling up his underwear. Come in. Come in."

"I left my overnight bag in the car."

"We'll manage."

In the front hallway, she helped him off with his coat. "What's up with Lindsay and Jordan? I stopped by this afternoon to make sure that Madison was all set."

"God bless that girl! She belongs in the nanny Hall of Fame." David sniffed and pulled on the end of his nose. "Tell the truth, I feel kind of guilty taking advantage of her." He kissed Claire again. "I decided not to mention that I was coming back early. They're still not expecting me until tomorrow."

Claire waggled a finger at him. "Such a bad man."

"I know." He beamed at her delightedly. "It's terrible."

Claire was hanging up David's coat as he walked into the living room. Her stomach dropped when she heard him saying, still jaunty but puzzled, "My goodness, what do we have here?"

When she saw him next, he was standing by the fire with a photograph in each hand, and his smile dying on his face. She'd been so overjoyed, she'd lost track of what she'd been up to before his knock. Lingering in the foyer, she felt half sick, not knowing what to say.

David dropped his hands to his sides, holding the two pictures, and gazed around the floor where the rest of the contents of Sid's file lay scattered. A serious, focused expression fell over his face.

He took another look at the photographs in his hands. "I see."

"David . . ."

He bent his knees and leaned to get a better look at the pictures of Beatrice and Evelyn Hatch. The shadows of the fire flickered over his face. "Uh-huh." When he looked up at Claire, his expression was half disbelief, half despair. "How could you?"

"David, I didn't . . ."

He spoke louder, waving at the floor. "I take it these are the photographs the FBI didn't find? The ones that Linda Ames convinced me never existed?"

Claire took a breath and swallowed. "Yes."

He let the prints in his hands drop onto the carpet. "How could you? How could you do something like this?" He pointed at the floor.

"David, I . . ."

"I knew you were upset about your friend, and you wanted to help him, but I guess I assumed that you would be . . . I mean, that you and I would be . . ."

"Of course, David, I . . ."

His face closed, and he stepped over the photographs toward the front door. "I need to get out of a here for a little bit, okay? I need to take a walk."

"David, it's . . ." But he'd moved quickly and was already opening the front door, ready to step out. "Let me at least get your raincoat." She hurried toward him.

"I don't . . ." He flapped his hand back at her. "I don't need it." Then the door closed, and he was gone.

The next ten minutes were among the longest in Claire's life. She was determined not to burst into tears—David might see it as a play for sympathy—but she couldn't get herself to think coherently. She had nothing to say, really, in her own defense, and she couldn't get her heart to slow down. What she'd done couldn't be undone. It might be the end of them. In a fog, she got up, retrieved a towel from her linen closet, and sat on the sofa holding the towel in her lap, waiting. She breathed and watched the fire die down. Once or twice, there was distant thunder.

The door, at last, rattled and opened, and David stepped back in. His hair, shoulders, and face were wet. Claire didn't say anything, merely got up and handed him the towel.

David took his time drying off, starting with his face and the back of his neck.

"It's chilly out there."

"David . . ."

"Give me a second here, okay?" He walked toward the sofa, picking up two of the prints on the way, and sat down. He placed the photographs on the coffee table and stared at them, frowning. Then he looked at Claire and shook his head. "Boy, did I ever make a mess of this case."

"You didn't."

"Sorry, Claire, but you're not the judge. I am. I should have realized that Cranmer probably ditched the photographs. It's so obvious now." He gazed into the fire for a while, looking out of breath. "Come over here, would you?"

Claire sat next to David, and he took her hand. He leaned back against the sofa cushions and didn't say anything for a while. Claire could only wait. It might be good-bye. He'd had all those helpful, romantic dinners with Dr. O'Leary.

Finally, he asked, "Did somebody tip you off ahead of time about the second search?"

"God, no. Elizabeth Spencer was worried about Ryan, so she stole the pictures before the search happened. Then she didn't know what to do with them, so she gave them to me. Even Sid doesn't know I have them."

"I see. I was imagining during my walk out there"—he nodded toward the door—"that Professor Cranmer probably gave the pictures to you, and you'd taken them. I just couldn't . . ."

"I wouldn't have done that."

"But you did take the handoff from Ms. Spencer."

"Well, that felt . . ."

"I know. In your position—I mean, if I were her teacher—I might have been tempted to do the same thing." He let out a joyless laugh. "I do remember, during the trial, thinking maybe the housecleaner had somehow come across them. What was his name again?"

"Jonathan something."

"Kind of like Agatha Christie. In England, it's the butler. In the United States, it's the housecleaner." Outside, the wind was picking up and the trees were creaking. David sighed. "Talk about a one-eyed judge."

"We're all one-eyed judges, David."

"Maybe." He looked at her, then turned back to the fire and spoke musingly. "Can't say I feel all that bad about not having to bury Professor Cranmer."

Claire looked down, kneading David's hand. "There's a line from *King Lear*, where the king, who is even crazier than Sid, says something like, 'I am more sinned against, than sinning.' Sid is kind of like that maybe."

"Maybe. I don't know. He deserved something. But he certainly . . ." He paused to think. "He certainly didn't deserve the beating he got." David took a sudden, deep breath and held it, as though he were having a cramp, then let it out slowly. "And he didn't deserve my getting cross with him for not pleading guilty to something he didn't do." He frowned. "I thought this was a routine case. It wasn't."

"We can all do better jobs, David. Things happen."

"Well, it's over now."

"Couldn't the case come back if you're reversed?"

"I doubt I'll get reversed. The government flubbed up badly. But now that the notice of appeal has been filed, I've recused myself." He gestured at the photographs. "If the court of appeals sends the case back, another judge will handle it." He started to say something, hesitated, and looked at her. "I was going to say, 'Some judge better than me,' but that would look like I was fishing, wanting you to tell me I did just fine."

"You'd catch a big fish, because that's exactly what I'd say."

"I should have done better." He tapped his chest. "That's what's in here." His eyes, turned to Claire, were intense. "But, really, can we do this? Two people like us? Should we even be trying?"

"David, listen." Claire took David's face in her hands and kissed him hard. "I really want to have a baby, okay?"

"But . . ." David looked confused. "That isn't what we're talking about."

"Of course it is."

"It is?"

"Yes, listen to me now, please. I really want a baby, but if I can't convince you . . ."

"Wait, wait. What I can't figure out is how we can ever manage, the way you are, and the way I am, and the way things keep happening. Things like this." He pointed at the two photographs at the coffee table.

"And what I'm saying is if I can't convince you to have a baby with me, I still want to be with you. I want to get married. That's the hardest thing, isn't it? It is for me."

"But won't train wrecks like this just keep happening? I mean, what do you plan to do about all these pictures, for example?" He nodded at the pile on the floor.

"I'm going to burn them."

"Oh my gosh, don't do that!"

Claire burst out laughing. "Jesus, David, you're impossible! What do you want me to do with them?"

David raised his hands in the air. "How do I know? Where have you been keeping them all this time?"

"I've had them in a safe-deposit box."

"Well, put them back until we figure something out. Don't burn them." He looked at her, almost indignant. "You can't burn them. It would be like the Taliban, or something, blowing up a Buddhist shrine because it's a different religion. Civilized people don't do that."

"Fine." Claire got up and began collecting the pictures. She was tucking them into Sid's accordion folder, her back to David, when he spoke again.

"And I'm open to negotiation."

She turned and looked at him. "You are?"

"Yes, I'm open to negotiation."

"About what?"

"About anything."

Claire put the file on the coffee table and returned to the sofa. An enormous amount of kissing and pawing and heavy breathing followed. After a certain interval, they took a break. By this time, they were stretched out on the couch, warmed by the remnants of the fire.

"I've just had an insight," David said into Claire's ear. "I think I may publish an article."

Claire cocked her head up. "Really. An article? And you're having this flash while we've been . . . ?"

"Uh-huh. Here's my title: Law Is to Justice, as Sex Is to Love."

Claire considered this for a minute. "Is that true?"

"It's true-ish."

"What exactly does it mean?"

"Who knows?"

"Come on."

David thought for a while. "I suppose it means that, ideally, one should be an expression of the other. When the two things get separated too far, for too long, you're going to have problems."

They lay on the sofa a few minutes longer before going upstairs. Sometime later, after they'd fallen asleep, the 50-percent possible thunderstorm broke and woke them up. The downpour drummed so heavily on the roof that it sounded as though it was raining blueberries.

47

The equinox arrived, and with it, Daylight Saving Time. As the spring eased in, patches of warmth in the breeze, the first sprinkling of daffodils, and the delicious smell of cow manure from the barns in Hadley signaled the final retreat of winter. In the woods, waxy shoots of skunk cabbage and fiddlehead ferns pushed their way up through the grimy undergrowth.

On one of these afternoons, on the way back from his piano lesson, Ethan Ames decided to stop by Professor Cranmer's. He knew he wasn't supposed to do this—his mom had been very clear—but he and the professor had kept their "little secret" so far, and Ethan was in the habit of dropping by. He liked to see Mick and Keith, and they seemed to like seeing him, too. There was also the harpsichord, which he and the professor had been working on, and the possibility of cupcakes. He wouldn't stay long.

He banged nice and loud, using the metal door knocker the way he always did, but nothing happened. It was a full minute before he saw the face of the weird housecleaner guy, Jonathan, peering at him from a gap in the curtains. Ethan couldn't tell how long Jonathan had been looking at him, and Jonathan ducked away as soon as he saw him.

Ethan hesitated, looking around the yard. He ought to just go, but he didn't want Jonathan to think he was playing some little kid's game, knocking and then running off. The day had gotten almost warm, and the two big forsythia bushes on either side of Professor Cranmer's walkway were covered in yellow flowers.

Ethan was just turning to go when the door sprang open, and Jonathan stood there, with a big smile. He'd never imagined Jonathan could smile like that.

"Is Professor Cranmer here?" Ethan asked.

"Sure." The smile stayed. "Come on in, little buddy."

"I better get home."

The smile dropped away. "Then what'd you knock for?" The smile appeared again. "No, seriously, he's right here." Jonathan pointed behind him. "He's upstairs. He wants to talk to you." His voice went up, sounding friendly. "Come on in, buddy."

"Well . . ."

"What's your name again?"

"Ethan."

"Sorry I called you 'Buddy,' Ethan. My uncle calls me Buddy all the time." Jonathan frowned and then smiled. "I don't really like it, to tell the truth."

"I . . . I probably ought to . . ." Ethan started to turn, but Jonathan reached out and grabbed his sleeve.

"Oh God, don't go now." He emphasized the word *now*. "Sid will be really disappointed, and I taught Keith a new trick." Jonathan pulled the door open wider. "It's cool. Come on in—you're here now anyway. A minute won't hurt."

Ethan stepped into the house, and Jonathan quickly closed the door behind him, twisting the dead bolt.

Ethan called out, "Professor Cranmer?"

"He's upstairs with Mick and Keith. Come on. I'll take you up."

It smelled normal, sort of perfumey and maybe of brownies. Ethan loved brownies. They never had them at home.

"Okay. Is that smell, like, brownies?"

Jonathan stared at Ethan with his mouth open. After a few seconds, his face cleared, and he said, "Yeah, he has them upstairs on a plate. He's put a big one with walnuts aside for you. Come on."

"I better go." Ethan turned back toward the door.

"Oh wow, no, Sid will be really sorry." Jonathan nodded upstairs. "Just go on up. I have to finish some stuff." Jonathan walked off toward the dining area. He looked over his shoulder and waved upstairs. "Go on. He wants to talk to you about the harpsichord."

"Okay." At least he'd get away from this guy.

Ethan ascended the stairs to the landing halfway up and called out again, "Professor Cranmer?"

A fat silence was pressing down on him from up there, and he didn't like it. Then he heard a meow and hurrying cat feet, and there was Mick, peering over the top step down at him. It was always hard to tell when a cat was happy, but he looked happy. Ethan hurried the rest of the way up and began rubbing Mick's head. He called out again, "Professor Cranmer?" Was he waiting to jump out at him? He and his mom had sometimes played that game, until Ethan got too good at it, and his mom told him they had to stop. No more scary surprises.

48

While Ethan was playing with Sid's cats, the Amherst Regional High School girls' softball team was taking the field for its first outdoor practice. They'd been working indoors for weeks, but now a break in the weather had finally allowed them to get into the fresh air and smell the mud. When David mentioned that Lindsay had taken over as the team's catcher, Claire, who was a baseball nut, pulled up the practice schedule and talked David into leaving work early to come watch. David arrived straight from court just as the practice was starting, still in his suit, tie, and khaki raincoat.

Since his dismissal of *United States v. Cranmer*, life in court had eased up enough to allow an outing like this. Two trials calendared to follow *Cranmer* had settled, and the gap in his schedule had given Judge Norcross time to make progress on his never-ending pile of pending opinions. Not surprisingly, the U.S. attorney's press release following the dismissal had been particularly frosty and promised a vigorous appeal. A "Pro and Con" article in *Massachusetts Lawyer's Weekly* had predicted that the court of appeals would reverse his ruling, but an accompanying rebuttal from a prominent defense attorney praised Norcross's action and opined forcefully that he deserved to, and would, be easily affirmed.

Norcross agreed with the "deserved to" part, but was not entirely confident of the "would be." The First Circuit could be stingy regarding the rights of criminal defendants. It irked Norcross that, while the appeal was pending, his defendant would be living life under the shadow of a possible reversal and retrial. If his ruling got tipped, Norcross would have given Professor Cranmer false hope and probably made everything worse.

But this was all part of life in Wonderland, and he couldn't do anything about it. Neither the "pro" nor the "con" article expressed any surprise that Norcross had recused himself after his ruling went up. The court of appeals regularly sent a case to a new judge after reversal, or the original judge might step aside voluntarily to make sure everything proceeded on a clean slate.

The far uglier case of *United States v. George Underwood* still festered on Judge Norcross's docket. A sealed motion to postpone the trial informed the judge that a plea bargain might be in the works. In its judge's-eyes-only memorandum, the government disclosed that an accomplice might still be out there. They must be hoping that a reduced sentence would tempt Underwood to identify his copredator and get him off the street.

David was tickled that his slightly looser schedule gave him the chance to join Claire for softball practice. He'd make up the time later in the week.

From their perch on the rickety aluminum grandstand, Claire pointed out Lindsay squatting behind the plate, warming up one of the pitchers, a tall black girl. The afternoon was cool and overcast, with an aggressive breeze combing ripples on the infield puddles. The first time the pitcher let fly, the ball rifled at Lindsay so fast that David half expected her to fling herself out of the way. Instead, Lindsay casually lifted her glove and nipped the ball from the air as though it was only a big bug.

Claire leaned over. "David, keep your mouth closed, please. You look presenile."

"I had no idea they threw that hard in girls' softball."

The team was in uniform, wearing black pants and deep maroon jerseys with white lettering. They still hadn't taken the field. Between pitches, the pitcher twiddled the ball in her hand, watching the catcher. Then, she'd rock back and underhand the ball in a blinding pinwheel motion, flinging her glove hand up in the air as she delivered. Lindsay seemed completely at home squatting behind the plate.

After four or five warm-up pitches, Lindsay stood and pushed her face mask on top of her head. She had a kind of dignity in the way she held herself that emphasized her height. As she walked out to the mound, her chest protector and shin guards made her move stiffly, and her slightly awkward stride, easy and deliberate, gave her a magnificent, heroic quality.

Lindsay approached the pitcher and put her hand on the girl's shoulder, leaned into her so their heads were almost touching, and began talking to her animatedly, gesturing with her glove. She bobbed her knees and mimicked the pitcher's delivery several times, obviously pointing something out. After a minute, the pitcher nodded, and Lindsay smacked her on the behind and trotted back to the plate. The coach shouted something, and the rest of the team ran out onto the field, whooping and waving their arms. One girl—the shortstop, it turned out—leaped high in the air right into the middle of a puddle between second and third base, making a huge splash that caused more laughter and hoots. Lindsay slid her face mask down, squatted, and smacked her fist into her mitt.

As the first batter took a couple practice swings, Norcross noticed Mike Patterson climbing toward them up the metal bleachers. Patterson nodded and took his seat two rows down, close enough to suggest a connection, but still at a certain distance. The public reverberations of *Cranmer* and the pending *Underwood* prosecution called for restraint.

After a while, Patterson turned, pointed at Lindsay, and asked back over his shoulder. "Your girl there, Judge?"

At the word *judge*, three of four heads twitched and glanced over at David. "My niece, Lindsay."

"Fine catcher. She's teaching Margaret a lot."

Claire chimed in. "The pitcher's your daughter?"

"Sure is."

"She's incredible," David said. "The speed!"

Patterson hesitated, maybe afraid it would sound like boasting, but it was clear he couldn't help himself. "It's her senior year. She's an early admit to Stanford."

"Wow." Claire was impressed.

"Physics." Patterson shook his head. "She wants to study physics. Can you believe that?"

Just then, the leadoff batter, a leftie, connected with a line drive that barely cleared the first baseman's leap. The bench hollered wildly, and the coach stepped into the field, clapping her hands, talking to the runner, and pointing.

David only caught a few words—"Watch her now, watch her"—and the coach stepped back to the sidelines. She pointed at Lindsay. "Be ready now!"

"This is going to be great," Claire said.

"What?"

"See how Lindsay's keeping an eye on the girl at first?"

The new batter was right handed, and the first pitch was high and toward the first base side. It made a loud *whop!* as it hit the pocket of Lindsay's glove. As the ball left Margaret's hand, the runner had danced toward second, hands dangling. Lindsay cocked her arm and feinted toward first, and the runner scuttled back to the bag.

"Uh-huh."

"Mouth, David, mouth." Claire pressed her shoulder into David and nodded down at Lindsay. "Okay, now watch how she sets up. See? Half a step toward first? I bet it's a pitchout."

This time, the ball sailed high and two feet toward the first base side of the plate. Meanwhile, the runner had skipped down the baseline, about a quarter of the way to second. Lindsay snatched the ball out of the air and immediately gunned it to first base. The runner dove back, hand outstretched, just as the tag slapped down.

The coach crossed her arms back and forth, giving the safe sign, and the first baseman, a stocky girl with a brunette ponytail, leaped into air indignantly, starting to protest.

This time David could hear the coach easily.

"It's a practice, Danielle! If I say she's safe, she's safe." She pointed at Lindsay. "Now get ready. Set up inside this time. High and tight."

"See that? See that?" Claire said.

David wasn't seeing anything. "Um . . ."

"She's having her jam the batter, to make the throw down to second harder." Claire was jiggling up and down. "Watch it, watch it! She's going . . ."

As Margaret delivered the ball, the runner, a short, agile girl, took off so fast David assumed she'd make second by a mile. But Lindsay, in one fluid motion, snatched the ball out from under the batter's chin, transferred it to her throwing hand, shoved the batter out of the way with her glove, stepped forward, and fired. The ball, a miracle of speed and accuracy, shot right over Margaret's ducked-down head. The second baseman leaned down and set her glove a foot to the first-base side of second, just off the ground. The ball smacked into the pocket, and the runner slid right into the tag. This time there was no argument. The base stealer wiped her hands on her thighs and trotted off the field, pumping her fist in the air. Even she was proud of Lindsay.

All the girls on the bench were screaming and chanting: "Po! Po! Po! Po!" Lindsay turned, pushed the face mask up onto her head, sniffed, and spat.

It was not a little dribbling girl's spit either. It was a nice big solo glob that sailed about six feet. Claire leaned back in delight, clapped her hands, and whooped.

"Well, David." She punched his shoulder. "If you were worried about Lindsay, you can relax." She yelled out, "Way to go, Lindsay!" Then she returned to David, continuing in a normal voice. "Any girl who can spit like that is going to be fine."

"Amazing. I can't remember anything so, so . . ."

"Beautiful?" Claire called down to Patterson, who was standing up, still clapping. "What's 'Po, Po, Po'?"

Patterson smiled and climbed up the creaky metal steps toward them, taking a seat next to Claire.

"Didn't you know? They call her 'Po,' which is short for Hippolyta, the . . ."

"The Amazon queen." Claire's smile broadened. "And the bride of Theseus. Cool!"

"Margie says they called her Hippo until they got to like her." Patterson turned his head and produced a sneeze so titanic it startled their neighbors. "Cold?" Claire asked.

"Allergies." Patterson looked apologetic. "Sorry. Ran out of tissues. Spring always does this to me."

Claire grabbed a Kleenex out of her purse. "Here you go."

"Thank heaven for the ladies." Patterson blew his nose and leaned forward to speak to David. "'Po' is also, as you know, Judge . . ."

"Yep," David said, turning to Claire. "It's Springfield street slang for the police."

"Folks in the neighborhood call out 'Po' when the cops are around." Patterson pointed at Lindsay. "Your niece is like the police. Nobody's going to steal when she's around."

"Chip off the old block." Claire smiled at David.

"I'm the judiciary, Claire. Not law enforcement."

"Picky picky."

David hugged his raincoat around him and looked over at Claire. Baseball of any sort always transformed her into some bubbling creature he hardly knew. She was still wonderful, and he still adored her, but it was like being in love with someone from a foreign country.

"I always root for the umpire," he said, to exasperate her.

"Oh, God, you would." Claire's cell phone burbled with a text, and she looked at it. "Rats!" She held it up to David. "Sid's meeting got over way early, and he needs a lift." At the mention of Sid Cranmer, David noticed that Agent Patterson made a point of looking intently out toward left field, as though he didn't hear.

Claire scowled at the phone. "He's over at UMass. His car's in the shop, and his ride crumped. I'm going to have to leave you boys." She kissed David. "See you tonight?"

"See you then." It was a casual kiss, just ordinary, but the warmth and softness of Claire's mouth erased the contents of David's brain for a few seconds. Somewhere out there in the actual world, somebody made a great catch, and more raucous screaming broke out. Claire, descending the grandstand, looked back over her shoulder at David and said "Bye-eye," doing her best bimbo imitation, making the word into two syllables—all ironically flirtatious. People's eyes flickered over to him, probably not picking up on the irony. He didn't care.

It felt strangely good to be left at the ball game with Agent Patterson, just two middle-aged men cheering for their girls. David knew instinctively that Patterson was too classy to start talking to him about his dismissal of *Cranmer*. Sitting there felt like some kind of closure. The situation was typical of the western Massachusetts scene. People knew each other, and sooner or later, everyone's lives crisscrossed.

Before long, the coach shouted something, and the girls in the field ran in and got ready to take their turns batting. The new cohort of fielders was plainly the second string. The replacement catcher let two balls get past her, and the second baseman dropped an easy pop-up. Margaret Patterson batted cleanup and hit the new pitcher's first offering over the center fielder's head into the parking lot. David and Patterson both stood and cheered like matching idiots as she trotted around the bases. At she stepped on home, she looked up at her dad and smiled—then looked at her friends on the bench and rolled her eyes.

As soon as they resumed their seats, Patterson's phone rang. He turned to the side and spoke in a low voice. David took the opportunity to return Patterson's earlier courtesy by shifting around to the side and pretending to be deaf. The rust-colored buds on a row of sugar maples up by the high school were bobbing against the milky sky. Springtime in New England.

At the end of the call, Patterson stood and said, "I have to go." He stared down at David, thinking, then added, "We might need to see you for an after-hours warrant application this evening. Will you be around?"

"I'll be in. Have Mr. Campanella call me. I can meet you at the Amherst police station." David handled after-hours warrant applications using a conference room at the local police station.

After some thought, Norcross had decided not to make a formal complaint about Campanella's conduct in *Cranmer*. So far, his boss, Buddy Hogan, had not done anything either. With the appeal pending, the U.S. attorney's office was taking the position that Campanella had done nothing wrong. Knowing Mr. Hogan, David assumed that once the court of appeals had its say, things might change.

"Seems Attorney Spade got his client Underwood to talk." Patterson lifted his head and gazed up at the overcast sky. When he looked back down, a sour expression had taken over his face. "Turns out our defendant's accomplice, who he calls Buddy, is Underwood's nephew—a kid named Jonathan. I'm going down to Springfield to help Paul debrief the defendant." He gave David a weary smile. "Paul is still unhappy with me about *Cranmer*. It won't hurt to do some fence mending."

David was not immediately bothered by Patterson's reference to someone named Jonathan. A lot of people had that name. But he nevertheless gave into an impulse to speak. "That's the name of Sid's cleaner, I think. I'm pretty sure Claire mentioned somebody named Jonathan turning up when she was visiting."

"Hmmm." Patterson took a deep breath and gazed down at the field, plainly not seeing much. "Maybe I'll swing by there. It's sort of on my way."

David stood up. "Maybe I will, too."

"I'd rather you didn't, Judge."

"Afraid that's too bad."

49

Ethan had never been upstairs in Professor Cranmer's house before. Three doors led off the carpeted landing, and he wasn't sure where he was supposed to go. He shouldn't be here. Mick was playing around his feet, and when he leaned down to give him a scratch, the cat grabbed at Ethan's hand, digging his claws in a little, and rolled over onto his back. A bedroom with a lot of books was facing Ethan, and he spotted Keith in there getting up off a pillow and doing a stretch. Ethan hurried into the bedroom, and Mick followed, jumping up onto the bed after Ethan sat on the edge. Both cats pushed onto Ethan's lap. They were very, very friendly, and their fur was so soft.

After a little while, something caught the corner of Ethan's eye. When he looked up, he saw Jonathan, standing in the doorway, which made him jump a little. With the carpet he hadn't heard Jonathan come up.

"Great cats, huh?" Jonathan said.

"Yeah."

"I love them." Jonathan stepped all the way into the bedroom and closed the door behind him.

This was bad. Ethan stopped petting the cats and asked, "Where's Professor Cranmer?" Jonathan leaned against the door. He had one hand kind of out of sight behind his back.

The cats were pushing at Ethan, but he ignored them. This was really not good.

Jonathan shrugged. "I don't know."

"He's not here?"

"Nah, I was fooling with you." Jonathan nodded over at the cats. "I wanted to show you some new tricks."

"Okay, but I better go."

"Why? You don't need to." Jonathan was a lot bigger than Ethan, and the room was not very large. The windows were high up, and the curtains were pulled across. No one would be able to see through them.

Ethan, still sitting on the bed, looked around the room. "You said Professor Cranmer was up here." There was a closet, but he wouldn't be able to hold the door closed. "You said there were brownies."

"I was just fooling around with you."

Ethan stood up. Maybe, if he moved fast, he could roll under the bed. Ethan noticed he was breathing hard. His hands were shaking a little.

"Do you know what a blow job is?" Jonathan asked. The smile came and went again. It was awful.

"Yes. Sort of."

"Have you ever given one?"

"No."

"Ever had anybody give one to you?"

"No. I don't . . . I don't want one."

"Why not? They're fun."

"I need to go now." Ethan took a step forward but stopped. He couldn't get closer to the door without getting closer to Jonathan, which was something he didn't want to do. "My mom will be worried. She'll be calling and stuff."

"Your mom won't be wondering about you for a while." Jonathan was breathing hard, too, but not as hard as Ethan was. "She won't think you're here. You're not even supposed to be here." Jonathan still had that one hand behind his back. He lifted the other hand, the free hand, and wagged a finger at Ethan. "You've been a naughty boy,

Ethan, and there's nobody here to help you now." Jonathan slowly pulled the hand behind his back out. It was holding a gun. "Do you know what this is?"

"Yes." Ethan's heart was beating like crazy. The room was getting funny. He couldn't think.

"It's Sid's. He got it in Vietnam."

"Okay."

"If I shoot you with this, it will hurt a lot and you'll die."

"I know."

"You're scared, right?"

"Uh-huh."

"I don't really want to shoot you." Jonathan looked down at the gun, then lifted it and pointed it at Ethan. He had his finger on the trigger, and he smiled. "Well, to tell the truth, I do, sort of." He closed one eye, aimed, and said, "Bang." Then he dropped his hand and pointed the gun down. "But I promise not to shoot you if you help me with something."

"People will hear if you shoot me."

"They might, but they won't think it's anything. They'll think it's, like, a car, or something falling off a truck or something. They won't care, and I'll be a long ways away before they find you and figure out what happened. They won't even know who did it."

"I don't—" Ethan began, but he couldn't think of how to finish.

"You don't, what?"

Ethan just shook his head.

"Okay, here's the deal. If I shoot you, you'll be dead. You won't feel anything then. But your mom, wow. Think how she'll feel." Jonathan raised his eyebrows and nodded at Ethan. "If you just help me with one little thing, you can go home, and everything will be fine. Don't be an asshole."

"What do I need to help you with?"

Jonathan stared at Ethan. His eyes went up and down Ethan's body. A car went by outside, then another.

"My zipper's stuck."

"Your zipper's stuck?"

"Uh-huh. My zipper's stuck." Jonathan looked down, tugged at his fly, and then looked back up. "I'm not kidding." He gave that awful smile again. "It's really stuck. I think it's because my dick is so big. I need you to come over here and help me unzip it and . . ."

There was the sound of the front door opening and some lady laughing downstairs. Right away, the cats jumped up off the bed and dashed to the closed door, mewing loudly.

Ethan called out. "Hello! I'm up here!" He should have yelled louder, but his voice was not working that well. He started to clear his throat.

"Shut up!" Jonathan whispered fiercely. Ethan took a step toward the door. Jonathan pointed the gun at him. "Stay right there." When Ethan looked uncertain, Jonathan pointed the gun down at the cats, still hissing. "I'll shoot Mick and Keith. Then I'll shoot you."

Professor Cranmer's voice came up the stairs, getting closer. "Hello?"

The female voice called out. "I'll put on the kettle."

Jonathan stuck his finger up to his lips and pointed the gun at Ethan. His eyes, all of a sudden, were wide and bugging out. He looked almost crazy.

Professor Cranmer was halfway up the stairs. "Ethan? Is that you?" The floor creaked as he turned up from the landing. "Jonathan? I'm home early."

Jonathan hurried over to Ethan, got behind him, and grabbed him around the waist. He pressed the barrel of the gun against Ethan's ear. Ethan's heart was pounding twice as fast now. Jonathan's breath smelled really bad, like old cheese. The barrel of the gun was cold, and it was scraping against his ear so hard it hurt. It felt like it was cutting him.

The door to the room opened, and Professor Cranmer stepped inside. When he saw Ethan and Jonathan, he looked surprised, his mouth dropped open, and his face looked confused and then just—Ethan couldn't think what—sort of scared, but also something else.

Jonathan broke in, using a low voice so the lady downstairs wouldn't hear. "Don't say a fucking word, Sid. Not one word."

Something happened then that was very surprising to Ethan, something that made him a tiny bit less frightened. After only a few seconds, Ethan could see that Professor Cranmer didn't look surprised or whatever anymore. Or maybe he was frightened underneath, but something bigger covered it up. His face just got very serious. He had his eyes on Jonathan as though he was sick and tired of everything, as though he hated Jonathan and everything all of a sudden. He stepped inside the room and closed the door behind him, not making a sound.

He spoke very quietly. "Let the boy go, Jonathan."

"Oh sure."

"Let Ethan go. You and I can settle this."

"Shut the fuck up."

The barrel of the gun was grinding into Ethan's ear so hard it felt like it might be bleeding. He gave out a little cry. He couldn't help it.

"You don't have to let him out of the room, Jonathan. Just let him come over here to where I am."

"Shut the—"

"You've got the gun. We won't go anywhere."

"You're fucking right."

"I promise we'll cooperate, Jonathan. You're hurting him."

"You're not the—"

"Come on. I'm worried you'll shoot him by accident. We'll do whatever you want."

A voice called up, the lady's voice. "Everything okay up there?"

Professor Cranmer called out. "Be down in a sec." You couldn't tell from his voice that anything was wrong at all.

"Black tea or herbal?"

Cranmer looked at Jonathan, very steady. Then he got close to smiling, and he called out, "Tension Tamer."

"You got it." Footsteps downstairs went off to the kitchen.

Jonathan gestured with his head over to the corner of the bedroom, farthest away from the door. "Get over there."

Professor Cranmer walked right over to where Jonathan pointed. He held his hands partway up and sort of out to the side, with his fingers sticking out, to show Jonathan he wasn't going to try anything.

The gun slid away from Ethan's ear—it was stinging like crazy—and Jonathan shoved him toward Professor Cranmer.

"Go over there and shut up."

There was a clatter downstairs in the kitchen. Nobody said anything. Jonathan had the gun hanging down at his side now, almost as though he'd forgotten about it, and he was breathing hard.

Professor Cranmer put a hand on Ethan's shoulder. "Jonathan . . ." Professor Cranmer began.

"Man, this sucks."

"Jonathan, listen . . ."

"Shut up. I'm trying to think."

"Okay."

Jonathan's eyes were going from side to side. "Is the basement unlocked?"

"Yes."

Jonathan looked like he was out of breath. "Okay, here's the deal. We're going downstairs, okay? You, me, the kid, and whoever the fuck that is in the kitchen."

"Whatever you want."

"Right. Whatever I want." Jonathan seemed to notice the gun. He turned it to the side and stared down at it, thinking. "That's your friend Claire, isn't it?"

"Yes."

"The judge's girlfriend."

"Well, I don't know about that."

"Bullshit." When Sid just kept looking at Jonathan without saying anything, Jonathan got angry. "You talk. I have ears. I'm not stupid."

"I know you're not stupid."

It seemed like Jonathan couldn't figure out what he wanted to do. After a little while, he said, "Looks like we may get a chance to go out big." When Professor Cranmer didn't say anything, Jonathan made up his mind. "Like I say, here's the deal: We go down to the kitchen and collect your friend Claire."

"Okay."

"Then, we all go in the basement."

"Okay."

"You tie the two of them up and put some tape over their mouths."

"Fine. Whatever you—"

"Then you and me will go for a drive in your car."

"Okay. Sounds good."

Jonathan went quiet, and his eyes started searching sideways. "When we go downstairs, you go first."

"Okay." Professor Cranmer took a step toward the door.

"Not yet." Jonathan pointed with his chin at Ethan. "You come here." Ethan looked up at Professor Cranmer, and Professor Cranmer nodded.

"Go ahead, Ethan. We're all going to be fine."

Ethan walked toward Jonathan. When he got close, Jonathan said, "Turn around."

Ethan turned around, and Jonathan put his left hand, the one without the gun, on Ethan's shoulder. "Okay, listen up." Jonathan was mostly talking to Ethan but loud enough for Professor Cranmer to hear. "As long as my hand is on your shoulder, you're fine. But if you try to run away, or jump somewhere, and my hand comes off your shoulder, you're dead, okay?" Ethan didn't say anything, and Jonathan shook him, not too hard. "Okay?"

"Okay."

Jonathan looked at Professor Cranmer. "If you try to run, you probably won't make it, but even if you do, the boy here is dead. And so is your friend in the kitchen. You understand?"

"I'm not going anywhere, Jonathan." Professor Cranmer looked at him. "You'll be fine, Ethan."

"Just walk right in front of the boy, just a couple steps in front."

"Whatever you say."

"Don't say 'whatever you say.' It's bullshit. I'm not fucking stupid, Sid. You'd screw me the first chance . . ."

"Of course I would. But you're not going to give me a chance."

"Damn straight."

"So I'm going to do whatever you tell me to do."

"Damn straight."

"I have an idea that might help. Can I say something?"

"No, you fucking can't." There was a long silence. Ethan couldn't see what Jonathan was up to, but he could feel him, standing there, and as he breathed, his stomach bumped the back of Ethan's head. Finally, Jonathan just said, "Shit. I'll never . . ." Then he let out a big shaky breath.

Professor Cranmer was standing there with his arms folded, not moving, as though he could stand there forever. He nodded over his shoulder toward the bedroom door. "Listen. When we get downstairs, and we're in the living room, I'm going to call out something to Claire before she sees us, to let her know we have a situation, so she won't be too startled, okay? If we just walk in on her like this, she might be really surprised, and we don't want any surprises."

Jonathan still didn't say anything. Professor Cranmer was looking past Ethan at Jonathan behind him, very hard. "Come on. I'm not going to say anything that will make things harder, Jonathan. I want the same thing you do. A nice, calm walk to the basement. Then you and I leave, and whatever happens after that, happens."

There was another pretty long silence, where Ethan wasn't sure what was going on, until finally Jonathan said, "I used your computer and screen name."

"I figured you might have."

"You didn't say anything to the cops."

"I wasn't sure. I didn't want to get you in trouble."

"Most of that shit was mine, but some of it was yours. You liked it, too."

"I know."

"And I wasn't the one who went in the chat rooms. That was fucking stupid, Sid. The cops watch them."

"You're right. I didn't know that."

Downstairs the teakettle began to whistle. Ethan could hear the lady moving around down there.

"This is all your fault."

"I know."

Another silence followed. Again, Ethan could feel Jonathan breathing. His fingers squeezed Ethan's shoulder, not too hard. "Okay, fuck it. Let's go."

They walked slowly down the stairs, Professor Cranmer first, maybe two steps in front, then Ethan with Jonathan's hand on his shoulder. The cats crowded down with them, and once, as they were jostling past, Jonathan stumbled a little. The barrel of the gun clunked the side of Ethan's head, and Jonathan said, "Sorry, man."

"It's okay," Ethan whispered.

When they got down into the living room, Professor Cranmer called out. "Claire. Just stay where you are in the kitchen, will you? Don't move. I have a little surprise for you. We have a kind of situation here. A couple people are with me. So, as the students like to tell us, just chill, will you, please?"

Professor Cranmer said, in a lower voice, to Jonathan. "Was that all right?"

"Just keep walking."

The lady, Claire, was standing by the island in the middle of the kitchen when they came in. She had the kettle in her hand, like she'd just been pouring the tea water, and when she saw Sid and Ethan, she started to smile, and then stopped.

Jonathan said, "Put the kettle down and walk over to that table. Away from the window." The lady's face dropped, but she didn't freak out. Ethan remembered seeing her once, talking to his mom.

"It's okay," Professor Cranmer said. "It's not as bad as it looks."

"Shut the fuck up."

50

Judge Norcross followed Agent Patterson from the high school to Sid Cranmer's house. Patterson slowly ran a red light at one point, keeping an eye on Norcross in the rearview mirror, but he didn't stick his flashing party hat on the roof. It was a serious situation but not, as far as he could tell, a crisis. Norcross stayed close behind him. How good would the judge be in a tight spot?

A banged-up, dark green Ford F-150 was sitting by the curb in front of the Cranmer address. It matched the general description of the vehicle present at the Ho Jo's when they grabbed Underwood. A red Prius was parked in the drive.

Patterson let his car drift two doors down before pulling over. Norcross, unfortunately, stopped smack in front of Cranmer's, creating a risk he might spook Jonathan, assuming the housecleaner was there and he was the guy they were looking for. Patterson wanted to watch the house for a bit and call for backup before approaching. He got out of his car and walked quickly over to where Norcross was just stepping onto the sidewalk.

"Hang on a second, okay?"

The judge looked at him sharply. "Claire." He gestured at the house. "Professor Lindemann is in there. That's her car."

Patterson couldn't exactly give Norcross orders, but he really didn't want him underfoot if things got interesting. To his relief, after some hesitation, the judge slid back into his car and closed the door, not too loudly.

Patterson slipped into the passenger seat. Norcross was staring at the house, making an awning of his hand to shade his eyes, which would have tipped off anyone's grandmother that they were doing surveillance. It probably didn't matter. There was no sign of anything wrong.

Patterson pulled out his phone. "I'm calling for backup. I think that's our guy's car." He nodded at the pickup. "If this is the right Jonathan, we don't want him going out a window." As Patterson began fingering the access code, he sneezed violently. "Dammit." He sniffed and shook his head.

Norcross nodded at his glove compartment. "Should be some Kleenex in there."

Groping inside, Patterson found something he really wasn't expecting. He pulled out a baggie of marijuana and held it up to the judge, raising his eyebrows.

Norcross looked at it, not changing expression. "Ah, that. Yes." He pulled on his nose and sniffed. "That's, uh . . ."

Patterson flipped the baggie back into the glove compartment. "I'm going to assume somebody has a prescription for that."

At that moment, a single, sharp gunshot came from inside Cranmer's house, large caliber, probably Cranmer's .45. Norcross flung his door open and had a foot out so fast that Patterson had to lunge across the seat, grab the shoulder of his raincoat, and yank him back in.

"Stay in the car."

"I can't just . . ." Norcross looked offended, but that was too bad.

"Stay put." Patterson got quickly out of the car. "This isn't a courtroom."

"Let me do something. I can't . . ."

"Call 911. Tell them to get here ASAP." Patterson drew his automatic from his shoulder holster. "And tell them we'll need an ambulance."

Gun pointed up, Patterson limped quickly down the walk toward Cranmer's front door, horribly aware of what a large, slow target he was making from inside the house. When the door suddenly swung open, he dodged to the side and pointed his gun. It was Claire Lindemann running for daylight, pulling a small boy behind her. An adult male voice was screaming in the background.

"You dumb motherfucker! I ought to fucking kill you."

The boy was crying and saying, "I'm sorry. I'm sorry." His glasses were askew and he was trying to push them up as he ran.

Claire's face was pale with fear. "Sid grabbed the gun." She looked over her shoulder back into the house. "Please hurry!"

"Take the boy over there." Patterson gestured toward the judge's car, where he saw Norcross, contrary to instructions, already out and coming toward them. Sirens were moaning in the distance. Some neighbor must have called right after the gunshot, even before Norcross got through.

The front door started to sway closed. Patterson kicked it open and hopped across the threshold as fast as he could, stepping to the side, gun in both hands, half expecting to get shot while he was lit up in the entry. What he saw in the house reminded him of Afghanistan, the interior of a hut after a raid. Blood was everywhere—splashed up against the walls, soaking into the light brown rug, spattering the hallway from the kitchen. A man, twentysomething, probably Jonathan, was kneeling over Sid Cranmer, who was curled up on the floor, hit good.

Jonathan seemed to be trying to do something to stop the bleeding, but Patterson could see it was a pumper. Jonathan had set the .45 on a table within easy reaching distance.

Sid was starting up, "Not there. Higher!"

"Fuck! You fucking fuck." Jonathan stood and raised his hands helplessly. They were covered in blood. Then he noticed Patterson, stood up straighter, and turned toward him.

"Move over there." Patterson gestured to the left to get Jonathan away from the gun.

"He's bleeding like shit."

"I said move over there." Patterson gestured again. "Put your hands up on the wall."

There was a smear of blood on Jonathan's cheek. "He fucking made me do it."

"Do what I said. There's an ambulance on the way."

Jonathan stared at Patterson. Something in his eyes seemed to change, some wall caving in behind them. "It's too late." He leaned and reached slowly for the gun on the table. Patterson knew immediately what Jonathan was up to and was almost desperate to stop him. He'd shot enough people to last him a lifetime.

He shouted, "Don't touch it! Don't touch it, Jonathan. Just move to the side, like I said."

Jonathan looked at his bloody hands, then up at Patterson. "I'm done." He picked up the gun and began to swing the barrel slowly, forcing Patterson, giving him plenty of time. "It's going to be one of us, man. Your choice."

Just before Jonathan had the gun lined up on him, Patterson fired twice, hitting Jonathan clean in the upper chest both times. The impact sent Jonathan staggering backward, tumbling over Sid, and sprawling into the kitchen. The .45 slid over the ceramic tiles and clunked against a chair leg. Jonathan didn't so much as squirm.

Patterson popped the safety on his gun, holstered it, then stepped quickly to where Sid lay writhing in a wad on the ground.

"Sid?"

"Fuck, it hurts."

Patterson kneeled down. "Where are you hit?"

"Up here." Sid was squeezing his hand over a wound high up on his inner thigh. Blood was pumping out through his fingers. "It's the femoral. I can't stop it." He breathed hard. "Shit. I'm losing it."

"Take your hand away." Patterson unhooked and yanked off his belt. "You need . . ."

"Serves me right for getting hollow points. It's all . . ."

Patterson worked as fast as he could, cinching the belt up high around Sid's upper leg. It was slippery as hell. "You're going to be okay. I'm getting something around it. We can stop the . . ." He pulled the belt as tight as he could. The blood flow eased, but only a little. He began groping at the wound, trying to find the artery and squeeze it off. "I'm just . . . I can feel it."

"It's too torn up. Oh God. I'm bleeding out." Sid tried to lift his head to look at his leg, but dropped back. "Christ, it hurts. Must have got the bone." As Patterson tried to pull the belt tighter, Cranmer shrieked out with the pain, shockingly loud, then gasped, fading. "Tell Ethan it's not his fault."

"Let me get my hand up here."

"I was all set to go, then he came by. Gave me another spring."

"I think I've got it. I'm close."

"Sorry about this. Had to do something. Taking us to the basement . . ." His voice was getting fainter.

"I know." Patterson was twisting his belt around Cranmer's upper thigh with one hand and pressing as hard as he could onto the wound with the other. "Would have done the same myself. Stay with me. You're going to be . . ."

"Tell Ethan. Even people who . . ." Cranmer was whispering now. Patterson could barely hear him. "Give him the cats."

Cranmer's eyes rolled up, and his head fell back. Soon after that, the pulsing spurt of the artery stopped. Patterson's arms were soaked up to his elbows, and his pants were drenched. Some time went by, probably not much, and then he heard car doors slamming and noticed blue lights bouncing off the ceiling. A uniformed Amherst cop was first through the door, with his gun out, looking scared. Couldn't blame him.

Patterson shouted and raised his hands. "Patterson, FBI." The cop lowered his gun. "Christ's sake, come help me. We got a bleeder. Maybe we can . . ." But Sid wasn't moving.

Two EMTs, a man and a woman, charged in after that and took over. After a short time, it was clear there was nothing they could do. Professor Cranmer was gone.

Patterson heaved himself onto his feet, walked to the far end of the living room, and dropped into the familiar wingback. His hands made bloody smears on the flowered pattern. Everything inside him, brain and bones, seemed to be sinking down into his gut. He couldn't move. After a while, one of the EMTs came and squatted down in front of him.

"Look at me, okay?" She was a young black woman. Her words went past him, and she repeated. "Just look at me, will you?"

"Okay." Patterson noticed that the EMT had a very pretty, very intelligent face. She reminded him of his daughter, but older, heavier.

"What's your name?"

He had to think for a second. "Mike." He cleared his throat. "Mike Patterson. FBI."

"Are you hit anywhere, Agent Patterson?"

"If he'd gotten them into the basement, they never would have come out again."

"I understand. Are you hit anywhere, Agent Patterson?"

"No." He glanced down. "I don't think so."

"Just keep looking at me, will you? You sure?" She reached up with a damp cloth and wiped his forehead. "You've got a nasty cut up here. Maybe caught a fragment?"

"Don't know how that happened."

"You have a lot of blood on you."

"It's mostly not mine."

The Amherst cop called from the kitchen. "Who's this other guy?"

"Suicide by cop," Patterson called out. "To hell . . ." He paused, listening as a siren wound down outside. Somehow, he'd forgotten what he'd started to say. After a few seconds, it came back. He cleared his throat and muttered to no one in particular, "To hell with him."

Patterson started to stand up, intending to go assist in the kitchen, but his ankle gave out. If the EMT hadn't grabbed him, he would have gone down right on his face.

51

Judge Norcross canceled court for the entire week following the death of Sidney Cranmer. Over dinner one night, he and Claire discussed whether he should attend the professor's funeral. It was scheduled for that Saturday at Johnson Chapel on the Amherst College campus. Claire would be one of the speakers.

"I want to be there," David said. "The case is over. It shouldn't be a problem."

David had made grilled swordfish, an easy, regular entrée that he was proud of and that Lindsay and Jordan both actually liked. The girls had finished up quickly, probably sensing that the adults wanted to talk. Lindsay, who was grumpy for some reason, had retreated upstairs to her room, and Jordan was watching television. It was a fairly normal evening.

"People might think it's kind of odd to see you there," Claire said.

"I don't care." David looked into Claire's eyes. "He wasn't a perfect guy, but as far as I'm concerned, he earned his spot in heaven."

The chapel, as it turned out, was packed for Sid's funeral. David noticed Elizabeth Spencer, looking very sad, coming in with a group of her friends. Linda Ames slipped into a pew directly in front of them. As the organ was warming up, Ames shifted around and whispered, "I'm going to be in court this Tuesday on the Kirkwood case, Judge. If you have a minute, I'd like to talk to you afterward about a personal matter."

People were nodding and smiling to each other as the organ drifted into a muted, high-church rendition of the Rolling Stones hit, "Sympathy for the Devil." Sid Cranmer would have loved it.

"No problem. Let Ruby know, and she'll bring you around to chambers."

Ames's new case involved the mayor of Kirkwood, a town west of Springfield, who was charged with extorting money from the municipal towing contractor. Norcross was curious how Ames would mount a defense. The government had her client starring in a secretly recorded video clip that was particularly embarrassing. At the payoff, when the government's cooperator had reached out with the cash, the mayor had looked at the wad of bills and said, in an offended tone, "What? No envelope?"

In court, at the Tuesday conference, Ames asked for ninety days to retain an investigator and to research and prepare pretrial motions.

Judge Norcross was surprised. "Is that much time really necessary?" The mayor needed a lot of help, but this was unusually long.

"I'll be honest, Your Honor. My son and I are going to Nantucket for the month of July. I've rented a place and . . ."

The assistant U.S. attorney, an African American woman out of Boston, stood. "The government has no objection, Your Honor. In view of . . ." She looked at Ames and nodded. "In view of everything that's happened."

After the conference, Ruby Johnson brought Ames around to chambers. Ames and Norcross shook hands, and Ames took a seat facing the judge across his desk. Before she had a chance to talk, Norcross got up and closed the door for privacy.

As he returned, he said, "Listen, before we get started, I want you to know how sorry I am about Professor Cranmer."

"It was hard for all of us."

"It must have been especially hard for you."

Norcross was puzzled by the cloudy look that came over Ames's face.

"It's true that it's hard." She looked to the side and shifted in her chair, gathering herself. "It's hard in complicated ways."

"Sorry. I'm not following you."

Ames sat up. "Sid gave up his life to save Ethan and Claire. I'll never forget him, or stop feeling grateful for that." She cleared her throat and spoke a little louder, approaching her courtroom voice. "On the other hand, Sid had no business letting Ethan visit him without telling me."

"I should have thought of that. I can see—"

"And I keep wondering—excuse me for interrupting—I keep wondering if Sid suspected that Jonathan had problems, tried to protect Jonathan for some reason, and ended up putting Ethan in danger." Ames's face had turned slightly pink as she spoke. She was twiddling her fingers on the arm of her chair. "If Sid came down from heaven right now, I wouldn't know whether to hug him or strangle him."

"I see what you're saying. Seems a lot of people felt that way about Professor Cranmer."

"It's very hard. Ethan's decided that the whole thing was all his fault, the fault of a ten-year-old who disobeyed his mom." Ames looked to side and shook her head. "I'm afraid he may even think he should have just done whatever awful thing Jonathan wanted him to do. He's so sealed up I can't reach him. That's why we need the time away." She took in a deep breath and blew it out. "Sorry. This isn't why I came here. It's horrible. Adults fuck up—excuse me, but I can't think of a better word—and kids pay the price."

"Take the whole summer if you need it."

"Thank you. We'll see."

It turned out that the main reason Ames had sought out the private conference was that she wanted Norcross to know that she'd decided to stop taking criminal cases. This was very bad news.

"Oh," Judge Norcross said when he'd heard of Ames's plans. "Oh, man, I wish you wouldn't do that."

Sid Cranmer had retained Ames, paying her out of his own pocket, but Ames was also a mainstay of Norcross's roster of attorneys who took low-fee appointments for indigent defendants. Losing her would be a heavy blow.

"I'm thinking of doing residential real estate or something. I'll die of boredom, but at least . . ."

"Think about it, please, Ms. Ames."

"Criminal cases just eat you up, Judge. And, with cases like Sid's, if you have a kid—"

Norcross interrupted. "Okay, none of those for a while."

Ames talked over him. "I think about your Underwood case, for example. I'm sorry, but I want the guy to be boiled in oil."

"Well, we'll leave that. But listen, I'll give you a break on any new appointments until the fall. Then we can talk again. How about that?"

Ames looked to the side long enough for Norcross to wonder what she was thinking. He made himself hold off saying anything more, giving her time, hoping her natural bent would bring her around.

Finally, she spoke, half to herself. "I am so hungry."

Judge Norcross quickly pulled open a desk drawer. "I think I have a granola bar somewhere in here. It's about a hundred years old."

"I skipped breakfast."

"We can split it."

Norcross unwrapped the bar and broke it in half. The two of them chewed in silence for a while, and then Linda Ames sighed and stood up.

"Thanks for the snack. I better be on my way." They shook hands.

"Think about what I said, will you, please?"

"I will."

When she was in the doorway, Norcross called after her. "You're cooking up something in the Kirkwood case that's going to complicate my life, aren't you?"

Ames gave him a quick, tight smile and raised her eyebrows. "Hope so."

52

One afternoon in the beginning of May, two weeks before spring term would be ending, Claire Lindemann ran into Darren Mattoon on the sidewalk outside Converse Hall. It was an unusually warm day, and the quad was exploding with lilacs, tulips, and grape hyacinths. The blossoms made bright borders around the buildings and leaping showers of violet along the edges of the lawns. The campus had never looked better.

Mattoon, by contrast, looked awful—his hair was off center, and his face was gray and unhealthy looking—but he managed a smile when he saw Claire.

"Hello there, kiddo." He produced his lopsided grin, still unable to resist a flirt. It was sad.

"Hello yourself." Claire hesitated, worried that a question might be tactless, but decided to go ahead. "So you'll be leaving us? I was sorry to hear that." This was not true, but one had to say these things.

"Yes." Darren's eyes flickered at her. "Las Vegas made me an offer I couldn't refuse." He looked down at the pavement. "It's a good town for a man to try his luck in. And I have close friends there." He looked at Claire, probing. "None as close as I hoped you might be."

"Well," Claire said. "I'm kind of taken."

"Should have realized that." He continued briskly. "Our friend Ryan Jaworski is transferring to the University of Chicago. His dad's on the board of trustees." Mattoon looked up at the sky unhappily. "They're giving Ryan pretrial diversion for lying to the FBI. If he behaves himself for a year, I'm told, they won't charge him with anything." He dropped his chin and frowned, looking depressed. "Kids like him always land on their feet."

Claire refused to conspire in Darren's despondency, going deliberately upbeat. "Well, there's good news, too. I'm told Elizabeth Spencer got into Harvard Medical School." After a pause, Claire decided to ask another sensitive question. It was turning out that she really didn't like Darren Mattoon very much after all. "How about you? How's your legal situation?"

"Oh, I'm fine. I didn't do anything wrong, you know." He spoke as though he was addressing a dim student. "At a trial, any case against me would depend on Ryan being a credible witness, which obviously he isn't. According to my lawyer, the U. S. attorney in Boston wants no more to do with any of this." Darren pressed on, pseudojocular but with a hint of nastiness. "By the way, I was talking to one of our legal studies professors here. He's positive your judge's *Cranmer* ruling would have been reversed."

"My sources say he'd definitely have been affirmed, but I'm biased."

Claire was more than ready to go. Darren, however, still seemed to be wrestling with something, not quite prepared to wrap the conversation up, and she didn't want to give him the satisfaction of being rude. He wouldn't be much longer.

"Can I ask you something?" He ran a hand back through his hair, trying unsuccessfully to dab it into shape. "What the hell was really going on with Sid? I still wonder whether he was into . . ."

"I don't know." Claire felt her voice going husky. She still couldn't talk about it, certainly not with this creep. Now that he was being real, it was worse than when he was phony. "It was complicated, I guess."

She pulled a Kleenex out of her purse and blew her nose, trying to make it look as though she was stifling a sneeze. She'd never forget Sid forcing the gun down and yelling, "Run!" Never forget the earsplitting crack of the shot, her panic as she grabbed Ethan's hand and took off, expecting any second to get a bullet in the back. Worst of all, she would never forget squatting in the driveway with David, trying to comfort Ethan, and hearing the sound of Sid's piercing last scream of pain.

But Darren couldn't let go of it. "I just don't get how it all happened." His eyes looked lost. "It all just seems so . . ."

Claire's voice was harder than she intended, but she didn't care. "No, you don't." Then she softened. "Probably none of us ever will. I better go." She gave Darren a noncontact kiss. She would always remember Sid. Always. But, as for this guy . . .

"Bye, Darren. I'm meeting David."

"Good-bye."

David and Susan O'Leary were visiting the grave of Emily Dickinson a few blocks from the center of Amherst. Susan had suggested combining a walk with their regular check-in about Lindsay and Jordan. She wanted to unkink herself, she said, after her long drive from Boston, and it was a nice, warm day. She was looking especially pretty.

As they strolled down North Pleasant Street, David brought Susan up to date on things. The girls still had good days and bad days, but their basic trajectory was better. Susan had been an incredible help. Soon, after the school year ended, Lindsay and Jordan would be returning to their father in Washington. Ray was back in his office at the Department of Commerce, happily firing people, and the girls' last couple visits down there had gone reasonably well. Their time in Amherst would soon be over. David was going to survive.

The air in the graveyard had a hallowed feel, carrying a stillness, and Susan took David's hand. "So, *rafiki yangu*, pretty soon you won't be needing me anymore."

As they stood by Emily's tombstone, her epitaph, "Called Back," prompted a smile from Susan.

"Makes her sound like a Volkswagen."

"Don't poke fun at our poetess, *memsahib*. This is sacred ground." David let go of Susan's hand. It felt too good.

Susan had parked near Amherst Coffee, which was in the center of town, and as they made their way back from the cemetery, she put her hand on his shoulder. "Can I ask you something? You've never, all this time, had me come to your house to meet the girls. I kept suggesting it, but you found an excuse not to every time. We always met up with them in town. It puzzled me."

"Well, you know, Suze, I didn't want things to get out of hand." David said this lightly, as though he were joking. But he wasn't, and he could tell Susan knew it.

Someone wearing headphones clattered by them on a skateboard; his tune was so loud David caught a few throbbing chords.

After a pause, Susan smiled, almost to herself. "I wouldn't have minded."

That stopped the conversation, and they strolled in silence up North Pleasant Street, past the pizza places and other student hangouts. David had a fleeting pang remembering Kenya and the sweetness of his time with Susan so many years ago now.

"Well, you remember the old Nairobi pop song." He quoted, "*Nilikupenda sana* . . ." In Swahili, it meant, "I loved you very much."

Susan completed the chorus. "*Lakini sasa sitaweza.*" Translated roughly, it was "but now I will not be able to." They crossed the town's main intersection, dominated by two banks, and turned up a side street toward the Amherst Cinema.

Outside the coffee shop next door, they stopped. "Well . . ." David began.

Claire appeared, coming around the corner, waving and smiling. Susan gave David a quick hug and whispered in his ear, "*Kwaheri, bwana.*"

"*Kwaheri.*"

Susan turned, not waiting for Claire to join them, and hurried down the street to where her car was parked. When Claire came up, she gave David a slightly longer than usual kiss. It felt as though she was marking her territory, which was fine with David.

She smiled at him. "I didn't catch what Dr. O'Leary was saying there. Something in your private language?"

"*Kwaheri.*" David touched Claire's face. "It means 'good-bye' in Swahili."

53

The end of David's life as he had known it arrived on a drizzly school day in late May. The occasion itself was not complicated, just a random interplay of force and fortune weaving their patterns.

As he stood in his pajamas and bathrobe, looking down from his bedroom window, the breeze rocking the hemlocks at the margin of the woods made him wince. Rain blew and clicked on the glass. They'd had a pleasant spate of warm days, and now this. Typical depressing, unpredictable New England weather.

When he went downstairs, he had to shove Marlene out into the yard with his foot to get her to go pee. Hurrying back in, she gave him a wounded look, walked to her bed in the mudroom, and flopped down with a melodramatic sigh.

Jordan was getting the sniffles and had to be called three times before she finally dragged herself out of bed. The coffee took forever. The only energized member of the family was Lindsay. Two of her teammates swung by to collect her early, and she bounced out the door in plenty of time, tossing her knapsack over her shoulder and shouting that she would be home after practice. The softball season was putting her into a good mood.

David breathed into his coffee, letting the steam soothe his eyelids. Seated with him at the kitchen counter, Jordan was working on her Eggo, chewing doggedly. The school bus was due in ten minutes.

On an impulse, David reached over and poked Jordan in the arm. "How about if I drive you to school today? It will give us a little extra time."

Jordan's eyes widened. She smiled with her mouth full. "Oh, that would be awesome!"

"We'll treat ourselves." David experienced a rush of happiness, despite the weather, buoyed by having winkled a smile out of a six-year-old. When had these girls acquired such power to rescue, or ruin, his day?

A half hour later, they were waiting at the bottom of the circular driveway in front of Crocker Farm Elementary. The rain was coming down harder, and the area was crowded with buses and cars converging from all directions. David was puzzled at how to manage the congestion. The windshield was steamy, and the wipers were leaving smears.

"You can let me out up there," Jordan said, nodding and gathering up her book bag. "I can run. Thank you so much!" After hesitating, she leaned over and gave David a quick kiss on the cheek. It left a cool spot and a blank in his brain of astonished joy. Once out of the car, she leaned through the open passenger door and pointed. "If you go that way? You can get out easier." She gave a little scream—"It's wet!"—slammed the door, and dashed off, lifting her legs high to avoid splattering.

The terrain between the car and the double doors leading into the school included an expanse of soggy lawn about twenty yards across, terminating in a wide, curving driveway. A hedge of arborvitae about five feet high ran between the right-hand side of the grassy area and the asphalt drive, stopping at the point where Jordan would cross to enter the school.

It was just the ordinary stuff of an ordinary school day. David watched Jordan as she scampered across the wet grass toward the main door of the school. Traffic was flowing along behind the dark green hedge irregularly, partly hidden. First with concern, and then with mounting apprehension, David watched the end of his life unfold.

To his right, a black Camry had stopped about halfway around the curving drive, not quite up to where the hedge began. The driver was leaning across the passenger seat, talking to a woman on the sidewalk. With her back turned like that, the driver of the Camry could not see Jordan, who was running at an angle toward a point at the far end of the hedge where her path would intersect with the curving blacktop drive. After a short interchange, the woman on the sidewalk laughed and waved the Camry on.

The driver sat up and took off with a jerk. Meanwhile, Jordan had broken into a trot across the lawn and into the path of the now swiftly approaching black car. Jordan very obviously did not see the car, which was screened by the arborvitae, coming toward her from the right. It was all happening very quickly and very slowly at the same time.

David started fumbling for the button to lower his window. Someone was behind him. The man—like him, wearing a tie—was getting impatient and tooted his horn, but David was trying to get his window down. It was taking forever.

He managed to shout, "Jordan!," while the window was half open, but she was picking up speed, and she didn't hear him. He could see the black Camry, oblivious, still coming, way too late to brake, and Jordan skipping from the wet grass onto the blacktop. He shouted again, louder, "Jordan, watch out!," and began struggling to unhook his seat belt.

He had just managed to get one leg out of the car, shouting for a third time, very loud now, "Jordan!," when the Camry, going at least twenty miles an hour, hit Jordan hard, knocking her down and sending her book bag in a flutter of paper onto the blacktop. The front end of the Camry bumped up over her, leaving one twisted, very skinny child's leg sticking out at an angle from behind the front left tire. The tire itself and part of the fender had blood on it. He could see the dark spatter of it clearly. Barely able to breathe, he began running.

Except, it didn't happen. It only happened like that in his imagination and not, this time, in real life. In fact, at the last moment, Jordan saw the Camry, squealed, and jumped back. The Camry came to an abrupt halt, rocking forward on its suspension but not skidding. It might not have been going as fast as David had feared.

The driver leaned out the window and called, "Sorry, Jordan!"

Jordan waved. "It's okay, Ms. Anderson!" Ms. Anderson waited as Jordan crossed the curving drive and dashed into the school. The doors closed behind her. David stepped back into his car, waved apologetically to the man behind him, and slowly drove off.

A short distance from the school, David pulled off onto a wide shoulder on the edge of one of Amherst's conservation areas. He sat for several minutes, catching his breath. The rain began to let up, just misting the windows. The car engine purred, and the wipers plodded back and forth.

Something had happened while David wasn't looking. He'd accepted early on, after Lindsay and Jordan came to live with him, that, if the situation required it, he would be obligated to give his life for them, the way poor Professor Cranmer had given his for Ethan and Claire. He wouldn't enjoy doing it, and he would be very frightened, but if the occasion arose where it was necessary, he would have the duty to do it. What he hadn't known was that this would be the least of the demands on him.

Getting killed for Lindsay or Jordan had the virtue of being unlikely and, if it happened, potentially noble. When he imagined, for example, throwing his body in front of a train to save Jordan, it made him feel sort of exalted, as though he would still be around afterward to congratulate himself and join in the general applause. Dying to save a small child like Jordan would, of course, probably make him feel better than dying to save an adolescent like Lindsay. Thinking of this, David smiled and rubbed the area under his eye. If he sacrificed his life for Lindsay, she'd probably just be annoyed.

Anyway, the problem with children was not an unlikely tragic gesture like this, but the inevitable, ignoble daily challenges—situations that regularly left him feeling helpless and stupid, dinners that nobody liked, wise observations or jokes of his, or attempts to introduce interesting topics of conversation that only provoked embarrassed side glances and silence. Mysteries he'd never plumb. He hadn't foreseen how skepticism about, and even scorn for, elders could be part of a child's process of maturation. Worst of all, the dirty little secret, which nobody told him, was that it was not possible to construct shields around children without unpeeling many of his own protective coverings—camouflage he'd been stitching together to protect himself since before he hit puberty. Now there were big holes in it.

Some days, he didn't even want to come home after work. He wanted to detour to a nice restaurant, maybe call Claire, have a couple glasses of wine, eat seafood, and let the girls fend for themselves for once. But when these fantasies arose, he immediately pictured Lindsay saying something unkind to Jordan and making her cry, or someone leaving a burner on, or forgetting to feed Marlene, or some darn thing, and he would end up hurrying home.

His old life was gone, and he was trapped. Even when the girls went back to Washington, it would not be over. If Ray mistreated or neglected them, he would hear it in their voices when he called on the phone—or he would feel it immediately when he visited—and his urge to bring them back to Amherst would be unbearable. Even if Ray managed with the girls somehow, part of David would be worrying about them until the day he died.

Soon, he could see, he and Claire would be starting their own endless journey down this path. Something dangerous had happened. David no longer worried about being a dad. He already was one.

AUTHOR'S NOTE

For more than thirty years, my position as a federal judge has placed me within a small cohort of people permitted to view child pornography legally—provided, of course, that the viewing occurs only in the context of a criminal prosecution. I wish I had never had this dubious privilege. The heartbreaking images one is required to examine linger in the mind, offering evidence of our species at its worst.

Defendants charged with these offenses vary greatly. They include vicious, unrepentant predators; outwardly upstanding citizens, otherwise law-abiding, drawn to a repulsive late-night obsession; pathetic loners, sometimes victims of abuse themselves; and teenagers or students trolling the Internet out of morbid curiosity. This novel, including the chat-room material, draws from my experience with these cases in federal court, but it does not track any specific case or defendant I handled. None of the characters in the story is modeled on any particular person.

It is important to underline as well that, though the story refers to the "Town of Amherst" and "Amherst College," and draws certain details of setting from both, the two are highly fictionalized. I could have concocted others names—Elm City or Norwottuck College or something—but the transparency of the ruse might have suggested that the book had some real-life events it had to obscure. It doesn't. My fondness for my hometown and, in particular, for Amherst College, a dynamic and courageously innovative institution, is enormous. Crimes like the ones described in this novel occur often, but not, up to now, in the town or at the college, so far as I know.

Finally, I must beg pardon if this story leads readers down some of the darker passages that judges routinely travel. It is not easy to write or to read about child sexual abuse. It is not easy to talk or even to think about it. On the other hand, we are learning that silence is false consolation and does little to help.

Michael A. Ponsor, U.S.D.J.
Springfield, Massachusetts
January 21, 2017

ACKNOWLEDGMENTS

It might be said, as with so many things, that it takes a village to write a novel. I am so thankful for the support of friends during this journey, including Ted and Esther Scott, Peter Shaw, Phyllis Joachim, Randall Paulsen, Sally Bowie, Brian Fay, Julie Perkins, Jennifer Kaplan, and Elizabeth Collins.

I am particularly grateful to my dear, lifelong friend, the superb poet Ellen Bass, whose line editing and insights took the early draft to another and finer level. The excellent writer, friend, and neighbor John Katzenbach also looked over the manuscript; his firmly grounded observations were very helpful and much appreciated.

My children, Anne and Joseph Ponsor, also offered helpful, very practical advice on points that their generational niche gave them special purchase on. From a loftier vantage, my parents, Ward and Yvonne Ponsor—still amazingly alive and kicking at ninety-six and ninety-three—and my sister, Valerie Pritchard, patiently listened to me, offered helpful perspective, and provided continuous encouragement.

Special thanks go to my fellow judges who read the draft, including my former boss and now dear friend, Senior Judge Joseph L.

Tauro; Chief Judge Patti B. Saris; Senior Judge Rya Zobel; and Judge William G. Young. My friend and colleague Judge Denise Casper, in particular, made several very insightful suggestions that I have adopted and that significantly improved the narrative. The warmth of this collegial spirit in our court has been a strong and positive force in my life for more than thirty years, including in my writing. No one, in all of history or on any known planet, has had better men and women to work with.

I have a deep feelings of appreciation for the attorneys who have appeared before me. Because I sit in a rather small community, in an essentially one-judge court, many of these lawyers have appeared before me numerous times over many years. For virtually all of them, I have not only great respect, but also real fondness. They are good people. My respect for the handful of assistant U.S. attorneys who have tried cases in front of me over the years is especially profound. Their work is morally challenging, and a conscientious AUSA can do as much to improve the quality of justice as any defense attorney or judge, often more. Prosecutors who handle child pornography cases carry an especially heavy emotional burden. I must emphasize than none of them would have made the mistakes that the inexperienced AUSA Campanella made in this book.

All the people at Open Road Integrated Media have been extraordinarily good at what they do and terrific to work with. From this group, I am most especially grateful to David Adams and Colleen Lindsay, for their energy, kindness, and competence, and to founder Jane Friedman, whose wisdom and experience still provide the soul of the Open Road operation.

My literary agent, Robin Straus, has been, as always, fantastic. Her guidance, both on the book and on the complex professional world she navigates so adroitly, has been invaluable. Without her, I would be nowhere. It doesn't hurt that she is a delightful friend and great fun to be around as well.

A wealth of material exists on the lonely, whimsical Oxford mathematics professor Charles Dodgson, aka Lewis Carroll, exploring his paradoxically very conventional and very odd life, his literary efforts, and his obsession, for some years, with very young girls. This is not intended to be an academic work, so I won't list all the books and articles I reviewed. The most prominent and helpful were Morton N. Cohen's *Lewis Carroll: A Biography*, Alfred A. Knopf, Inc. (New York, 1995); Jenny Woolf's *The Mystery of Lewis Carroll*, St. Martin's Griffin (New York, 2011); and Robert Douglas-Fairhurst's *The Story of Alice*, the Belknap Press of Harvard University Press (Cambridge, Mass., 2015). I also took great delight in rereading *The Annotated Alice*, with an introduction and notes by Martin Gardner, W. W. Norton & Company (New York and London, 2000). Whatever may have been Prof. Dodgson's demons, he was an amazingly creative storyteller.

Next to my wife, my closest, best, most essential ally in writing this book has been Maggie Crawford, my editor. Helping anyone write is tricky; helping me requires something well above average. Maggie has been brilliant. She has been gracious. She has been meticulous through years of hard work and the exchange of, by now, an extremely plump file of drafts and emails. Whatever the virtues of this book may be, they have been immensely enhanced by her careful assistance. No words can convey the extent of my gratitude to her.

Finally, there is my adored wife, Nancy. The fundamentals of the book, its blocks of granite, emerged from conversations with her. Every tap on the chisel from then on has had the benefit of her perceptive mind and sharp ears. Nancy's generous, passionate spirit dazzles me every day. Whenever I see her, or even think of her, a green light turns on inside me, I smile, and life makes sense.

ABOUT THE AUTHOR

Michael Ponsor graduated from Harvard, received a Rhodes Scholarship, and studied for two years at Pembroke College, Oxford. As an undergraduate, he spent a year teaching in Kabete, Kenya, just outside Nairobi. After taking his law degree from Yale and clerking in federal court in Boston, he began his legal career, specializing in criminal defense. He moved to Amherst, Massachusetts, in 1978, where he practiced as a trial attorney in his own firm until his appointment in 1984 as a U.S. magistrate judge in Springfield, Massachusetts. In 1994, President Bill Clinton appointed him a life-tenured U.S. district judge. From 2000 to 2001, he presided over a five-month death penalty trial, the first in Massachusetts in over fifty years. Judge Ponsor continues to serve as a senior U.S. district judge in the United States District Court for the District of Massachusetts, Western Division, with responsibility for federal criminal and civil cases in the four counties of western Massachusetts. *The One-Eyed Judge* is his second novel featuring Judge Norcross.

ABOUT THE AUTHOR

THE JUDGE NORCROSS NOVELS

FROM OPEN ROAD MEDIA